SATANTANGO *is proof that the devil has all the good times.*

Set in an isolated hamlet, SATANTANGO *unfolds over the course of a few rain-soaked days.*

Only a dozen inhabitants remain in the bleak village, rank with the stench of failed schemes, betrayals, failure, infidelity, sudden hopes, and aborted dreams.

At the center of SATANTANGO *is the eponymous drunken dance.*

"Their world," in the words of the renowned translator, George Szirtes, "is rough and ready, lost somewhere between the comic and tragic, in one small insignificant corner of the cosmos. Theirs is the dance of death."

Into their world comes, it seems, a Messiah . . .

P9-AOZ-308

SATANTANGO

ALSO BY LÁSZLÓ KRASZNAHORKAI
FROM NEW DIRECTIONS

Animalinside
The Melancholy of Resistance
War & War

FORTHCOMING
Seiobo There Below

László Krasznahorkai

SATANTANGO

Translated from the Hungarian
by George Szirtes

A NEW DIRECTIONS BOOK

Grateful acknowledgment to the Hungarian Cultural Fund,
which supported the translation of this book.

 Nemzeti
Kulturális
Alap

 National
Cultural Fund
of Hungary

Originally published in Hungarian as *Sátántango* in 1985.
Published by arrangement with S. Fischer Verlag, Frankfurt.

Manufactured in the United States of America
Published simultaneously in Canada by Penguin Books Canada Ltd.
New Directions Books are printed on acid-free paper.
First published as a New Directions Book in 2012
Design by Erik Rieselbach

Library of Congress Cataloging-in-Publication Data
Krasznahorkai, László.
[Sátántangó. English]
Satantango / László Krasznahorkai ;
translated from the Hungarian by George Szirtes.
p. cm.
ISBN 978-0-8112-1734-7 (acid-free paper)
I. Szirtes, George, 1948– II. Title.
PH3281.K8866S2813 2012
894'.51134—dc23
2011051922

New Directions Books are published for James Laughlin
by New Directions Publishing Corporation
80 Eighth Avenue, New York 10011

THE DANCES

SATANTANGO

In that case, I'll miss the thing by waiting for it. —FK

THE FIRST PART

I

NEWS OF THEIR COMING

One morning near the end of October not long before the first drops of the mercilessly long autumn rains began to fall on the cracked and saline soil on the western side of the estate (later the stinking yellow sea of mud would render footpaths impassable and put the town too beyond reach) Futaki woke to hear bells. The closest possible source was a lonely chapel about four kilometers southwest on the old Hochmeiss estate but not only did that have no bell but the tower had collapsed during the war and at that distance it was too far to hear anything. And in any case they did not sound distant to him, these ringing-booming bells; their triumphal clangor was swept along by the wind and seemed to come from somewhere close by ("It's as if they were coming from the mill ..."). He propped himself on his elbows on the pillow so as to look out of the mousehole-sized kitchen window that was partly misted up, and directed his gaze to the faint blue dawn sky but the field was still and silent, bathed only in the now ever fainter bell sound, and the only light to be seen was the one glimmering in the doctor's window whose house was set well apart from the others on the far side, and that was only because its occupant had for years been unable to sleep in the dark. Futaki held his breath because he wanted to know where the noise came from: he couldn't afford to lose a single stray note of the rapidly fading clangor, however remote ("You must be asleep, Futaki …"). Despite his lameness he was well known for his light tread and he hobbled across the ice-cold stone floor of the kitchen soundless as a cat, opened the windows and leaned out ("Is no one awake? Can't people hear it? Is there nobody else around?"). A sharp damp gust hit him straight in the face so he had to close his eyes for a moment and, apart from the cockcrow, a distant bark, and the fierce howling of the wind that had sprung up just a few minutes earlier, there was nothing to hear however hard he listened but the dull beating of his own heart, as if the whole thing had been merely a kind of game or ghostly half-dream ("… It's as if somebody out there wants to scare me"). He gazed sadly at the threatening sky, at the burned-out remnants of a locust-plagued summer, and suddenly saw on the twig of an acacia, as in a vision, the progress of spring, summer, fall and winter, as if the whole of time were a frivolous interlude in the much greater spaces of eternity, a brilliant conjuring trick to produce something apparently orderly out of chaos, to establish a vantage point from which chance might begin to look like necessity … and he saw himself nailed to the cross of his own cradle and coffin, painfully trying to tear his body away, only, eventually, to deliver himself—utterly naked, without identifying mark, stripped down to essentials—into the care of the people whose duty it was to wash the corpses, people obeying an order snapped out in the dry air against a background loud with torturers and flayers of skin, where he was obliged to regard the human condition without a trace of pity, without a single possibility of any way back to life, because by then he would know for certain that all his life he had been playing with cheaters who had marked the cards and who would, in the end, strip him even of his last means of defense, of that hope of someday finding his way back home. He turned his head toward the east, once the home of a thriving industry, now nothing but a set of dilapidated and deserted buildings, watching while the first rays of a

swollen red sun broke through the topmost beams of a derelict farmhouse from which the roof tiles had been stripped. "I really should
come to a decision. I can't stay here any longer." He snuck back under
the warm duvet again and rested his head on his arm, but could not
close his eyes; at first it had been the ghostly bells that had frightened
him but now it was the threatening silence that followed: anything
might happen now, he felt. But he did not move a muscle, not until the
objects around him, that had so far been merely listening, started up a
nervous conversation (the sideboard gave a creak, a saucepan rattled,
a china plate slid back into the rack) at which point he turned away
from the sour smell of the perspiring Mrs. Schmidt, felt with his hand
for the glass of water left standing by the bed and drained it at one gulp.
Having done so he was free of his childish terror: he sighed, wiped his
sweating brow and, knowing that Schmidt and Kráner were only just
now rounding up the cattle to drive them west from the Szikes toward
the farm byres in the west where they would eventually receive eight
months' worth of hard-earned wages, and that this would take a good
couple of hours, he decided to try and get a bit more sleep. He closed
his eyes, turned on his side, put his arm around the woman and had
almost succeeded in nodding off when he heard the bells again. "For
God's sake!" He pushed aside the duvet but the moment his naked cal-
loused feet touched the stone floor the bells suddenly stopped ("As if
someone had given a signal...") ... He sat hunched on the edge of the
bed his hands clasped in his lap till the empty glass caught his attention. His throat was dry, his right leg was suffering shooting pains, and
now he didn't dare to either get up or go back under the covers. "I am
leaving by tomorrow at the very latest." He surveyed the vaguely functioning articles in the bare kitchen, from the cooking range filthy with
burned fat and leftover scraps to the basket without a handle under the
bed, the rickety table, the dusty icons hanging on the wall, and the
saucepans, his eye finally resting on the tiny window and the bare

branches of the acacia bending across the Halicses' house with its dented roof and teetering chimney, the smoke billowing from it, and said, "I'll take what's mine and go tonight!... No later than tomorrow at any rate. Tomorrow morning." "Dear God!" Mrs. Schmidt cried, waking suddenly, and stared about her in the dusk, terrified, her chest heaving, but when she saw that everything looked back at her with a familiar expression she gave a relieved sigh and slumped back on the pillow. "What's the matter? Bad dreams?" Futaki asked her. Mrs. Schmidt was staring at the ceiling in fright. "Good Lord, really horrible dreams!" She sighed again and put her hand on her heart. "Such things! Me?!... Who'd have imagined?... There I was sitting in the room and ... suddenly there was a knock at the window. I didn't dare to open it, just stood there, peeking through the curtains. I only saw his back because by now he was shaking the door handle, and then his mouth as he bellowed. God knows what he was saying. He was unshaven and it seemed his eyes were made of glass ... it was horrible ... Then I remembered I had only given the key one turn the previous night and knew that by the time I got there it would be too late so I quickly slammed the kitchen door, but then I realized I didn't have the key. I wanted to scream but no sound came from my throat. Then I don't exactly recall why or how but suddenly Mrs. Halics was at the window making faces—you know what it's like when she makes faces—and anyway, there she was staring into the kitchen and then, I don't know how, she vanished, though by that time the man outside was kicking at the door and would have been through it in a minute, and I thought of the bread knife and dashed over to the cupboard but the drawer was jammed and I kept trying to open it ... I thought I would die of terror ... Then I heard him smash the door open and he was coming down the hall. I still couldn't open the drawer. Suddenly he was there at the kitchen door just as I finally succeeded in opening the drawer to grab the knife, and he was getting closer waving his arms about ... but I don't know ... suddenly he was lying on the floor in the corner by the window and, yes, he had a lot of red and blue saucepans with him that started flying about the kitchen ... and I felt the floor move under me and, just imagine, the whole kitchen set off, like a car ... and I can't remember anything after that ..." she ended and laughed in relief. "We're a fine pair," Futaki shook his head. "I woke—to what do you think?—to someone ringing bells ..." "What!" the woman stared at him in astonishment: "Someone was ringing bells? Where?" "I don't understand it either. In fact not once but twice, one after the other ..." It was Mrs. Schmidt's turn to shake her head. "You—you'll go crazy." "Or I might have dreamed it all," grumbled Futaki nervously: "Mark my words, something is going to happen today." The woman turned to him angrily. "You're always saying that, just shut up, can't you?" Suddenly they heard the gate creaking open at the back and stared each other in fright. "It must be him," whispered Mrs. Schmidt. "I can feel it." Futaki sat up in shock. "But that's impossible! How could he have got back so soon ..." "How should I know ...! Go! Go now!" He leapt out of bed, grabbed his clothes, stuck them under his arm, shut the door behind him, and dressed. "My stick. I left my stick out there!" The Schmidts hadn't used the room since spring. Green mildew covered the cracked and peeling walls, but the clothes in the cupboard, a cupboard that was regularly cleaned, were also mildewed, as were the towels and all the bedding, and a couple of weeks was all it took for the cutlery saved in the drawer for special occasions to develop a coating of rust, and what with the legs of the big lace-covered table having worked loose, the curtains having yellowed and the lightbulb having gone out, they decided one day to move into the kitchen and stay there, and since there was nothing they could do to stop it happening anyway, they left the room to be colonized by spiders and mice. He leaned against the doorjamb and wondered how he might get out without being seen. The situation seemed pretty hopeless because he would have to pass through the kitchen and he felt too decrepit to clamber through the window where he would, in any case, be observed by Mrs. Kráner or Mrs. Halics who spent half their lives peeking through their curtains to keep an eye on affairs outside. Besides which, his stick, if Schmidt should discover it, would immediately betray the fact that he was hiding somewhere in the house, and if that happened he might not receive his share at all since he knew Schmidt did not consider such a thing a joking matter; that he would promptly be run off the estate to which he had rushed seven years before in response to news of its success— two years after the estate had been set up—at a time when he was hungry and had only a single pair of ragged trousers plus a faded overcoat with empty pockets to stand up in. Mrs. Schmidt ran into the hall while he put his ear to the door. "No complaining, sweetheart!" he heard Schmidt's hoarse voice: "You do as I tell you. Is that clear?" Futaki felt a hot rush of blood. "My money!" He felt trapped. But he had no time to think so decided to climb out of the window after all because "something has to be done right away." He was about to open the window catch when he heard Schmidt moving down the hall. "He's going to take a leak!" He tiptoed back to the door and held his breath to listen. Once he heard Schmidt close the door to the backyard, he carefully slipped into the kitchen where he took one look at a nervously fidgeting Mrs. Schmidt, silently hurried to the front door, stepped out and, once he was sure his neighbor was back inside, gave the door a good clatter as if he were just arriving. "What's up? Nobody at home? Hey, Schmidt!" he shouted as loud as he could, then—so as not to leave him any time to escape—immediately opened the door and blocked Schmidt's way out of the kitchen. "Well, well!" he asked in a mocking voice. "Where are we going in such a hurry, pal?" Schmidt was utterly at a loss for words: "No, well I'll tell you, buddy! Don't you worry, pal. I'll help you remember all right!" he continued with a deep frown. "You wanted to make off with the money! Am I right? Guessed

8

right the first try?" Schmidt still said nothing but just kept blinking. Futaki shook his head. "Well, pal. Who would have thought it?" They went back into the kitchen and sat down facing each other. Schmidt was nervously fiddling with objects on the stove. "Listen, pal ..." Schmidt stuttered: "I can explain ..." Futaki waved him away. "I don't need any explanations! Tell me, is Kráner in on this?" Schmidt was forced to nod. "Up to a point." "Sons of bitches!" Futaki raged. "You thought you'd put one over on me." He bowed his head and thought. "And now? What happens now?" he eventually asked. Schmidt spread his arms. He was angry: "What do you mean: what now? You're one of us, buddy." "What do you mean?" Futaki inquired, mentally calculating the sums. "Let's split it three ways," Schmidt answered reluctantly: "But keep your mouth shut." "You won't have to worry about that." Mrs. Schmidt was standing by the range and gave a despairing sigh. "Have you lost your minds? Do you think you can get away with this?" Schmidt acted as though he hadn't heard her. He fixed his eye on Futaki. "There, you can't say we haven't cleared it up. But there's something else I want to say to you, buddy. You can't rat me out now." "We've made a deal, haven't we?" "Yes, of course, there's no doubt about that, not for a second!" Schmidt continued, his voice rising to a plaintive whine. "All I ask is ... I want you to lend me your share for a short time! Just for a year! While we settle down somewhere ..." "And what other part of your anatomy do you want me to suck?!" Futaki snapped back at him. Schmidt flopped forward and grasped the edge of the table. "I wouldn't ask you if you yourself hadn't said you wouldn't be leaving here now. What do you need it all for? And it's just for a year ... a year, that's all! ... We have to have it, you understand, we just have to. I can't buy anything with the rags I'm standing up in. I can't even get a plot of land. Lend me ten at least, eh?" "No way!" Futaki answered: "I don't give a damn. I don't want to rot here either!" Schmidt shook his head, so angry he was practically crying, then began again, obstinate but ever more helpless, his elbows propped on the kitchen table that rocked each time he moved as if taking his part, begging his partner to "have a heart," hoping his "pal" might respond to his pitiful gestures, and it wouldn't have taken much more effort since Futaki had almost decided to give in when his eye suddenly lit on the million specks of dust swirling in a thin beam of sunlight and his nose became aware of the dank smell of the kitchen. Suddenly there was a sour taste on his tongue and he thought it was death. Ever since the works had been split up, since people had been in as much of a rush to get away as they had been to come here, and since he—along with a few families, and the doctor, and the headmaster who, like him, had nowhere else to go—had found himself unable to move, it had been the same, day after day, tasting the same narrow range of food, knowing that death meant getting used to, first the soup, then to the meat dishes, then, finally, to go on to consuming the very walls, chewing long laborious mouthfuls before swallowing, slowly sipping at the wine rarely enough set in front of him, or the water. He sometimes felt an irresistible desire to break off a chunk of nitrous plaster in the machine hall of the old enginehouse where he lived and to cram it into his mouth so that he might recognize the taste of the *Vigilance!* sign among the disturbing riot of normally ordered flavors. Death, he felt, was only a kind of warning rather than a desperate and permanent end. "It's not as if I'm asking for a gift," Schmidt continued, growing tired: "It's a loan. You understand? A loan. I'll return every last cent of it in precisely a year." They sat at the table, both of them worn out. Schmidt's eyes were burning from exhaustion, Futaki was furiously studying the mysterious patterns of the stone tiling. He mustn't show he is afraid, he thought, though he would have found it hard to explain what it was he was afraid of. "Just tell me this. How many times did I go out to Szikes, all by myself, in that intolerable heat where a man is scared to breathe the air in case it sets fire to his insides?! Who got hold of the wood? Who built that sheepfold?! I have contributed just as much as you, or Kráner, or Halics! And now you have the nerve to touch me for a loan. Oh yes, and it'll all be returned next time I see you, eh?!" "In other words," Schmidt replied, affronted, "you don't trust me." "Damn right!" Futaki snapped back. "You and Kráner meet up before dawn, planning to make off with all the money and then you expect me to trust you?! Do you take me for an idiot?" They sat silently together. The woman was clattering dishes by the stove. Schmidt looked defeated. Futaki's hands trembled as he rolled a cigarette and got up from the table, limped over to the window, leaned on his stick with his left hand and watched rain billowing over the rooftops. The trees were leaning with the wind, their bare branches describing threatening arcs in the air. He thought of their roots, the life-giving sap, of the soaked earth and of the silence, of the unspoken feeling of completion he so dreaded. "In that case tell me ...!" he asked in a hesitant manner, "Why did you come back, this once ..." "Why? why?!" Schmidt grumbled. "Because that's what occurred to us—and before we could think better of it we were on the way home, and back ... And then there was the woman ... Would I have left her here? ..." Futaki nodded understandingly. "What about the Kráners?" he asked after a while. "What's your arrangement with them?" "They're stuck here, like us. They want to head north. Mrs. Kráner heard there was an old neglected orchard or something there. We'll meet by the crossroads after dark. That's what we arranged." Futaki gave a sigh: "A long day ahead. What about the others? Like Halics? ..." Schmidt rubbed his fingers together despondently: "How should I know? Halics will probably sleep the whole day. There was a big party yesterday at the Horgoses. His highness, the manager, can go to hell on the first bus! If there's any trouble on his account, I'll drown the sonofabitch in the next ditch, so relax, pal, relax." They decided to wait in the kitchen till night fell. Futaki drew up a chair by the window so he could keep an eye on the houses opposite while Schmidt was overcome by sleep, slumped over the table, and began to snore. The woman brought the big iron-strapped military trunk out from behind the cupboards, wiped away the dust, inside and out, then wordlessly began packing their things. "It's raining," said Futaki. "I can hear," replied the woman. The weak sunlight only just succeeded in penetrating a jumbled mass of clouds that was slowly proceeding eastwards: the light in the kitchen dimmed as if it were dusk and it was hard to know whether the gently vibrating patches on the wall were merely shadows or symptoms of the despair underlying their faintly hopeful thoughts. "I'll go south," Futaki declared, gazing at the rain. "At least the winters are shorter there. I'll rent a little land near some town that's growing and spend the day dangling my feet in a bowl of hot water ..." Raindrops were gently trickling down both sides of the window because of the finger-wide crack that ran all the way from the wooden beam to the window frame, slowly filling it up then pushing their way along the beam where they divided once more into drops that began to drip into Futaki's lap, while he, being so absorbed in his visions of faraway places that he couldn't get back to reality, failed to notice that he was actually wet. "Or I might go and take a job as a night watchman in a chocolate factory ... or perhaps as janitor in a girls' boarding school ... and I'll try to forget everything, I'll do nothing but soak my feet in a bowl of hot water each night, while this filthy life passes ..." The rain that had been gently pouring till now suddenly turned into a veritable deluge, like a river breaking over a dam, drowning the already choking fields, the lowest lying of which were riddled with serpentine channels, and though it was impossible to see anything through the glass he did not turn away but stared at the worm-eaten wooden frame from which the putty had dropped out, when suddenly a vague form appeared at the window, one that eventually could be made out to be a human face, though he couldn't tell at first whose it was, until he succeeded in picking out a pair of startled eyes, at which point he saw "his own careworn features" and recognized them with a shock like a stab of pain since he felt that what the rain was doing to his face was exactly what time would do. It would wash it away. There was in that reflection something enormous and alien, a kind of emptiness radiating from it, moving toward him, compounded of layers of shame, pride and fear. Suddenly he felt the sour taste in his mouth again and he remembered the bells tolling at dawn, the glass of water, the bed, the acacia bough, the cold flagstones in the kitchen and, thinking of it all, he made a bitter face. "A bowl of hot water!... Devil take it!... Don't I bathe my feet every day ...?" he pouted. Somewhere behind him there was the sound of choked-off sobbing. "And what's bugging you then?" Mrs. Schmidt did not answer him but turned away, her shoulders shaking with the sobs. "You hear me? What's the matter with you?" The woman looked up at him, then simply sat down on the nearby stool and blew her nose like someone for whom speech was pointless. "Why don't you say something?" Futaki insisted: "What the hell is wrong with you?" "Where on earth can we go!" erupted Mrs. Schmidt: "The first town we come to some policeman is bound to stop us! Don't you understand? They won't even ask our names!" "What are you blathering about?" Futaki angrily retorted: "We will be loaded with money, and as for you ..." "That's exactly what I mean!" the woman interrupted him: "The money! You at least might have some sense! To go away with this rotten old trunk ... like a band of beggars!" Futaki was furious. "That's enough, now! Keep out of this. It has nothing to do with you. Your job is to shut up." Mrs. Schmidt would not let it rest. "What?" she snapped: "What's my job?" "Forget it," Futaki answered quietly. "Keep it down or you'll wake him up." Time was passing very slowly and, luckily for them, the alarm clock had long ago stopped working so there wasn't even the sound of ticking to remind them of time, nevertheless the woman gazed at the still hands as she gave the paprika stew the occasional stir while the two men sat wearily by the steaming plates in front of them, not touching their spoons despite Mrs. Schmidt's constant badgering for them to get on with it ("What are you waiting for? Do you want to eat at night, soaked to the bone in the mud?"). They did not turn the light on although objects washed into each other during the agonizing wait, the pans by the wall coming to life along with the icons and it even seemed there was someone in the bed. They hoped to escape these hallucinatory visions by stealing glances at one another but all three faces radiated helplessness, and while they knew they couldn't get started till nightfall (because they were sure that Mrs. Halics or the manager would be sitting at their windows watching the path to Szikes with even greater anxiety now that Schmidt and Kráner were almost half a day late), every so often Schmidt or the woman made a move as if to say, screw caution, let's make a start. "They're off to see a movie," Futaki quietly declared. "Mrs. Halics, Mrs. Kráner and the manager, Halics." "Mrs. Kráner?" Schmidt snapped: "Where?" And he rushed to the window. "He's right. He's damn right," Mrs. Schmidt nodded. "Hush!" Schmidt turned on her: "Don't be in such a hurry, sweetheart!" Futaki calmed him: "That's a smart woman. We have to wait till dark anyway, don't we? And this way no one gets suspicious, right?" Schmidt was edgy but sat back down at the table and buried his face in his hands. Futaki carried on despondently puffing smoke by the window. Mrs. Schmidt drew out a length of twine from the depths of the kitchen cupboard and, because the locks were too rusty to close, tied the trunk up with it and set it down by the door before sitting down next to her husband and clasping her hands. "What are we waiting for?" asked Futaki. "Let's split up the money." Schmidt stole a glance at his wife. "Don't we have plenty of time for that, pal?" Futaki rose and joined them at the table. He spread his legs and, rubbing his stubbled chin, fixed his eyes on Schmidt: "I say we split it up." Schmidt ran a hand over his brow. "What are you worried about? You'll get your share when it's time." "Then what are you waiting for, pal?" "What's with the fuss? Let's wait till we get Kráner's contribution." Futaki smiled. "Look, it's very simple. We just halve what you've got there. Then when we get what's owing we'll split that up at the crossroads." "All right," Schmidt agreed. "Fetch the flashlight." "I'll get it," the woman leapt up, agitated. Schmidt plunged his hand into his trench coat and brought out a package tied round with string, somewhat drenched through. "Wait," cried Mrs. Schmidt and quickly wiped the table with a rag. "Now." Schmidt shoved a piece of paper under the nose of Futaki ("The document," he said, "just so you see I am not trying to cheat you") who tipped his head to one side and briefly took stock of it before pronouncing: "Let's get counting." He pressed the flashlight into the woman's hand and watched the bank notes with shining eyes as they passed through Schmidt's stubby fingers and slowly piled up at the far side of the table, and, as he watched, his anger slowly evaporated, because now he understood how "a man's head might get so confused by the sight of so much cash that he'd risk a lot to possess it." Suddenly he felt his stomach cramp up, his mouth filled with saliva and, as the sweat-spotted wad in Schmidt's hand began to shrink and swell the piles on the other side of the table, the flickering unsteady light in Mrs. Schmidt's hand seemed to be shining in his eyes as if she were deliberately doing it to blind him and he felt dizzy and weak, recovering only when Schmidt's cracked voice announced: "That's the precise amount!" But just as he was reaching forward to take his half share somebody right by the window shouted: "Are you in, Mrs. Schmidt, darling?" Schmidt snatched the flashlight from his wife's hand and snapped it off, pointing to the table, whispering: "Quick, hide it!" Mrs. Schmidt, lightning fast, swept it all together and stuffed the bills between her breasts, mouthing almost silently: "Miss-us Ha-lics!" Futaki sprang to conceal himself between the range and the cupboard, back tight against the wall, visible only as two phosphorescent points, as if he were a cat. "Go out and tell her to go to hell!"

Schmidt whispered, escorting her as far as the door where she froze for an instant before giving a sigh and stepping out into the hall, clearing her throat as she did so. "All right, all right, I'm going!" "We'll be fine providing she didn't see the light!" Schmidt whispered to Futaki though he himself did not really believe that, and having hidden himself behind the door was so nervous he had a hard time standing still. "If she dares take a step in I'll throttle her," he thought in desperation and swallowed hard. Those early morning bells, Mrs. Halics's unexpected appearance—it must be a conspiracy, there must be some significant connection, and as the slowly drifting smoke enveloped him it fired his imagination once more. "Maybe there'll be life on the estate yet? They might bring new machines, new people might come, everything could start all over again. They could mend the walls, give the buildings a fresh coat of limewash and get the pump house going. They might need a machinist, mightn't they?" Mrs. Schmidt stood in the door, her face pale. "You can come out," she said in a hoarse voice and turned on the light. Schmidt leapt over to her, blinking furiously. "What are you doing? Turn it off! They might see us!" Mrs. Schmidt shook her head. "Forget it. Everyone knows I'm at home, don't they?" Schmidt was obliged to nod in acknowledgment as he grabbed her arm. "So what happened? Did she notice the light?" "Yes," Mrs. Schmidt replied, "but I told her I was so nervous on account of you still not having returned that I fell asleep waiting and when I suddenly woke and turned the light on the bulb blew. I said I was just changing the bulb when she called out and that was why the flashlight was on …" Schmidt murmured in approval then grew anxious again: "What about us? What did she say … did she spot us?" "No, I'm certain she didn't." Schmidt breathed a sigh of relief. "Then what in God's name did she want?" The woman looked blank. "She's gone mad," she replied quietly. "No surprise there," Schmidt remarked. "She said …," Mrs. Schmidt added, her voice hesitant, looking now at Schmidt, now at the tensely attentive Futaki, "she said that Irimiás and Petrina were coming down the road ... they're on their way to the estate! And that they might already have arrived at the bar ..." For a minute or so neither Futaki nor Schmidt was capable of saying anything. "Apparently the driver of the long-distance bus ... he saw them in town ...," the woman broke the silence and bit her lip. "And that he set out—they set out— for the estate in this filthy weather, worse than judgment day ... The driver saw them as he turned off for Elek, that's where he has his farmstead, as he was hurrying home." Futaki sprang to his feet: "Irimiás? And Petrina?" Schmidt gave a laugh. "That woman! Mrs. Halics really has gone mad this time. She's been at her Bible too much. It's gone to her head." Mrs. Schmidt stood stock-still. Then she spread out her helpless arms and ran over to the range and flung herself on the stool, propping her head on her hand: "If it's true ..." Schmidt turned on her, impatient: "But they're dead!" "If it turns out to be true ...," Futaki repeated quietly as if completing Mrs. Schmidt's line of thought, "then the Horgos kid was simply lying ..." Mrs. Schmidt suddenly raised her head to look at Futaki. "And we had only his word for it," she said. "That's right," Futaki nodded and lit another cigarette, his hand trembling. "And do you remember? I said back then there was something not quite right about the story ... there was something about it I didn't like. But no one listened to me ... and eventually I gave in and accepted it." Mrs. Schmidt kept her eyes on Futaki as if she were trying to transfer her thoughts to him. "He lied. The kid simply lied. It's not so hard to imagine. In fact it's very easy to imagine ..." Schmidt stared nervously, now at him, now at his wife. "It's not Mrs. Halics who's gone mad, it's you two." Neither Futaki nor Mrs. Schmidt ventured an answer but looked at each other. "Have you lost your mind?!" Schmidt burst out and took a step toward Futaki: "You, you old cripple!" But Futaki shook his head. "No, my friend. No ... though you're right, Mrs. Halics hasn't gone mad," he told Schmidt, then turned to the woman, announcing: "I'm sure it's true. I'm going down to the bar." Schmidt closed his eyes and tried to govern his temper. "Eighteen months! Eighteen months they've been dead. Everyone knows that! People don't joke about such things. Don't fall for it. It's just a trap! You understand? A trap!" But Futaki hadn't even heard him, he was already buttoning his coat. "It'll be all right, you'll see," he declared, and you could tell by the firmness of his voice that his mind was made up. "Irimiás," he added, smiling and he put his hand on Schmidt's shoulder, "is a great magician. He could turn a pile of cow shit into a mansion if he wanted to." Schmidt lost his head entirely. He grabbed hold of Futaki's coat and yanked him closer. "You're the one who's a pile of cow shit, buddy," he grimaced, "and that's all you'll ever be, let me tell you, a pile of shit. You think I'm going to let a pea-brain like you do me down? No, pal, no. You're not going to get in my way!" Futaki calmly returned his gaze. "I've no intention of getting in your way, pal." "Yes? And what will become of the money?" Futaki bowed his head. "You can split it with Kráner. You can pretend that nothing's happened." Schmidt sprang to the door and barred their way. "Idiots!" he screamed: "You're idiots! Go fuck yourselves, the pair of you! But as for my money . . . ," he raised his finger, "you will deposit that on the table." He looked menacingly at the woman. "You hear me, you lousy . . . You'll leave the money right here. Understand?!" Mrs. Schmidt made no move. A peculiar, unaccustomed light flashed in her eyes. She slowly rose and moved toward Schmidt. Every muscle of her face was tense, her lips had grown extraordinarily narrow and Schmidt found himself the object of such intense contempt and mockery that he was forced to step back and gaze at the woman in astonishment. "Don't you go screaming at me, you moron," said Mrs. Schmidt quite quietly: "I'm going out. You can do what you like." Futaki was picking his nose. "Look pal," he added, his voice also quiet, "if they are really here you won't be able to escape Irimiás anyway, you know that yourself. And what happens then? . . ."

Schmidt felt his way over to the table and slumped in a chair. "The dead resurrected!" he muttered to himself. "And these two happy to take the bait ... Ha ha ha. I can't help laughing!" He brought his fist down on the table. "Can't you see what the game is?! They must have suspected something and now they want to lure us out ... Futaki, old man, you at least should have a drop of sense in you ..." But Futaki wasn't listening; he was standing by the window, his hands locked together. "Do you remember?" he said. "The time the rent was nine days late, while he ..." Mrs. Schmidt brusquely cut him off: "He always got us out of a mess." "Filthy traitors. I might have guessed," Schmidt mumbled. Futaki moved away from the window and stood behind him. "If you're really so skeptical," he advised Schmidt, "let's send your wife on ahead ... She can say she is looking for you ... and so on ..." "But you can bet your life on it—it's true," the woman added. The money remained in Mrs. Schmidt's bosom since Schmidt himself was quite convinced that was the best place for it though he insisted he would far rather it were secured there with a piece of string and they had to work hard to persuade him to sit down again because he was off somewhere to look for something. "All right, I'm going," said Mrs. Schmidt and was immediately in her coat, pulling on her boots and was off running, soon disappearing into the darkness through the ditches surrounding the carriageway leading to the bar, avoiding the deeper puddles, not once turning back to look at them, leaving them there, two faces by the window, the rain washing over them. Futaki rolled a cigarette and blew out smoke, happy and hopeful, all tension gone, the weight lifted from him, dreamily contemplating the ceiling; he was thinking of the machine hall in the pump house, already hearing the cough, the splutter, the painful but successful sound of machines long silent starting up again, and it was as though he could smell the freshly limewashed walls ... when they heard the outside door open and Schmidt had just enough time to leap to his feet before Mrs. Kráner was announcing:

"They're here! Have you heard?!" Futaki stood and nodded and put his hat on. Schmidt had collapsed at the table. "My husband," Mrs. Kráner gabbled, "he's already started and just sent me across to tell you, if you didn't know already though I'm sure you know, we could see through our window that Mrs. Halics had dropped by, but I've got to go, I don't want to bother you, and as for the money, my husband said, forget it, it's not for the likes of us, he said and . . . he's right because why hide and run, with never a moment of peace, who wants that, and Irimiás, well you'll see, and Petrina, I knew that it couldn't be true, any of it, so help me, I never trusted that sneaky Horgos kid, you can tell from his eyes, you can see for yourselves how he made it all up and kept it up till we believed him, I tell you, I knew from the start . . ." Schmidt examined her suspiciously. "So you're in on it too," he said and gave a short bitter laugh. Mrs. Kráner raised her eyebrows at that and disappeared through the door in confusion. "Are you coming, buddy?" Futaki inquired after a while and suddenly they were both at the door. Schmidt led with Futaki hobbling behind with his stick, the wind snapping at the edges of his coat as he held on to his hat to prevent it flying away into the mud and tapped his blind way in the darkness, while the rain poured pitilessly down washing away both Schmidt's curses and his own words of encouragement that eventually resolved into a repeated phrase: "Don't go regretting anything, old man! You'll see. It'll be cushy for us. Pure gold. A real golden age!"

II

WE ARE RESURRECTED

The clock above their heads shows a quarter before ten but what else should they be waiting for? They know what the neon light with its piercing buzz is doing on that ceiling with its hairline cracks and what the timeless echo of those slamming doors is all about; they know why those heavy boots with their half-moon metaled heels are clattering down those strangely high, tiled corridors, just as they suspect why the lights at the back have not been lit and why everything looks so tired and dim; and they would bow their heads in humble acknowledgment and with a degree of complicit satisfaction before this magnificently constructed system if only it were not the two of them sitting on these benches polished to a dull glow by the rumps of the hundreds upon hundreds who have occupied them before, obliged to keep their eyes on the aluminum handle of door Number Twenty-Four, so that, having gained admittance, they should be able to make use of the two or three minutes ("It's nothing, just ...") to dispel "the shadow of suspicion that has fallen ..." For what else is there to discuss except this ridiculous misunderstanding that has arisen on account of procedures initiated by some no doubt conscientious but overzealous official? ... And so the words prepared for the occasion tumble over each other and begin sparring round as in a whirlpool, having formed the occasional frail, if painfully useless, sentence that, like a hastily improvised bridge, is capable of bearing only the weight of three hesitant steps before there's the sound of a crack, when it bends, and then with one faint, final snap collapses under them so that time and time again they find themselves back in the whirlpool they entered last night when they received the sheet with its official stamp and formal summons. The precise, dry, unfamiliar language ("the shadow of suspicion that has fallen") left them in no doubt that it was not a matter of proving their innocence—for to deny the charge or, conversely, to demand a hearing, would be a waste of time—if only the opportunity might arise for a general chat where they might state their position regarding an all-but-forgotten matter, establish their identities and perhaps modify a few personal details. In the past, seemingly endless, months, ever since a stupid difference of opinion so slight it's hardly worth mentioning, had led to their being cut off from normal life, their earlier, now clearly frivolous, views had matured to a firm conviction, and if opportunity arose they could answer correctly any questions regarding such general ideas as might be grouped together under the heading of a "guiding principle" with startling certainty and without any torturous inner struggle; in other words they were beyond surprise now. And as regards this self-consuming and constantly recurring state of panic they could take courage and put it down to "the bitter experience of the past" because "no man could have got out of such a hole without some injury." The big hand is moving steadily closer to twelve when an official appears at the top of the stairs, his hands behind him, moving with light steps, his whey-colored eyes clearly fixed ahead of him until they are drawn to the two strange characters sitting there, when a faint flush of blood enters his gray, hitherto dead-looking face and he stops, raises himself on tiptoe, and then, with a tired grimace, turns away again to disappear down the stairs, taking a moment only to look up at the other clock hanging beneath the NO SMOKING notice by which time his face has returned to its normal gray. The taller of the two men assures his companion, saying, "The two clocks say different times, but it could be that neither of them is right. Our clock here," he continues, pointing to the one above them with his long, slender and refined index finger, "is very late, while that one there measures not so much time as, well, the eternal reality of the exploited, and we to it are as the bough of a tree to the rain that falls upon it: in other words we are helpless." Though his voice is quiet it is a deep, musical, manly voice that fills the bare corridor. His companion who, it is obvious at a glance, is as different "as chalk from cheese" from the individual radiating such confidence, resilience and firmness of purpose, fixes his dull button-like eyes on the other's timeworn, suffering-hardened face and his whole being is suddenly suffused by passion. "Bough of a tree to the rain ..." he turns the phrase over in his mouth as if it were fine wine, trying to guess its vintage, realizing somewhat indifferently that it is beyond him. "You're a poet, old man, you really are!" he adds and marks it with a deep nod like someone frightened by the idea that he has inadvertently stumbled on some truth. He slides further up the bench so that his head might be at the same level as the other man's, sinks his hands into the pockets of the winter coat that seems to have been made for a giant and searches among the screws, sweets, nails, the postcard of the seaside, the alpaca spoon, the empty frame of a pair of spectacles and some loose Kalmopyrin tablets that are to be found in there until he discovers the piece of sweat-soaked paper and his brow begins to perspire. "If we don't put the lid on ..." He tries to prevent the words escaping his lips but it's too late. The creases on the taller man's face grow deeper, his lips tighten and his eyelids slowly close since he too finds it hard to suppress his emotions. Though they both know they made a mistake that morning in immediately demanding an explanation and bursting in through the marked door and not stopping till they reached the innermost room: not because they received no explanation, they never even met the boss, since no sooner had they got there than he simply told the secretaries in the outer office ("Find out who these people are!") and they found themselves outside the door. How could they have been so stupid? What a mistake! Now they were piling one mistake on top of another since even three days were not enough to recover from such bad luck. Because ever since they had been released to take a deep breath of the air of liberty and to cover every inch of those dusty streets and neglected parks, the sight of homesteads declining into autumnal yellow made them feel practically newborn, and they had taken strength from the sleepy expressions of the men and women they passed, from their bowed heads, from the slow gaze of melancholy youths leaning against a wall, the shadow of some as yet undefined ill fortune had followed them around, like something without a shape, and they could glimpse it in a pair of eyes that flashed up at them, or a movement here or there that would betray its presence as admonitory, inevitable. And just to crown all this ("Call me Petrina, I call that terrifying . . .") the incident last night at the deserted station when—who knows, who could have suspected that someone else might want to spend the night on the bench next to the door that led to the platform?—a spotty-faced lout of a lad stepped through the revolving doors and, without a moment's hesitation, strode over to them and pressed the summons into their hands. "Will there never be an end to this?" the taller one had asked the stupid-looking messenger and it is this that now comes to his shorter companion's mind when he timidly remarks: "They are doing this deliberately, you know, in order to . . ." The taller one smiles wearily. "Don't exaggerate. Just listen closely. Pay more attention. It's stopped again." The other man jerks back at this as if suddenly caught in some guilty act, is embarrassed, makes a waving movement and reaches for his improbably large ears, trying to smooth them down while flashing his toothless gums. "As fate dictates," he says. The taller man regards him with raised eyebrows for a while then turns away before registering his abhorrence. "Ugh! How ugly you are!" he exclaims and turns back from time to time as if he could not believe his eyes. The jug-eared one shrinks despondently away, his pear-shaped little head hardly visible above his turned-up collar. "You can't judge by appearances ...," he mutters, wounded. At that moment the door opens and a man with a squashed nose and the look of a professional wrestler steps through with a considerable amount of fuss but instead of dignifying the two characters who rush to greet him with a glance — or saying, "Please come with me!"— marches past them and disappears behind a door at the end of the corridor. They stare at each other indignantly (as though they had reached the end of their tether), hang about for a while, desperate and ready to do anything, just one step from committing some unforgivable act when the door snaps open once again and a little fat man sticks his head out. "What are you waiting for?" he asks mockingly, then, with a wholly inappropriate gesture and a harsh "Aha!" flings the door wide before them. The large office inside is like a stockroom with five or six plainclothesmen bent over heavy shiny desks, above them a neon light like a vibrating halo, though there is a distant corner where the darkness has been squatting for many years, where even the light filtering through the closed slats of the blinds vanishes and disappears as if the dank air beneath were swallowing it all. Though the clerks are silently scribbling (some of them are wearing black patches on their elbows, others have glasses slipping down their noses) there is a constant whispering sound: one or another of them quickly casts half an eye at the visitors, squinting at them, sizing them up with barely concealed malice, as if speculating when they might make the one wrong move that will betray them, when the worn old overcoat might flap aside to reveal a flea-bitten butt, or when the holes in the shoes might reveal socks in need of darning. "What's going on here!"

the taller one thunders as he crosses the threshold of the stockroom-like space ahead of the other, for there in the room he sees a man in shirtsleeves on all fours on the floor feverishly looking for something under his dark-brown desk. He keeps his presence of mind though: he takes a few steps forward, stops, fixes his eyes on the ceiling so as tactfully to ignore the embarrassing position of the man he must talk to. "Begging your pardon, sir!" he begins in his most charming manner. "We haven't forgotten our obligations. Here we are ready to comply with your request as expressed in your letter of last night, according to which you wish to have a few words with us. We are citizens, honest citizens, of this country and therefore would like—voluntarily, that goes without saying—to offer you our services, services that, if I may be so bold as to remind you, you have been kind enough to draw upon for a good many years, albeit in an irregular fashion. It will hardly have escaped your attention that there has been a regrettable intermission in these services when you have had to do without us. We guarantee, as employees of your organization, that, now, as always in the past, we reject shoddy work and indeed any other kind of disappointment. We are perfectionists. Believe us, sir, when we say that we offer you the same high standard of work to which you have been accustomed. Delighted to be at your service." His companion nods and is clearly moved, barely able to prevent himself from grasping his comrade's hand and giving it a firm shake. The chief meanwhile has got up off the floor, gulps down a white pill and, after struggling a little, manages to swallow it without a sip of water. He dusts off his knees and takes his place behind the desk. He crosses his arms and leans heavily on his worn old fake-leather folder, glaring at the two strange figures before him who are standing vaguely at attention, looking at something over his head. His mouth twists in pain and settles all the lineaments of his face into a sour mask. Without moving his elbows he shakes a cigarette free of the pack, puts it in his mouth and lights it. "What were you saying?" he asks suspiciously, his expression puzzled, his feet twitching a nervous little dance under the table. The question hangs uselessly in the air while the two apparent derelicts stand stock-still, patiently listening. "Are you that shoemaker fellow?" the chief tries again and continues blowing out a long plume of smoke that rises above the tower of files on his desk and begins to swirl around him so it is minutes before his face becomes visible again. "No, sir ...," the jug-eared one replies as if deeply insulted. "We were summoned to appear here at eight o'clock ..." "Aha!" the chief exclaims with satisfaction: "And why did you not appear on time?" The jug-eared man looks up accusingly from under his brow. "There must be some misunderstanding, if I may ... We were here precisely on time, don't you remember?" "As I understand it ..." "No chief, you don't understand anything!" the little fellow cuts him off, suddenly full of life: "The thing is that we, that is to say the man next to me and I, sure, we can do anything. We can make you furniture, farm your chickens, castrate your pigs, deal with your real estate, and repair anything, even things thought to be beyond salvation. You want us to be market traders—that's fine. We can do anything you want. But come off it!" he snarls. "Don't make us laugh! You know very well our job is to supply information, if I may put it like that. We're on your payroll, if you care to remember. Our position, if you know what I mean, is ..." The chief leans back in exhaustion, slowly examines them, his brow clears, he springs to his feet, opens a little door in the back wall and calls back to them from the threshold: "Just wait here. But no monkey business ... you know what I mean!" Within a couple of minutes a tall, blond, blue-eyed man, rank of captain, appears before them, sits down at the table, carelessly stretches out his legs, and gives them a benign smile. "Do you have any papers?" he inquires politely. The jug-eared one searches in his enormously large pockets. "Paper? Certainly!" he announces in delight: "Just a moment!" He produces a slightly rumpled but perfectly clean sheet of writing paper and puts it down in front of the captain. "Would you like a pen too?" the taller man inquires and reaches for his inside pocket. The captain's face darkens for an instant then opens in a cheerful smile. "Very funny," he grins. "You two certainly have a sense of humor." Jug Ears modestly casts his eyes down. "True enough, you don't get anywhere without it, chief . . ." "Yes, but let's get to the point," the captain grows serious: "Do you have papers of any other sort?" "Of course, chief. Give me a moment . . . !" He reaches into his pocket again and pulls out the summons. Flourishing it in the air with a gesture of triumph he puts it down on the table. The captain glances at it, then his face reddens and he bellows at them: "Can't you read!? Fucking idiots! Which floor does it say?" The question is so unexpected that they take a step back. Jug Ears nods furiously. "Of course . . . ," he answers for want of anything better to say. The officer tips his head to one side. "What does it say?" "The second . . . ," the other replies and, by way of explanation, adds, "I beg to report." "Then what are you doing here!? How did you get here!? Have you any idea what this office deals with?!" Both men shake their heads, feeling weak. "This is the RP section — Registry of Prostitutes," the captain bellows at them leaning forward in his chair. But there is no sign of surprise. The shorter man shakes his head as if to say he doesn't believe the captain, and purses his lips in thought, while his companion stands beside him with his legs crossed apparently studying the landscape picture on the wall. The officer props an elbow on the table to support his head and starts massaging his brow. His back is as straight as the road to righteousness, his chest is deep and wide, his uniform crisply washed and ironed, his perfectly starched blindingly white collar in splendid harmony with his fresh, rosy-cheeked countenance. One lock of his otherwise immaculately wavy hair is hanging over his sky-blue eyes and lends an irresistible charm to his whole appearance, an appearance that radiates a childlike innocence. "Let's start," he says in a stern, southern singsong voice, "with your IDs." Jug Ears produces two ragged-edged packages from his back pocket and pushes aside one of those big towers of files so that he might smooth the package out before handing it over but the captain snatches it from his hand with the impatience of youth and flicks through the pages military fashion without even looking at them. "What do they call you?" he asks the shorter man. "Petrina, at your service." "Is that your name?" Jug Ears nods in melancholy fashion. "I would like to have your full name," says the officer leaning forward. "That's it, sir, that's all there is," Petrina answers with wide-eyed innocence then turns to his companion and whispers, "What can *I* do about it?" "What are you, a gypsy?" the captain snaps at him. "What, me?" Petrina asks, perfectly shocked: "Me, a gypsy?" "Then stop fooling about! Give me your name!" Jug Ears glances helplessly at his friend, then shrugs, looking utterly confused, as if unwilling to take responsibility for what he is about to say. "Well, Sándor-Ferenc-István … er … András." The officer leafs through the ID document and notes menacingly, "It says József here." Petrina looks as though he has been poleaxed. "Surely not, chief, sir! Would you mind showing me …." "Stay right there!" the captain orders him, unwilling to put up with any more nonsense. The taller man's face shows no sign of anxiety, not even interest, and when the officer asks him his name, he blinks a little as if his mind had been elsewhere and courteously replies: "I beg you pardon, I didn't get that." "Your name!" "Irimiás!" His answer rings out, as if he were proud of it. The captain puts a cigarette in the side of his mouth, lights it with a clumsy movement, throws the burning match into the ashtray and puts it out with the matchbox. "I see. So you too have only one name." Irimiás nods cheerfully: "Of course, sir. Doesn't everyone?" The officer looks deep into his eyes, opens the door ("Is that all you have to say?") and waves to them to follow him. They follow a couple steps behind him past the clerks with their sly looks, past the desks of the office outside, into the corridor and set off up the stairs. It is even darker here and they almost trip over the turns of the stairs. A crude iron balustrade runs alongside them, its polished and worn underside streaked with rust as they move from step to step. Everywhere there is the sense of everything having been thoroughly cleaned and not even the heavy fishlike smell that follows them everywhere can quite mask it.

UPPER FLOOR
FLOOR 1
FLOOR 2

The captain, slender as an officer of the hussars, proceeds before them with long ringing strides, his shining, half-length military boots almost musical as they strike against the polished ceramic tiles; he casts not a single look back at them but they are acutely aware he is considering everything about them, all the way from Petrina's laborer's boots to Irimiás's dazzlingly loud red tie, having perhaps memorized such details, or maybe because the thin skin stretched over the back of his neck is capable of receiving deeper impressions than the naked eye can discover. "Identification!" he barks at a lushly mustached, swarthy, large lump of a sergeant as they step through another door marked 24, into a smoky, stuffy hall, not slowing for an instant, indicating with a wave of his fingers that those leaping to their feet at his entrance should sit down, while snapping out his orders: "Follow me! I want the files! I want the reports! Give me extension 109! Then a line to town!" before he disappears behind a glazed door on the left. The sergeant remains stiffly at attention then, as he hears the lock click, wipes his arm across his sweating brow, sits down at the desk opposite the entrance and pushes a printed form in front of them. "Fill it out," he tells them, exhausted: "And sit down. But first read the instructions on the back of the page." There is no movement of air in the hall. There are three rows of neon lights on the ceiling, the illumination is dazzling: the wooden blinds are closed here too. Clerks are running about nervously between a mass of desks: when they occasionally find themselves obstructing another's path in the narrow gangways between tables they impatiently push each other aside with brief apologetic smiles as a result of which the desks are shifted a few centimeters every time, leaving sharp scrape marks on the floor. Some refuse to move out of the way though the piles of work in front of them have grown into huge towers. They clearly prefer to spend most of their working time bickering with their colleagues, carping at them for constantly shoving them in the back or pushing their desks aside. Some perch in their red fake-leather chairs like jockeys, telephone receiver in one hand, a steaming cup of coffee in the other. From wall to wall, from the back of the hall to the front, there are aging female typists sitting in rows that are straight as a die, pecking at their machines. Petrina watches their feverish labor with astonishment, prodding Irimiás with his elbow though the other man simply nods, busily studying the "Instructions" on the back of the form. "Do you suppose there's a cafeteria here?" whispers Petrina but his companion irritably gestures for him to be quiet. Then he looks up from the document and starts sniffing the air, asking: "Can you smell it?" and points upward. "It smells marshy here," Petrina declares. The sergeant looks at them, beckons them closer and whispers: "Everything is rotting in this place ... Twice in the last three weeks they've had to limewash the walls." There is a shrewd light in his deep-set, puffy eyes, his jowls constricted by his tight collar. "Shall I tell you something?" he asks with a knowing smile. He moves close so they can feel the steam of his breath. He starts to laugh silently as if unable to stop himself. Then he speaks, emphasizing each individual word like a set of land mines: "I suppose you think you can get out of this," he smiles, then adds: "But you're screwed." He looks mightily pleased with himself and taps the table three times as though repeating what he had just said. Irimiás gives a superior smile and goes back to study-ing the document while Petrina stares in horror at the sergeant who suddenly bites his lower lip, gives them a contemptuous look and leans indifferently back in his chair, once again simply part of the dense ma-trix of background noise. Once they have completed their forms he leads them into the captain's office, all trace of fatigue, of the almost terminal exhaustion that had seemed to be his lot, vanishing from his features, his steps firm, his movements crisp, his speech military and sharp. The furnishings of the office suggest a measure of comfort. To the left of the writing desk stands an enormous potted plant on whose deep luxurious green the eye may rest, while in the corner by the door a leather sofa stretches complete with two leather armchairs and a smoking table of "modern" design. The window is covered by a heavy set of poisonously green velvet curtains: a strip of red carpet runs over the parquet flooring from the door to the desk. You can sense rather than see the fine dust sifting slowly from the ceiling, a dust hallowed and dignified by countless years. There is a portrait of some military figure on the wall. "Sit down!" the officer orders, pointing to three wooden chairs in a tight row in the far corner: "'I want us to understand each other ..." He leans back in his high-backed chair, pressing against the bone-colored wood, and fixes his eye on some distant point, some faint mark on the ceiling, while his voice, a surprisingly singsong voice, swims toward them through a clearing cloud of cigarette smoke, as though he were speaking from elsewhere, not from within the stifling fug that catches at their throats. "You've been summoned because you have endangered the project by your absence. No doubt you have no-ticed I've not given precise details. The nature of the project has noth-ing to do with you. I myself am inclined to forget the whole matter, but whether I do or not, depends on you. I hope we understand each other." He lets his words hang there for a moment, timelessly signifi-cant. They are like fossils cushioned by damp moss. "I suggest we put the past aside," he continues. "That is providing you accept my terms regarding the future." Petrina is picking his nose; Irimiás trying to free his coat from under his companion's rear. "You have no choice. If you say no I shall make sure you're put away so long your hair will be gray by the time you get out." "I beg your pardon, chief, but what are you talking about?" Irimiás interrupts. The officer continues as though he hasn't heard him: "You have three days. Did it never occur to you that you should have been working? I know exactly what you've been up to. I give you three days. I think you should appreciate what is at stake here. I'm not making any wild promises beyond that, but three days you'll get." Irimiás considers protesting but thinks better of it. Petrina is genuinely terrified. "I'm fucked if I understand any of this, if you'll pardon the expression..." The captain lets it go, pretends not to have heard, and carries on as if he were delivering himself of a verdict, a verdict that expects to be met with complaint but is willing to ignore it. "Listen carefully because I won't say this again: no more delays, no more fooling around, no more trouble. All that is over. From now on you do what I say. Is that clear?" Jug Ears turns to Irimiás. "What's he talking about?" "I haven't the faintest idea," Irimiás rumbles back. The captain shifts his gaze from the ceiling and his eyes darken. "Will you please shut up," he drawls in his old-fashioned, singsong voice. Petrina sits, almost lies, on the chair, blinking in panic, his hands clasped across his chest, the back of his neck against the chair back, his heavy winter coat spread about him like petals. Irimiás is sitting upright, his mind working feverishly. His pointed shoes are a blinding bright yellow. "We have our rights," he sniffs, the skin on his nose forming delicate wrinkles. The captain is annoyed and blows out smoke, a brief sign of exhaustion flickering across his face. "Rights!" he exclaims: "You talk of rights! The law for your type is simply something to be exploited! Something to cover your back when you get into trouble! But that's all over... I'm not arguing with you because this isn't a debating club, you hear? I suggest you quickly get used to the idea that you do as I say. You will act legally from now on. You work within the law." Irimiás massages his knees with sweaty palms: "What law?" The captain frowns. "The law of relative power," he says, his face pale, his fingers turning white on the arms of the chair. "The law of the land. The people's law. Do these concepts mean nothing to you?" he asks, employing the less intimate form of "you" for the first time. Petrina is roused to speak ("What's going on here? Are we *te* or *maga* now? Are we fellow workers or not? Which is it? If you ask me I prefer ...") but Irimiás restrains him, saying: "Captain, you know what law we're talking about as well as we do. That's why we're here. Whatever you may think of us, we are law-abiding citizens. We are aware of our duties. I would like to remind you that we have frequently demonstrated that to be the case. We are on the side of the law as much as you are. So why all these threats? ..." The captain smiles mockingly, fixes his big, sincere eyes on Irimiás's inscrutable features and though the words sound friendly enough they can see there's real fury at the back of them. "I know everything about you ... but the truth is ... ," he gives a great sigh, "I have to admit I am none the wiser for that." "That's good," the relieved Petrina prods his companion, then casts an endearing look at the captain who recoils from his gaze and stares threateningly back. "Because, you know, I can't work when I'm tense! I simply can't deal with it!" and then Petrina anticipates the officer, seeing and feeling that this is going to end badly: "Isn't it better to talk like this, rather than ..." "You just shut that flabby face of yours!" the captain screams at him and leaps from his chair. "What do you think? Who the hell are you, you pair of cheapskates?! You think you can banter your way past me?!" He sits back down, enraged. "You think we're on the same side!? ..." Petrina is immediately on his feet, waving his hands about in panic, trying to salvage what he can of the situation. "No, of course not, for God's sake, beg to report we, how shall I put it, we wouldn't dream of it! ..." The captain says nothing, not a word, but lights another cigarette and stares fixedly ahead of him. Petrina stands there at a loss and gestures to Irimiás for help. "I've had enough of you two. That's it!" the officer announces in a steely voice: "I've had enough of the Irimiás-Petrina duo. I am fed up with creatures like you, miserable dogs who think I am answerable to them!" Irimiás quickly intervenes. "Captain, you know us. Why can't things remain as they were? Ask . . . ("Ask Szabó," Petrina helps him out) . . . Sergeant Major Szabó. There's never been any trouble." "Szabó has been retired," the captain answers bitterly, "I have taken over his files." Petrina leans over to him and squeezes his arm. "And here we are, just sitting here like a flock of sheep! . . . Many congratulations, chief, my heartiest congratulations!" The captain is irritated and pushes Petrina's hand away. "Back to your place! What do you think you're doing!" He shakes his head hopelessly then, because he sees they are genuinely shocked, he assumes a friendlier manner. "All right, now listen. I want us to understand each other. Please note, it is quiet here now. People are satisfied. That's just how it should be. But if they read the papers properly they would know that there is a real crisis out there. We are not going to allow that crisis to hem us in and destroy all we have achieved! That's a big responsibility, you understand, a serious responsibility! We are not going to allow ourselves the luxury of having characters like you wandering around wherever where they please. We don't want whispers and rumors here. I know you can be useful to the project. I know you have ideas. Don't think for an instant I don't know that! But I'm not interested in what you did in the past—you got what you deserved for that. You are to adapt yourselves to the new situation! Is that clear?!" Now Irimiás shakes his head. "Not at all, captain, sir. Nobody can make us do anything we don't want to. But when it comes to duty we will do what we can in our own way . . ." The captain leaps up again, his eyes bulging, his mouth starting to tremble. "What do you mean no one can make you do anything you don't want to?! Who the hell are you to talk back to me?! Fuck you, you rotten, hopeless bastards! Filthy bums! You will report to me tomorrow morning at eight o'clock sharp! Now get lost! Scram!" So saying, he turns his back on them and his body gives a convulsive shudder. Irimiás lopes toward the door, his head hanging and before drawing it closed behind him in order to follow Petrina who—like a snake—is already slipping out of the room, he glances back a last time. The captain is rubbing his brow and his face . . . it is as if he were covered in armor; gray, dull, yet metallic; he seems to be swallowing light, some secret power is entering his skin; the decay resurrected from the cavity of the bones, liberated, is filling every cell of his body as if it were blood spreading to the extremities thereby announcing its unquenchable power. In that briefest of moments the rosy glow of health vanishes, the muscles tighten and once more the body begins to reflect light rather than absorb it, glittering and silvery, and the finely arched nose, the delicately chiseled cheekbones and the microscopically thin wrinkles are replaced by a new nose, new bones, new wrinkles that wipe away all memory of what had preceded them to preserve in a single mass everything which, years from now, will find itself interred six feet under. Irimiás closes the door behind him and begins to walk faster, crossing the busy hall to catch up with Petrina who is already out in the corridor, not even looking back to see whether his companion has followed him because he feels that if he did turn to see he might be called back in again. The light percolates through heavy clouds, the town breathes through their scarves, an unfriendly wind swirls down the street, houses, sidewalk and roadway soaking helplessly under the downpour. Old women are sitting at their windows gazing at the dusk through net curtains, their hearts contracting at the sight of faces fleeing beneath the eaves outside, their faces full of such wrongs and sorrows that not even the steaming cookies baked in hot ceramic stoves can banish them. Irimiás strides furiously through the town, Petrina following him on little feet, complaining, indignant, getting left behind, occasionally stopping for a minute to recover his breath, his coat billowing in the wind. "Where now?" he asks miserably. But Irimiás does not hear him, moves ahead, muttering imprecations: "He'll regret this ... he'll regret this, the bastard ..." Petrina walks faster. "Let's just forget the whole shitty business!" he suggests, but his companion is not listening. Petrina raises his voice. "Let's head up river and see if we can get some action there ..." Irimiás neither sees nor hears him. "I'll wring his neck ...," he tells his partner and demonstrates how. But Petrina is just as stubborn. "There's so much we could do once we're there ... There's the fishing for example, you know what I mean ... Or, listen: say there's some lazy wealthy guy who, let us say, wants something built ..." Having stopped in front of a bar, Petrina puts his hand in his pocket and counts their money and then they go through the glazed door. Inside there are only a few people hanging around, a transistor radio in the lap of the old woman minding the toilets is ringing out noon bells; the sticky wiping up cloth, the tables with damp pools ready to witness a thousand little resurrections are mostly unoccupied for now, tipping this way and that; four or five men with cavernous faces, their elbows propped on tables some way from each other, are wearing disillusioned expressions or slyly eyeing the waitress, or staring into their glasses or studying letters, absentmindedly sipping at coffees, or cheap spirits or wine. A damp and bitter stench blends with cigarette smoke, sour breath rising to the blackened ceiling; beside the door, next to a smashed oil heater, a bedraggled rain-soaked dog trembles and stares panic-stricken outside. "Shift those lazy asses of yours!" shrieks a cleaning woman as she proceeds past the tables with a scrunched-up rag. Behind the counter, a girl with flaming red hair and a baby face is propping up a shelf laden with stale desserts and a few bottles of expensive champagne while painting her fingernails. On the drinkers' side of the counter leans a stocky waitress, cigarette in one hand and a dime novel in the other, licking her lips in excitement every time she turns the page. On the walls a ring of dusty lamps serves for atmosphere. "A single, blended," says Petrina and leans on the counter next to his companion. The waitress doesn't even look up from her book. "And a Silver Kossuth," adds Irimiás. The girl behind the bar, clearly bored, levers herself away from the shelf, carefully puts down the bottle of nail polish, and pours out the drinks, her movements slow and sluggish, only taking the odd glance at what she is doing, then pushes one toward Irimiás. "Seven-seventy," she drawls. But neither man moves. Irimiás looks into the girl's face and their eyes meet. "The order was for a single!" he growls. The girl quickly looks away and fills two more glasses. "Sorry!" she says, a little abashed. "And I seem to remember ordering a pack of cigarettes too," Irimiás continues in a low voice. "Eleven-ninety," the girl gabbles, glancing over at her colleague who is stifling a giggle and waves at her to leave off. Too late. "What's so funny?" All eyes are fixed on them. The smile freezes on the waitress's face, she nervously adjusts her bra strap through her apron then shrugs. Suddenly everything has fallen quiet. Next to the window opening onto the street sits a fat man in a bus driver's cap: he watches Irimiás in astonishment then quickly finishes his piccolo and clumsily slams the glass down on the table. "Excuse me . . . ," he stutters, seeing how everyone is looking at him. And at that point, one cannot quite tell from where, a gentle humming begins. Everyone is breathlessly watching everyone else because for a moment it seems as though it is a person, a living person doing the humming. They steal glances at each other: the humming becomes a tad louder. Irimiás raises his glass then slowly puts it down again. "Is someone humming here?" he mutters in irritation. "Is someone making a joke?! What the hell is it? A machine? Or, or might it be . . . the lamps? No, it is a person after all. Could it be that old bat by the toilets? Or that asshole over there in the gym shoes? What is this? Some kind of dissent?" Then it suddenly stops. Now there's only the silence, the suspicious glances. The glass is trembling in Irimiás's hand; Petrina is nervously drumming on the counter. Everyone is sitting still, looking down, no one dares move. The old woman at the washrooms tugs the sleeve of the waitress. "Should we call the police?" The girl behind the bar can't stop giggling out of sheer nervousness so, to bring things to a head, she quickly turns on the tap in the sink and begins making a noise with the beer glasses. "We will blow them all up," says Irimiás in a strangled voice, then repeats it in a ringing bass: "We'll blow up the lot of them. We'll blow them up one by one. Cowards! Worms!" He turns to Petrina. "One stick of dynamite per jacket! That one there," he indicates someone behind him with his thumb, "will get one stuffed in his pocket. That one," he continues, glancing toward the fire, "will find one under his pillow. There'll be bombs up chimney flues, under doormats, bombs hung from chandeliers, bombs stuffed up their assholes!" The girl behind the bar and the waitress move closer to each other for comfort at the end of the counter. The patrons stare at each other in fright. Petrina weighs them up, his eyes full of hatred. "Blow up their bridges. Their houses. The whole town. The parks. Their mornings. Their mail. One by one, we'll do it properly, everything in the proper order ..." Irimiás purses his lips and blows out smoke, pushing his glass to and fro in pools of beer. "Because one has to finish what one has started." "True enough, no point in shilly-shallying," Petrina nods furiously: "We'll bomb them in stages!" "All the towns. One after the other!" Irimiás continues as if in a dream. "The villages. The remotest little shack!" "Boom! Boom! Boom!" cries Petrina, waving his arms around: "You hear! Then BLAAM! The end, gentlemen." He pulls a twenty from his pocket, throws it down on the counter right in the middle of a pool of beer, the paper slowly drawing the liquid up. Irimiás too moves away from the bar and opens the door but then turns back. "A couple of days, that's all you have left! Irimiás will blow you to pieces!" he spits out by way of parting, curls his lip and, by way of a grand finale, runs his gaze slowly over the terrified larval faces. The stench of sewers mixed with mud, puddles, the smell of the odd crack of lightning, wind tugging at tiles, power lines, empty nests; the stifling heat behind low ill-fitting windows ... impatient, annoyed half-words of lovers embracing ... demanding wails of babies, their cries sliding off into the tin-smell of dusk; streets pliable, parks soaked to their roots lying obedient to the rain, bare oaks, half-broken dry flowers, scorched grass all prostrate, humbled by the storm, sacrifices strewn at the executioner's feet. Petrina wheezes at Irimiás's heels. "Are we going to see Steigerwald?" But his companion does not hear him. He has turned up the collar of his houndstooth coat, his hands thrust deep into his pockets, his head raised, and is hurrying blindly from street to street, never slowing, never looking back, his soaked cigarette drooping from his mouth, though he doesn't even notice it, while Petrina continues to curse the world with an inexhaustible supply of imprecations, his bow legs buckling every so often and, when he falls twenty paces behind Irimiás, vainly shouting after him ("Hey! Wait for me! Don't be in such a rush! What am I, a cow in a stampede?") though the other pays no attention at all and, to make matters worse, he treads in a puddle up to his ankles, gives a great puff, leans against the wall of a house and mutters, "I can't keep up with this ..." But, after a couple of minutes, Irimiás reappears, his wet hair hanging over his eyes, his pointed bright-yellow shoes caked in mud. Water drips off Petrina. "Look at these," he says pointing to his ears, "Gooseflesh, frozen ..." Irimiás nods reluctantly, clears his throat and says, "We're going to the estate." Petrina stares at him, his eyes popping out. "What ... ? Now?! The two of us?! To the estate?!" Irimiás pulls another cigarette from the pack, lights it and quickly blows the smoke out. "Yes. Right now." Petrina leans against the wall. "Listen here, old friend, master, savior, slave driver! You'll be the death of me! I am frozen through, I'm hungry, I want to find somewhere warm where I can dry out and eat and I have no desire at all, God

40

knows, to tramp out to the estate in this foul weather, in fact I am quite disinclined to follow you, to run after you like a lunatic, damn your already damned soul! Damn it!" Irimiás gives a wave and replies indifferently, "If you don't want to stay with me go where you please." And he is gone. "Where are you going? Where are you off to now?" Petrina shouts after him in anger, setting off to follow him. "Where would you go without me?... Stop for a second. Come on!" The rain eases off a little as they leave the town. Night descends. No stars, no moon. At the Elek crossroads, a hundred yards ahead of them, a shadow sways; only later do they discover it is a man in a trenchcoat; he enters a field and the darkness swallows him. On either side of the highway there are gloomy patches of woodland as far as the eye can see, mud covering everything and, since the fading light blurs all clear outlines, consuming all traces of color, stable forms begin to move while things that should move stand as if petrified, so the whole highway is like a strange vessel run aground, idling and rocking on a muddy ocean. Not a bird is stirring to leave its mark on the sky that has hardened to a solid mass that, like a morning mist, hovers above the ground, only a solitary frightened deer rises and sinks in the distance—as if the mud itself were breathing—preparing to flee in the far distance. "Dear God!" Petrina sighs. "When I think it will be morning before we get there I get cramp in my legs! Why didn't we ask Steigerwald if we could borrow his truck? And that coat too! What am I? A circus strongman??!" Irimiás stops, puts his foot up on a milestone, pulls out a cigarette, they both take one, and light them using their hands as shelter. "Can I ask you something, killer?" "What?" "Why are we going to the estate?" "Why? Do you have anywhere to sleep? Do you have anything to eat? Money? Either you stop your eternal whining or I strangle you." "OK. Fine. I understand, this much anyway. But tomorrow we've got to go back, haven't we?" Irimiás grinds his teeth but says nothing. Petrina gives another sigh. "Look friend, you really could have thought of something else with that clever head of yours! I don't want to stay with those people the way I am. I can't stand being in one place. Petrina was born under open skies, that's where he's lived all his life and that's where he'll die." Irimiás dismisses him with a bitter gesture: "We're in the shit, friend. There's nothing we can do about that for a while. We have to stay with them." Petrina wrings his hands. "Master! Please don't say things like that! My heart is already pounding." "OK, OK, don't crap in your pants. We'll take their money then we'll move on. We'll manage somehow ..." They set off again. "You think they have money?" Petrina asks anxiously. "Peasants always have something." They proceed without speaking, mile after mile, they must be roughly halfway between the turnoff and the local bar; occasionally a star twinkles in front of them only to vanish again in the dense dark; sometimes the moon shines through the mist and, like the two exhausted figures on the paved road below, escapes with them across the celestial battlefield, pushing its way past every obstacle toward its target, right until dawn. "I wonder what the bumpkins will say when they see us." "It'll be a surprise," Irimiás replies over his shoulder. Petrina picks up the pace. "What makes you think they'll be there at all?" he asks in his anxiety. "I figure they'll have made tracks ages ago. They must have that much intelligence." "Intelligence?" grins Irimiás. "Them? Servants is what they were and that's what they'll remain until they die. They'll be sitting in the kitchen, shitting themselves in the corner, taking the odd look out of the window to see what the others are doing. I know these people like the back of my hand." "I don't know how you can be so sure of that, friend," says Petrina. "My hunch is that there won't be anyone there. Empty houses, the tiles fallen or stolen, at best one or two starved rats in the mill ..." "No-o-o," Irimiás confidently retorts. "They'll be sitting in exactly the same place, on the same filthy stools, stuffing themselves with the same filthy spuds and paprika every night, having no idea what's happened. They'll be eyeing each other suspiciously, only breaking the silence to belch. They are waiting. They're waiting patiently, like the long-suffering lot they are, in the firm conviction that someone has conned them. They are waiting, belly to the ground, like cats at pig-killing time, hoping for scraps. They are like servants that work at a castle where the master has shot himself: they hang around at an utter loss as to what to do ..." "Enough poetry, boss, I am terrified enough already!" Petrina tries to calm himself while pressing his rumbling stomach. But Irimiás pays him no attention, he's on a roll. "They are slaves who have lost their master but can't live without what they call pride, honor and courage. That's what keeps their souls in place even if at the back of their thick skulls they sense these qualities aren't their own, that they've simply enjoyed living in the shadow of their masters ..." "Enough," Petrina groans and rubs his eyes because the water keeps running down his flat forehead: "Look, don't be cross, but I just can't bear listening to such stuff right now! ... You can tell me all about them tomorrow, for now I'd sooner you talked about a good steaming bowl of bean soup!" But Irimiás ignores this too and goes on undisturbed. "Then, wherever the shadow falls they follow, like a flock of sheep, because they can't do without a shadow, just as they can't do without pomp and splendor either," ("For God's sake! Cut it out old man, please! ..." Petrina cries in his agony) "they'll do anything not to be left alone with the remnants of pomp and splendor, because when they are left alone they go mad: like mad dogs they fall on whatever remains and tear it to bits. Give them a well-heated room, a cauldron bubbling with paprika stew, a few dogs, and they'll be dancing on the table every night, and even happier under warm bedclothes, panting away, with a tasty piece of the neighbor's stout wife to tuck into ... Are you listening to me Petrina?" "Ayayay," the other sighs in reply and adds in hope: "Why? Have you finished?" By now they can see the blown-over fences of the roadside houses, the tumbledown shed, the rusty water tank, when right beside them, a hoarse voice calls them from behind a high stack of weeds: "Wait! It's me!" A twelve- or thir-teen-year-old boy, completely chilled and soaked to the bone, wearing trousers rolled up to the knee, rushes toward them, drenched, trem-bling, his eyes shining. Petrina is the first to recognize him. "So it's you … ? What are you doing here, you little good-for-nothing!?" "I've been hiding here for hours …," he announces with pride, and quickly looks down. His long hair hangs in knots over his spotty face, a cigarette glowing between his bent fingers. Irimiás takes patient stock of the boy who steals the odd look at him but immediately lowers his eyes again. "So what do you want?" Petrina quizzes him, shaking his head. The boy steals another glance at Irimiás. "You promised …" he starts, stutters and stops, "that … that if …" "Come on boy, spit it out!" Irimiás hassles him. "That if I told people that you were …" the boy finally blurts out kicking the ground all the while, "… dead, then you'd fix me up with Mrs. Schmidt …" Petrina pulls the boy's ear and snaps at him: "What's this? No sooner hatched and out of the egg but you already want to climb up ladies' skirts, you little scoundrel! What next?!" The boy frees himself and shouts, his eyes flashing in anger, "I tell you what you should be pulling, you old goat. The skin off your dick!" If Irimiás did not intervene there'd be a fight. "Enough!" he bellows. "How did you know we were on the way?" The boy stands a careful distance from Petrina, rubbing his ear. "That's my business. It doesn't matter anyway … Everyone knows by now. The driver told them." Petrina is cursing, looking up at the sky but Irimiás gestures for him to be quiet ("Use your brains! Leave him alone!") and turns to the boy: "What driver?" "Kelemen. He lives by the Elek turning, that's where he saw you." "Kelemen? He's become a bus driver?" "Yeah, since spring, on the cross-country route. But the bus isn't in service at the moment so he has time to loaf around …" "OK," says Irimiás and sets off. The boy hurries to keep pace with him. "I did what you asked me to do. I hope you'll keep your part of …" "I generally keep my promises," Irimiás answers coolly. The boy follows him like a shadow; sometimes he catches up with him and squints up at his face then falls behind again. Petrina trails still further behind, a long way back, and though they can't make out his voice they are aware he is continually cursing the ceaseless rain, the mud, the boy, and the world at large ("to hell with it all!"). "I still have the photograph!" says the boy some two hundred yards on. But Irimiás does not hear him or pretends not to have heard, his head raised high he is striding down the middle of the road, slicing the darkness with his hooked nose and sharp chin. The kid tries again: "Don't you want to see the photograph?" Irimiás turns slowly to look at him. "What photograph?" Petrina has caught up with them. "Do you want to see?" Irimiás nods. "Stop beating around the bush, you little devil," Petrina hurries him. "You won't be cross?" "No. OK?" "You must let me hold it!" the boy adds and reaches into his shirt. In the photograph they are standing in front of a street vendor, Irimiás on the right, his hair combed and parted on the side, wearing a houndstooth-check jacket and a red tie, the crease on his trousers broken at his knee; Petrina is beside him in a pair of satin britches and an outsize undershirt, the sun shining through his jug ears. Irimiás has screwed up his eyes and gives a mocking smile, Petrina is solemn and ceremonial; his eyes happen to be closed, his mouth slightly open. Someone's hand intrudes into the picture on the left, the fingers holding a banknote, a fifty. Behind them a merry-go-round that has been tipped over, or is in process of being tipped over. "Well, would you look at that!" Petrina remarks in delight, "It's really us, friend. I'll be darned if it isn't! Pass it over, let me get a better look at that old mug of mine." The boy pushes his hand away. "Nah! Get lost! You think this is a free show I'm giving here! Get your filthy paws off," and so saying he slips the photo back in its little clear plastic sleeve and back inside his shirt. "Aw, come on kid!" Petrina purrs, pleading. "Let's have another look. I hardly had a chance to see anything." "If you want to see more of it ... then ..." the boy hesitates, "then you'll have to fix me up with the bar owner's wife. She has nice big tits too!" Petrina curses and sets off. ("What next, you brat!") The boy slaps him on the back then rushes after Irimiás. Petrina fishes in the air after him for a while then he remembers the photograph, smiles and hums, and walks a little faster. They're at the crossroads: from here it's only half an hour. The boy looks at Irimiás adoringly, leaping now to the left, now to the right of him ... "Mari is screwing the bar owner ..." he loudly explains as he goes, taking the odd puff at his cigarette that has burned right down to his fingers by now. "... Mrs. Schmidt does it with the cripple, has for a long time, the headmaster does it to himself ... Really repulsive ... you can't begin to imagine, ugh! ... My sister has gone totally crazy, does nothing but listen and spy, she spies on everyone all the time, Ma beats her but it's no use, nothing is of any use, it's like people said, she will remain gaga all her life ... believe it or not, the doctor just sits at home all the time, doing nothing, absolutely nothing! Just sits there all day, all night, he even sleeps in his chair, and his whole place smells, it's like a rat's nest, the light on day and night, not that it matters to him, he sits there smoking high-class cigarettes, you'll see, it's just like I told you. And, I almost forgot, today's the day when Schmidt and Kráner are bringing the money home for the poultry, yes, that's what they've all been doing since February, except Ma, because the filthy swine did not include her. The mill? Nobody goes there, the place is full of rooks, and my sisters because that's where they go to whore, but what idiots, just imagine! Ma takes all their money and all they do is sit and weep! I wouldn't let that happen, you can be sure of that. There in the bar? That doesn't work any more. The landlord's wife is so full of herself now, she's swollen up like a cow's ass, but luckily she has moved into the town house at last and will stay there till spring, because she said she wasn't going to stay here up to her neck in mud, and, you have to laugh, the landlord has to go home once a month and when he comes back it's like he's had the shit kicked out of him, she lays into him so … In any case he has sold that great Pannón bike he had and bought some crap machine that he's having to push around all the time, and everyone's around, the whole estate when it starts up—because he is always delivering something to somebody—but then everyone has to push it, that's if the engine starts at all … And, yes, he tells everyone that he has won some county race riding that wreck, you have to laugh! He's with my little sister for now because we owe him for seed since last year …" By now the window of the bar is visible, glowing ahead of them, but there is no sound, not a single word to be heard, as if the place were deserted, not a soul … but now, someone is playing the harmonica … Irimiás scrapes the mud off his lead-heavy shoes, clears his throat, cautiously opens the door, and the rain begins again, while to the east, swift as memory, the sky brightens, scarlet and pale blue and leans against the undulating horizon, to be followed by the sun, like a beggar daily panting up to his spot on the temple steps, full of heartbreak and misery, ready to establish the world of shadows, to separate the trees one from the other, to raise, out of the freezing, confusing homogeneity of night in which they seem to have been trapped like flies in a web, a clearly defined earth and sky with distinct animals and men, the darkness still in flight at the edge of things, somewhere on the far side on the western horizon, where its countless terrors vanish one by one like a desperate, confused, defeated army.

III

TO KNOW SOMETHING

At the end of the Paleozoic era the whole of Central Europe begins to sink. Naturally, our Hungarian homeland is part of this process. In the new geological circumstances the hill masses of the Paleozoic era sink ever lower until they reach rock bottom, at which point the sedimental sea inundates and covers them. As the sinking continues the territory of Hungary becomes the northwestern basin of that part of the sea that covers Southern Europe. The sea continues to dominate the region right through the Mesozoic era. The doctor was sitting by the window feeling morose, his shoulder up against the cold, damp wall and he didn't even have to move his head to look through the gap between the dirty floral curtain inherited from his mother and the rotten window frame in order to see the estate, but had only to raise his eyes from his book, take a brief glance to note the slightest change and if it now and then happened — say if he was utterly lost in thought or because he had focused on one of the remotest points of the estate—that his eyes missed something, his exceedingly sharp ears immediately came to his aid, though it was rare for him to be lost in thought and rarer still for him to rise in his fur-collared winter coat from the heavily blanketed, stuffed armchair— its position precisely determined by the cumulative experience of his everyday activities, successfully reducing to a minimum the number of possible occasions on which he would have to leave his observation post by the window. Of course, on a day-to-day basis this was by no means an easy task. On the contrary: he had to collect and arrange, in the optimal fashion, all that was necessary for eating, drinking, smoking, diary writing, and reading as well as the countless other little necessary details of daily life and, what was more, it meant he had to give up the idea of letting the odd slip—due entirely to some personal weakness—go unpunished, for, if he did so, he would be acting against his own interests, since an error due to distraction or carelessness increased the danger and the consequences were far graver than a man might think: one superfluous movement might mask a sign of the onset of vulnerability; a matchstick or brandy glass in the wrong place was a monument to the destructive effects of declining memory, not to mention the fact that it necessitated further modifications of behavior, so, sooner or later, it would mean reconsidering the place of the cigarette, the notebook, the knife and the pencil too, and soon "the whole system of optimal movement" would be obliged to change, chaos would ensue and all would be lost. It had not been the work of a moment establishing the best conditions for observation, no, it had taken years, a series of day-by-day refinements—a process of self-flagellation, punishment, and wave after wave of nausea following endless errors—but with the passing of initial uncertainty, and the occasional bout of despair, the time came when he no longer had to watch each and every distinct movement, when objects finally arrived at their fixed, final positions and he himself could assume firm, automatic control of his sphere of action at the most minute level, at which point he could admit to himself, without any danger of self-deception or overconfidence, that his life was capable of functioning perfectly. Of course it took a while, even months after achieving this, for the fear to leave him because he knew that however faultless his assessment of his situation in the neighborhood might be, he still, alas, depended on others for his supplies of food, spirits, cigarettes and other invaluable items. His anxieties about Mrs. Kráner, whom he had entrusted with his food shopping, and his doubts about the bar owner, immediately proved to be unfounded: the woman was punctilious and it had proved possible to wean her off the practice of appearing at the most inopportune moments with the some exotic foodstuff she had purloined on the estate, crying, "Don't let it cool down, doctor." As regards the drink he bought it in large quantities at long intervals, either buying it himself, or— more frequently—as a kind of insurance, entrusting the landlord with the task, since the latter feared that the unpredictable doctor might one day withdraw his confidence thereby depriving him of an assured income, and therefore did his utmost to satisfy the doctor in every particular, even when those particulars seemed downright stupid to him. So there was nothing to fear regarding these two people and as for the other residents of the estate, they had long abandoned hope that they might encroach on his privacy with a sudden attack of fever, stomach upset or general accident as pretext without at least a warning call since they were all convinced that, with his withdrawal of such privileges, his professionalism and reliability had also vanished. While this was clearly something of an exaggeration the feeling was not entirely unfounded since he dedicated the greatest part of what strength remained to him to preserving his powers of memory and letting all inessential matters take care of themselves. Despite all this he still lived in a constant state of anxiety because—as he noted in his diary with conspicuous regularity—"these things take all my attention!" so it didn't matter whether it was Mrs. Kráner or the landlord he spotted at his door, he would scrutinize either silently for minutes on end, looking deep into their eyes, checking to see whether they would look down, noting how quickly they averted their gaze, to see, in other words, how far their eyes betrayed them, revealing their suspicion, curiosity and fear, from which evidence he endeavored to tell whether they were still willing to stick to the agreement on which their financial arrangements depended, and only allowing them to approach once he was satisfied. He kept contact to a minimum, refusing to return their greetings, casting only a glance at the full bags they carried, watching their clumsy movements with such an unfriendly expression on his face, hearing their awkwardly formulated questions and excuses so impatiently, muttering away the whole time, that they (particularly Mrs. Kráner) constantly bit off their sentences, quickly put away the money he had put out for them and hastened away without counting it. This more or less explained why he was so nervous about being anywhere near the door: it made him feel decidedly ill, gave him a headache or made him feel breathless every time he was obliged (due to some carelessness on their part) to get up out of the armchair and fetch something from the far end of the room, so that each time he did (only after a long preliminary struggle with himself) he strove to be through with it as quickly as possible, although, no matter how quickly he accomplished it, by the time he got back to his chair his day had been ruined and he was seized by a mysterious bottomless anxiety, so the hand holding the pencil or the glass began to tremble and he filled his journal with nervous little jottings that, naturally, he scrubbed out with crude, furious movements. It was no wonder then that everything in this accursed corner of the estate was upside-down: the mud that had been trailed in had dried in thick layers on the wholly rotten, disintegrating floorboards; weeds grew by the wall nearest the door and off to the right lay a barely recognizable hat that had been trampled flat, surrounded by remnants of food, plastic bags, a few empty medicine bottles, bits of notepaper and worn-down pencils. The doctor—quite contrary, some believed, to his perhaps exaggerated and probably pathological love of order—did nothing to remedy this intolerable situation; he was convinced that his small corner of the estate was part of the hostile outside world and this was all the evidence he needed to justify his fear, anxiety, restlessness and uncertainty, for there was only a single "defensive wall" to protect him, the rest being "vulnerable." The room opened on to a dark corridor where weeds grew, this being the way to the toilet whose cistern had not worked for years, its absence being remedied by a bucket that Mrs. Kráner was obliged to refill three days a week. At one end of the corridor were two doors with great rusty locks hanging from them; the other end led outside. Mrs. Kráner, who had her own keys to the place, could always smell the strong sour stench as soon as she entered: it got into her clothes and, as she always insisted, it settled in her skin as well so it was no use trying to wash it off, even washing twice, on the days when she was "visiting the doctor": her efforts were pointless. That was the reason she gave Mrs. Halics and Mrs. Schmidt for the brief time she spent indoors: she was simply incapable of enduring the stench for more than two minutes at a time, because "I tell you, that smell is unbearable, simply unbearable, I don't even know how it is possible to live with such a terrible smell. He is after all an educated man and can see . . ." The doctor ignored the unbearable smell as he did everything else that did not directly impinge on his observation post, and the more he ignored such things the more attention and expertise he devoted to maintaining the order around him—the food, the cutlery, the cigarettes, the matches and the book—all with the correct distance between them on the table, the windowsill, the area round the armchair and the fiercely aggressive rot on the already ruined floorboards, and at dusk he would feel a warm glow, a degree of contentment, on surveying the suddenly darkening room, recognizing that everything was under his firm, omnipotent control. He had been aware for months that there was no point in further experimentation but then he realized that, even if he wanted to, he was unable to make the slightest change to any of it; no modification could conclusively be proved better because he was afraid that in itself the desire for change was only a subtle sign of his failing memory. So, doing nothing, he simply remained on the alert, careful to preserve his failing memory against the decay that consumed everything around him, much as he had done from the moment that he—once the closing of the estate had been announced and he personally had decided to stay behind and survive on what remained until "the decision to reverse the closure should be taken"—had gone up to the mill with the elder Horgos girl to observe the terrible racket of the abandonment of the place, with everyone rushing round and shouting, the trucks in the distance like refugees fleeing the scene, when it seemed to him that the mill's death sentence had brought the whole estate to a condition of near collapse, and from that day on he felt too weak to halt by himself the triumphal progress of the wrecking process, however he might try, there being nothing he could do in the face of the power that ruined houses, walls, trees and fields, the birds that dived from their high stations, the beasts that scurried forth, and all human bodies, desires and hopes, knowing he wouldn't, in any case, have the strength, however he tried, to resist this treacherous assault on humanity; and, knowing this, he understood, just in time, that the best he could do was to use his memory to fend off the sinister, underhanded process of decay, trusting in the fact that since all that mason might build, carpenter might construct, woman might stitch, indeed all that men and women had brought forth with bitter tears was bound to turn to an undifferentiated, runny, underground, mysteriously ordained mush, his memory would remain lively and clear, right until his organs surrendered and "conformed to the contract whereby their business affairs were wound up," that is to say until his bones and flesh fell prey to the vultures hovering over death and decay. He decided to watch everything very carefully and to record it constantly, all with the aim of not missing the smallest detail, because he realized with a shock that to ignore the apparently insignificant was to admit that one was condemned to sit defenseless on the parapet connecting the rising and falling members of the bridge between chaos and comprehensible order. However apparently insignificant the event, whether it be the ring of tobacco ash surrounding the table, the direction from which the wild geese first appeared, or a series of seemingly meaningless human movements, he couldn't afford to take his eyes off it and must note it all down, since only by doing so could he hope not to vanish one day and fall a silent captive to the infernal arrangement whereby the world decomposes but is at the same time constantly in the process of self-construction. It was not, however, enough to remember things conscientiously: that "was insufficient in itself," not up to the task: one had to compile and comprehend such signs as still remained in order to discover the means whereby the perfectly maintained memory's sphere of influence might be extended and sustained over a period. The best course then, thought the doctor during his visit to the mill, would be "to reduce to a minimum such events as would tend to increase the number of things I have to keep an eye on," and that very night, having told the useless Horgos girl to clear off home, informing her he no longer required her services, he set up his observation post by the window and began planning the elements of a system that some people might consider insane. Dawn was beginning to break outside and in the distance four ragged crows were wheeling menacingly above the Szikes, so he adjusted the blanket round his shoulders and automatically lit a cigarette. *During the Cretaceous period, it has since been discovered, there were two classes of material that comprised the body of our homeland. An inner mass shows signs of more regular sinking. A trough-like region develops that is progressively filled in and all but buried by a kind of basin deposit. At the periphery of the trough on the other hand we find signs of folding, that is to say a synclinal system is in formation ... And now a new chapter begins in the history of the landmass that is inner Hungary, a new developmental stage in which, as by a process of reaction, the heretofore close relationship between the framework of outer folds and the inner mass breaks down. The tensions within the earth's crust seek an equilibrium which does in fact duly follow when the unyielding inner mass that had hitherto been the determinant begins to collapse and sink, thereby bringing into existence one of the most beautiful basin groups in Europe, and as the sinking continues, the basin is filled by the neogene sea.* He looked up from his book and saw an unexpected wind had suddenly sprung up as if intent on trashing the area; in the east the horizon was flooded by bright red sunlight and then, all at once, the orb itself appeared, pale and wan in a heap of lowering cloud. On the narrow path beside the Schmidts' and the headmaster's houses the acacias were panicking, shaking their tiny crowns in surrender; the wind was wildly driving dense balls of dead leaves before it and a terrified black cat darted through the fence of the headmaster's house. He pushed aside his book, pulled out his journal and shivered in the cool draft that crept through the window. He stubbed out his cigarette on the wooden arm of his chair, put on his glasses, ran his eye over what he had written in the night, then noted by way of continuation: "Storm coming, must put the window rags in place for the evening. Futaki still inside. A cat in the headmaster's, one I haven't seen before. What the hell is a cat doing here?! It must have been frightened by something, it squeezed through such a narrow gap ... its spine practically flat against the ground, it only took a moment. I can't sleep. I have a headache." He drained the contents of his *pálinka* glass then immediately refilled it to the same level. He removed his spectacles and closed his eyes. He saw a vague, barely distinguishable figure, a tall awkward man with a large body dashing into the darkness: only later did he notice that the road, that "crooked road littered with many obstacles," came to a sudden end. He did not wait for the figure to fall down the chasm but opened his eyes in fear. Suddenly it was as if a bell were tolling, though only for a moment, then silence. A bell? And quite close, too! ... Or so it seemed for a moment. Very close. He surveyed the estate with an icy expression. He saw a blurred face in the Schmidts' window and quickly recognized Futaki's creased features: he looked scared, leaning out of the open window, searching intently for something above the houses. What did he want? The doctor pulled a notebook marked FUTAKI from among the pile of writings at the end of the able and found the relevant page. "Futaki is frightened of something. He was looking out of the window at dawn with a startled expression. Futaki fears death." He threw back his *pálinka* and quickly refilled the glass. He lit a cigarette and remarked aloud: "You'll all cheese it soon. You too are going to cheese it, Futaki. Don't get so worked up." After a few moments the rain began to fall. Soon enough it was pouring down, quickly filling the shallower ditches; tiny streams were already zigzagging in every direction like liquid lightning. The doctor watched all this, deeply absorbed, then set to making a rough sketch of the scene in his notebook, carefully and conscientiously marking the smallest puddle, the direction of the current and, having finished, noting the time underneath. The room slowly brightened: the bare bulb hanging from the ceiling threw a cold light over it. The doctor forced himself up from the chair, pushed away the blanket and turned the light off before settling back again. He took a can of fish and some cheese from the cardboard box at the left-hand side of the chair. The cheese had grown moldy here and there and the doctor took some time examining it before throwing it into the litter basket by the door. He opened the can and slowly and methodically chewed his way through mouthfuls before swallowing them. Then he threw back another glass of *pálinka*. He was no longer cold but kept the blankets around him for a while. He laid his book in his lap then suddenly filled up his glass. *It is interesting to note at the end of the Ponticum era, when the great lowland sea had mostly subsided leaving a large shallow lake roughly the size of the Balaton, how much destruction was caused by the combined forces of the wind and water in the beating of the waves.* What is this supposed to be, prophecy or geological history? the doctor fumed. He turned the page. *At the same time the entire area of the Lowlands begins to rise and so the waters of lesser lakes start to drain off to more distant territories too. Without the epirogenetic elevation of this central Tisian mass we could not begin to explain the rapid disappearance of the Levantine lakes. In the Pleistocene era, after the disappearance of the various standing waters, only minor lakes, marshes and bogs remained as signs of the lost inland sea* ... The text, in Dr. Benda's local edition, did not sound at all convincing, the evidence insufficient, the crude logic of the argument not worth taking seriously, or so he felt without having any knowledge of the subject, uncertain even of the technical terms employed; nevertheless, as he read, the history of the earth that had seemed so solid, so fixed under and around him, came alive, though the unknown author's awkward, unpolished style — the book being written now in the present and now in the past tense — confused him, so he couldn't be sure whether he was reading a work of prophecy regarding the earth's condition after the demise of humanity or a proper work of geological history based on the planet on which he actually lived. His imagination was bewitched almost to the point of paralysis by the notion that this estate with its rich, generous soil was, only a few million years ago, covered by the sea ... that it had alternated between sea and dry land, and suddenly — even as he conscientiously noted down the stocky, swaying figure of Schmidt in his soggy quilted jacket and boots heavy with mud appearing on the path from Szikes, hurrying as if he feared being spotted, sliding in through the back door of his house — he was lost in successive waves of time, coolly aware of the minimal speck of his own being, seeing himself as the defenseless, helpless victim of the earth's crust, the brittle arc of his life between birth and death caught up in the dumb struggle between surging seas and rising hills, and it was as if he could already feel the gentle tremor beneath the chair supporting his bloated body, a tremor that might be the harbinger of seas about to break in on him, a pointless warning to flee before its all-encompassing power made escape impossible, and he could see himself running, part of a desperate, terrified stampede comprising stags, bears, rabbits, deer, rats, insects and reptiles, dogs and men, just so many futile, meaningless lives in the common, incomprehensible devastation, while above them flapped clouds of birds, dropping in exhaustion, offering the only possible hope. For a few minutes he was contemplating a vague plan, thinking it might be better to abandon his earlier experiments and thus make available the energy required "to liberate himself from desire," to gradually wean himself off food, alcohol and cigarettes, to opt for silence rather than the constant struggle of naming things and so, after a few months, or perhaps just one or two weeks, he might reach a condition entirely without waste and instead of leaving a trail behind him to dissolve in the terminal silence that was in any case urgently calling to him ... but within a few moments all this seemed quite ridiculous, and maybe it was, after all, little more than fear or the sense of his own dignity that made him feel vulnerable, so he downed the prepared *pálinka* then filled his glass again because an empty glass always made him feel a little nervous. Then he lit another cigarette and set to making more notes. "Futaki slips carefully through the door and waits outside a short time. Then he knocks and shouts something. He hurries back in. The Schmidts are still inside. The headmaster has gone out through the back carrying his trash can. Mrs. Kráner sneaks around her gate, watching. I'm tired, I should sleep. What day is it?" He pushed his glasses up on his brow, put down his pencil and rubbed the red mark on the bridge of his nose. He could only see vague patches in the cataract of rain outside, the odd clear-then-blurred top of some tree when, somewhere under the constant thunder, he heard the agonized howling of dogs in the distance. "As if they were being tortured." He saw dogs hanging by their feet in the lee of some obscure hut or shack, their noses being roasted by a depraved adolescent wielding matches: he paid close attention and made further notes. "It seems to be stopping ... no, it has started again."

For minutes on end he could not tell whether he was really hearing howls of pain, or whether it was simply that his years of long, exhausting work had rendered him incapable of distinguishing between the general noise and ancient prehistoric screams that were somehow preserved in time ("The evidence of suffering does not disappear without trace," he hopefully remarked) and now were being raised by the rain, like dust. Then, suddenly, he heard other noises: whimpers, wails and a stifled human sobbing, which—like the houses and trees that were solidifying into blotches—would sometimes rise clear of, or sink back into, the monotonous hum of the rain. "Cosmic *wirtschaft*," he wrote in his notebook. "My hearing is going." He looked out of the window, drained his glass, but this time forgot immediately to refill it. A great wave of heat passed through him, his brow and thick neck covered in sweat; he felt mildly dizzy and there was a pain, a kind of tightening around his heart. He did not find this at all surprising for ever since yesterday night, when he was woken from a brief, restless two hours of dreamless sleep by a nearby cry, he had been continuously drinking (the "capacious demijohn" at his right had only enough *pálinka* left for one more day), and furthermore, he had hardly eaten anything. He got up to relieve himself but, surveying the pile of rubbish towering before the door, he thought better of it. "Later. It'll wait," he said aloud but did not sit back down and took a few steps close to the table toward the far wall in case movement might help "the painful tightening." The sweat was running in streams from his armpits down his fat flanks: he felt weak. The blanket slipped from his shoulders as he went but he lacked the strength to readjust it. He sat back in the armchair, filled another glass, thinking that might help, and he was right, a few minutes later he could breathe more easily and was sweating less. The rain beating at the windowpane made it more difficult to see anything so he decided to suspend his surveillance for a little while, knowing that he would not miss anything since he was attentive to "the slightest noise, the slightest rustle" and would notice it immediately, even those delicate noises that emanated from within, from his heart or his stomach. Soon he had fallen into an anxious sleep. The empty glass he had been holding in his hand slipped to the floor without breaking, his head slumped forward, saliva trickled from the side of his mouth. Everything seemed to have been waiting for just this moment. The place suddenly went dark as if someone had stood in front of the window: the colors of the ceiling, the door, the curtain, the window and the floor all deepened, the tuft of hair that formed the doctor's forelock began to grow more rapidly as did the nails on his short, puffy fingers; the table and the chair both gave a creak and even the house sank a little deeper into the soil as part of the insidious revolt. The weeds at the foot of the wall at the back of the house began to spurt, the creased notebooks scattered here and there attempted to smooth themselves out with one or two sharp movements, the rafters in the roof groaned, the emboldened rats ran down the hall with a greater freedom. He woke dizzy, with a bad taste in his mouth. He didn't know and could only guess at the time having forgotten to wind his waterproof, shockproof, frostproof, highly reliable "Rocket" wristwatch—and the small hand had just passed the eleven on the dial. The shirt he was wearing was wet through with sweat and made him feel cold, as though he was perishing, and his headache—though he couldn't be sure of this— seemed to be concentrated at the back of his neck. He filled his glass and was surprised to note that he had misjudged the situation: there was not enough *pálinka* for a day, only for a couple of hours at the most. "I shall have to go into town," he thought nervously. "I can refill the demijohn at Mopsz's. But the damn bus is out of service! If only it would stop raining I could go on foot." He looked out of the window and was annoyed to find that the rain had washed out the road. What was more, if the old road could not be used, then he could not set out on the metaled way because it might be tomorrow morning before he got there. He decided to eat something and postpone the decision. He opened another can and, leaning forward, began to spoon it into his mouth. He had just finished and was preparing to make new notes comparing the current width of the flooded ditches and traffic with their conditions at dawn, remarking on the differences, when he heard a noise at the entrance door. Somebody was fiddling with a key in the lock. The doctor put his notes away and leaned back in his chair, ill-tempered. "Hello, doctor," said Mrs. Kráner, stopping on the threshold. "It's only me." She knew she had to wait and, sure enough, the doctor did not miss the opportunity to examine her face in the usual ruthless, slow, detailed manner. Mrs. Kráner bore this humbly without in the least understanding the procedure ("Let him gaze his fill, let him conduct his examination, if he enjoys it so much!" she used to say at home to her husband), then stepped forward as the doctor beckoned her in. "I've only come 'cause, as you can see, we've got heavy rain, and, as I said to my husband at lunchtime, this will take time to clear, and then it'll be snow next." The doctor did not answer but looked sullenly in front of him. "I talked it over with my husband and we thought that since I can't go anyway, as there is no bus till the spring, we should speak to the bar owner because there's a car there, and then we could bring a lot of things in one trip, enough even for two or three weeks, said my husband. Then, in the spring, we'll think about what to do after that." The doctor was breathing heavily. "So does that mean you can no longer do the job?" It seemed Mrs. Kráner was prepared for this question. "Of course not, I mean why wouldn't I do it, you know me doctor, there's been no problem ever, but as you can see for yourself, sir, there is no bus and when it's raining like this, as the doctor knows, said my husband, he'll understand, 'cause how am I going to get into town on foot, and it would be better for you too, sir, if Mopsz drove here, you could get so much more ..." "Fine, Mrs. Kráner, you may go." The woman turned toward the door. "Then you will talk to him, I mean the landlo—" "I'll speak to whomsoever I want to speak to," the doctor thundered. Mrs. Kráner left but she had barely taken a few steps down the corridor when she quickly turned back. "Oh look, I forgot. The keys." "What about the keys?" "Where should I put them?" "Put them anywhere you like." Mrs. Kráner's house was near the doctor's so he could observe her for only a short time as she made her slow, painful way back over the cloying mud. He searched among his clutch of papers, found the notebook headed MRS. KRÁNER and jotted down: "K resigned. She can't do it any more. I should ask the landlord. She had no problem walking in the rain last spring. She is up to no good. She was confused but not to be swerved from her purpose. She's cooking something up. But what the devil is it?" In the course of the afternoon he read the rest of the notes he had made on her but it didn't help: it might be that his suspicions were unfounded and all that was happening was that the woman has spent the whole day dreaming at home and now she was getting things confused … The doctor knew Mrs. Kráner's kitchen of old, well remembered that narrow constantly overheated cubbyhole and knew that that stuffy, ill-smelling nook was a breeding ground for feeble, childish plans; that stupid, perfectly ridiculous desires sometimes caught her unaware there, drifting before her like steam from a saucepan. Clearly, that's what must have happened now: steam had raised the lid of the pan. Then, as so many times before, would come the moment of bitter realization and Mrs. Kráner would rush around at breakneck speed to remedy that which she had ruined the previous day. The noise of the rain seemed to have grown a little fainter but then it pelted down again. Mrs. Kráner would be proved right: it really was the first great rain of the season. The doctor thought back to last year's autumn and to those of earlier years and knew that this was how it would have to be; that, apart from a brief break of sunshine that lasted a few hours, or at most a day or two, it would pour down steadily, without a pause, right until the first frosts so that the roads would become impassable and they would be shut off from the outside world, from town and from the railways; that the constant rain would turn the soil into one enormous sea of mud, and the animals would vanish into the woods the other side of the Szikes, into the narrow park of the Hochmeiss estate or into the overgrown park of Weinkheim Manor because the mud would kill off all forms of life, rot the vegetation and there would be nothing left, just the ankle-deep cart tracks of the end of summer that had filled up with water up to your boot tops, and these pools and puddles of water, as well as the nearby canal, would be covered over with frogspawn and reeds and tangled weeds that in the evening or early twilight, when the moon's dead light reflected off them, would glitter all over the body of the land like a galaxy of tiny silvery blind eyes gazing up at the sky. Mrs. Halics passed before the window and crossed opposite him to the far side to rattle the window at Schmidt's. A few minutes earlier he seemed to have heard snatches of conversation which led him to think that there must be some trouble with Halics again and that the lanky Mrs. Halics must be calling on Mrs. Schmidt for help. "Clearly, Halics must be drunk again. The woman is animatedly explaining something to Mrs. Schmidt who appears to be looking at her in astonishment or fear. I can't see too well. The headmaster has appeared now, chasing the cat. Then he sets off toward the cultural center with a projector under his arm. The others are drifting that way too now, yes: there's going to be a film show." He threw back another glass of *pálinka* and lit a cigarette. "What a business!" he muttered under his breath. It was getting toward evening so he rose to put the lamp on. Suddenly he felt extremely dizzy but was still capable of making his way over to the light switch. He lit the lamp but was incapable of taking a single step back. He stumbled over something, struck his head forcefully against the wall, and collapsed where he stood, right under the switch. When he recovered consciousness and finally succeeded in hauling himself upright the first thing he noticed was a little trickle of blood from his forehead. He had no idea how much time had passed since he lost consciousness. He returned to his usual place. "It seems I am very drunk," he thought then drank quite a small measure of *pálinka* because he did not fancy a cigarette. He stared ahead of him with a somewhat foolish expression: recovery was proving difficult. He adjusted the blanket on his shoulders and looked out into the pitch darkness through the gap. Even though his senses were dulled by the *pálinka* he was aware that certain aches and pains were struggling to enter his consciousness, much as he was determined not to acknowledge them. "I have suffered a slight blow, that's all." He thought back to the conversation with Mrs. Kráner in the afternoon and tried to decide what to do next. He couldn't set out now, in this weather, though his *pálinka* needed urgent replenishment. He did not want to think about how he would replace Mrs. Kráner—that was if she did not change her mind—since it was not only the problem of provisions but all those truly insignificant yet necessary little tasks round the house that would have to be addressed, not at all a simple matter, and that was why, for the time being, he concentrated on trying to work out a practical plan regarding what to do in the face of other unexpected events (tomorrow would have been the day for Mrs. Kráner to see the landlord) and get hold of enough drink to see him through until "a proper solution" could be found. Obviously he had to speak with the landlord. But how could he send him a message? Through whom? Taking into account his current condition, he did not want to even consider the possibility of setting out for the bar himself. Later, however, he thought it best not to leave the task to anyone else, since the landlord was bound to water the liquor and would later defend himself by claiming that he didn't know that "the doctor was the customer." He decided to wait a little, collect himself, and then to make his own way there. He tapped his brow a few times and dabbed at the wound with water from the jug on the table using his handkerchief. This did not relieve his headache in the slightest but he did not dare risk the whole enterprise by looking for medication. He tried, if not to sleep, then at least to snooze a while, but was obliged to keep his eyes open because of the terrible images that rushed in on him once they were closed. He used his feet to push out the ancient old genuine leather suitcase he kept under the table and pulled a few foreign magazines out of it. The magazines—bought at random, much like his books—came from the secondhand bookshop at Kisrománváros, the smaller Romanian borough in town, the one owned by the Swabian, Schwarzenfeld, who boasted of his Jewish ancestors, and who once a year, in the winter months when the tourist season was over and he closed the shop for lack of trade, would set off on a round of business trips to the greater and lesser communities of the area, at which time he never failed to visit the doctor in whom he was delighted to meet "a man of culture it was an honor to know." The doctor paid no great heed to the names of the magazines, preferring to look at the pictures in order—as now—to pass the time. He particularly enjoyed looking through photo spreads of the wars in Asia, at scenes that never seemed very distant or exotic to him, and which, he was convinced, were photographed somewhere nearby, to the extent that one or another face seemed so familiar he would spend a long, anxious time trying to identify it. He arranged and ranked the best pictures, and regular examination made their various pages familiar so he quickly found his favorites. There was one special picture—though the rank of favorites did change in due course—an aerial shot, that greatly appealed to him: an enormous, ragged procession winding over a desertlike terrain leaving behind them the ruins of an embattled town billowing smoke and flames, while ahead, waiting for them, there was only a large, spreading dark area like an admonitory blot. And what made the photograph particularly worthy of note was the equipment appropriate to a military observation post that—redundant at first sight—was just about visible in the bottom left-hand corner. He felt the picture was important enough to deserve close attention because it demonstrated with great confidence, in real depth, the "all but heroic history" of a perfectly conducted piece of research focused on essentials, research in which observer and observed were at an optimal distance from each other and where minuteness of observation was given particular emphasis, to the extent that he often imagined himself behind the lens, waiting for the precise moment when he might press the button on the camera with absolute certainty. Even now it was this picture he had picked up almost without thinking: he was familiar with it down to the most minute detail but every time he looked at it he lived in hope of discovering something he hadn't yet noticed. However, despite wearing his glasses, it all looked a little blurry to him this time. He put the magazines away and took "one last nip" before setting out. He struggled to put on his fur-lined winter coat, folded the blankets and left the house, swaying a little. The cold fresh air hit him hard. He tapped his pocket to check he had his wallet and notebook, adjusted his wide-brimmed hat and started uncertainly in the direction of the mill. He could have chosen a shorter route to the bar but that would have meant passing first the Kráners' then the Halicses' house, not to mention the fact that he was bound to bump into "some dumb ass" near the Cultural Center or the generator, someone who would detain him against his will and engage him in some crude or sly form of interrogation, disguised with so-called gratitude to satisfy the person's repulsive curiosity. It was hard making progress in the mud and what was worse he could barely see his way in the darkness, but proceeding through the backyard of his house he found his way to the path that led to the mill and he was more or less familiar with that, though he hadn't recovered his sense of balance so he swayed and tottered as he went, as a result of which it often happened that he miscalculated a step and bumped into a tree or stumbled over a low bush. He fought for breath, his chest heaving, and there was still that tight feeling around his heart he had endured since the afternoon. He walked faster to reach the mill as

67

quickly as he could so that he might shelter from the rain, and he no longer tried to avoid the lurking puddles along the path, plowing through them ankle-deep if he had to. His boots were clogged with mud, his fur-lined coat was growing ever heavier. He shouldered open the stiff doors of the mill, sank down on a wooden chest and struggled for breath for several minutes. He could feel the blood pulsing through his neck, his legs were numb, his hands trembled. He was on the ground floor of the abandoned building, with two stories above him. The silence was overwhelming. Ever since anything halfway useful had been removed from here, this vast, dark, dry space rang with its own emptiness: to the right of the door there were a few old fruit crates, an iron trough of uncertain function, and a crudely banged-together wooden box saying IN CASE OF FIRE without any sand in it. The doctor removed his boots, took off his socks and squeezed the water from them. He searched for a cigarette but the pack had soaked through and there was not one fit to smoke. The weak light that filtered through the open door was enough to see the floor and the boxes like patches of semi-dark distinguished from the greater darkness. He seemed to hear the scurrying of rats. "Rats? Here?" he marveled and took a few steps forward into the deep core of the building. He put on his glasses and peered, blinking, at the dense darkness. But there was no noise now, so he went back for his hat, socks and boots and put them on. He tried to strike a match by rubbing it against the lining of his coat. It worked and, by its briefly flickering light, he could make out the bottom of the stairs rising three or four yards away by the far wall. For no particular reason he took a few hesitant steps up them. But the match soon burned down and he had neither reason nor desire to repeat the exercise. He stood for a moment in the darkness, felt for the wall, and would have made his way back down to set out for the road to the bar when he heard a quite faint noise. "It must be rats after all." The scurrying sound seemed to be coming from a long way off, somewhere at the very top of the building. He put his hand to the wall again and, tapping it, began to climb the stairs once more, but he had only climbed a few steps when the noise grew louder. "That's not rats. It's like brushwood snapping." Having reached the first turning of the stair, the noise, though low, was now clearly that of snatches of conversation. Right at the back of the middle story, about twenty to twenty-five meters away from the stiff statue-like figure of the listening doctor, two girls were sitting on the floor around a flickering brushwood fire. The fire brought their features into sharp relief and produced great vibrating shadows on the high ceiling. The girls were clearly involved in some deep conversation, looking not at each other but into the dancing flames rising from the glowing brushwood. "What are you doing here?" the doctor asked and moved toward them. They leapt up in fright but then one of them gave a relieved laugh. "Oh, is that you, doctor?" The doctor joined them by the fire and sat down. "I'll warm myself a bit," he said. "That's if you don't mind." The two girls sat down with him, their legs beneath them and giggled quietly. "I don't suppose you have a cigarette?" asked the doctor, not looking up from the fire. "Mine have turned to sponge in the rain." "Of course, take one," answered one of them. "It's there, by your feet, next to you." The doctor lit it and slowly blew out the smoke. "The rain, you know," one of the girls explained. "It's what Mari and I were grumbling about just now: no work alas, business is bad"—she gave a hoarse laugh—"so, you know, we're stuck here." The doctor turned to warm his side. He had not met the two Horgos girls since he had dismissed the elder one. He knew they spent the day at the mill, indifferently waiting for a "customer" to appear or for the landlord to summon them. They rarely ventured onto the estate. "We didn't think it worthwhile to wait," the elder Horgos girl continued. "There are days, you know, when they turn up one after the other, and other days when there's no visitors, nothing happens and we just sit here. There are times when we almost leap on each other, the two of us, it's so cold. And it's scary being here by ourselves . . ." The younger Horgos girl gave a raucous laugh. "Oh we're so scared!" and lisped, like a little girl, "it's horrible here, just the two of us." This elicited a brief shriek from both of them. "May I take another cigarette?" the doctor grumbled. "Take one, of course you may take one, why should I say no, especially to you?!" The younger one was falling about with still more laughter and, imitating her sister's voice, repeated, "Why should I say no, especially to you! That's good, that's well said!" Eventually they stopped their giggling and stared, exhausted, into the fire. The doctor was enjoying the heat and thought to stay a little longer, to dry out and warm up, then pull himself together and set out for the bar. He stared dozily into the fire, faintly whistling as he breathed in and out. The elder Horgos girl broke the silence. Her voice was tired, hoarse and bitter. "You know, I am over twenty now, and she will soon be twenty herself. When I think about it—and that's what we were talking about just now when you turned up—I wonder where all this is leading us. A girl gets fed up. Have you any idea how much we can put away in savings? Can you imagine?! Ah, I could kill people sometimes!" The doctor gazed at the fire in silence. The younger Horgos girl stared indifferently straight ahead of her: her legs were spread and she was leaning back on her hands, nodding. "We have to support the little criminal, the idiot child Esti, not to mention mother, though she can't do much apart from complain about this or that, or ask where we have stowed the money, and demand we give her the money, the money this and the money that—and what's with them all!? Believe me, they are quite capable of robbing us of our last pair of panties! And as for us finally going into town and leaving this filthy hole, if you could only have heard the abuse hurled at us! What on earth did we think we were doing, blah, blah, blah? . . . The fact is we are utterly fed up with this life, isn't that right, Mari, haven't we had enough of it?" The younger Horgos waved a bored hand. "Forget it! Don't rock the boat! You either go or stay! You can't say anyone is keeping you here." Her older sister immediately rounded on her. "Yes, you'd like it if I pissed off, wouldn't you? You'd do all right here by yourself! Well, that's exactly why I'm not going! If I go, you go too!" Baby Horgos made an ugly face: "OK, but don't moan so much, you'll make me cry already!" Horgos the elder had a reply ready but could not get to the end of it because her words were lost in a volley of throaty coughing. "No sweat, Mari, there'll be cash enough here today, cash by the sack full!" she broke the silence. "Just see what's going to happen here pretty soon, just see if I'm not right!" The other turned to her, annoyed. "They should have been here ages ago. Something doesn't smell right about this, that's my feeling." "Aah, leave off. Don't bother your head about it. I know Kráner and all the rest. He'll be here right enough, panting and chasing tail, the same as ever." "You don't imagine he's going to cough it up? All that money?" The doctor raised his head. "What money?" he asked. The elder Horgos made an impatient gesture with her hand. "Forget it, doc, just sit there and make yourself warm, and don't pay any attention to us." So he sat a while longer then begged two more cigarettes and a dry match and started down the stairs. He got to the door without any trouble: the rain was slanting in through the gap. His headache was a little better and he no longer felt dizzy in the slightest, there was only the tightness in his chest that didn't want to go away. His feet quickly grew accustomed to the dark and felt perfectly at home, knowing his way along the path. He made rapid progress in view of his condition, only rarely brushing against a branch or some shrub; so he pressed forward, his head held to one side so the rain wouldn't beat at it so hard. He stopped for a couple of minutes under the eaves of the shed before the weighbridge but soon went on in a fury, silence and darkness before and behind him. He cursed Mrs. Kráner aloud and dreamed up various forms of revenge all of which he immediately forgot. He was tired again and there were moments he felt he simply had to sit down somewhere or else he would collapse. He turned down the metaled road that led to the bar and decided not to stop until he'd got there. "It's a hundred steps, no more, that's all that remains," he chivied himself. There was a hopeful light filtering from the bar door and through its tiny window, the one single point in the darkness to guide him. He was ridiculously close now yet it seemed the filtered light was not getting any closer but, rather, moving away from him. "It's nothing, it will pass, I'm just not feeling well," he declared and stopped for a moment. He looked up at the sky and the gale slammed a fistful of rain into his face: what he needed more than anything right now was help. But the weakness that suddenly overcame him left just as suddenly. He turned off the metalled roadway and there he was, right in front of the bar door, when a faint voice below him called out: "Mr. Doctor!" It was the youngest of the Horgos children, little Esti, clinging to his coat. Her straw-blonde hair and her cardigan hanging down to her ankles were completely soaked through. She hung her head but carried on clinging to him as though she were not doing it just to amuse herself. "Is that you, little Esti? What do you want?" The little girl made no reply. "What are you doing out here at this hour of the night?" The doctor was shocked for a moment then tried impatiently to free himself, but little Esti clung on to him as though her life depended on it and would not let him go. "Let go of me! What's the matter with you! Where's your mother?!" The doctor seized the girl who suddenly pulled her hand away only to grab hold of his sleeve and to continue standing there in silence, looking down at the ground. The doctor nervously struck her on the arm to free himself but stumbled on the mud scraper and, however he waved his arms, finished up full length in the mud. The little girl was frightened and ran to the bar window, watching him, ready to run as the vast body rose and moved toward her. "Come here. Come here at once!" Esti leaned against the windowsill then pushed away and ran off down the metaled road on little duck feet. "That's all

I need!" the doctor muttered furiously to himself, then shouted after the little girl. "That's all I needed! Where are you rushing off to?! Stop now, stop! Come back here at once!" He stood before the bar door not knowing what to do, to go about his errand or to go after the child. "Her mother is in there drinking, her sisters are whoring at the mill, her brother, well ... who knows which store he is robbing in town right this minute, and she is running around in the rain with only a thin dress on ... the sky should fall in on the lot of them!" He stepped onto the metaled road and shouted out in the darkness. "Esti! I won't harm you! Have you gone mad?! Come back here at once!" There was no answer. He set off after her and cursed himself for leaving his house in the first place. He was soaked to the skin, he wasn't feeling well anyway, and now this half-wit clinging child! ... He felt too much had happened to him since he stepped out of his home and that everything was now mixed up in his head. Bitterly, he decided that all the order he had patiently, painstakingly constructed over the years was proving highly fragile, and it gave him even more pain to realize that he himself—despite his big strong constitution—was also on the verge of collapse: look, just one short walk to the bar ("And I took a rest too!") which really was no great distance, and here he was, out of breath, tight in the chest, his legs weak and all strength gone from his body. And the worst thing was that he had been rushing around mindlessly, swept this way and that without the faintest idea why he should be pelting like a lunatic after a child down the metaled road in the driving rain. He shouted one last time in the direction the child might have been going then stopped, furious, admitting he'd never catch her anyway. It was high time he pulled himself together. He turned back and was astounded to observe that he seemed to have moved a long way from the bar. He started toward it but after a couple of steps the whole world went dark in an instant and he felt his legs sliding in the mud; for a brief moment he was aware that he was falling to the ground and rolling somewhere, then, finally, he lost consciousness. It took him a lot of effort and a long time to come to himself. He couldn't remember how he had got here. His mouth was full of mud and the earthy taste suddenly made him feel sick. His coat too was covered in mud, his legs had stiffened because of the cold and damp, but curiously enough the three cigarettes he had begged from the Horgos girls, which he was firmly gripping in his fist so they wouldn't get wet, were perfectly intact. He quickly tucked them back in his pocket and tried to stand up. His legs, however, kept slipping on the sides of the muddy ditch and it was only after a sustained effort that he managed to get back on the proper road. "My heart! My heart!" The thought flashed through his mind and he grabbed at his chest in fear. He felt extremely weak and he knew he had to get to the hospital as quickly as he could. But the rain made that impossible: ever new waves of it were beating down at an angle to the road with unrelenting power. "I must rest. Find a tree ... or go on to the bar? No, I have to rest somewhere." He left the road and took shelter under a nearby old acacia. He drew his legs under him so he wouldn't have to sit directly on the ground. He tried hard not to think about anything, but stared stiffly ahead of him. A few minutes passed like this, or it might have been hours, he couldn't tell. In the east, the horizon was slowly brightening. The doctor watched the light's ruthless progress across the field, his spirit broken but still nursing some vague hope. The light gave him hope but he was afraid of it too. He would have loved to be lying down in a warm, friendly room, under the tender gaze of pale-skinned young nurses, with a bowl of hot soup before him, spooning it into his mouth, then turning to the wall. He noticed three figures proceeding down the road parallel to the road-sweeper's house. They were a long way off, hopelessly far off, he couldn't hear them, only see them, but he could tell that the smallest figure, a child, was passionately explaining something to one of them, while the other adult followed a few strides behind. When they finally came level with him he recognized them: he tried crying out but the wind must have blown his voice away because they took no notice at all but continued on their way to the bar. By the time he started to wonder at seeing these two big-time rogues, people he thought were dead, right in front of him, he had forgotten it all: his leg began to hurt with a sharp pain and his throat was dry. Morning found him on the road heading for town. He had no desire to turn back to the bar. He reeled rather than walked, full of confused thoughts, frightened by voices that broke every so often above him. A crowd of rooks seemed to be hanging around, following him; it distinctly looked like they were on his tracks, never letting him out of their sight. By the afternoon, when he reached the fork to Elek, he didn't have enough strength to get up on the cart; it was left to the homeward-bound Kelemen to haul him onto the thoroughly wet straw behind the seat. He felt light-headed and the admonitory words of the driver kept echoing through his skull: "Doctor, sir, you shouldn't have! You really shouldn't have!"

IV

THE WORK OF THE SPIDER I

∞

Turn the fire on!" said Kerekes, the farmer. Autumnal horseflies were buzzing around the cracked lampshade, describing drowsy figures of eight in its weak light, time and again colliding with the filthy porcelain, so that after each dull little thud their bodies fell back into the magnetic paths they themselves had woven, to continue this endless cycle, albeit on a tight closed circuit until the light went out; but the compassionate hand that had the power to undertake such action was still supporting the unshaven face. The landlord's ears were full of the sounds of the rain that never seemed to want to stop, and he was watching the horseflies through sleepy eyes, blinking and muttering: "Devil take the lot of you." Halics was sitting in the corner by the door on an iron-framed if rather unsteady chair, his waterproof coat buttoned up to the chin, a coat that, if he wished to sit down at all, he had to raise to groin level because the fact was the rain and wind had not spared either him or his coat, disfiguring and softening them both. Halics's whole body felt as though it had lost definition and, as for his coat, it had lost whatever resistance to water it once had nor could it protect him from the roaring cataract of fate, or, as he tended to say, "the rain of death in the heart," a rain that beat, day and night, against both his withered heart and defenseless organs. The pool of water around his boots was growing ever wider, the empty glass in his hand was growing heavier, and however he tried not to hear, there, behind him, his elbows propped on the so-called billiards table and his sightless eyes turned to the landlord, was Kerekes, slurping his beer slowly through his teeth, then greedily swallowing it with great glugs. "I said turn it on ...," he repeated, then turned his head slightly to the right so he would not miss a single sound. The smell of mold rising from the floor at the corners of the room surrounded the vanguard cockroaches working their way down the back walls, with the main cockroach army following them to swarm across the oily floor. The landlord responded with an obscene gesture, meeting Halics's watery eyes with a sly, conspiratorial smile, but hearing the farmer's words of warning ("Don't point, shit face!") he shrank back in the chair with fright. Behind the tin-topped counter a poster spotted with lime bloomed at a crooked angle on the wall while on the far side, beyond the circle of light emanating from the lamp, next to a faded Coca-Cola ad, stood an iron clothes hook with a dusty forgotten hat and work coat dangling from it, the coat stiff as an airborne statue; anyone glancing at it might have mistaken it for a hanged man. Kerekes started off in the direction of the landlord, an empty bottle in his hand. The floor creaked under him and he pitched slightly forward, his enormous body looming above everything else. For a moment he was like a bull springing over a fence: he seemed to occupy every available inch of space. Halics saw the landlord disappear behind the stockroom door and heard him quickly shoot the bolt and, frightened as he was, because something had actually happened, Halics took some consolation in realizing that, for once, he did not have to take shelter behind the towering sacks of artificial fertilizer that years ago had been piled one on top of the other and had never been moved, or between rows of garden implements and containers of foul-smelling pig swill with his back up against the ice-cold steel door, and he even felt a certain flutter of joy, or maybe just a smidgen of satisfaction at the thought that the master of all that store of glittering wine was now cowering behind locked doors, desperately waiting for some reassuring sound, his life threatened by the powerfully built farmer. "Another bottle!" Kerekes angrily demanded. He pulled a fistful of paper money from his pocket, but having moved too fast he dropped the money— which, after a moment of dignified drifting in the air, landed right next to his enormous boots. Because he was aware—if only briefly—of the rules governing the actions of other persons, the degree to which they were predictable or unpredictable, and knowing what he himself should most certainly do, Halics rose, waited a few seconds to see whether the farmer would bend down to retrieve the cash, cleared his throat, then went over, took out his own last few dimes and opened his palm. The coins clinked as they ran all over the place, then—as the very last one finally settled—he knelt down on the floor to gather them up. "Pick up my hundred too," Kerekes boomed at him and Halics, knowing the ways of the world (" ... I can see right through you!"), silently, obediently, slavishly picked up the money and handed it over, all the time brimming with hatred. "It was just the denomination he got wrong!..." he said to himself, still frightened. "Just the denomination." Then, at a gruff question from the farmer ("So, where are you?!") he sprang to his feet, brushed his knees down and hopefully, since he couldn't be certain whether the farmer was addressing the landlord or him, leaned against the bar at a safe distance from Kerekes, who—was it possible?—appeared to be hesitating, so that when Halics finally spoke his frail, hardly audible voice ("Well, how long do we have to wait?") reverberated in the silence and could not be retracted. Nevertheless, obliged as he was to stand near someone as physically powerful as Kerekes and having distanced himself as far as he could from the words he had so carelessly uttered, he felt he had forged some vague comradeship with Kerekes, the only sort of which he was capable, not only because of his easily wounded self-regard but because his very cells protested against the possibility that he should behave differently from any other coward: terrified complicity was the only available option. By the time the farmer slowly turned to him the obligation to remain loyal, something that had long been part of Halics's character, had given way to something else: he felt oddly moved in discovering that a stray remark of his should have hit the mark. It was so unexpected. He wasn't prepared to find that his own voice—the voice in which he had just spoken, a voice not in the least prepared—could deflect and, to some degree, neutralize the farmer's clear surprise, so he quickly, as a sign of immediate and unconditional withdrawal, added: "Though of course, it's nothing to do with me ..." Kerekes was beginning to lose his temper again. He lowered his head and registered the fact that there before him on the counter stood a row of washed wine glasses: he had just raised his fist when, at that precise moment, the landlord emerged from the stockroom and stood on the threshold. He rubbed his eyes and leaned against the doorframe, the two minutes spent at the back of his emporium being sufficient to wipe away his sudden and, when you came to consider it, ridiculous, panic ("How aggressive he is! Damn animal!"), so the damage to his self-esteem could be only skin-deep after all, nothing really serious, and, if the big farmer did get under his skin, it was simply "another stone dropped down a bottomless well." "Another bottle!" Kerekes demanded, and put the money down on the counter. And seeing how the landlord was still keeping a careful distance, added, "Don't be afraid, you idiot. I won't hurt you. Just stop pointing." By the time he returned to his chair at the "billiard table" and sat down carefully for fear of someone pulling the chair out from under him, the landlord's chin was propped on his other hand, his whey-colored foxy eyes clouded over with uncertainty and a sort of tangible longing, his fingers long, refined, and polished with long years of laboring on the periphery of that same palm, his shoulders fallen in, his belly a conspicuous paunch, not a muscle of his body moving apart from the toes inside his well-worn shoes: all in the close warmth of perpetual servility—the kind of servility that renders the skin torpid and the palm sweaty—shining from his white-as-chalk face. Then the lamp that had been hanging motionless from the ceiling began to sway and its narrow aureole of light—no bigger than a slice of bread—that left most of the ceiling and the tops of the walls in shadow, offering only enough light to see the three men, the cookies, the dried noodles for soup, the counter covered with wine glasses and bottles of *pálinka,* the chairs, the dead flies—gave the bar the air of a ship in a storm in the early evening dusk. Kerekes opened the bottle, dragged the glass over with his free hand, and sat there for some minutes without moving, bottle in one hand, glass in the other, as if he had forgotten what to do next. Now that everything had gone quiet, in the absolute dark of his blindness he felt as if he were deaf too, that everything around him had become weightless, right down to his own body, his ass, his arms, and the legs spread wide below him, and that any capacity he might have had in the realms of touch, or taste, or smell, had also deserted him, leaving nothing but the throbbing of blood and the calm workings of his organs to disturb his utter lack of consciousness, the mysterious core of his anxiety having withdrawn into its own infernal darkness, into the forbidden territories of the imagination, whence it was obliged, time and again, to break free. Halics didn't know what to make of the situation, and shifted here and there in his excitement because he sensed Kerekes was watching him. It would have been too presumptuous to interpret his unexpected immobility as a gradually unfolding form of invitation; on the contrary, he suspected that the dead eyes turned toward him constituted a threat, but however he racked his brains he couldn't remember having committed any offense for which he ought to bear immediate responsibility, all the more so since in the hard hours, when "a man of sorrows" like him was plunged deep into the liberating waters of self-knowledge, he had confessed to himself that his comfortable life, which had slipped uneventfully into his fifty-second year, was as insignificant in the great rank of competing lives as cigarette smoke in a burning train. This brief, unlocated sense of guilt (was it in fact guilt at all? since if it was true, as the saying goes, that "once the flame of guilt has gone out it's no more than a dead match," the minimal light remaining is easily identified with some problem in the conscience) vanished just at the moment it might have penetrated his soul more deeply, which had entered on the next phase of hysteria, affecting the roof of his mouth, his throat, his gullet and stomach, all because of something he had prepared himself for far earlier, that being the arrival of the Schmidts and the settling of what was "due to him." The cold bar only made the situation worse, and a single glance at the wine racks piled behind the landlord's low stool set his hysterical imagination spinning into a whirlpool that threatened to swallow him completely, especially now that, finally, he heard the glug of wine being poured into the farmer's glass, and couldn't resist looking, some greater power drawing his eyes to the tiny momentary pearls of poured wine. The landlord listened, his eyes cast down, as Halics's boots creaked across the floor and didn't even look up when he felt his sour breath, feeling no desire at all to confront the beads of perspiration on Halics's face, because he knew that, for the third time that evening, he'd give in. "Look friend," Halics carefully cleared his throat, "just a glass, just one!" and he gave the landlord a perfectly sincere look, even raising a finger. "The Schmidts will be here, you know, very soon ..." He raised the newly filled glass with closed eyes, very slowly, and drank in small sips, his head tipped back and, once the glass was empty, he kept a little in his mouth so the very last drop might dribble down his throat. "Neat little wine ... ," he smacked his lips in confusion as he gently, somewhat indecisively, put the glass down on the counter like one living in hope right down to the very last moment, then slowly turned away and grumbled to himself ("Pig swill!") before ambling back to his chair. Kerekes leaned his heavy head on the green baize of the "billiards table"; the landlord, who was bathed in lamplight, scratched his numb ass then started flapping at the spiderwebs with his dishcloth. "Halics, listen! You hear me?... You! What's going on out there?" Halics stared uncomprehending, straight in front of him. "Where?" The landlord repeated it. "Oh, in the cultural center? Well," he scratched his head, "nothing in particular." "OK, but what's playing there now?" "Ach," Halics waved, "I've seen it at least three times. Actually I just took my wife and left her there and came straight over." The landlord sat back on his stool, leaned against the wall and lit a cigarette. "At least tell me what film they're showing tonight!" "That whats-itsname ... *Scandal in Soho.*" "Really?" nodded the landlord. The table beside Halics made a creaking noise and the rotting wood of the bar gave a slow sigh like the quiet easy movement of an old carriage wheel over the buzzing chorus of horseflies: it conjured the past but it also spoke of perpetual decay. And as the wood creaked, the wind outside, like a helpless hand searching through a dusty book for some vanished main clause, kept asking the same question time and again, hoping to give a "cheap imitation of a proper answer" to the banks of solid mud, to establish some common dynamic between tree, air and earth, and to seek through invisible cracks in the door and walls the first and orig-inal sound, of Halics belching. The farmer was snoring on the "bil-liards table," the saliva trickling from his open mouth. Suddenly, like a distant rumble on the horizon, from a vague shape that is slowly get-ting closer, though you can't quite tell whether it's a herd of cows being driven home, a school bus, or the sound of a marching military band, from the deep pit of Kerekes's stomach rose a quite unclassifiable grumble that eventually reached his lips and issued forth in words like "... bitch" and "really" and "or" and "more" though that was all they could make out. The grumbling culminated in a single movement, a blow aimed at someone or something. His glass tipped over and the pool of wine on the baize cloth assumed the shape of a flattened dog before absorbing various other shapes into itself as it soaked in, ending up in a form of uncertain character (but had it soaked in? or had it simply run between the strands of cloth to lie on the surface of the riven boards to establish a series of isolated and conjoined pools ... though none of this was of the least significance as far as Halics was concerned because ...). In any case Halics made a hissing noise, "Damn your drunk mug!" and shook his fist in the direction of Kerekes, helpless with rage, as if not wanting to believe his eyes, turning to the landlord to mutter a furious explanation: "Now the bastard spills the stuff!" The latter gave Halics a long significant look before finally glancing over at the farmer, not in fact directly at him, but in his general direction, just enough to register the damage. He appraised the inexperienced Halics with a supercilious smile then, giving several little nods, changed the subject. "What a huge ox of a man, a real animal, eh?" Halics stared in confusion at the mocking light glimmering under the landlord's half-closed eyelids, shook his head and took a long look at the bull-like figure of the prostate farmer. "What do you think?" he numbly asked. "How much does a beast like him need to eat?" "Eat!?" the landlord snorted. "He doesn't eat, he feeds!" Halics went over to the bar and leaned against it. "He eats half a pig at a sitting. You believe me" "Sure, I believe you." Kerekes gave a loud snore and that shut them up. They looked at the enormous, immovable body, the big bloodshot head and the muddy boots protruding from under the shadowy reaches of the "billiards table" in astonishment and fear, the way people take stock of a sleeping predator, doubly assured of safety by the bars and by sleep itself. Halics was seeking—and indeed had found!—a minute or a second's worth of comradeship with the landlord, if only in the way a caged hyena and a freely circling vulture discover a warm, mutual unselfconscious partnership that welcomes any disaster ... But they were awakened from this reverie by an enormous clap, as if the sky was cracking open above them. Immediately after the bar was lit by a great flash, so you could practically smell the lightning. "That was really close," Halics would have remarked, but at the same time someone started beating powerfully at the door. The landlord leapt to attention but didn't immediately rush over because, for a moment, he was sure there must be some connection between the lightning and the knocking at the door. He only gathered himself together and set to open up when whoever was outside started bellowing. "So it's you and ... ?" The landlord's back was in the way so Halics saw nothing at first, then two big heavy boots became visible, then a windbreaker, and finally Kelemen's puffy face hove into sight, his soaked driver's hat perched on top. Halics stared at him, his eyes wide. The new arrival cursed as he shook his coat free of water and threw it angrily on top of the stove before turning on the landlord who was still struggling with the bolt and had his back to him. "Are you all deaf in here! There I am trying to wrestle with that bloody door, almost struck by lightning, and nobody comes to open it!" The landlord retreated behind the counter, poured a glass of *pálinka* and pushed it in front of the old man. "Given the noise of the thunder it's really not that surprising ..." the landlord answered by way of excuse. He was fiercely scrutinizing the newcomer, trying quickly to guess what had brought him here in the rain, why the glass was trembling in his hand, and what he was hiding. But neither he nor Halics asked him anything yet, because there was another great crack in the sky and all the rain seemed to fall at once, in one great sack-full, battering at the roof. The old man tried as best he could to wring the water out of his broadcloth cap, pushed it back into shape, replaced it on his head and, with a careworn look, threw back the *pálinka*. Now, for the first time since searching for the lost track in dense darkness, a track no one could remember using (the track covered in weeds and rank grass), the excited profiles of his two horses flashed before him as they, inexplicably, kept glancing back at their helpless but determined master, their tails nervously twitching, and he heard again their heavy panting over the squeak and creak of the cart as it rattled over dangerous potholes, and he saw himself standing in the driver's seat, then holding onto the reins, up to his ankles in mud, leaning against the driving wind in his face, and it was only now he really believed what had happened, that, but for Irimiás and Petrina, he'd never have set off, because there was "no power greater than theirs" that could have forced him, because he felt quite certain now that it was true because he saw himself in the shadow of their great power, like a common foot soldier on the battlefield when he senses rather than hears the order given by his commanding officer and goes about his duties without anyone having told him to do so. And so the images moved silently past his eyes in ever more stilted sequence, as if everything man might hold dear and consider vital to protect existed as part of some independent, indissoluble system, and while one's memory was still functional enough to furnish it with a degree of certainty and bring into existence its lightly fleeting *now*, as well as validating the living strands of the rules of the system in the open field of events, one was forced to bridge the gap between memory and life not with a sense of freedom but rather bound by the cramped satisfaction simply of being the possessor of the memory; and so at this stage, given the first opportunity of bringing these things to mind, he felt the terror in everything that had happened, though pretty soon he would begin to cling to the memory with an ever-greater jealous possessiveness, however often "in the few years still remaining to him" the memory recurred, right down to the last time he conjured these images while leaning out of the tiny north-facing window of the farmhouse at the most miserable time of night, alone and sleepless, waiting for dawn. "Where have you just come from?" the landlord eventually asked. "From home." Halics looked surprised and took a step nearer. "But that's at least half a day's journey!" The visitor silently lit a cigarette. "On foot?" asked the landlord in uncertainty. "Of course not. Horses. Cart. The old track." He had been warmed through by the drink now and he looked at each face in turn, blinking a little, but he hadn't yet told them what he wanted to tell them, nor did he know how to begin, because the moment wasn't quite right, or, to put it more precisely, he was unable to decide about the moment because he didn't know what it was he was hoping for, and even if it was plain to him that the sense of vacancy and tedium radiated by the very walls was only an appearance, and even if this spot was to be the site of as yet invisible but therefore all the more feverish forces in the coming hours, and even if the wild cries of the party that would soon engulf them were already audible but not yet present, he was, nevertheless, expecting far more than this, a more feverish sense of anticipation than the landlord and Halics were able to offer, and so he felt fate was letting him down badly by presenting him with just these two people: a landlord from whom "a veritable chasm" divided him, because the people he regarded as the "traveling public," or, more strictly, as the generic "Passengers" were, to the landlord, merely "guests . . ."; and Halics, a "flat tire" of a man to whom expressions such as "discipline, firmness of purpose, fighting spirit and reliability" meant nothing now, nor ever had. The landlord was tensely watching the shadows in the nape of the driver's neck, his breathing slow and careful. Halics meanwhile was convinced—at least until the driver started his story—that "someone must have died." News quickly spread on the estate and the half hour it took before the landlord returned was plenty enough for Halics, who was in touching distance, secretly to examine what was really behind the labels on those bottles on the shelf, the ones saying RIZLING, a name that was filled with various associations for him, and there was even enough time, in the presence of a sleeping figure and another vaguely nodding off, to make a lightning quick test of his long-stated hypothesis that when wine was watered down the color of the mixture—because it was quite a different matter he had in mind!—bore an easily confusable likeness to the wine's original color. At the same time as he successfully concluded his inspection, Mrs.

Halics, who was on her way to the bar, thought she saw a star falling from the sky above the mill. She stopped dead in her tracks and put her hand to her heart, but however keenly and stubbornly she scanned the sky, a sky that seemed to be full of ringing bells, she was obliged to admit that it was probably just her eyes sparkling with the unexpected excitement—nevertheless, the uncertainty, the mere possibility of a decisive event as against the oppressive sight of the desolate landscape, pressed on her so heavily that she changed her mind, turned back to the house, took out her ragged Bible from under the pile of crisply ironed washing, and, with an increasing sense of guilt, set off again down the metaled road by the sign that used to bear the name of the estate, and walked the hundred and seven steps or so to the bar against the driving rain while her mind sought to grasp the developing state of affairs. In order to gain a little time, because in her agitated state the words were merely clanging around in her head, and because she wanted to convey her message ("we are living in apocalyptic times!") with a blinding, irresistible clarity, she stopped at the bar door and waited until a phrase came to her, only throwing open the door and crossing the threshold once she felt sure it was the right phrase, the right word, at which point she entered, to the astonishment of all within, with the single cry of RESURRECTION!—a word whose power was such as to increase the spellbinding effect of her entrance, the term itself being enough to demand attention. Hearing it the farmer's head snapped back in fear, the driver leapt from his place as if he had been stabbed, and the landlord started back so violently and so suddenly that he hit his head against the wall and was knocked semiconscious as a result. Soon after that they recognized Mrs. Halics. The landlord couldn't stop himself shouting at her ("For God's sake, Mrs. Halics, what in heaven's name is the matter with you!?") then attempted to screw the broken bolt back in the door. Halics was overcome with embarrassment and tried to drag his overexcitedly gabbling wife over to the nearest chair (which was no easy matter: "Come along with you, for God's sake, look at the rain coming in!"), attempting to calm her by simply nodding to everything she said, her speech being a blend of high pathos and whimpering terror that ended only when Mrs. Halics noticed the landlord and the driver giving each other a mocking look and cried out in fury: "It's nothing to laugh at! There's nothing in the least bit funny about it!" at which point Halics finally managed to push her into the chair next to his at the corner table. There she retreated into a wounded silence, clutching the Bible to her bosom, looking over the heads of the others into a kind of heavenly haze, her eyes misting over with a blissful sense of certainty derived from above. In her own mind she stood, straight as a post, high above a magnetic field of bent heads and backs, the proud unassailable place she occupied in the inn, a space she was unwilling to vacate, like a vent in the closed bar, a vent through which foul air could escape so that numbing, frozen, poisonous drafts from outside might rush in and take its place. In the tense silence the continual buzzing of the horseflies was the only audible sound, that and the constant rain beating down in the distance, and, uniting the two, the ever more frequent *scritch-scratch* of the bent acacia trees outside, and the strange nightshift work of the bugs in the table legs and in various parts of the counter whose irregular pulse measured out the small parcels of time, apportioning the narrow space into which a word, a sentence or a movement might perfectly fit. The entire end-of-October night was beating with a single pulse, its own strange rhythm sounding through trees and rain and mud in a manner beyond words or vision: a vision present in the low light, in the slow passage of darkness, in the blurred shadows, in the working of tired muscles; in the silence, in its human subjects, in the undulating surface of the metaled road; in the hair moving to a different beat than do the dissolving fibers of the body; growth and decay on their divergent paths; all these thousands of echoing rhythms, this confusing clatter of night noises, all parts of an apparently common stream, that is the attempt to forget despair; though behind things other things appear as if by mischief, and once beyond the power of the eye they no longer hang together. So with the door left open as if forever, with the lock that will never open. There is a chasm, a crevice. The landlord, having discovered it was a waste of energy trying to find a firm patch in the rotten door, threw the bolt aside and made do with a wedge then sat back on his stool with a curse ("The gap's still a gap," he eventually muttered, resigned to the fact), so that his body at least might get a rest and so be able to resist the spiraling anxiety that—as he well knew—would soon overtake him. Because it was all in vain: he no sooner felt a sudden and violent desire to be revenged on Mrs. Halics than the desire was overtaken by a precipitous descent into despondency. He took a look around the tables, estimated how much wine and *pálinka* there was left, then got up and pulled the storeroom door closed behind him. Now that no one could see him, he gave his rage free rein, shaking his fist and making terrifying faces, keenly aware of the smell of rust ("the smell of love . . ." as he often had occasion to term it when the Horgos girls had pitched their headquarters there) and running his eye straight down the line of untouched goods as he always did when wanting to think over some pressing problem, toward the window that was protected from potential roadside thieves by two iron bars of a finger's thickness each, as well as a dense weave of cobwebs, then back along the sacks of flour, past the high piles of foodstuff right down to the little desk where he kept his business books, his notes, his tobacco and various personal belongings, and finally back to the small window where—having already made a discourteous remark regarding the Creator who was trying to ruin his life with these "filthy spiders," without feeling any particularly keen emotion either way—he turned to his right and, stepping over a pile of spilt grain, soon reached the iron door again. It was all nonsense: he didn't believe in any kind of resurrection and was happy to leave such humbug to Mrs. Halics who was well acquainted with humbug of all sorts, though one might

of course feel a certain uneasiness if it suddenly turned out that someone thought dead should turn out to be alive. He'd had no reason at
that time to doubt what the Horgos kid had firmly stated, he even drew
him aside to "interrogate him" more intensely about the details; and,
though some of the smaller details made him question the foundations
on which the story was built because they were "not as solid as they
might be," he never once assumed the story itself to be false. Because,
he asked himself, what reason would the Horgos kid have for telling
such a whopping lie? He himself, of course, was firmly of the opinion
that the kid was as rotten as could be but no one could tell him the boy
was capable of making up such a story without any outside help, or
indeed encouragement. But, at the same time, he was pretty certain
that (while someone might indeed have seen the dead in town), death
was death, and that's it. He wasn't in the least surprised: it's just what
you'd expect of Irimiás. As far as he was concerned nothing was too
strange to be believed about that lousy vagrant, because it was perfectly
clear that he and his companion were a pair of filthy scoundrels. He
resolved that whenever and however they arrived he would stand quite
firm: the wine had to be paid for. In the long run it wasn't his problem—they might be ghosts for all he knew—but anyone that wants to
drink here has to pay up. Why should he be the loser? He hadn't
"worked his fingers to the bone" all his life; he hadn't set up this business by sheer hard slog so that "a bunch of idle tramps" should swig his
wine for free. People didn't sell on credit, and grand gestures—that
kind of thing—were not his style. In any case he did not think it impossible that Irimiás really *had* been hit by a car. Why? Hadn't anyone but
him ever heard of a case of apparent death? So someone had succeeded
in dragging people back into this miserable life, so what!? In his opinion, this was not beyond the ability of modern medicine, though it was
an act of considerable carelessness, if so. One way or the other, he
wasn't interested; he was not the kind of man to run scared of a figure

suspected to be dead. He sat down at his desk and, having blown the dust off his account book, leafed through it, pulled out a piece of paper and a blunt much-chewed pencil stub and, feverishly adding up the figures on the last page, scribbled some meaningless numbers while incoherently mumbling to himself:

10 x 16 b. @ 4 x 4
9 x 16 s. @ 4 x 4
8 x 16 w. @ 4 x 4
owe. 2 cases 31.50
3 cases 5.60
5 cases 3.00

Fully absorbed, he gazed at the column of numbers sloping right to left with pride while feeling an infinite hatred for the world that made it possible for filthy scoundrels to target people like him for their latest outrage; normally he was capable of sublimating his sudden bouts of fury ("He's a good-natured man!" his wife used to say to neighbors in town) and contempt to the greater ambitions of his life: in order that these should come true, he knew he should be ready for anything at any time. One misjudged word, one hurried calculation and every-thing would be ruined. But "sometimes a man can't govern his tem-perament" and trouble always comes of it. The landlord was happy enough with his given condition but had suddenly discovered how to develop the foundations of a great ambition. Even in his youth, in fact as a child, he could calculate, right down to a penny, the benefit to be gained from the hatred and disgust that surrounded him. And having discovered this—it was obvious—he couldn't then make the same mistake! Nevertheless he was subject to occasional fits of temper and whenever he was in the grip of one of these he would retire to his storeroom so he could vent his rage without inopportune witnesses.

He understood circumspection. Even at times like this he remained circumspect in case he caused some damage. He'd kick the wall or—at worst—would smash an empty wine rack against the metal door, let him "have his fit" there! But he really couldn't allow himself this now because they might be able to hear it in the bar. So now, as so often before, he took refuge in numbers. Because there is in numbers a mysterious evidentiary quality, a stupidly undervalued "grave simplicity" and, as a product of the tension between these two ideas a spine-tingling concept might arise, one that proclaimed: *"Perspectives do exist."* But did there exist a series of numbers that might defeat this bony, gray-haired, lifeless-looking, horse-faced heap of trash—that piece of shit, that parasite who belonged in a cesspit, known as Irimiás? What number could possibly vanquish that infinitely treacherous scoundrel straight from hell? Treacherous? Unfathomable? There weren't words for him! No description could do him justice. Words wouldn't do it—it wasn't a matter of words. Sheer strength was required. That's what was needed to put paid to him! Strength, not a lot of feeble chatter! He drew a line through what he had written but the numbers behind the lines remained legible, sparkling with significance. It was no longer just a matter of the beer, soft drinks and wine to be found in various cases, as far as the landlord was concerned. Far from it! The numbers were becoming ever more significant. He couldn't help noticing that as the importance of the numbers grew, so did he. He was positively swelling. The greater the significance of the numbers the "greater my own significance." For a couple of years now the consciousness of his own extraordinary grandeur had constrained him. Limber now, he ran over to the soft drinks to check that he had remembered it all correctly. It worried him that his left hand had started shaking uncontrollably. He had eventually to face the oppressive issue of, "What to do?" "What does Irimiás want?" He heard a hoarse voice in the corner that made his blood freeze for a moment because he thought that, on top of everything else, those infernal spiders had learned to speak. He wiped his brow, leaned against the sacks of flour and lit a cigarette. "So he drinks free for fourteen days and he dares show his mug here again! He's back! But not just any old how! It's like he thought it wasn't enough. I'm going to throw these drunken pigs out of here! I'll turn off all the lights! I'll nail up the door! I'll put a barrier over the entrance!" He was quite hysterical now. His mind was sprinting down the usual self-made channels. "Let me see. He came to the estate saying, "If you need money you should plant onions everywhere." That's all. "What sort of onions?" I asked. "Red onions," he said. So I planted onions everywhere. And it worked. Then I bought the bar from the Swabian. Greatness is always compounded of simple things. And four days after I open up he comes in and dares tell me that I (yes, I!) owe it all to him, and he gets drinks on credit for fourteen days without even a word of thanks! And now? Perhaps he's come to take it all back. TAKE BACK WHAT'S MINE! Good God! What's the world coming to when anyone can walk in one day and without so much as a by your leave, tell you he's the boss now! What's this country coming to? Is nothing sacred anymore? Ah no, no my friends! There are laws against that kind of thing!" His eyes slowly cleared and he calmed down. Calmly he counted the cases of soft drinks. "Of course!" he cried slapping his forehead. "Trouble comes when you get into a bit of a panic." He took out his ledger, opened his notebook and once more put a line through the last page, starting all over again with the same pride.

<pre>
        9 x 16 s. @ 4x4
       11 x 16 b. @ 4x4
        8 x 16 w. @ 4x4
       Owe. 3 c.   31.50
            2 cases   3.00
            5. c   5.60
</pre>

He slammed the pencil down on the desk, slipped the notebook into the ledger, slid them both into the desk drawer, rubbed his knees and opened the bolt of the steel door. "Let's see it through." Mrs. Halics was the only one to have noticed "how long he had spent in that dreadful room" and now her piercing eyes were following his every movement. Halics was listening, startled, to the driver's loud story. He made his body as small as possible, sinking his hands deep into his pockets, so as to reduce the area open to assault, in case someone "should break in on us now." It was quite enough that the driver should appear in this extraordinary weather, so tousled and excited (he hadn't visited the estate since last summer), exactly the way some strangers in ragged ankle-length coats might enter a quiet family dinner to announce in tired voices the confusing and terrifying news that war has broken out, and having done so lean against the cupboard, drain a glass of home-brewed *pálinka*, never to be seen in the region again. Because what should he make of this sudden resurrection, this feverish rushing around in circles. He didn't like everything changing around him: he took it badly. The chairs and tables had moved, the pale imprint of their legs remained on the oily floor: the cases of wine by the wall were shifting into a different order and the top of the counter was unnaturally clean. At other times the ashtrays "might as well be stacked in a pile" since everyone sprinkled ash on the floor anyway, but now, behold! Every table was bright with its own ashtray! The door was still wedged, the cigarette butts had been swept into a corner! What was all this about? Not to mention those damned spiders, that make it impossible to sit down without having to sweep cobwebs off one's clothes ... "What do I care in the end. If only that female creature would go to hell ..." Kelemen waited for his glass to be filled before he stood up. "I'm just going to give my waist a bit of exercise!" he said and loudly groaning bent back and forth a few times, then, with one grand gesture, upset his *pálinka*. "Believe me, it's as true as I am sitting here. The place suddenly went so quiet even the dog slunk behind the stove without even a squeak! Me, I just sat there, my eyes popping out, not believing what they saw! But there they were, right in front of me, large as life and twice as natural!" Mrs. Halics gave him a cool look. "Just tell me then, were you any the wiser for it?" The driver turned round in anger. "Wiser for what?" "Did you not learn anything?" Mrs. Halics sadly continued, and with the Bible still in her hand, pointed to Kelemen's glass. "See, you're still on the booze." The old man snorted. "What? Me? Me drunk? What makes you think you can speak like that to me?" Halics gave a great gulp and intervened by way of apology. "Don't take it seriously, Mr. Kelemen. She's always like this, I'm afraid." "What do you mean, don't take it seriously!" the man snapped back: "What do you think I am?!" The landlord dutifully stepped in. "Take it easy. Carry on please, do carry on. I'm interested." Mrs. Halics turned to her husband, clearly upset. "How can you sit there so calm, as if nothing had happened?! That man there has insulted your wife! Can you believe it?!" The contempt she radiated was so absolute that the words stuck in Kelemen's mouth, even though he wasn't quite through with the subject. "Now ... where was I?" he asked the landlord, then blew his nose before carefully folding his handkerchief again, crease to crease ... "Oh yes, how the girls behind the bar started making rude comments and then ..." Halics shook his head: "No, you hadn't got as far as that." Kelemen angrily slammed his glass down on the table. "I can't go on like this!" The landlord cast a warning glance at Halics then waved at Kelemen. "No need to make a fuss about it ..." "No, indeed. I'm through!" he retorted and pointed to Halics: "Get a load of him! Like he was there! He knows better!" "Forget them," the landlord assured him: "They don't understand. Believe me, they don't understand." Kelemen was mollified and started nodding. The drink had warmed him to the bone, his puffy face had grown red and even his nose seemed to have swollen ... "So, there we were, the girls behind the bar ... And I thought that Irimiás would give them a box on the ear then and there, but no! They were just like this lot here ... I recognized them all: there was the driver of the firewood truck, two stops down from the forest, then the gym teacher from the nearby school, a night waiter from the restaurant and a good few others. So. I make no bones about it, I admired Irimiás's restraint ... but to be fair, to be fair to him that is, what was he to do with them? What do you do with people like that? I waited till they took a sip of their blended, because that's what the pair of them were drinking (yes, I tell you, blended), then once they'd sat down at a table I went over to them. When Irimiás recognized me, I mean ... I mean he immediately embraced me and said: Well, my friend, fancy seeing you here. And he waved the bar girls over and they came skipping over like they were crickets or something, though it wasn't table service, and he immediately ordered a round." "A round? ... ," the landlord asked in astonishment. "A round," insisted Kelemen: "What's so strange about that? I could see he didn't feel like talking so I started chatting with Petrina. He told me everything." Mrs. Halics leaned forward anxious not to miss this. "Oh yes, everything. He's just the kind of man people tell everything," she dryly remarked. And before the driver could turn round to face "the old witch," the landlord leaned over the bar and put a hand on his shoulder. "I told you, take no notice. Meanwhile Irimiás? ..." Kelemen controlled himself and made no move. "Irimiás merely nodded now and then. He didn't say a lot. He was thinking about something." The landlord took a gulp. "You say he was ... thinking ... about something? ..." "Yes, quite so. Eventually he simply said: Time to go. We'll meet again, Kelemen." Not long after that I myself left because it was impossible ... I can only put up with so much bad company and in any case I still had some business in Kisrománváros with Hochan, the butcher. It was already dark by the time I set off for home but at the slaughterhouse I popped into The Measure. I bumped into the younger Tóth boy there, who had been my neighbor on the estate at Póstelek. It was he who told me that Irimiás, or so he said, had spent the afternoon with Steigerwald, the gun dealer who went broke, and that they were talking about some kind of ammunition, at least that's what the Steigerwald kids told him in the street. So then I set off home. And before I got to the fork at Elek—you know the Feketes' place?—and I'm not sure why myself, I looked back. I immediately knew it could only be them though they were still some way off. I went on a while but only so far that I could see the road forking and it was true, my eyes were not playing tricks on me, it really was them. They turned down the proper road without a moment's hesitation. Then, once I got home, I realized where they're going, what for and why." The landlord leaned forward with satisfaction and kept a skeptical eye on Kelemen: he guessed that what he heard was just a part, a very small part, of what had actually happened and that even the bit he heard was probably made up. He had enough respect for Kelemen to know that the man was probably saving the best for later when it would have much more effect. After all, he reasoned, no one tells you everything up front, which meant he never believed anyone, and certainly not the driver now, not a single word, though he did pay considerable heed to what he said. He was sure that even if he wanted to tell the truth in a straightforward fashion the man was incapable of doing that, so he never assumed too much about the first version of events, merely noting that, "Something might have happened." But what precisely happened, that could only be determined by a maximum joint effort, by hearing ever newer and newer versions of the story, so that there was never anything to do but wait, wait for the truth to assemble itself, as it might at any moment, at which point further details of the event might become clear, though that entailed a superhuman effort of concentration recalling in what order the individual incidents comprising the story actually appeared. "Which way, where, and why," he asked with a sly smile. "Plenty to be getting on with, don't you think?" came the answer. "Could be," the landlord coldly replied. Halics drew closer to his wife ("What terrible things to hear, dear Jesus! It's enough to make a man's hair stand on end ...") who slowly moved her head to examine the flaccid skin of her husband's face, his cataract-gray eyes, and low protruding brow. Close up, his sagging skin reminded her of those horrible slaughterhouses, of slabs of meat and ham folding in on each other; his cataract-gray eyes of water covered in frog-spawn in the courtyard wells of long-abandoned houses; and his low jutting brow of "the brows of murderers whose photographs you see in the national papers and can never forget." And so, whatever momentary fellow feeling she might have had for Halics immediately left her to be replaced by another, scarcely appropriate feeling whose object could be summed up in a single sentence: *the Grace of Jesus!* She dismissed the harsh sense of obligation to love her husband, "because a dog has more honor than he has," but what next? It must, after all, be written in the book of fate. There might perhaps be a quiet corner of heaven prepared for her, but what of Halics? What could his sinful crude soul expect? Mrs. Halics believed in providence and placed her hope in the powers of purgatory. She waved the Bible. "It would be better for you to be reading this!" she declared severely, "while you still have time!" "Me? You know, that I don't ..." "You!" Mrs. Halics cut in: "Yes, you! At least you won't be completely unprepared for the end times." Halics was not moved by these grave words; nevertheless he took the book from her with a sour grimace because "one might as well get some peace." On receiving the weight of the book in his hands he gave a nod of acknowledgment and opened it on the first page. But Mrs. Halics snatched the book from his hands. "No! Not the Creation, you idiot!" she cried and, with one well-practiced movement, went straight to the Book of Revelations. Halics found the first sentence rather difficult but didn't spend time struggling with it because, Mrs. Halics's attention being less keenly focused on him, it was enough to pretend to read. And though the words never made it as far as his brain, the smell of the pages had a pleasing effect on him, and he could listen with half an ear to the conversation between Kerekes and the landlord, and between the driver and the landlord ("Is it still raining?" "Yup," and "What's up with him?" "Drunk as a newt") because, the terror roused by the prospect of Irimiás having evaporated, he was slowly recovering his sense of orientation and had some idea of the distance between the counter and himself, as well as a notion of the dryness of his throat and of the security of being sheltered in the world of the bar. He felt immediately better that he was able to sit here, whiling away his time "among other people," certain in the knowledge that harm was less likely to befall him in company. "I'll have my wine by tonight. Who cares about the rest!" And when he saw Mrs. Schmidt at the door, another shudder of "mischievous little hope" ran up his soft spine. "Who knows? When all is said and done I might even get my money." But, being under the sharp eye of Mrs. Halics, he didn't have much time for dreaming, so he closed his eyes and leant over the book like a school dunce facing an exam, struggling with his teacher's uncompromising glare on one side and the temptations of the hot summer beyond the classroom on the other. Because in Halics's eyes Mrs. Schmidt was the embodiment of summer, a never-to-be season unattainable to one acquainted only with "the ruins of autumn, a winter without desire" and a hyperactive but frustrating spring. "Oh, Mrs. Schmidt!" the landlord leapt to his feet with a faint smile and while Kelemen was swaying here and there, looking on the floor for the door wedge so that the door could be kept closed, he led the woman over to the table he tended to work at, waited for her to sit then bent close to her ear so he could breathe in the powerful, rough scent of cologne rising from her hair that just about overcame the bitter tang of her hair gel. He didn't really know which he preferred: the scent of Easter or the exciting aroma that, come spring, leads a man—as it does the bull in the field—to the focus of desire. Halics couldn't even begin to imagine what had happened to her husband ... "What horrible weather. What can I bring you?" Mrs. Schmidt shoved the landlord aside with her "delicious, practically edible elbow" and looked around. "Cherry *pálinka?*" the landlord persisted confidentially, continuing to smile. "No," replied Mrs. Schmidt. "Well, maybe just a drop." Mrs. Halics followed every movement of the landlord, her eyes sparkling with hatred, her lips trembling, her face burning; the fury in her whole body now suppressed, now rising, with the irresistible sense of injustice over what was owing to her, and now she couldn't make up her mind what to do, whether to march out of "this notorious den of vice" or to give that lecherous swine of a landlord a sharp box on the ears for trying to inveigle innocent creatures into his wicked web by craftily getting the innocent soul drunk. She would much have preferred to rush to Mrs. Schmidt's defense ("I'd sit her on my lap and be nice to her ...") so she should not be subject to the landlord's attempts "to force himself on her," but there was nothing she could do. She knew she must not betray her feelings because they were bound to be misunderstood (weren't they always gossiping behind her back about precisely this?) but feared the poor girl might be seduced by such wiles and dreaded what would await her at the end. She sat there, her tears welling up, her body overblown, the weight of the whole world on her shoulders. "And have you heard?" asked the landlord with disarming courtesy. He put the glass of *pálinka* down in front of Mrs. Schmidt and, as far as possible, tried to hide his potbelly by breathing in. "She's heard! She's heard all right!" Mrs. Halics blurted out from her corner. The landlord sat back in his place with a solemn expression, his lips tight, while Mrs. Schmidt delicately raised her glass to her mouth using only two fingers before—as if having properly considered the matter—throwing back its contents and swallowing it all in one manlike gulp. "And are you all sure it was them?" "Absolutely sure!" the landlord retorted: "No mistake." Mrs.

Schmidt's entire being was filled with excitement; she felt her skin tingling all over, myriad scraps of thought swirling chaotically in her head, so she grabbed the edge of the table with her left hand in case she should betray herself in this great rush of happiness. She still had to pick her own things out of the big military chest, consider what she would need and what not, if, tomorrow morning—or perhaps this very night—they were to set off, because she was not in any doubt whatsoever that the unusual—unusual? fantastic rather!—visit of Irimiás (how like him! she proudly thought) could be no accident. She herself remembered his words to the letter ... but could they ever be forgotten? And all this now, at the last possible hour! These last few months since the terrible moment she had first heard the news of his death had completely destroyed her faith: she had given up all hope, abandoned all her best-loved plans, and would have resigned herself to a kind of poverty-stricken—and preposterous—bid to escape, just to be away from here. Ah, but you stupid people of little faith! Hadn't she always known that this miserable existence owed her something? There was after all something to hope for, to wait for! Now at last, there would be an end to her sufferings, her agonies! How often had she dreamed of it, imagined it? And now here it was. Here! The greatest moment of her life! Her eyes shone with hatred and something like contempt as she gazed at the shadowy faces around her. Inside, she was almost bursting with happiness. "I'm leaving! Drop dead the lot of you, just the way you are. I hope you get struck by lightning. Why don't you all just kick the bucket. Drop dead right now!" She was suddenly full of big, indefinite (but chiefly big) plans: she saw lights; rows of illuminated shops with the latest music, expensive slips, stockings and hats ("Hats!") floated before her; soft furs cool to the touch, brilliantly lit hotels, lavish breakfasts, grand shopping trips and nights, the NIGHTS, dancing ... she closed her eyes so that she might hear the rustling, the wild hubbub, the immeasurably joyful clamor. And, under her closed eyelids, there appeared to her the jealously guarded dream of her childhood, the dream that had been driven into exile (the dream relived a hundred, no a thousand times, of "afternoon tea at the salon ...") but her wildly beating heart was, at the same time, beset by the same old despair at all those delights—all those many delights—that she had already missed! How would she now—at this stage of her life—cope in entirely new circumstances? What was she to do in the "real life" about to break in on her? She was still just about able to use a knife and fork for eating, but how to manage those thousands of items of make-up, the paints, the powders, the lotions? how should she respond "when acquaintances greeted her"? how to receive a compliment? how to choose or wear her clothes? and should they—God forbid—have a car as well, then what was she to do? She decided to pay heed only to her first instinct and in any case, she would just keep her eyes peeled. If she could bear to live with a man as repulsive as that beetroot-faced halfwit Schmidt, why worry about the hazards of life with someone like Irimiás?! There was only one man she knew—Irimiás—who could thrill her so deeply in both bed and life; Irimiás who had more virtue in his little finger than all the men in the world put together, whose word was worth more than all the gold ... In any case, *men?!* ... Where were the men around here, except him? Schmidt with his stinking feet? Futaki with his gimpy leg and soaked trousers? The landlord—this thing here, with his potbelly, rotten teeth and foul breath? She was familiar with "all the filthy beds in the district" but she had never met one man to compare with Irimiás, before or since. "The miserable faces of these miserable people! What are they doing here? The same piercing, unbearable stench everywhere, even in the walls. How come I'm here? In this fetid swamp. What a dump it is! What a bunch of filthy polecats!" "Ah well," sighed Halics, "what can you do, that Schmidt is one lucky son of a bitch." He gazed lustfully at the woman's broad shoulders, her substantial thighs, her black hair wound into a knot, and that beautiful vast bosom delicious even under a thick coat, not to mention in the imagination ... (He gets up to offer her a glass of *pálinka*. And then? Then, they get to talking, and he asks her to marry him. But you're already married, she says. No matter, he answers.) The landlord put another glass of *pálinka* down in front of Mrs. Schmidt, and while she drank it off in little sips her mouth filled with saliva. Mrs. Halics's back was covered in gooseflesh. There could be no more doubt that the landlord had given her another glass of *pálinka*, though she hadn't asked for it, and that she had drunk it. "Now they're lovers!" She closed her eyes so no one else would see what she felt. Fury and frustration ran through her veins from head to toe. This time she all but lost control. She felt trapped because there was nothing she could do against them; after all it was not just that they were "constantly mouthing off" but that she had to sit here helplessly while they went about their wicked affairs. But suddenly a great light brightened her terrible darkness—she could have sworn it was a beam directly from heaven—and she inwardly cried out: "I am a sinner!" She grabbed her Bible in panic and, lips moving silently, but screaming inside, she instinctively started mouthing the Our Father. "By morning?" the driver cried. "It can't have been later than seven, half past seven at most, when I met them at the fork in the road, and, OK ... I did the journey in, let's say, three or four hours, though the horses often had to slow down to walking pace in that mud, so for them, four or five hours might be enough shall we say?!" The landlord raised a finger. "It will be the morning at least, you wait and see. The road is full of ridges and potholes! The old road leads directly here, of course, it's straight as an arrow, but they'd have to come by the metaled road. And the metaled road goes a long way around, it's like having to skirt an ocean. Don't even bother to argue: I am from these parts myself." Kelemen could hardly keep his eyes open by now, and was reduced to waving and leaning his head on the counter, where he pretty soon fell asleep.

At the back of the room Kerekes slowly raised his terrifying shaven head, covered in the scars of old injuries, his dreams practically nailing him to the "billiards table." He listened to the driving rain for a few minutes, rubbed his numb thighs, gave a shudder on account of the cold then turned on the landlord. "Dumb ass! Why is that fucking stove not working?!" The obscenity had a certain effect. "Fair enough," added Mrs. Halics: "It'd be nice to have a bit of warmth." The landlord lost his temper. "Tell me, honestly, what are *you* gabbing on about? What!? This isn't a waiting room. It's a bar!" Kerekes rounded on him: "If it's not warm in here in ten minutes, I'll wring your neck!" "OK, OK. What's the point of shouting?" the landlord caved in, then looked over to Mrs. Schmidt and gave her a cheesy grin. "What time is it?" The landlord glanced at his watch. "Eleven. Twelve at most. We'll know when the others arrive." "What others?" asked Kerekes. "I'm just saying." The farmer leaned on the "billiards table," gave a yawn, and reached for his glass. "Who's taken my wine?" he asked in a flat voice. "You spilled it." "You're lying, you dumb ass." The landlord spread his palms, "No, really, you did spill it." "Then bring me another." The smoke slowly billowed across the tables and in the distance they heard the sound—now there, now gone—of furious barking. Mrs. Schmidt sniffed the air. "What's that smell? It wasn't there before," she asked, startled. "It's just the spiders. Or the oil," the landlord replied in unctuous tones, and knelt down by the stove to light it. Mrs. Schmidt shook her head. She put her nose to her trench coat and sniffed it both inside and out, then the chair, then got down on her knees and proceeded to inquire further. Her face was practically up against the floor when she suddenly stood up straight and declared, "It's an earth smell."

V

UNRAVELING

I t wasn't easy. Back then it had taken her two days to work out where
she should plant her foot, what to grab for support and how to squeeze
herself through what looked to be the impossibly narrow hole left by a
few slats that opened under the eaves at the back of the house; now, of
course, it took only half a minute and was only mildly risky, entailing
one well-chosen movement to leap onto the woodpile covered with a
black tarpaulin, grabbing the gutter, slipping her left foot into the gap
and sliding it to one side, then forcefully entering, head first, while
kicking against the support with her free foot, and there she was inside
the old pigeon loft in the attic, in that single domain whose secrets were
known to her alone, where she had no need to fear her elder brother's
sudden inexplicable assaults, though she did have to be careful not to
awaken the suspicions of her mother and elder sister on account of
her long absence, because, should they discover her secret, they would
immediately ban her from the loft, and then all further efforts would
be in vain. But what did all that matter now! She pulled off her soaked
sweater, adjusted her favorite pink outfit with its white collar and sat
herself at "the window" where she closed her eyes and shivered, ready
to jump, listening to the roar of rain on the tiles. Her mother was asleep
in the house somewhere below, her sisters hadn't yet returned though

it was time for tea, so she was practically certain that no one would look for her that afternoon, with the possible exception of Sanyi, and nobody ever knew where to find him which made all his appearances sudden and unexpected, as if he were seeking the answer to some long-ignored riddle of the estate, a secret that could only be discovered by means of a sudden surprise attack. The fact was she had no real reason to be frightened, because no one ever did look for her; on the contrary, she had been firmly told to stay away, particularly—and this was often the case—when there was a visitor at the house. She had found herself in this no-man's-land because she was incapable of obeying orders; she wasn't allowed to be anywhere near the door nor to wander too far because she knew she could be summoned any time ("Go fetch me a bottle of wine. On the double!" or "Get me three packs of cigarettes, my girl, Kossuth brand, you won't forget, will you?"), and should she fail but once in her mission she'd never be let into the house again. Because there was nothing else left to her: her mother, when she was sent home from the special school "by mutual agreement," put her to kitchen work, but her fear of disapproval—when plates broke on the floor, or enamel chipped off the pan, or when the cobweb remained in the corner, or when the soup turned out tasteless, or the paprika stew too salty—made her incapable of completing the simplest tasks at last, so there was nothing for it but to chase her from the kitchen too. From that time on, her days were filled with cramping anxiety and she hid herself behind the barn or sometimes at the end of the house under the eaves because from there she could keep an eye on the kitchen door so that, though they couldn't see her from there, if they called she could appear immediately. Having to be constantly on the alert soon played havoc with her emotions: her attention was almost exclusively restricted to the kitchen door, but she registered that with such keen sharpness it almost amounted to acute pain, every detail of the door impinging on her at once, the two dirty panes of glass above it, through which she glimpsed flashes of lace curtains fixed there with drawing pins, and below it, splashes of dried mud, and the line of the door handle as it bent toward the ground; in other words a terrifying network of shapes, colors, lines; not only that, but the precise condition of the door itself as it changed according to her curiously chopped-up sense of time, in which possible dangers presented themselves every moment. When any period of immobility came to a sudden end everything around her shifted with it: the walls of the house sped by her as did the crooked arc of the eaves, the window altered position, the pigsty and the neglected flowerbed drifted past her from left to right, the earth under her feet shifted, and she seemed to be standing in front of her mother or elder sister who suddenly appeared before her, without her being able to see the open door. The brief moment it took her to blink was enough for her to recognize them, since that was all she needed, because the shadowy forms of her mother and sister were constantly imprinted on the scene before her in the throbbing air: she could sense their presence without seeing them, she knew they were there, that she was facing

them

down there,

just as she knew that they were rising above her to the point that if she once looked up and saw them, their image might crack right across, because their intolerable right to tower above her was so unarguable that the vision she had of them might well be enough to explode them. The ringing silence extended only as far as the unmoving door, beyond that she struggled to distinguish her mother or sister's angry command from the pounding noise ("You're enough to give anyone a heart attack! Why are you rushing around like that? There's nothing for you here! Go on, get out and play somewhere!") that quickly faded as she ran away to hide behind the barn or under the eaves, so that relief might overcome panic, of which she was never quite free because it could start again at any time. Of course, there was no playing for her, not that she had a doll, or a storybook, or a glass marble to hand with which—if any stranger should appear in the yard or if the people inside glanced out of the window to check on her—she might pretend to be engaged in a game, but she dared not, because her constant state of alert had prevented her, for a long time now, from being immersed in any kind of game. Not merely because her brother's rapidly changing moods determined what objects presented themselves to her to play with—ruthlessly deciding what things she might keep and for how long—but because of the games she was expected to play, that she might play as a kind of defense to satisfy her mother and sister's expectations of "the kind of games she should play," for, this way, they were not forced to endure the daily shame of her ("If we let her!") "peeping at us, like a sick thing, watching everything we do." Only up here, in the old unused pigeon loft, did she feel at all safe: here, she didn't have to play; there was no door "that people might walk through" (her father having nailed up the door as the first stage of some never executed plan in the dim and distant past) and no window "that people might look through," since she herself had taped two color photographs torn from newspapers across the projecting pigeonholes so that there might be "a nice view," one of them showing a seashore with setting sun, the other a snow-covered mountain peak with a reindeer in the foreground. Of course, everything was all over now, forever. A draft blew through the space once occupied by the old attic flap: she shuddered. She felt for her sweater but it wasn't dry yet so she took one of her greatest treasures, a scrap of white lace rescued from among the rags in the back kitchen and spread it over herself rather than go down into the house, wake her mother, and ask her for some dry clothes. She wouldn't have believed herself so daring, not even one day before could she have imagined it. Had she got soaked yesterday she would immediately have changed her clothes because she knew that, if she fell ill and had to be confined to bed, her mother and sisters couldn't abide her crying. But how could she have suspected that as late as yesterday morning, there would be this event, like an explosion that did not knock things flat, but, on the contrary, made things stronger and that, having been purged by "a belief built on the tempting sense of dignity," she'd been able to sleep and dream in peace. She had noticed a few days earlier that something had happened to her brother: he held his spoon differently, closed the door after him in a different way, would wake suddenly on the iron bedstead beside her in the kitchen, and spent the whole day puzzling over something. Yesterday after breakfast he came over to the barn but instead of pulling her up by her hair or—what was worse—simply standing behind her until she burst into tears, he pulled a piece of Balaton Slice candy from his pocket and pressed it into her hand. Little Esti didn't know what to make of it and she suspected something bad might happen in the afternoon when Sanyi shared with her "the most fantastic secret ever." She never doubted the truth of what her brother told her, and was far more inclined to disbelieve and find inexplicable the fact that Sanyi had chosen her of all people to ask for help, she "who was completely unreliable." But the hope that this wouldn't turn out to be just another trap overcame her anxiety that it would; so, before the question could be resolved, Esti—immediately and quite unconditionally—agreed to everything. Not that she could have done anything else, of course, because Sanyi would have forced a "yes" out of her anyway, but there was no need because once he had revealed to her the secret of the money tree he immediately won her unqualified confidence. Once Sanyi had "finally" finished, he looked to see what effect he had had on his sister's "dumb mug"; she was practically in tears with this unexpected burst of happiness, though she knew from bitter experience that crying was not an advisable course with her brother. Confused, she handed over the little treasure she had scraped together since Easter, as her contribution to the "can't lose" experiment, because she had intended this collection of dimes she had picked up from visitors to the house for Sanyi anyway, and she didn't know how to tell him that she had hidden it away for months and lied about it, just so that it—her savings—should remain a secret ... But her brother showed no great curiosity and, in any case, the joy she felt at being able, at last, to take part in her brother's secret adventures immediately overcame any sense of confusion. What she couldn't explain was why he should be burdening her with this dangerous confidence and why he should risk failure in this way since he couldn't possibly believe that his sister was capable of executing a mission that demanded "courage, endurance and the will to victory." On the other hand she couldn't forget that beneath all the harsh suffering he inflicted on her, under all the ruthless cruelty, there'd been one time, when she was ill, that Sanyi allowed her to creep into the kitchen bed with him and even let her cuddle him a little and so fall asleep. That would explain it. And there was that other time, some years ago, at her father's funeral, when, having understood that death, which was "the most direct way to heaven and the angels," was not only the result of God's will, but was something that could be chosen, and she herself was determined to find out how that worked, it was her brother who had enlightened her. She couldn't possibly have worked it out by herself: she needed him to tell her what exactly to do, a solution she might perhaps have stumbled on by herself, which was that "rat poison would do the trick too." And then yesterday, when she woke at dawn, when she had finally overcome her fear and decided to wait no longer, and was feeling a real desire to be raised to heaven, and a mighty wind seemed to be lifting her, so that she saw the earth beneath her receding further and further, the houses, trees, the fields, the canal, the whole world shrinking below and she was already standing at heaven's gate, among the angels who lived in a blaze of scarlet—it was again Sanyi with his talk of the secret money tree who had yanked her back from that magical yet terrifying height, and so, at dusk they set out together—together!—for the canal, her brother happily whistling and carrying the spade on his back, she a couple of strides behind, excitedly clutching her little hoard of money, tied up in a handkerchief. Sanyi dug a hole in the canal bank in his customary silence and, rather than chasing her away, even let her place the money at the bottom of it. He instructed her more strictly that the money-seeds they had sown should be generously watered twice daily, once in the morning, once in the evening ("or it all dries up!") then sent her home telling her she should return "precisely" an hour later with the watering can, because he had to utter "some magic spells" while she was gone, and he had to be absolutely alone while he uttered them. Little Esti conscientiously went about her task and slept badly that night, dreaming of being pursued by escaped dogs, but when she woke in the morning and saw it was raining heavily outside, everything took on a more cheerful air, a warm miasma of happiness settling over her. She immediately went back to the canal so she could be certain of giving the magic seeds a truly thorough soaking in case they weren't getting as much water as they needed. At lunch she whispered to Sanyi—she didn't want to disturb her mother who was asleep because she'd been making hay all night—that she hadn't seen anything so far, "... nothing, simply nothing," but he argued that it would take at least three, possibly four, days for the shoots to appear, and there would certainly be nothing till then, and even that depended on whether "the spot had been properly watered." "After that," he added impatiently, in a voice that brooked no contradiction, "there's no need for you to spend the whole damn day crouching there to watch it ... that won't do any good. It's enough for you to be there twice a day, once in the morning, once in the evening. That's all. Do you understand, retard?" Giving her a grin, he left the house and Esti decided to stay up in the loft until the evening if need be. "Until the shoots come through!" How often, after that, did she close her eyes so she might imagine the shoot rising and growing ever more lush, its boughs soon bending under the tremendous weight when she, with her little basket with the torn handles, might—abracadabra!—gather up the fruits, go home and tumble the coins out on the table!... How they would all stare! From that day on she would be given a clean room to sleep in, one with a big bed with a really big eiderdown, and there would be nothing for any of them to do other than to make a daily visit to the canal, fill the basket, and dance and drink cup after cup of cocoa, and the angels would be there too, fleets of them, all sitting around the kitchen table ... She wrinkled her brow ("Hang on a minute!") and, bending from side to side, began to sing:

Yesterday's one day,
Add today, makes two days,
Tomorrow's the third day,
Tomorrow's tomorrow makes four.

"Maybe it only needs two more nights' sleep?" she thought in her excitement. "But wait!" she suddenly stopped. "That's not right!" She took her thumb from her mouth, pulled her other hand out from under the lace cover, and tried counting again

Yesterday's one day.
Today makes two
Two and one makes three days
Tomorrow, ah tomorrow,
Makes three, plus one, makes four.

"Of course! So it might be tonight! Tonight!" Outside the water rushed, unobstructed, from the tiles, in a hard, straight line and beat at the earth by the walls of the Horgos farm, forming an ever-deeper moat, as if every individual drop of rain were the product of some hidden intent, first to isolate the house and maroon its occupants, then slowly, millimeter by millimeter, to soak through the mud to the foundation stones beneath and so wash away the whole thing; so that, in the unremittingly brief time allowed for the purpose, the walls might crack, the windows shift and the doors be forced from their frames; so that the chimney might lean and collapse, the nails might fall from the crumbling walls, and the mirrors hanging from them might darken; so that the whole shambles of a house with its cheap patchwork might vanish under water like a ship that had sprung a leak sadly proclaiming the pointlessness of the miserable war between rain, earth, and man's fragile, best intentions, a roof being no defense. Below her the darkness was almost complete, only through the opening did some faint light, like thick rolling fog, seep in. Everything around her was calm. She leaned against one of the rafters and because something of her earlier joy still lingered she closed—"Now's the moment!"—her eyes ... She had been seven the first time her father took her into town, at the time of the national cattle fair; he had let her wander around among the tents, and this was how she met Korin, who had lost both eyes in the last war and who was kept alive by the little money he earned by playing the harmonica at markets and bars at festival time. It was from him she learned that blindness "was a magical condition, my girl" and that he, meaning Korin, was not in the least sorry, but, on the contrary, glad, and grateful to God for "this eternal dusk of mine," so he just laughed when someone tried to describe the "colors" of this poor worldly life to him. Little Esti listened to him, mesmerized, and the next time they went to the fair she went straight to him, when the blind man revealed to her that the way into this magical world was not "barred to her either, and that she had only to close her eyes for a long time to be there." But her first efforts frightened her: she saw flames leaping, pulsing colors and a horde of furiously fleeting shapes, as well as hearing a continuous low humming and thumping noise nearby. She didn't dare approach Kerekes for advice, Kerekes who spent his time in the bar from fall through to spring, so she only discovered the secret solution much later when she caught a serious lung disease and the doctor was hastily summoned to spend the night at her bedside. With the fat, enormous, silent doctor beside her, she felt secure at last, the fever having numbed her senses, a tremor of joy ran through her, she closed her eyes, and then she finally saw what Korin had been talking about. In the magical country she saw her father with his hat on his head, wearing a long coat, holding a horse by the reins, driving the cart into the yard, taking from it a bowl of sugar, a sugarloaf, and a thousand other items brought from the market, and spreading them across the table. She realized that the gates of the kingdom would only be opened to her when "her skin felt hot all over," when her body and eyelids started to shudder. Her excited imagination usually tended to conjure her dead father as he slowly vanished over the fields, the dust rising before him and in his wake as the wind blew; and, increasingly often, she would see her brother too as he winked cheerfully at her, or sleeping beside her on the iron bed, the way he appeared to her now. His dreaming face calm, his hair over his eyes, one arm dangling from the bed; and now his skin contracts, his fingers begin to move, suddenly he turns over and the covers slide from him. "Where is he now?" The magic kingdom buzzed and rattled and drifted away as she opened her eyes. She had a headache, her skin was on fire with fever, her limbs felt very heavy. And suddenly, as she looked through the "window" it occurred to her that she couldn't just wait here for the ill-omened mist to clear all by itself; she understood that till she proved herself deserving of her brother's irrational good mood, she was risking losing his trust, and, furthermore, that this was her first, and possibly last, opportunity of gaining it; she couldn't afford to lose it because Sanyi knew the "triumphant, mad, contrary" nature of the world, without him life would be a matter of blindly stumbling between fury and murderous pity, between the thousand dangers presented by anger and waste. She was frightened, but she understood that something had to be done now, and because this wasn't a feeling previously known to her, it was balanced by a flash of momentary, confused ambition suggesting that, if she could earn her brother's respect, together they could "conquer" the world. And so, slowly, unnoticeably, the magical treasure, the broken-handled basket, the golden boughs bending with coins, drifted from the narrow confines of her attention and their qualities were transferred, by adulation, to her brother. She felt she was standing on a bridge which connected her old terrors to the things that had terrified her just the day before: she had only to cross over to the other side where Sanyi was impatiently waiting for her, and there everything that had hitherto mystified her would be explained. Now she understood what her brother had meant when he insisted on winning—"We have to win, do you understand, retard? Win!"—because she herself was moved by the hope of winning, and while she still felt that there could be no winners at the end if only because nothing ever ended, the words Sanyi had spoken yesterday ("People here make a mess of everything, it's one mess after another, but we know how to straighten things out, don't we, retard?...") had rendered all objections ridiculous; each failure was an act of heroism. She took her thumb out of her mouth, gripped the lace curtain even tighter, and started walking around the loft so as to feel less cold. What to do? How could she prove she was capable of "winning"? She looked around the loft for inspiration. The beams above her rose in a sinister fashion, rusty nails and old carpenter's hooks hanging from them. Her heart beat wildly. Suddenly she heard a noise from below. Sanyi? Her sisters? Carefully, silently, she let herself down onto the woodpile, then slunk by the wall as far as the kitchen window, pressing her face to the cold glass. "It's Micur!" The black cat sat on the kitchen table, happily lapping up the remnants of the paprika stew from the red saucepan. The lid of the pan rolled along the floor right into the corner. "Oh, Micur!" Silently, she opened the door, threw the cat down on the floor

and quickly replaced the lid on the pan, at which point an idea occurred to her. She turned around slowly, her eyes seeking Micur. "I'm
stronger than her," the thought flashed across her mind. The cat ran
over to her and rubbed herself against her legs. Esti tiptoed over to the
coatrack and, picking the green nylon net bag from one of the hooks,
silently made her way back to the cat. "Come along now!" Micur obediently strolled over and allowed Esti to put her into the bag. Her indifference didn't last long, of course: her legs slipping through the holes
without finding any firm ground, she let out a scared yowl. "What's up
now?" came a voice from the other room. "Who's out there?" Esti
stopped in fright. "It's me ... only me ..." "What the fuck are you doing
messing around in there. Get out now. Go play somewhere!" Esti said
nothing, but holding her breath, stepped out into the yard, the cat still
yowling in the bag. She reached the corner of the farmstead without
further trouble, stopped there to take a deep breath, then set off at a
run because she felt the whole world was waiting to leap on her. When
eventually, at the third try, she succeeded in reaching her hiding place,
she leaned gasping against one of the rafters and didn't look back but
knew that below her—all around the woodpile—the barn, the garden,
the mud, and the darkness were helplessly rushing at each other, their
faces contorted with fury, like hungry dogs that have missed a meal.
She gave Micur her freedom and the black cat immediately glossed
over to the opening before turning round and sniffing its way round
the loft, occasionally raising its head, listening for the silence, then rubbing itself against Esti's legs, raising its tail in pleasure and, once its
mistress had sat down in front of the "window," it settled in her lap.
"You've had it," Esti whispered as Micur started purring. "Don't think
I'll feel sorry for you! You can defend yourself if you like, if you think
you can, but it won't do any good ..." She pushed the cat off her lap,
went over to the opening and, using some planks leaning against the
tiles, closed it off. She waited a little while so her eyes could get used

to the darkness then slowly set out toward Micur. The cat did not suspect anything and allowed Esti to grab it and raise it high, and only started struggling when its mistress threw herself to the ground and began wildly rolling about with it from corner to corner. Esti's fingers closed around its neck like handcuffs and so quickly did she lift the cat up then turn over again, so the cat was underneath her, that Micur was frozen with terror for a second, and quite incapable of defending itself. The struggle couldn't last for long though. The cat quickly seized the first available opportunity to sink its claws deep into her mistress's hands. But Esti too had suddenly lost confidence, and however furiously she railed at the cat ("Come on then! Where are you? Go on, go for me! Go for me!") Micur was unwilling to try her strength against her, in fact it was she who had to be careful not to squash the cat under her palms when they next rolled over. She stared in desperation at the fleeing cat who stared back with her strangely luminous eyes, fur on end, prepared to leap. What to do? Should she try again? But how? She made a frightening face and pretended she was about to rush at the cat as a result of which the cat sprang to the opposite corner. After that she made just one sudden move—raising her hand and stamping her foot then suddenly leaping closer to the cat—and this was enough for Micur, ever more desperate, to throw herself into a yet more defensible corner, not even caring that she was cutting herself on the hooks and rusty nails, that she was crashing full tilt against the tiles, the king post, or the planks covering the opening. Both of them knew, with absolute certainty, where the other one was: Esti could immediately tell the cat's precise whereabouts on account of its luminous eyes, by the noise as it touched the tiles, or the dull thump of its body as it landed; as for herself, her position was clearly perceptible even from the faint whirlwind she created in moving her arms through the dense air. The joy and pride that swelled within her from moment to moment sent her imagination into feverish overdrive, so she felt she hardly needed to stir, her power being such that it must bear down on the cat with irresistible force; in fact the consciousness of her own inexhaustible grandeur ("I can do anything, absolutely anything with you . . . !") confused her a little at first, presenting her with a completely unknown universe, a universe with her at the center, unable to decide anything given the vast range of choice available to her, though the moment of indecisiveness, that happy sense of saturation was soon enough broken, and she could see herself stabbing through Micur's terrified, sparkling eyes with their deathly glow, or in one movement ripping off her forepaws, or simply hanging her from every damn hook or cramp at once. Her body felt strangely heavy and she felt an ever-keener, ever more alien kind of self-consciousness. The fierce desire for victory had all but vanquished her old self, but she knew whichever way she turned she was bound to trip, to fall right through the floor and that, at that last moment, the sense of determination and superiority positively radiating from her would be deeply injured. She stood there stiffly, watching the phosphorescent glow in the cat's eyes, and suddenly realized something that had never before occurred to her: looking into the light of those eyes she understood the terror, the despair that might almost make another being turn against itself; the helplessness whose last hope was to offer itself up as prey on the chance that that way it might yet escape. And those eyes were like spotlights cutting through the darkness, unexpectedly illuminating the last few minutes, the moments of their struggle when they were now apart, now clinging to each other, and Esti watched helplessly as everything she had slowly and painfully constructed in and of herself was laid flat as if at a single blow. The rafters, the "window," the planks, the tiles, the hooks and the walled-off entrance to the loft once again drifted back into her consciousness though—like a highly disciplined army waiting for the word of command—they had moved from their appointed places; the lighter objects were receding little by little, the heavier ones, strangely enough, were getting closer, as if everything had sunk to the bottom of a pond where the light no longer reached and where the direction, speed and momentum of their movements would be determined by weight. Micur lay flattened on the rotting boards across a spread of dried pigeon droppings, every muscle tense to the point of snapping, the outlines of her body a little lost against the darkness, so the cat seemed to be swimming toward her in the dense air, and she only came to full consciousness of what she had done when she *seemed* to feel the cat's warm, violently pulsating stomach and the skin with its various lacerations and the blood trickling between them. She was choking with shame and regret: she knew her victory could never be made good now. If she started moving toward her, to stroke her, it would be in vain, Micur would just run away. And that this was how it would remain forever: useless now to call her, useless to hold her in her lap, Micur would always be at the ready, her eyes would always retain the terrifying, *ineradicable* memory of this flirtation with death that would force her to make the last move. Until now she had always believed that it was failure only that was intolerable, but now she understood that victory too was intolerable, because the most shameful element of the desperate struggle was not that she remained on top, but that there was no chance of defeat. It flashed through her mind that they could try again ("... if she clawed ... should she bite ...") but she quickly realized that there was nothing she could do about it: she was simply the stronger. The fever was burning her up, sweat covered her brow. And then she caught the smell. Her first reaction was fear because she thought there was someone else in the loft with them. She only discovered what had happened when Micur—because Esti had taken an uncertain step toward the "window" ("What is this smell?") and the cat thought her mistress was about to attack her again—slipped by her into the opposite corner. "You've shat yourself!" she cried furiously. "You dared shit yourself!" The smell immediately filled the loft. She held her breath

121

and leaned over the mess. "And you've pissed as well!" She ran toward the opening, took a deep breath, then returned to the scene of the crime, and used a broken piece of plank to prod the mess into an old piece of newspaper and threatened Micur with it. "I'd like to make you eat it!" She stopped suddenly as if her words had finally caught up with her, ran to the opening and pushed aside the slats. "And I thought you were frightened! I even felt sorry for you!" Quick as lightning, so as to allow no time for escape, she dropped down onto the woodpile and threw the stinking paper package into the darkness, to let the invisible monsters hidden there, ever on the lookout for scraps, gobble it up, then crept under the eaves and stole over to the kitchen door. She carefully opened the door to find her mother loudly snoring. "I'm going to do it. I dare. Yes, I dare." She shivered in the heat, her head heavy, her legs weak. Quietly, she opened the pantry door. "A thing that shits itself! Well, you deserve it!" She took the milk pan from the shelf, filled a bowl and tiptoed back into the kitchen. "Too late for anything else, anyway." She removed her mother's yellow cardigan from the rack and very slowly, so as not to make any noise, she went out into the yard. "First, the cardigan." She wanted to put the bowl down on the ground so she could simply slip the cardigan on but as she bent down the edge of it trailed into the mud. She quickly straightened up again with the cardigan in one hand and the bowl in the other. What to do!? The rain slanted in beneath the eaves, the lace curtain was already soaked through on one side. Carefully, uncertainly, wary of spilling the milk, she started backing away ("I'll hang the cardigan out on the woodpile and then …"), but, suddenly, she stopped, because she remembered she had left the cat's dish by the step. It only occurred to her what she should do when she returned to the kitchen door: if she draped the cardigan over her head she could just about put the bowl down and so—finally being ready to move over to the woodpile with the bowl full of milk in one hand and the deep cat's dish in the other—everything looked much easier. Having control of the situation, she felt she had found the key to the tasks that lay ahead. She took the dish up first, then successfully went back for the bowl. She covered the opening with the slats again and started calling Micur in the pitch dark. "Micur! Micur! Where are you? Puss, puss, I have a treat for you!" The cat had flattened itself against the furthest corner and was watching from there as its mistress reached under one of the boards beneath the "window" and pulled out a paper bag, sprinkled some of its contents into the dish, then poured milk on top of it. "Hang on, this won't work." She left the dish and went over to the opening—Micur gave a nervous twitch— but however far she moved the slats no light came through it now. Apart from the battering of rain on the tiles the only noise to be heard was the howling of dogs in the distance. Lost for ideas, she stood there like an orphan, the cardigan hanging down to her knees. She longed to flee this dark place, escaping the oppressive silence, and because she no longer felt secure there, she was scared alone, in case something might leap out at her from a dark corner, or that she herself might walk right into an icy extended hand. "Must get on!" she cried aloud and as if clinging to the sound of her own voice she took a step toward the cat. Micur did not move. "What's the matter? Not hungry?" She started calling it in cajoling tones and very soon the cat did not leap aside when she took another step toward it. And then the opportunity presented itself: Micur—perhaps trusting the voice for a second—allowed Esti to get close, so, quick as lightning, she leapt on the cat, first holding it tight to the floor, then cleverly, avoiding those scratching claws, she raised it and carried it over to the dish waiting by the "window." "Now, go on, eat! Nice treat!" she cried in a trembling voice and with one forceful movement pressed the cat's face into the milk. It was in vain for Micur to try to escape, and it was as if it understood that all further resistance was pointless, because it stayed quite still, and its mistress, when she finally released it, couldn't tell whether she had drowned the cat, or if the cat were merely "pretending," because it was lying by the empty dish as if it were already dead. Esti slowly backed into the furthest possible corner, covered her eyes with both hands so as not to see the threatening, deathly darkness, and stuck her thumbs in her ears at the same time because, suddenly, out of the silence a host of clicking, crackling, hammering noises homed in on her. But she felt no trace of terror because she knew that time was on her side and that she had only to wait for the noise to die away by itself the way a robbed and defeated army deserts its general after the initial panic and chaos, fleeing the battlefield, or, if flight was impossible, seeking out the enemy to plead for mercy. A long time after, once the silence had swallowed the last burst of noise, she felt neither hurried nor becalmed— she was no longer concerned about what she should do but knew precisely where to step, her movements faultless and properly directed: it was as if she was rising above the field of battle and her vanquished foes. She found the curled, stiff body of the cat and, her face flushed with the fever, dropped down into the yard, looked round her, and proudly set off on the path to the canal because her instincts whispered she would find Sanyi there. Her heart beat loudly as she imagined "the face he would make" when she presented him with the corpse that would be cold by then and her throat tightened with joy when she noticed how the poplars leaned over the farm behind her like old women jealously, scoldingly, following the path of the bride as she leaves them behind, clutching the dead body of Micur, forever extended, holding it by the legs, away from her body. It wasn't a long way but it still took longer than usual for her to reach the canal, because, at every third step, her feet sank into the mud and she slithered to and fro in the heavy boots she had inherited from her sisters and, what was more, the "shitty creature" was growing steadily heavier too so she continually had to be shifting it from one hand to the other. But she wasn't discouraged, nor did she take any notice of the pouring rain, and was only sorry she couldn't fly like the wind to be at Sanyi's side, and so she blamed no one but herself when she finally arrived and saw there was not a blessed soul around. "Now where could he be?" She dropped the corpse in the mud, massaged her aching arms, burning with fatigue then, forgetting everything, leaned over the seedlings only to stop in mid-movement, breathless, as if hit by a stray bullet straight to the heart, uncomprehending and quite alone. The magical spot had been disturbed and the stick they had used to mark the spot lay on the ground in the rain, broken in two where the carefully tended earth had been piled, the earth her imagination had dwelt on and cultivated all this time, and now she was confronted by just a hole in the ground, like a hollow eye socket, a hole half filled with water. She threw herself on the ground in despair and started digging away at the crudely scraped hollow. Then she jumped up and gathered all her strength to out-shout the night towering above her, but her strained voice ("Sany-i! Sany-i! Come here!...") was lost in the overpowering din of wind and rain. She stood on the bank, quite lost as to what to do, which way to run. Eventually she set off along the side of the canal but quickly turned back and started rushing in the opposite direction, but within a few yards had stopped again and turned toward the metaled road. She found the going slow and ever harder because her feet would sink in the mud up to the ankle, the ground having been all but washed away, and she'd have to stop, pull her foot up, step out of her boot, then balancing on one leg, spend time extricating the boot from the mud. She reached the road exhausted and when she surveyed the deserted terrain—the moon appeared for a second above her head—she suddenly felt she had taken the wrong direction, that it might have been better to look for him at home first. But which way home? What if she went by the path round Horgos's field and Sanyi was returning by the Hochmeiss route? And what if he was in town?... What if he got a lift from the landlord?... But what to do without him?... She dared not admit to herself that the fever had seriously weakened her and that it was the light flickering in the distant window that really drew her. She had only taken a few steps when a voice to one side of her demanded: "Your money or your life!" Esti let out a cry of terror and started running. "What's this, little squirrel! You shitting yourself?...," the voice continued in the dark and gave a hoarse laugh. Hearing this the little girl's fear evaporated and, relieved, she ran back. "Come ... come quick! The money!... The money tree!" Sanyi slowly stepped out onto the metaled road, straightened himself and grinned. "Wow! That's ma's cardigan! You'll get a thorough beating for that. You'll spend next week in bed! Moron!" He dug his left hand deep into his pocket, his right holding a lit cigarette. Esti smiled in confusion, bowed her head and simply continued where she had left off. "The money tree!... Someone!..." She didn't raise her head to look at him because she knew how much Sanyi hated making eye contact with her. The boy looked Esti up and down, and blew smoke in her face. "What news from the asylum?" He blew his cheeks out like someone who can barely suppress laughter, then suddenly his face turned stony. "If you don't scram at once, I'll give you such a smack, sweetheart, your thick head will drop off! That's all I need is to be seen here with you ... People would be laughing at me the rest of the week. Now, go on, disappear!" He quickly looked round over his shoulder and, clearly agitated, scanned the metaled road as it vanished into the dark, then — as if his sister were already gone — looked over her head toward the distant lit window with a puzzled expression, as if he was trying to work something out. Esti was perfectly terrified now. What had happened? What could have happened for Sanyi to revert to ... Had she done something wrong? Had she made a mistake? She tried again. "The money we seeded ... It's been stolen ... Stolen!" "Stolen?" the boy shouted impatiently. "Well, well! Stolen, you say? And who stole it?" "I, I don't know ... some ..." Sanyi gave her a cold look. "You giving me lip? You dare to give me lip?" Esti quickly shook her head in fright. "Oh, right. That's what it sounded like." He drew on his cigarette and suddenly turned around again, tensely watching the bend in the road, as if he were waiting for someone, then turned back to his sister and looked at her, his face full of fury. "Can't you even stand up straight!" The little girl immediately straightened her back but kept her head bowed, staring at her boots in the mud, her straw-blonde hair tumbling over her face. Sanyi lost his temper. "What's wrong with you!? Fuck off! Understand?!" He stroked his pimply, fluffy chin then, seeing that Esti hadn't moved, was forced to speak again: "I needed the money, see! So what!?" He stopped for a moment but his sister was still there, she hadn't shifted an inch. "In any case, for fuck's sake, that money was mine. Is that clear?" Esti nodded in fright. "The money ... was mine too. How *dare* you hide it from me!?" He grinned with satisfaction. "Be glad that you got away with the little you have! I could have just taken it from you!" Esti nodded understandingly, and started slowly backing away because she feared her brother was about to hit her. "Anyway," he added with a conspiratorial smile, "I've got some really cool wine here. Do you want a sip? I'll let you have a bit. Do you want a drag of this? There." And he extended the by-now-dead cigarette toward her. Esti made a tentative effort to reach for it, but almost immediately snatched her hand back. "No? OK. Now listen, I'll tell you something. You'll never amount to anything. You were born a retard, and that's what you'll remain." The little girl screwed up her courage. "So you ... knew?" "Knew what, bug? What the fuck did I know?" "You knew ... that ... that ... the money plant ... never ... never?..." Sanyi lost his temper again. "What? Don't try to put one over on me. You should have tumbled to that much earlier, you retard! You think I'm going to believe you never had a clue? You're not that soft in the head ..." He took out a match and lit the cigarette, shielding it with his hand. "Brilliant! So you're the one upset! Rather than being happy that I'm paying some attention to you!" He blew out

127

the smoke and blinked. "Right! Session over! I haven't got the time to stand here debating with idiots. Scram, little baby. Scram!" and he prodded Esti with his forefinger, but the moment she set off at a run, he shouted after her. "Come back here! Closer! Closer, I said. Good. What's that in your pocket?" He reached into her cardigan pocket and pulled out the paper bag. "Fucking hell! What's this?!" He raised the bag and examined the writing. "For fuck's sake! This is rat poison! Where did you get this?!" Esti couldn't get a word out. Sanyi bit his lip. "Fine. I know anyway . . . It's from the barn and you *stole* it! Right?" He pressed the bag. "So what did you want it for, my little retard? Be nice and tell big bro!" Esti didn't move a muscle. "I see it now. A pile of dead bodies back home, right?" the boy continued, laughing. "And I'm next in line, eh? OK. Now let's see if you have a spark of courage in you! There you are!" He pushed the bag back in the cardigan pocket. "But be careful. I've got my eyes on you!" Esti started running toward the bar, waddling a little, like a duck. "Easy now! Be careful!" Sanyi shouted after her: "Don't use it all at once!" He stood for a while in the rain, his shoulders hunched, his head up, holding his breath, listening to the noises of the night, then fixed his eye on the distant window, squeezed a zit on his face, then he too started to run, turned off by the road mender's house and vanished into the darkness. Esti, who kept looking back, saw him for a split second, his cigarette alight in his hand, like a comet fading, never to reappear, its trace remaining for a few minutes in the dark sky, its outlines growing blurred, eventually absorbed in the heavy night haze that snapped its jaw around her now, the road beneath her immediately snuffed out so she felt as though she were swimming through the dark without any support, weightless, quite isolated. She was running toward the flickering light of the bar window as if that could compensate for the lost glow of her brother's cigarette, and more than once she shuddered in the cold when she reached it and hung on to the bar's projecting windowsill, because her clothes were completely soaked through and the lace curtain was clinging to her hot body, and it felt like ice. She stood on tiptoe but couldn't quite reach the window so had to jump to look inside and because her breath misted the glass she was only able to hear a confused babble inside, the clinking of a glass, some more glass breaking, and snatches of laughter that quickly melted into the louder sound of human conversation. Her head was pounding: she felt a flock of invisible birds were screaming and circling her. She pulled back from the light of the window, leaned her back against the wall and dreamily stared at the ground with its patch of light from the window. That was why it was only at the last possible moment that she became aware of heavy steps and the sound of gasping as someone emerged from the road and mounted the steps to the door. There was no time to escape now so she just stood by the wall, her feet rooted to the ground, hoping she wouldn't be noticed. She only moved when she saw it was the doctor, and ran to him in a panic. She clutched at his soaked coat and would have most happily hidden herself inside it, the only reason she didn't burst into tears was because the doctor did not embrace her and so she simply stood before him, her head hung low, her heart racing, the blood throbbing in her ears, and she didn't really take in the fact that the doctor was saying something, she understood only that he was impatiently wanting to be rid of her and, not being able to make out the words, her original relief was quickly succeeded by an incomprehensible bitterness because rather than hugging her he was sending her away. She couldn't understand what had happened to the doctor, to the one man who once "had spent the whole night at her bedside, wiping the perspiration from her brow," why she had to wrestle with him to hold on to him and to prevent him from pushing her away but, in any case, she simply couldn't let go of the edge of his coat and only gave up when she saw that everything around them—suddenly—was caving in and rising up, and it was hopeless trying to detain the doctor because, at last, it was all over, and she watched terrified as the earth opened under them and the doctor disappeared in the bottomless pit. She started to run, with a chorus of baying voices, like wild dogs, pursuing her and she felt it was the end, that she could do no more, that the howling voices were bound to seize her and grind her into the mud, when it suddenly fell silent, with only the humming of the wind and the soft explosions of a million tiny raindrops covering the ground around her. She only dared slow down a little when she reached the edge of the Hochmeiss estate but she couldn't stop. The wind drove the rain into her face, the cardigan had come unbuttoned and she couldn't stop coughing. Sanyi's frightening words and the nasty incident with the doctor bore down on her with such force that she was incapable of thinking; it was little things that drew her attention: her bootlaces had come undone ... the cardigan was unbuttoned ... did she still have the paper bag? ... By the time she reached the canal and stopped at the hole in the ground a curious calm had settled on her. "Yes," she thought. "Yes, the angels see this and understand it." She looked at the disturbed earth around the hole, the water dripping from her brow into her eyes, and the ground before her started, ever so gently, to undulate. She tied up her laces, buttoned the cardigan and tried to fill the hole by pushing the earth with her foot. She stopped and left it. She turned to one side and saw Micur's dead body extended on the ground. The cat's fur had soaked up the water, her eyes were staring glassily into nothing, her stomach was strangely sagging. "You're coming with me," she said quietly to the corpse and lifted it out of the mud. She hugged it close, and thoughtfully, decisively, set off. She followed the course of the canal for a while then turned off before the Kerekes farm, reaching the long, winding path round the Pósteleki estate, which, having cut across the metaled road into town, leads straight past the ruins of Weinkheim Castle, toward the fogbound Pósteleki woods. She tried to walk so that the lining of her boots rubbed less painfully against her heels because she knew she had a long way to go: she had to be at Weinkheim Manor by daybreak.

She was glad she wasn't alone and Micur was warming her stomach a little. "Yes," she quietly repeated to herself, "the angels see this and understand it." She felt a more naked kind of peace now: the trees, the road, the rain, even the night, all radiated calm. "Whatever happens is good," she thought. Everything was simple at last, forever. She saw the rows of naked acacia on either side of the road, the landscape that vanished into the dark within a few yards of her, was aware of the rain and the stifling smell of mud, and knew for certain that what she was doing was absolutely right. She thought over the events of the day and smiled as she understood how they all connected up: she felt it was neither chance, nor accident, but an unutterably beautiful logic that was holding them together. She also knew she was not alone, since everything and everyone—her father up above, her mother, her siblings, the doctor, the cat, these acacias, this muddy track, this sky and the night below it—all depended on her, just as she depended on everything else. "What a great champion I might become! I just have to keep going." She squeezed Micur still closer, looked up at the unchanging sky and quickly stopped. "I'll make myself useful once I'm there." The sky was slowly beginning to lighten in the east, and by the time the first beams of the sun touched the ruined walls of Weinkheim Castle and streamed through the gaps and the enormous window spaces into the burnt-out, overgrown rooms, Esti had made all the preparations. She laid Micur down on her right, and once she had divided the remaining contents in brotherly fashion, half and half, and had succeeded in swallowing her half with a little rainwater to wash it down, she placed the paper bag on her left side on a rotten board, because she wanted to be sure her brother wouldn't miss it. She lay down in the middle, stretched out her legs and relaxed. She brushed the hair from her forehead, put her thumb in her mouth, and closed her eyes. No need to worry. She knew perfectly well her guardian angels were already on the way.

THE WORK OF THE SPIDER II

The Devil's Tit, Satantango

W hat is behind me still remains ahead of me. Can't a man rest?"
Futaki said to himself in a low mood, when, treading soft as a
cat, leaning on his stick, he caught up with the stubbornly silent
Schmidt, and the now silent, now howling Mrs. Schmidt at the "personal table" to the right of the counter, and dropped heavily into the
chair, letting the woman's words slip by him ("As far as I can see you
must be drunk! I think it's gone to my own head a little, I shouldn't mix
my drinks like that, but ... But you're such a gentleman ...") as he
grabbed the new bottle and slid it to the middle of the table with a foolish look on his face, wondering why he should feel so glum all of a sudden, because, really, there was absolutely no reason to be so gloomy,
after all, today wasn't just any old day, because he knew the landlord
would be proved to be right and that "they had only a few short hours
to wait" for Irimiás and Petrina to arrive and that their arrival would
put an end to years of "wretched misery," break the damp silence, and
stop that infernal funereal bell, the one that wouldn't let people rest in
bed in the early morning, so they had to stand there helplessly, dripping with sweat while everything slowly fell to pieces. Schmidt who
had refused to say a word ever since they set foot in the bar (and would
only mumble, turning his back on "the whole damn thing" in the great

din when Kráner and Mrs. Schmidt shared out the money) now raised his head, laid furiously into his wife as she swayed precariously on the edge of her chair ("It's all gone to your head, not to mention your ass!... You're drunk as a newt") then turned to Futaki who was just about to fill their glasses. "Don't give her any more, damn it! Can't you see the state she's in?!" Futaki didn't answer or try to make any excuses, he simply gestured that he totally agreed with him, and quickly put the bottle down again. He had spent hours trying to explain it to Schmidt, but the man just shook his head: according to him, "they'd had their one chance and had blown it" by sitting here in the bar like "gutless sheep" instead of using the confusion created by Irimiás and Petrina to quietly make off with the money and, better still, "Kráner might have been left here to rot ..." However Futaki went on about how, from tomorrow on, everything would be different, that Schmidt should just calm down, because they'd really struck it lucky this time, Schmidt simply made a mocking face and kept quiet, and so it all went on until Futaki realized that they could never see eye to eye since while his old chum might be willing to accept that Irimiás was "a real opportunity," he would not agree that there was no other option: without him (and without Petrina too, of course) they'd just be stumbling about like the blind, without a clue, ranting on, fighting each other, "like condemned horses at the slaughterhouse." Somewhere deep inside him he did—of course—understand Schmidt's resistance, since they had spent years cursed with bad luck, though he thought the sheer hope that Irimiás would look after things and that everything would improve as a result might mean that they could finally "make it all work" because Irimiás was the only man capable of "holding together things that just fall apart when we're in charge." What would it matter then that an indeterminate sum of money had gone up in smoke? At least they need not feel so bitter about things, watching helplessly, day after day, the plaster falling off the walls, the walls cracking, the roofs sagging; nor would they have to put up with the ever slower beating of their hearts and the growing numbness of their limbs. Because Futaki was certain that neither this week-on-week, month-on-month cycle of failure in which the same but increasingly confused schemes suddenly and inevitably crumbled into ash, nor the ever fainter longing for freedom, constituted a real danger: on the contrary, these were the forces that held them together, because bad luck and utter annihilation were far from the same thing, but right now, in this most recent state of affairs, failure was out of the question. It was as if the real threat came from elsewhere, from somewhere beneath their feet, though its source was bound to be uncertain: a man will suddenly find silence frightening, he fears to move, he squats in a corner that he hopes might protect him: even chewing becomes a torture there and swallowing agony, so eventually he doesn't even notice that everything around him has slowed, that he is ever more hemmed in, and then discovers that his strategic withdrawal is in fact nothing less than petrification. Futaki glanced around in fright, lit a cigarette, his hands trembling, and greedily drank up what was in his glass. "I shouldn't be drinking," he berated himself. "Every time I do I can't help thinking of coffins." He stretched out his legs, leaned comfortably back in his chair, and decided to indulge in no more fearful thoughts; he closed his eyes and let the warmth, the wine and noise radiate his bones. And the ridiculous panic that had seized hold of him one moment was gone the next: now he was listening only to the cheerful banter around him and was so moved he could barely hold back a tear because his earlier anxiety had been succeeded by gratitude for the privilege of being able, after all his sufferings, to sit in this hubbub, excited and optimistic, safe from everything he had just had to confront. If, having consumed eight and a half glasses, he had had enough strength left, he would have hugged each of his sweating, gesticulating companions if only because he couldn't resist the desire to give formal shape to this profound emotion. The trouble was he had unexpectedly developed a violent headache, felt suddenly hot, his stomach was heaving and his brow was covered in sweat. He sank back into himself, quite weak, and tried to alleviate his condition by breathing deeply, so he never even heard the words of Mrs. Schmidt ("What's with you? Gone deaf or something? Hey, Futaki, you feeling sick?") who, seeing Futaki massaging his stomach, his face pale and clearly suffering, just waved ("Ah well. Someone else you shouldn't count on!...") and turned to face the landlord who had long been staring at her with the most lustful expression. "This heat is unbearable! János, do something for heaven's sake!" But it was as if he hadn't heard her "in this hellish din": he simply spread his hands, and without responding to Mrs. Schmidt and her nonsense about the heater, gave her a deeply meaningful nod. Having realized that her efforts had been in vain, the woman sat angrily down and unbuttoned the top button of her lemon-yellow blouse, to the gratification of the landlord who regarded her with pleasure, delighted his patient work had borne the desired fruit. For hours now, secretly, and with commendable diligence, he had been turning up the fire, and finally, with one quick movement, he had raised and slid aside the oil-heater's control—who, after all, would have noticed that in all the hubbub?—so that Mrs. Schmidt might be "liberated" from, first, her coat and then her cardigan, her charms acting on him with even greater power than before. For some unaccountable reason she had always rejected his advances, his every effort—though he never ever gave up—meeting with failure, and the agonies he suffered through her rejections increased each time. But he was patient and waited, and continued waiting, because he knew from the first time he surprised Mrs. Schmidt at the mill, in the arms of a young tractor-driver—when instead of leaping to her feet and running away in shame, she just carried on, letting him stand there, his throat dry, until the young man finally brought her to a climax—that it would take a long-term campaign to win her. However, ever since it had come to his attention a few days ago, that the bonds between Futaki and Mrs.

Schmidt had, so to speak, "loosened," he was hardly able to conceal his delight because he felt it was his turn now, that this was his opportunity once and for all. Now, weakening at the sight of Mrs. Schmidt delicately pinching the blouse about her breasts and using the garment to fan herself, his hands began to shake uncontrollably and his eyes all but misted over. "Those shoulders! Those two sweet little thighs rubbing against each other! Those hips. And those tits, dear lord!..." His eyes wanted to seize the Entirety at once, but in his excitement he could only concentrate on the "maddening sequence" of the Details. The blood drained from his face, he felt dizzy: he was practically begging to catch Mrs. Schmidt's indifferent ("It's like he's some kind of simpleton...") eyes and, since he was incapable of freeing himself from the illusion that he could sum up every situation in life, from the simplest to the most complex, in one pithy phrase, he asked himself, "Wouldn't any man spare the oil for a woman like this?" It was all one happy dream. Ah, but if he had known how hopeless it was, how unsuited he was to her desires, he would anxiously have retreated to the storeroom once again to nurse his fresh wounds, protected there from the hostile looks of others, and escape the gleeful mocking he would have had to face. Because he couldn't even begin to guess that what he took for the come-on looks of Mrs. Schmidt, apparently aimed at Kráner, Halics, the headmaster, and he himself, and the way she led them into this dangerous whirlpool of desire with her languorously extended limbs, was only her way of filling the time while every inch of her imagination was given over to Irimiás, her memories of him beating at "the grassy cliffs of her consciousness like a roaring sea in a storm" that, combined with exciting visions of their future life together, served to intensify her hatred and loathing of the world around her, a world to which "she must soon bid adieu." And if, now and then, it happened that she swayed her hips or allowed greedy eyes to feast on the sight of her notable bosom, it was not just to make the remaining, highly tedious hours fly faster, but because it was preparation for the much longed for meeting with Irimiás, at which point their two hearts "might be conjoined in recollected pleasures." Kráner and Halics (and even the headmaster)—unlike the landlord—were perfectly clear there was no hope for them: their arrows of desire dropped at Mrs. Schmidt's feet with a hollow sound, but this way, at least, they could remain resigned to the pointlessness of their desire: the desire, at least, would survive without its object. The bald, thin, tall ("but sinewy . . .") figure of the headmaster, with his disproportionately small head, sat, resentfully, by his glass of wine, behind Kerekes, in the corner. It was pure chance he had heard of the prospective arrival of Irimiás, he, the only educated man in the district! Except, that is, for the perpetually drunk doctor. Who do these people think they are? What do they think they're up to? If he hadn't eventually had enough of Schmidt and Kráner's ridiculous unpunctuality and closed up the Culture Center, having placed the projector, as he was bound to in writing, in a secure place, and decided to "catch up with the news" at the bar, he might never have heard about the return of Irimiás and Petrina . . . And what would these people do without him? Who would protect their interests? Did they think he'd accept whatever Irimiás was likely to propose, just as it was, no questions asked? Who else was likely to put himself forward as the leader of such a rabble? Someone had to grasp the nettle, to prepare a plan and organize "all the necessaries" into a proper list! As his first fit of rage passed ("These people are hopeless! What to do? Surely we must be methodical about this, we can't leave everything from one day to the next . . .") his attention was divided between Mrs. Schmidt and the detailed working out of such a plan, but he quickly dropped the latter because he was firmly of the opinion, based on long years of experience, that "at any given time one should concentrate only on one given thing." He was convinced that this woman was different from the others. It could be no accident that she had rejected the crude, animal advances of the other locals, one after the other. Mrs. Schmidt, he felt, needed "a serious man, a man of some substance" not someone of Schmidt's kind, Schmidt, whose coarse character was not in the least fitted to her thoughtful, simple, yet refined soul. And, "in the last analysis," it was no wonder that the woman was attracted to him—there could be no question that she was—it was enough to know that she was the only one on the estate who had never tried to make fun of him, not even that time the school was closed down, and that she had continued to address him as "headmaster." And that must be because the way this woman behaved toward him—quite apart from the issue of attraction, that is to say with clear and obvious respect—showed that she knew he was just waiting for the right moment (which would be when the right people, proper first-rate figures in both human and professional terms, reassumed the official positions they had relinquished to make room for that vulgar horde of clowns in what could only be a strategic, temporary retreat) to renovate the building and "energetically to set about" teaching again. Mrs. Schmidt, of course—why deny it?—was a very good-looking woman; the photographs he had of her (he'd taken them years ago on a cheap, but all the more reliable, camera) were far superior, in his opinion, to the "highly provocative" kind he saw in *Füles*, the games and puzzles magazine, with which he tried to chase away those sleepless, endless nights filled with anxiety ... But, possibly as a result of the generally recognized effect of yet another emptied bottle of wine, his normally clear, methodical, organized thoughts suddenly failed him: his stomach began to heave, the "veins" in his head started pounding, and he was almost ready to leap to his feet, ignoring the babblings of these primitive "peasants," and invite the woman to his table, when his excited gaze, roving here and there over the hidden promises of Mrs. Schmidt's body, suddenly met her own indifferent gaze across the snoring figure of Kerekes slumped over the billiards table, and the shock of her utter indifference seemed to cut right through him, brought a blush to his face and led him to retreat behind the farmer's vast bulk so that he might be "alone with his shame" or at least to give up the idea, for an hour or so, much like Halics who—having seen that Mrs. Schmidt, though sitting opposite him, had not heard him, or, if she had heard him, simply didn't want to hear his gripping account of long familiar events—abruptly stopped in mid-sentence and let Kráner carry on shouting and quarrelling with the ever more furious driver, but—"excuse me!"—without him, for he wasn't going to get himself into a stew about it, and, having resolved this, he swept the cobwebs off his clothes and glared in frustration at the greasy, self-satisfied mug of the landlord as he made eyes at Mrs. Schmidt, because—after considerable thought—he had concluded that, since "shits like him had no place in the world," the profusion of cobwebs must be a new kind of ruse, part of the landlord's guile. What an utter scoundrel the man was! It wasn't enough for him to be constantly annoying people with his childish nonsense, now he had to make eyes at Mrs. Schmidt too. Because this woman was his alone ... or would be soon because even a blind man could see that she'd smiled at him at least twice, and he had, after all, smiled back! ... Given all this—for it was plain to see, especially with eyes as sharp as his were generally acknowledged to be—that there was no limit to the depths to which this brigand, this shameless exploiter, this disgraceful con man, was prepared to stoop! ... The man was loaded with money, his storeroom was packed to the rafters with wine, brandy and food, never mind what was in the bar itself, not to mention the car outside, and yet he wanted more! And more, and more. The man was insatiable! And now he had to be drooling over Mrs. Schmidt too! This time he's gone too far! Halics was made of sterner stuff: he was not going put up with such impertinence! Everyone thinks he's just some timid little mouse, but that's just appearances, the outer man. Well, let them bring on Irimiás and Petrina! The inner man was capable of things they could never dream of! He threw back his wine, squinted over at his stony, all-observing wife and reached for a quick refill but, to his greatest surprise—he distinctly remembered there being at least two glassfuls remaining—the bottle was empty. "Someone's stolen my wine!" he cried and leapt to his feet, glaring, but, not meeting with a single pair of startled, guilty eyes, he grumbled and sat back in his chair. The tobacco smoke was so dense now you could barely see through it: the oil heater pumped out heat, its top glowing bright red, so everyone was pouring with sweat. The noise grew louder and louder because the loudest people, Kráner, Kelemen, Mrs. Kráner, and when she had recovered her strength, Mrs. Schmidt, all tried to shout over the racket and now, on top of it all, Kerekes had woken up and was demanding another bottle from the landlord. "That's what you think, pal!" Kráner stumbled forward. Glass in hand he was waving his arms around right under Kelemen's nose, the veins on his forehead standing out, his cataract-gray eyes glittering with menace. "I'm not your 'pal,'" the driver leapt to his feet, having completely lost his temper. "I've never been anyone's 'pal,' understand?!" The landlord tried to calm them from behind his counter ("Just leave it, will you? Your noise is enough to give a man a splitting headache!") but Kelemen skirted around Futaki's table and ran over to the counter. "Well, you tell him then! Someone's got to tell him!" The landlord picked his nose. "Tell him what? Can't you just forget it, can't you see he's upsetting everyone!" But instead of calming down Kelemen grew angrier still. "So you don't get it either! Are you all stupid?!" he bellowed, and started beating his fists on the counter: "When I ... yes, I ... got friendly with Irimiás ... near Novosibirsk ... in the prisoner-of-war camp, there was no Petrina then! Understand?! Petrina was nowhere!" "What do you mean nowhere? He must have been somewhere, mustn't he?" Kelemen was practically frothing at the mouth and gave the counter a great kick. "Look, if I say he was nowhere, he was nowhere. Simply ... nowhere!" "OK, OK," the landlord tried to pacify him: "Whatever you say; now just be nice, go back to your table and stop kicking my counter to pieces!" Kráner made a face and shouted over Futaki's head: "Where were you?! And how did you get to be at Novosibirsk or what the fuck? Look pal, if you can't hold your liquor, stop drinking!" Kelemen stared at the landlord, with an agonized expression, then turned to Kráner, and having shaken his head to convey the right mixture of fury and bitterness, flapped his hand in a rather grand way at the extraordinary ignorance of the man ... He swayed back to his table and tried to calm himself by sitting in a comfortable position but miscalculated, upset the chair and, dragging it with him, ended up sprawling on the floor. This was too much for Kráner who burst out laughing. "What's the matter with you ... You lunk...You big drunk lunk?!... My sides are splitting! And that this ... this ... he ... he claims ... To have been a prisoner of war at ... No, it's too much!..." His eyes bulging, his hand clutching his belly, he managed to make his way over to the Schmidts' table, stopped behind Mrs. Schmidt and abruptly gave her a big sudden hug. "Did you hear that ...," he started, his voice still choked by laughter: "This man—this man here—he has been trying to tell me ... did you hear him?!..." "No I didn't, but in any case I'm not interested!" Mrs. Schmidt snapped back, trying to free herself from Kráner's spade-like hands. "And you can take your filthy paws off me!" Kráner let that pass and leaned against her with the full weight of his body, then—as if by mere accident—he slid his hand down Mrs. Schmidt's open blouse. "Ooh! It's lovely and warm in here," he grinned but the woman, with one furious movement, freed herself, turned round and, summoning her full power, struck him a heavy blow. "You!" she bellowed at Schmidt when she saw that Kráner hadn't stopped grinning. "You just sit there! How can you tolerate it?! His hands were all over me!?" With an enormous effort, Schmidt raised his head from the table, but this being the limits of his strength, slumped right back again. "What are you beefing about?" he muttered and started a bout of hiccupping. "Just ... let ...

hands ... go wherever! At least someone is enjoying them ... selves ..."
But by this time the landlord had sprung into action and went at
Kráner like a fighting cockerel. "You think this is some kind of bor-
dello! You think that's what this place is! A whorehouse!?" But Kráner
just stood there, more bull than rooster, not flinching, but looking at
him sidelong, before suddenly brightening. "Whorehouse! That's it
precisely, pal! That's what it is!" He put his arm round the landlord and
started dragging him toward the door. "This way, pal! Let's get out of
this shitty hole! Let's go down to the mill! Now that's what I call life
down there ... Come on, don't hang back! ..." But the landlord succeeded in escaping him, and quickly skipped back behind the bar, waiting, by way of satisfaction, for the "drunken idiot" to notice at last that
his stocky wife had long been waiting by the door, hands on hips, her
eyes flashing. "I can't hear you! Go on, tell me too!" she hissed into her
husband's ear when he bumped into her. "Where do you think you're
going?! Up your mother's ass?!" Kráner immediately sobered up.
"Me?" he looked at her uncomprehendingly: "Me? Why should I be
going anywhere? I'm not going anywhere because I want my one and
only little darling, and no one else!" Mrs. Kráner disengaged herself
from her husband's arms and carried on, stabbing her finger at him. "I'll
give you 'little darling' and no mistake, and you sober up by morning
or little darling will give you a black eye you won't forget!" Though two
heads shorter than he was, she grabbed the meek-as-a-lamb Kráner's
shirtsleeve and pushed him down into the chair: "You dare stand up
again without my say-so, I tell you, you'll regret it ..." She filled her own
glass, drained it in anger, looked round, gave a great sigh and turned to
Mrs. Halics ("A den of vice, that's what this is! But there'll be tears and
wailing and gnashing of teeth yet, just like the prophet says!") who was
watching events with a grim satisfaction. "Where was I?" Mrs. Kráner
picked up her broken conversation, waving an admonitory finger at her
husband as he carefully reached for a glass. "Oh yes! In other words my

husband is a decent man, I can't complain, and there's the truth! It's just the booze, you know, the booze! If it weren't for that, butter wouldn't melt in his mouth, believe you me, butter wouldn't melt. He can be such a thoroughly good man when he wants to be! And he can work, you know, work as hard as two men! Well, so what if he has a fault or two, dear God! Who doesn't have faults, Mrs. Halics, my dear, tell me that? There's no such man anywhere. None that walk the earth, anyway. What? He can't stand people being rude to him? Yes, that's the one thing he gets really sore about, my husband. That time with the doctor, that happened because, well, you know what the doctor is like, treating people like they're his dogs! An intelligent man would let it pass, and pull himself together, because it's only the doctor, after all, and the whole thing doesn't amount to much, best to ignore it, end of story. In any case he's nowhere near so bad a man as he seems. I should know Mrs. Halics darling, because don't I know him through and through, his every little foible, after all these years!?" Futaki put out a careful hand as he leaned on his stick and teetered toward the door, his hair tousled, his shirt hanging out at the back, his face white as lime. With great difficulty he removed the wedge and stepped outside, but the shock of fresh air immediately laid him on his back. The rain was beating down as hard as ever, each drop "a sure messenger of doom," exploding against the moss-covered tiles of the bar roof, against the trunk and branches of the acacia, on the uneven glimmering surface of the metaled road above and, down below the road, on the space by the door where Futaki's bent, shivering body sprawled in the mud. He lay there for long minutes, as if unconscious in the dark, and when he eventually managed to relax, he immediately fell asleep, so if it hadn't occurred to the landlord, some half an hour later, to wonder where he'd got to, to find him and shake him into consciousness ("Hey! Have you gone crazy or something?! Get up! Do you want pneumonia?!") he might have remained there till the morning. Dizzy, he leant against the wall of the bar, rejecting the landlord's offer ("Come along, lean on me, you'll get soaked to the bone out here, so stop it ...") and just stood, stupid and drained under the pitiless power of the rain, seeing but not understanding the unstable world around him until—another half hour later—he was utterly soaked and he suddenly noticed he was sober again. He nipped round the corner of the building to piss by an old bare acacia and, while doing so, looked up at the sky, feeling tiny and quite helpless—and while an endless stream of water gushed from him in powerful masculine fashion he experienced a fresh wave of melancholy. He continued gazing at the sky, examining it, thinking that somewhere—however far away—there must be an end to the great tent extended above them, since "it is ordained that all things must end." "We are born into this sty of a world," he thought, his mind still pounding, "like pigs rolling in our own muck, with no idea what all that jostling at the teats amounts to, why we're engaged in this perpetual hoof-to-hoof combat on the path that leads to the trough, or to our beds at dusk." He buttoned himself up and moved to one side to be directly under the rain. "Go wash my old bones," he grumbled. "Give them a good wash, since this ancient piece of shit won't be around much longer." He stood there, his eyes closed, his head thrown back because he longed to be free of the obstinate, ever-recurring desire to know at last, now that he was near the end, the answer to the question: "What is the point of Futaki?" Because it would be best to resign himself now, to resign himself to that last moment when his body dropped into the last ditch, to drop into it with the same enthusiastic thud you expect from a baby saying hello to the world for the first time; and then he thought again of the sty and of the pigs because he felt—though it would have been hard to put the feeling into words, his mouth being so dry—that no one ever suspected that the reassuring self-evident providence that took care of us all on a daily basis would ("At one unavoidable dawn hour") be simply the light flashing off the butcher's knife, and that that would be at the time when we least expected it, a time when we wouldn't even know why we should be facing that incomprehensible and terrifying last goodbye. "And there's no escape and nothing to be done about it," he thought as he shook his tangled locks, in ever-deeper melancholy, "for who could possibly comprehend the idea that someone who, for whatever reason, would happily carry on living forever, should be kicked off the face of the planet and spend eternity with worms in some dark, stinking marsh." Futaki had, in his youth, been "a lover of machines" and retained that love even now when he resembled nothing so much as a small drenched bird, muddied and fouled with his own vomit; and because he knew the precision and order demanded even of the workings of a simple pump he thought that, if a functioning universal principle did exist somewhere ("as it plainly does in machines!"), then ("you can bet your life on it!") even a world as mad as this must be subject to reason. He stood at a loss in the pouring rain then, without any warning, started furiously accusing himself. "What an idiotic blockhead you are, Futaki! First you roll around like a pig in muck, then you stand here like a lost sheep ... Have you lost what little brain you had? And, as if you didn't know it was the last thing you should do, you get totally smashed! On an empty stomach!" He shook his head in anger, looked himself up and down, and full of shame, started to wipe his clothes down without much success. With his trousers and shirt still covered in mud he quickly found his stick in the dark and tried to sneak back into the bar unnoticed to get some help from the landlord. "Feeling better now?" the landlord asked, winking, ushering him into the storeroom. "There's a bowl and some soap, don't worry about it, you can use this to dry yourself with." He stood there with arms folded and did not move until Futaki had finished washing, though he knew he could have left him alone, but had decided it was better if he stayed, because "you never know what devil gets into people." "Brush your trousers off as best you can, and wash that shirt," he said. "You can let it dry off on the stove! Until it's ready you can put this on!" Futaki thanked him, wrapped the ragged and cobwebbed old coat around him, smoothed back his dripping hair and followed the landlord out of the storeroom. He didn't go back to rejoin the Schmidts but settled instead next to the stove and spread his shirt over the back of it, asking the landlord, "Got anything to eat?" "Just some milk chocolate and these croissants," the landlord replied. "Give me two croissants!" said Futaki, but by the time the landlord returned with the tray the heat had overcome him and he was asleep. It was late now and the only people still awake were Mrs. Kráner, the headmaster, Kerekes and Mrs. Halics (who, now that everyone was exhausted, took the liberty of raising her unsuspecting husband's glass of Riesling to her lips), so Futaki greeted the landlord's laden tray ("Fresh croissants, help yourself!") with a quiet mumble of refusal and the croissants were returned untouched. "Fine, drop dead ... Give these corpses half an hour and it'll be resurrection time again ...," the landlord muttered in fury, stretching his stiff limbs before mentally making a quick calculation as to "how things stand." It all looked pretty hopeless because the takings fell far short of what he had originally anticipated and he could only hope that a shot of coffee would bring "the drunken rabble" to their senses. Beyond the financial loss (because, "heigh-ho," lack of income also amounted to loss) what most annoyed him was that he had been just one step away from getting Mrs. Schmidt into the storeroom when she went out like a light and suddenly fell asleep, which forced him to think of Irimiás again (though he had decided he would not let the thought "bother him because things would take their own course") conscious that they'd be arriving soon and then it would "all" be over. "Waiting, waiting, nothing but waiting ...," he fretted, then leapt to his feet because he remembered that he had put the croissants back on the shelf without covering them in cellophane, though "these bastards" would soon be up again and he'd be dashing round with the tray for hours. He was long used to the state of perpetual readiness and had been ever since he got over his first wave of anger, just as he was no longer anxious to find the last owner of the bar, "that blasted Swabian" and tell him "there was nothing in the contract about spiders." Back then, just two days before opening the bar, having got over his shock, he had tried every possible way of eliminating the creatures but, discovering that it was impossible, he realized there was nothing for it but to talk to the Swabian again in the hope of persuading him to drop the asking price a little. But he had vanished off the face of the earth, which was distinctly not the case with the spiders who continued "joyfully cavorting" about the place, so he was obliged to resign himself for the rest of his life to the fact there was nothing to be done about it, that he could pursue them with rags and cloths and crawl from bed in the middle of the night, but, even so, he could only deal with "the majority of them" at best. Fortunately this never became a major subject of conversation because as long as he stayed open and people shifted from place to place, the spiders couldn't "go around wrecking the place": even they weren't capable of "covering anything that moved in cobwebs . . ." The trouble always started after the last customer had gone and he had locked up, washed the dirty glasses, put things away and closed the ledger, at the point when he started to clean up, because then every corner, every table and chair leg, every window, the stove, the rising rank of nooks and shelves and even the line of ashtrays on the counter would be covered in fine webs. And the situation deteriorated from there because having once finished and lain down in the storeroom, quietly cursing, he could hardly sleep because he knew that, within a few hours, he himself would not be spared. Given this, it was no wonder that he shrank, disgusted, from anything that reminded him of cobwebs, and it often happened that when he could no longer bear it he would attack the iron bars over the windows but—luckily—because he went at them with his bare hands he couldn't really damage them. "And all this is nothing compared ...," he complained to his wife. Because the scariest thing was that he never once saw an actual spider though at that time he'd stay awake all night behind the counter, but it was as if they sensed his presence watching them, and they simply wouldn't appear. Even after he had resigned himself to the situation he still hoped—just once—to set eyes on one of them. So it became a habit with him, from time to time—without ever stopping what he was otherwise doing—to cast his eyes carefully around the place, just as he was examining the corners now. Nothing. He gave a sigh, wiped the counter down, gathered together all the bottles off the tables then left the bar to relieve himself behind a tree. "Someone's coming," he ceremoniously announced on his return. The whole bar was immediately on its feet. "Somebody? What do you mean somebody?" cried Mrs. Kráner, quite pale. "Alone?" "Alone," the landlord calmly replied. "And Petrina?" Halics spread his hands. "I told you it's just one man. That's all I know!" "Well then ... it can't be him," Futaki determined. "Quite right, not him," the rest muttered ... They sat back in their places, lit cigarettes in disappointment or took a sip from their glasses and only a few glanced up when Mrs. Horgos walked into the bar but even those then turned away again partly because, while not particularly old, she looked like an ancient hag and partly because she was not much liked on the estate ("There's nothing sacred for that woman!" Mrs. Kráner declared). Mrs. Horgos shook the rain off her coat then, without a word, strode over to the counter. "What will you have?" the landlord coldly asked. "Give me a bottle of beer. It's hell out there," Mrs. Horgos croaked. She looked round the bar, hard-eyed, not out of curiosity, it seemed, but as if she had arrived just in time to bear witness to a crime. Her gaze finally settled on Halics. She flashed her red toothless gums and remarked to the landlord. "They seem to be having a fine time." Scorn radiated from her wrinkled crow's face, the water still dripping from a coat that seemed to have gathered on her back like a hump. She raised the bottle to her mouth and greedily started drinking. The beer ran over her chin and the landlord watched in disgust as it dribbled from there onto her neck. "Have you seen my daughter?" Mrs. Horgos asked. "The little one." "No," the landlord gruffly replied. "She hasn't been here." The woman croaked and spat on the floor. She took a single cigarette from her pocket, lit it, and blew smoke in the landlord's face. "You know, the thing is," she said, "we had a bit of a party with Halics yesterday and now the shit doesn't even have the manners to say hello. I've been asleep all day. I wake up this evening and there's nobody around, not Mari, not Juli, not little Sanyi, not one of them. But never mind that. The little one has skipped off somewhere, I'll give her a hiding she won't forget when she turns up. You know how it is." The landlord didn't say anything. Mrs. Horgos drained the remainder of the bottle and immediately ordered another. "So she wasn't here," she muttered, grimacing. "The little whore!" The landlord curled his toes. "I'm sure she must be somewhere on the farm. She's not the kind to run away," he said. "Sure she is!" the woman snapped back. "Fuck her! I hope she gets what's coming to her, the sooner the better. It's practically dawn and she's out in this rain. No wonder I'm so worn out I'm in bed all the time." "And where have you left the girlies?" Kráner shouted over. "What's that got to do with you?" Mrs. Horgos spat back, full of fury: "They're my girls!" Kráner grinned. "OK, OK, no need to bite my head off!" "I'm not biting your head off, but you just mind your own business!" It was quiet. Mrs. Horgos turned her back on the drinkers, leaned an elbow on the counter and, tipping her head back, took another great gulp. "I need it for my bad stomach. It's the only medicine that helps at times like this." "I know," the landlord nodded. "Do you want some coffee?" The woman shook her head, "No, I'd be throwing up all night. What good is coffee? Useless!" She picked the bottle up again and drained it to the last drop. "Good night then. I'm off now. If you see any of them tell them to get back home and be quick about it. I'm not going to hang around all night. Not at my age!" She pushed a twenty at the landlord, put away the change and started for the door. "Tell the girlies there's no hurry— tell them to take their time," Kráner laughed behind her back. Mrs. Horgos muttered something and spat once on the floor by way of goodbye as the landlord opened the door for her. Halics, who was still a regular at the farm, didn't even "spare her a glance of his beady eye" because ever since he had woken he had been staring at the empty bottle in front of him and was only concerned about discovering whether someone had been playing tricks on him. He scanned the pub with eagle eyes and, settling finally on the landlord, decided to watch the man like a hawk and to expose him at the earliest opportunity for the scoundrel he was. He closed his eyes again and let his head fall to his chest because he was incapable of remaining conscious for more than a few minutes at a time before sleep overcame him. "Almost dawn," noted Mrs. Kráner. "I have a feeling they're not coming." If only!" muttered the landlord, wiping his brow as he went round with a thermos full of coffee. "Don't panic," Kráner retorted. "They'll come when they are good and ready." "Of course," added Futaki. "It won't be long now, you'll see." He took slow sips of his steaming coffee, touched his drying shirt, then lit a cigarette and fell to wondering what Irimiás would do once he got here. The pumps and generators could certainly do with a complete overhaul for a start. The whole engine room needed a new coat of limewash and the windows and doors would have to be repaired because there was such a draft there it gave you a head- ache all the time. It wouldn't be easy, of course, because the buildings were in a poor state, the gardens overrun by weeds, and people had carried away anything usable from the old industrial building leaving nothing but the bare walls so it looked like a bombed site. But there is no such word as "can't" for Irimiás! And then of course you'd need luck, because there's no point in anything without luck! But luck comes with intelligence! And Irimiás's mind was sharp as a razor. Even back then, Futaki recalled with a smile, when he was appointed boss of the works, it was to him everyone ran in case of trouble, the managers too, because, as Petrina said at the time, Irimiás was "an angel of hope to hopeless people with hopeless difficulties." But there was nothing to be done with bottomless stupidity: no wonder he walked away in the end. And the moment he vanished things ran straight downhill and the community plunged to ever-lower depths. First cold and ice, then foot-and-mouth disease with piles of dead sheep, then wages a week late because there wasn't enough money to pay them, ... though by the time it got to that state everyone was saying it was all over, and that they'd have to close up shop. And that's what happened. Those who had somewhere to go cleared off as fast as they could; those who didn't stayed behind. And so began the quarrels, the arguments, the hopeless plans where everyone knew better than anyone else what should be done, or else pretended that nothing had happened. Eventually everyone was resigned to the sense of helplessness, hoping for miracles, watching the clock with ever greater anxiety, counting the weeks and months until even time lost its importance and they sat around all day in the kitchen, getting a few pennies from here and there that they immediately drank away in the bar. Latterly he himself had got used to staying in the old engine room, only leaving it to call at the bar or round at the Schmidts' place. Like the others, he no longer believed that anything could change. He had resigned himself to staying here for the rest of his life because there was nothing he could do about it. Could an old head like his set itself to anything new? That was how he had thought but no longer: that was all over now. Irimiás would be here soon "to shake things up good and proper" ... He twisted and turned excitedly in his chair because more than once he seemed to hear someone trying to open the door, but he told himself to calm down ("Patience! Patience ...") and asked the landlord for another cup of coffee. Futaki was not alone: the excitement was tangible everywhere in the bar, particularly when Kráner looked out through the glazed door and ceremonially declared: "It's getting lighter at the horizon," at which point everyone suddenly came to life, the wine started flowing again, and Mrs. Kráner's voice rose over the rest, shouting: "What is this? A funeral?!" Swinging her enormous hips she took a turn around the bar, ending up in front of Kerekes. "You there! Wake up! Play us something on your accordion!" The farmer raised his head and gave a great belch. "Talk to the landlord. It's his instrument, not mine." "Hey, landlord!" Mrs. Kráner shouted. "Where's your accordion?" "Got it, just bringing it . . ." he muttered, disappearing into the storeroom. "But then you'll really have to drink." He made his way to the food shelves, took out the cobweb-covered instrument, gave it a perfunctory cleaning, then holding it across his middle, took it over to Kerekes. "Careful now! She's a bit temperamental . . ." Kerekes waved him away, put his shoulders through the straps, ran his hands over the keys of the instrument, then leaned forward to finish his glass. "So where's the wine?!" Mrs. Kráner was swaying around in the middle of the room with her eyes closed. "Go on, bring him a bottle!" she harried the landlord, and stamped her foot impatiently. "What's with you, you lazy scum! Don't fall asleep on me!" She put her hands on her hips and upbraided the laughing menfolk. "Cowards! Worms! Don't any of you have the guts to take a turn with me?!" Halics was not going to be called a coward by anyone and leapt to his feet, pretending not to hear his wife calling ("You stay where you are!"). He bounded up to Mrs. Kráner. "Time for a tango!" he cried and straightened his back. Kerekes didn't even give them a glance so Halics simply grabbed Mrs. Kráner by the waist and started dancing. The others cleared a space for them, clapping, cheering, and encouraging them, so not even Schmidt could stop himself laughing because they did present a truly irresistible spectacle, Halics, at least a head shorter than his partner, cavorting around Mrs. Kráner while she swung those enormous hips of hers without moving her feet. It was as if a wasp had got into Halics's shirt and he was trying to get it out. The first *csárdás* finished to loud cheers, Halics's breast was bursting with pride and he could barely refrain from bellowing at the approving crowd: "See! See! That's me! That's Halics!" The next two turns of *csárdás* were even more spectacular, Halics surpassing himself with a series of complex, quite inimitable maneuvers, though he did interrupt these with one or two statuesque poses in which he would all but freeze, with his left or right arm above his head, his body seemingly hollowed out, waiting for the next heavy beat so that he might extend his extraordinary and unique moment of glory with more demonic caperings around the puffing and whooping figure of Mrs. Kráner. Each time a dance was over, Halics would demand a tango, and when Kerekes finally relented and struck up a well-known tune, beating out the rhythm with his great heavy boots, the headmaster could no longer resist and strode up to Mrs. Schmidt, who had been woken by the racket around her, and whispered in her ear: "May I have the pleasure?" Once they started, finally he could clap his right hand on Mrs. Schmidt's back, and the scent of her cologne immediately overwhelmed him and held him entranced, so the dance began a little clumsily, if only because he was desperate to hug her close and lose himself in her hot, radiant breasts; in fact he had to exercise supreme self-control to maintain the "obligatory distance" between them. But it wasn't an altogether hopeless situation because Mrs. Schmidt dreamily pressed herself ever closer to him, so close, in fact, he thought his blood would boil over, and when the music took a still more romantic turn she actually rested her tearful cheeks on the headmaster's shoulder ("You know dancing is my one weakness ..."). At that point the headmaster could bear it no longer and awkwardly kissed the soft folds of Mrs. Schmidt's neck: then, having realized what he'd just done, he immediately straightened up but didn't get to apologize because the woman silently yanked him back to her. Mrs. Halics, whose mood had changed from fierce and active hatred to dumb contempt, naturally observed all this: nothing could remain hidden from her. She was fully aware of what was going on. "But my Lord, our Savior, is with me," she muttered, firm in her faith, and was only wondering why judgment was so slow in coming: where was the hellfire that would surely destroy them all? "What are they waiting for, up there?!" she thought. "How could they look down on this seething nest of wickedness 'straight out of Sodom and Gomorrah' and yet do nothing?!" Because she was so sure that judgment was imminent, she waited ever more impatiently for her own moment of judgment and absolution, even though, as she had to admit, she had sometimes—if only for the odd minute—been tempted by the devil himself to take a nip of wine, and then, under the influence of the Evil One, been constrained to look with sinful desire upon the devil-possessed Mrs. Schmidt's undulating figure. But God exercised firm governance over her soul and she would fight Satan alone, if need be: just let Irimiás, he who had risen from his own ashes, arrive in time to support her, for she could not be expected, all by herself, to bring an end to the headmaster's invidious assault. She could not help but see that the devil had gained a complete, if momentary victory—that being the devil's aim—over those gathered in the bar, for, with the exception of Futaki and Kerekes, they were all on their feet, and even those who could not grab a part of either Mrs. Kráner or Mrs. Schmidt stood close to them, waiting for the dance to end so they could take their turn. Kerekes was tireless, beating out the rhythm with his foot behind "the billiards table," and the impatient dancers would not allow him any time to rest and drain a glass between numbers, but kept putting ever more bottles beside him on the table, so he would not flag in his efforts. Nor did Kerekes object but kept going, one tango after another, then simply repeating the same one over and over again, though nobody noticed. Of course Mrs. Kráner couldn't keep pace; her breath came short, the sweat poured off her, her legs were burning and she didn't even wait for the next dance to finish but suddenly turned on her heels, left the excited headmaster and dropped back in her chair. Halics ran after her with a pleading, accusing look: "Rosie, my dear, my one and only, you're not going to leave me like that, are you? It would have been my turn next!" Mrs. Kráner was wiping herself down with a napkin and waved him away, gasping, "What are you thinking! I'm no longer twenty!" Halics quickly filled a glass and pressed it into her hand. "Drink this, Rosie darling! Then ...!" "There won't be any 'then'!" Mrs. Kráner retorted, laughing. "I don't have the energy, not like you youngsters!" "As concerns that, Rosie dear, I'm not exactly a child myself! No, but there's a way, Rosie dear!..." But he was unable to continue because his eyes now wandered to the woman's rising and falling bosom. He took a swallow, cleared his throat and said, "I'll get you a croissant!" "Yes, that'd be nice," Mrs. Kráner said gently once he'd gone, and wiped her dripping brow. And while Halics was fetching the tray she gazed at the ever-energetic Mrs. Schmidt who twirled dreamily from one man to the other in the course of the tango. "Now, let's get this down you," said Halics and sat down very close to her. He leaned back comfortably in his chair, one arm around Mrs. Kráner—without risking anything since his wife had finally fallen asleep by the wall. Silently they munched the dry croissants one after the other, which is how it must have happened that the next time they reached for one their eyes met, because there was only one croissant left. "There's such a draft in here, can't you feel it?" the woman said, fidgeting. Halics gazed deeply into her eyes, his own eyes squinting because of the drink. "You know what, Rosie darling," he said, pressing the last croissant into her hand. "Let's both eat it, OK? You start from this side, me from the other, until we get to the middle. And you know what, sweetheart? We'll stop the draft in the door with the rest!" Mrs. Kráner burst out laughing. "You're always pulling my leg! When's that hole in your head going to heal up? Very good ... the door ... stop the draft ... !" But Halics was determined. "But Rosie dear, it was you who said there was a draft! I'm not pulling your leg. Go on, take a bite!" And so saying he pressed one end of the croissant into her mouth and immediately clamped his teeth round the other end. As soon as he did so the croissant broke in two and fell into their laps, but they—their mouths just opposite each other!—stayed there unmoving, and then, when Halics started feeling dizzy, he summed up his courage and kissed the woman on the mouth. Mrs. Kráner blinked in confusion and pushed the passionate Halics away from her. "Now now, Lajos! That's not allowed! Don't act like a fool! What are you thinking!? Anyone might be watching!" She adjusted her skirt. It was only once the window and the glazed part of the door were bright with morning that the dance was over. The landlord and Kelemen were both leaning on the counter, the headmaster had flopped across the table next to Schmidt and Mrs. Schmidt, Futaki and Kráner looked like an engaged couple leaning against each other and Mrs. Halics's head had dropped onto her chest. They were all fast asleep. Mrs. Kráner and Halics carried on whispering for a while but didn't have enough strength to get up and bring a bottle of wine over from the counter, and so, in the general air of peaceful snoring, they too were eventually overcome by the desire to sleep. Only Kerekes remained awake. He waited until the whispering had stopped then got up, stretched his limbs, and silently and carefully set off to skirt the tables. He felt around for bottles that still had something left in them, then removed them and set them out in a row on "the billiards table"; he examined the glasses too and whenever he found a drop of wine in one he quickly downed it. His enormous shadow followed him like a ghost across the wall, sometimes drifting onto the ceiling, then, once its master took his uncertain place again, it too rested, in the corner at the back. He swept the cobwebs off the scars and fresh scratches on his frightening face, and then—as best he could—he poured the remnant wine into a single glass and, puffing, set greedily to drinking. And so he drank on without a break until the very last drop vanished into his great gut. He leaned back in his chair, opened his mouth and tried belching a few times, then, not succeeding, he put his hand on his stomach and rambled his way into the corner where he stuck a finger down his throat and started vomiting. Having finished he straightened up and wiped his mouth with his hand. "So that's done with," he grumbled, and retired behind "the billiards table" again. He picked up the accordion and struck up a sentimental, melancholy tune. He swayed his enormous body back and forth in time to the gentle lilting of the music and when he got to the middle of it a tear appeared in the corner of his numb eyelid. If anyone had appeared then and asked him what suddenly bothered him he wouldn't have been able to say. He was alone with the puffing sound of the instrument and he didn't mind being overcome, quite swept away by the slow military air. There was no reason to stop playing it and when he got to the end he started it again, without a break, like a child among sleeping adults, full of a happy sense of satisfaction since, apart from him, no one else was in any position to listen. The velvety sound of the accordion stimulated the spiders of the bar to a new frenzy of activity. Every glass, every bottle, every cup and every ashtray was quickly veiled over with a light tissue of webs. The table and chair legs were woven into a cocoon and then—with the aid of one or another secret narrow strand—they were all connected up, as if it were a matter of some importance that the spiders, flattened in their secret, remote corners, should be properly advised of every slight tremor, each microscopic shift, and would be so as long as this strange, all-but-invisible network remained intact. They wove over the faces, hands, and feet of the sleepers too, then, lightning-quick, retreated to their hidey-holes so that given one barely perceptible vibration, they would be ready to start again. The horseflies who were seeking safety from the spiders in movement and night tirelessly described their figures of eight around the faintly flickering lamp. Kerekes played on, half-asleep, his semiconscious brain full of bombs and crashing planes, of soldiers fleeing the field, and of burning towns, one image rapidly succeeding the other with dizzying speed: and when they entered, it was so silent, and they so unnoticed, that they stopped in astonishment, surveying the scene before them, so Kerekes only sensed, rather than knew, that Irimiás and Petrina had arrived.

THE SECOND PART

VI

IRIMIÁS MAKES A SPEECH

My friends! I confess, I come to you at a difficult time. If my eyes do not deceive me I see that no one has missed the chance to be present at this fateful meeting ... And many of you, trusting, no doubt, that I will be ready to supply you with an explanation for recent events, events that no sane person could describe as anything but an incomprehensible tragedy, seem to have arrived even before the time we arranged only yesterday ... But what can I say to you, ladies and gentlemen? What else can I say but that ... I am shaken, in other words, I am cast down ... Believe me, I too am utterly confused, so you must forgive me if, for now, I cannot find quite the right words, and that, instead of addressing you as I should, my throat, like yours, is still tight with the shock we all feel, so please don't be surprised if, on this devastating morning for us all, I am, like you, left helpless and without words, because, I must admit, it does not help me speak when I recall how last night, as we were standing in horror by the lately discovered body of this child, and I suggested that we should try to grab some sleep, we are once again gathered together in the hope that, perhaps now, on the morrow of the event, we might be able to face life with a clearer head, though, believe me, I am as utterly at a loss as you are, and my confusion has only increased with the morning ... I know I should pull myself together, but am sure you will understand if just at this moment I am incapable of saying or doing anything except share, deeply share, the agony of an unfortunate mother, a mother's constant, never-to-be-alleviated grief ... because I don't think I need to tell you twice that the grief of losing— just like that, from one minute to the next—those dearest to our hearts is, my friends, quite beyond measure. I doubt if anyone now gathered here could fail to understand any part of this. The tragedy involves each and every one of us, because, as we know full well, we are all responsible for what has happened. The hardest thing we must face in this situation is the obligation, through clenched teeth, with lumps in our throats, to examine the case ... Because—and I really must emphasize this most intensely—there is nothing more important, before the officials arrive, before the police begin their own inquiries, than that we, the witnesses, we in our positions of responsibility, should accurately reconstruct events and discover what brought about this horrifying tragedy resulting in the terrible death of an innocent child. It's best we prepare ourselves, for we are the people the official local agencies will regard as primarily responsible for the catastrophe. Yes, my friends. Us! But surely we should not be surprised at this. Because, if we are honest with ourselves, we must admit that, with a little care, a touch more foresight and some proper circumspection, we could have prevented the tragedy, couldn't we? Consider that this defenseless creature, she who we might rightly regard now

as God's little outcast, this little lamb, was liable to all kinds
of danger, prey to any tramp or passerby—to anything and
everything my friends, being out all night, soaked through
to the bone in that heavy rain, out in the wild wind, easy
prey to all the elements ... and, through our blind thoughtlessness, our unforgivable wicked thoughtlessness, she was
left wandering around like a stray dog, here in our vicinity,
practically in our midst, driven here and there by all kinds of
forces while never straying too far from us. She might possibly have been looking through that very window, watching you, ladies and gentlemen, as you danced drunkenly
through the night, and as, I cannot deny it, we ourselves
passed, passed while she watched us from behind a tree or
from the depths of a haystack, while we were stumbling
rain-beaten and exhausted past the well-known milestones,
our destination Almássy Manor—indeed, her path lay near
to us, so close to us we might have reached out and touched
her and no one, you understand, no one hurried to help
her or strained to catch her voice, because it's certain that
at the moment of death she must have cried out to us—to
someone!—but the wind blew away the sound, and she was
lost in the tumult you yourself were making, you, ladies and
gentlemen! What brought about this terrible combination
of chance factors, you will ask, what pitiless whim of fate? ...
Don't misunderstand me, I am not accusing any particular
person here ... I am not accusing the mother who might
never again enjoy a night of peaceful slumber because she
cannot forgive herself for the fact that, on this one fateful
day, she woke too late. Nor do I—like you, my friends—
accuse the victim's brother, this fine upstanding young man
with a bright future, who was the last to see her alive, just

two hundred yards from here, barely two hundred yards from you, ladies and gentlemen, you, who, suspecting nothing, were patiently waiting for us to appear, only to fall into a dull drunken sleep … I am not accusing any particular person of anything and yet … let me put this question to you: are we not all to blame? Would it not be more befitting if, instead of offering cheap excuses, we confessed that, yes, we are indeed guilty? Because—and in this respect Mrs. Halics is undoubtedly right—we should not kid ourselves, hoping to put our consciences at rest by pretending that all that has happened was merely a peculiar accident, a coming together of chance events we could do nothing about … It wouldn't take me a minute to prove you wrong about that! Let us take stock, piece by piece, each one of us in turn … let us analyze the dreadful moment and examine its several parts, because the big question—and we should not forget this, ladies and gentlemen!—is what actually happened here yesterday morning. I went through the particulars of the night over and over again before I stumbled on the truth! Please don't think it is just a matter of not knowing *how* the tragedy came about, since the fact is we don't even know *what it is* that has happened … The details we are aware of, the various confessions we have heard, are so contradictory that it would take a genius, a man with sprouts for brains, as you put it round here, to see through the rather convenient fog and make out the truth … All we know is that the child is dead. That's not a lot, you must admit! That's why, I thought later, once I could lie down on the bed in the storeroom that this kind gentleman, the landlord, had selflessly offered up to me, that's why there is no other way than to go through the events step by step—and I remain convinced that that's the only correct procedure open to us … We must collate all the most seemingly insignificant details, so please don't hesitate to recall what might appear to you to be unimportant. Think hard about what you might have missed telling me yesterday, because this is the only way we will find both an explanation and some kind of defense in the most demanding moments of the public examination to come ... Let us use the brief time available to us, since who can we trust but ourselves—no one else can lay bare the story of this momentous night and morning ...

The grave words rang mournfully through the bar: it was like the continuous tolling of furiously beaten bells, the sound of which served less to direct them to the source of their problems than simply to terrify them. The company—their faces reflecting the terrible dreams of the night before, choked up with memories of foreboding images between dreams and waking—surrounded Irimiás, anxious, silent, spellbound, as if they had only just woken, their clothes rumpled, their hair tangled, some with the pressure marks of pillows still on their faces, waiting benumbed for him to explain why the world had turned upside down while they were sleeping ... it was all a terrible mess. Irimiás was sitting in their midst, his legs crossed, leaning back majestically in his chair, trying to avoid looking into all those bloodshot, dark-ringed eyes, his own eyes staring boldly ahead, his high cheekbones, his broken hawk-like nose and his jutting, freshly shaven chin tilted above everyone's head, his hair, having grown right down his neck, curled up on both sides, and, every now and then, when he came to a more significant passage, he would raise his thick, close, wild eyebrows as well as his finger to direct his listeners' eyes to wherever he chose.

But before we set out on this dangerous road, I must tell you something. You, my friends, deluged us with questions when we arrived yesterday at dawn: you cut across each other, explaining, demanding, stating and withdrawing, begging and suggesting, enthusing and grumbling, and now, in response to this chaotic welcome, I want to address two issues, though I might already have broached them with you individually ... Someone asked me to "reveal the secret," as some of you called it, of our "disappearance" about eighteen months ago ... Well, ladies and gentlemen, there is no "secret"; let me nail this once and for all: there was no secret of any kind. Recently we have had to fulfill certain obligations—I might call these obligations a mission—of which it is enough, for now, to say that it is deeply connected to our being here now. And having said that, I must rob you of another illusion because, to put it in your terms, our unexpected meeting is really pure chance. Our route—that is to say mine and that of my friend and highly valuable assistant—led us to Almásssy Manor, being obliged—for certain reasons—to make an emergency visit there in order to take what we might call a survey. When we set out, my friends, we did not expect to find you here: in fact we weren't even sure whether this bar would still be open ... so, as you see, it was indeed a surprise for us to see you all again, to come upon you as if nothing had happened. I can't deny it felt good to see old familiar faces, but, at the same time—and I won't hide this from you—I was at the same time concerned to see that you, my friends, were still stuck here—do protest if you find "stuck" too strong a word—stuck here, at the back of beyond, years after having often enough decided to move on, to leave this dead end and to seek your fortunes elsewhere. When we last saw each other, some eighteen months ago, you were standing in front of the bar, waving goodbye to us as we disappeared around the bend, and

I remember very clearly how many great plans, how many wonderful ideas were ready, just waiting to be put into action, and how excited you were about them. Now I find you all still here, in precisely the same condition as before, in fact more ragged and, forgive the expression, ladies and gentlemen, duller than before! So, what happened? What became of your great plans and brilliant ideas?!... Ah, but I see I am digressing somewhat ... To repeat, my friends, our appearance among you is a matter of pure chance. And while the extraordinarily pressing business that brooks no delay should have brought us here some time ago—we should have arrived in Almássy Manor by noon yesterday—in view of our long-standing friendship I have decided, ladies and gentlemen, not to leave you in the lurch, not just because this tragedy—though at some remove—touches me too since the fact is we ourselves were in the vicinity when it happened, not to mention that I do faintly remember the victim's unforgettable presence among us and that my good relations with her family impose on me an unavoidable obligation, but also because I see this tragedy as a direct result of your condition here, and in the circumstances I simply can't desert you. I have already answered your second question by telling you this, but let me repeat it, just so there will not be any later misunderstanding. Having heard that we were on our way you were too hasty in assuming that we were intending to see you because, as I have already mentioned, it hadn't occurred to us that you would still be here. Nor can I deny that this delay is a little inconvenient, because we should have been in town by now, but if this is the way things have fallen out let's get something over with as quickly as possible and draw a line under this tragedy. And if, perhaps, any time should remain after that I'll try to do something for you, though, I must confess, at the moment I am utterly at a loss to think what that could be.

. . . . .

What has fate done to you, my unfortunate friends? I could be referring to our friend Futaki here, with his endless, depressing talk of flaking plaster, stripped roofs, crumbling walls and corroded bricks, the sour taste of defeat haunting everything he says. Why waste time on small material details? Why not talk, instead, of the failure of imagination, of the narrowing of perspective, of the ragged clothes you stand in? Should we not be discussing your utter inability to do anything at all? Please don't be surprised if I use harsher terms than usual, but I am inclined to speak my mind now, to be honest with you. Because, believe me, pussyfooting and treading carefully around your sensitivities will only make things worse! And if you really think, as the headmaster told me yesterday, dropping his voice, that "the estate is cursed" then why don't you gather your courage in both hands and do something about it?! This low, cowardly, shallow way of thinking can have serious consequences, friends, if you don't mind me saying so! Your helplessness is culpable, your cowardice culpable, culpable, ladies and gentlemen! Because—and mark this well!—it is not only other people one can ruin, but oneself!... And that is a graver fault, my friends, and indeed, if you think about it carefully, you will see that every sin we commit against ourselves is an act of self-humiliation.

The locals were huddled together in fear and now, after the last of these thundering sentences had died away, they had to close their eyes, not only because of his fiery words but because his very eyes seemed to be burning holes in them ... Mrs. Halics's expression was pure sackcloth-and-ashes as she absorbed the ringing denunciation, and she stooped before him in almost sexual ecstasy. Mrs. Kráner hugged her husband so close that he had, from time to time, to ask her to loosen her grip. Mrs. Schmidt sat pale at the "staff table," occasionally drawing her hands across her brow as if trying to wipe away the red blotches that kept appearing there in faint waves of ungovernable pride ... Mrs. Horgos, unlike the men who—without precisely understanding these veiled indictments—were spellbound and feared the ever-fiercer passion rising in them, observed events with a keen curiosity, occasionally peeking out from behind her crumpled handkerchief.

I know, I know, of course ... Nothing is so simple! But before you excuse yourselves—blaming the intolerable pressure of the situation or because you feel helpless when faced by the facts—consider little Esti for a moment, whose unexpected death caused you such consternation ... You say you are innocent, friends, that's what you say for now ... But what would you say if I now asked you how we should refer to this unfortunate child? ... Should we call her an innocent victim? A martyr to chance? The sacrifical lamb of those without sin?! ... So, you see. Let's just say that she herself was the innocent party? Right? But if she was the embodiment of innocence then you, ladies and gentlemen, are the embodiment of guilt, every one of you! Feel free to reject the charge if you think it is without foundation! ... Ah, but you are silent! So you agree with me. And you do well to agree with me because, as you see, we are on the threshold of a liberating confession ... Because by now you all know, *know* rather than just suspect, what has happened here. Am I right? I'd like to hear each and every one of you to say it now in chorus ... No? Nothing to say, my friends? Well of course, of course, I understand how hard it is, even now when it's all perfectly obvious. After all, we're hardly in a position to resurrect this child! But believe me, that's exactly what we have to do now! Because you will be stronger for the confrontation. A clean confession is, as you know, as good as absolution. The soul is freed, the will is released, and we are once again capable of holding our heads high! Think of that, my friends! The landlord will quickly convey the coffin to town while we remain here with the weight of the tragedy dragging at our souls, but not enfeebled, not uncleansed, not cringing in cowardice, because, our hearts broken, we have confessed our sin and can stand unabashed in the searching beam of judgment ... Now let's not waste any more time, since we understand that Esti's death was a punishment and warning to us, and that her sacrifice serves, ladies and gentlemen, as a pointer to a better, fairer future.

Their sleepless, troubled eyes were veiled over with tears and, hearing these words, an uncertain, wary, yet unstoppable wave of relief washed over their faces, while, here and there, a brief, almost impersonal sigh escaped from them. It was like fierce sunlight curing a cold. After all, this was precisely what they'd been waiting for all these hours—these liberating words pointing to the lasting prospect of "a better, fairer future" and their disappointed looks now radiated hope and trust, belief and enthusiasm, decision and the sense of an ever more steely will as they faced Irimiás ...

And you know, when I think back over what I saw when we first arrived and crossed the threshold, the way you, my friends, were strewn across the room, dribbling, unconscious, slumped in chairs or over tables, your clothes in rags, covered in sweat, I must confess my heart aches and I become incapable of judging you, because that was a sight I shall never forget. I will recall it whenever anything threatens to deflect me from the mission with which God has entrusted me. Because that prospect made me see the full misery of people cut off forever, deprived of everything: I saw the unlucky, the outcasts, the indigent and defenseless masses, and your snuffling, snoring and grunting made me hear the imperative of their cry for help, a call I must obey as long as I live, until I too am dust and ashes ... I see it as a sign, a special sign, for why else should I have set out once again but to take my place at the head of an ever more powerful, ever-rising, fully justified fury, a fury that demands the heads of the truly guilty ... We know each other well, my friends. I am an open book to you. You know how I have moved around the world for years, for decades, and have bitter experience of the fact that, despite every promise, despite all pretense, despite the thick veil of lying words, nothing has really changed ... Poverty remains poverty and those two extra spoonfuls of food we receive are nothing but thin air. And in these last eighteen months I have discovered that all I have done so far also counts for nothing—I should not have been wasting my time on tiny details, I have to find a much more thoroughgoing solution if I am to help ... And that's why I have finally decided to seize the opportunity: I want now to gather together a few people in order to establish a model economy that offers a secure existence and binds together a small band of the dispossessed, that is to say ... Do you begin to understand me? ... What I want is to establish a small island for a few people with nothing left to lose, a small island free of exploitation, where people work *for*, not *against* each other, where everyone has plenty and peace and security and can go to sleep at night like a proper human being ... Once news of such an island gets around I know the islands will multiply like mushrooms: there will be ever more of us and eventually everything that seemed merely an idle dream will suddenly become possible, possible for you, and you, and you, and you. I felt, in fact I knew, that now this plan had to be realized as soon as I got here. And since I myself have lived here and belong here, here must be the place to realize the plan. That, I now discover, is the real reason I set out for Almássy Manor with my friend and helper, and that, friends, is why we are meeting now. The main building is, as I recall, still in a reasonable state, and the other buildings can soon be put right. Getting the lease is child's play. There remains only one problem, a big problem, but let's not worry ourselves about that just now ...

An excited hubbub surrounded him: he lit a cigarette and stared straight ahead with a solemn expression, lost in thought, the furrows on his brow deepening as he bit his lips. Behind him by the stove Petrina was quite overcome with admiration and gazed at the back of the "genius"'s head. Then Futaki and Kráner spoke at once: "What's the problem?"

I don't think I need to burden you with that just yet. I know you are thinking: Why shouldn't we be those people? ... Indeed, my friends, it isn't a wholly impossible idea. The kind of people I need are those with nothing to lose and—and this is the most important thing—they should not be afraid of taking a risk. Because my plan is undoubtedly risky. If anyone interested, you understand, *anyone*, gets cold feet then I'll be gone—just like that! These are hard times. I can't bring the plan to fruition straightaway ... I have to be prepared—and am in fact prepared in case I meet with an obstacle that I can't immediately overcome—to withdraw temporarily. Though that would be merely a strategic withdrawal, and I would simply be waiting for the next opportune moment.

The same question was now being fired at him from every direction. "OK, tell us about the big problem? Couldn't we ... Maybe despite that ... Somehow ..."

Look here, my friends ... It's not such a great secret really and there is nothing to stop me telling you. I just wonder what use the knowledge will be to you? ... In any case, there's nothing you can do to help me at the moment. For my part, I would be happy to help you once things here have improved, but for now this other business needs my entire attention. To tell you the truth, the estate looks like a hopeless case to me right now ... the best I could do, maybe, would be to find one or another of you honest work, a decent living somewhere, but your whole situation is new to me so you will understand that for now it's impossible. I'd have to give the matter some proper thought ... You'd like to remain together? I understand, of course I do, but what can I do in that case? ... Pardon? What was that? You mean the problem. What's the problem? Well look, I've already told

175

you that it makes no sense keeping anything from you. The problem is money, ladies and gentlemen, money, because without a penny, of course, there's nothing to be done, the deal is dead ... the cost of the lease, the outlay on contracts, the rebuilding, the investment, the whole business of production, requires, as you know, a certain, what they call, capital investment ... but that's a complex matter, my friends, and why go into that now? What's that? ... Really? ... You've got the money? ... But how? Oh, I see. You mean the value of the cattle, the herd. Well, that's fair enough ...

There was real fever in the company now; Futaki had already sprung to his feet, grabbed a table, put it down in front of Irimiás and reached into his pocket. He displayed his contribution to the others and threw it on the table. Within minutes he was followed, first by Kráner, then, one after the other, by the rest, all pledging their cash on top of Futaki's contribution. The gray-faced landlord ran back and forth behind his counter, stopping dead every so often, and standing on tiptoe so he could see better. Irimiás rubbed his eyes in exhaustion; the cigarette in his hand went out. He looked on without expression as Futaki, Kráner, Halics, Schmidt, the headmaster and Mrs. Kráner tried to outdo each other in their enthusiasm to demonstrate their readiness and commitment. So the pile of money on the table rose ever higher. Finally Irimiás rose, went over to Petrina, stood beside him and moved his hand for silence. The room fell quiet.

My friends! I can't deny your enthusiasm is deeply touching ... But you haven't thought it over properly. No, you haven't! No protests, please. You can't be serious about this! Surely you can't be capable of committing your hard-earned small savings, won with such superhuman effort, suddenly, just like that to a spur-of-the-moment idea, sacrificing everything, risking all, on a venture that's full of risks? Oh, my friends! I am extremely grateful for this moving demonstration, but no! I can't take it from you ... not for what seems likely to be several months ... Really? ... the bitterly scrimped savings of a whole year? ... What can you be thinking?! My scheme is, after all, fraught with as yet unpredictable risks of all sorts! The forces I am up against could delay realization of the plan for months, even years! And you wish to sacrifice your hard-earned cash for that? And should I accept it—after having just confessed to being unable to help you in the immediate future? No, ladies and gentlemen! I can't do it. Please take your money back and put it away safely! I'll get the necessary resources one way or the other. I'm not willing to let you risk so much. Landlord, if you could just stand still for a moment, would you please be kind enough to bring me a spritzer ... Thank you ... Wait! Let no one refuse! I invite my dear friends to have a drink on me ... Go on, landlord, don't even think about it ... Drink up, my friends ... and think. Think well. Calm yourselves and think it over once more ... Make no rash decisions. I have told you what this is about and what the risks are. You should only agree to it if you are utterly decided. Consider the possibility that you might lose this hard-earned sum and that then you might, just might, have to begin again from scratch ... No, no, friend Futaki, I do believe that's something of an exaggeration ... That I am ... that you talk about salvation ... Please don't embarrass me like that! Yes ... that's a little closer to the mark, friend Kráner ... "Well-wisher" is a term I can more readily accept, "a well-wisher" is what I certainly am ... I see you are

177

not to be convinced. OK, OK, fine . . . Ladies! Gentlemen! Can I have a little quiet please! Let's not forget why we are gathered here this morning! All right! Thank you! . . . Please sit down in your places . . . Yes . . . Indeed . . . Thank you, my friends . . . Thank you!

Irimiás waited for everyone to return to their chairs, returned to his own, stood there, cleared his throat, threw out his arms in a gesture of emotion, then let them drop helplessly to his sides, raising his slightly tearful eyes to the ceiling. Behind the deeply moved company, the Horgos family—now quite isolated from the others—stared at each other, helplessly confused. The landlord was emotionally scrubbing the top of the counter with his drying-up cloth, polishing the cake tray and the glasses, then sat back on his stool but, however he tried, he could not tear his eyes away from the great pile of money in front of Irimiás.

Now, my most dear friends . . . What can I say! Our paths have crossed by chance but fate demands that, from this hour on, we stick together, inseparably together . . . Though I worry for you, ladies and gentlemen, on account of the chance you are taking. I must confess your trust moves me . . . it feels good to be the subject of an affection of which I do not feel myself worthy . . . But let's not forget how we have arrived in this situation! Let's not forget! Let us always remember, let us never forget, the cost! What a cost! Ladies and gentlemen! I hope you will agree with me when I suggest that a small part of this sum, this money in front of me, should cover the cost of the funeral, so that the unfortunate mother might be saved the burden—as a gesture to the child who went to her final sleep most certainly for us or because of us . . . Because, in the end, it is impossible to decide whether it was for us or because of us that she died. We cannot prove the case either way. But the question will remain in our hearts forever, as will the child's memory, a child whose life might have been lost for this precise purpose ... so that the star that governs our lives might rise at last ... Who knows, my friends ... But life is harsh, and it has dealt harshly with us in this matter.

V

THE PERSPECTIVE,

AS SEEN FROM THE FRONT

For years after, Mrs. Halics would insist that as Irimiás, Petrina and the "demon child" who had in the end attached himself to them, disappeared down the road leading to town in the pattering rain, leaving those that remained standing around silently in front of the bar because the figure of their savior had not quite vanished in the bend of the road, the air above their heads was suddenly filled with brightly colored butterflies. Where they came from no one knew but you could clearly hear the gentle angelic music from on high. And though she was perhaps alone in such an opinion, this much was certain: they had only just begun to believe in what had happened, and were only now capable of realizing that they weren't the subject of some lulling but false vision with a bitter awakening to follow, but an enthusiastic, specially chosen band that had just passed through the painful process of liberation; and as long as they could still see Irimiás, recall his clear instructions, and be cheered by his words of encouragement, they could keep at bay the fear that something terrible might happen at any moment, something that might sweep away their fragile sense of victory and leave it utterly in tatters, for they also knew that, once he had gone, the glowing sparks of enthusiasm could quickly turn to ashes; and so, in order that the time should seem longer between striking the agreement and the farewells that would inevitably follow, they had tried to delay Irimiás and Petrina's departure by a variety of artful distractions; by discussing the weather, or complaining about their rheumatism, or opening new bottles of wine, babbling all the while—as if their lives depended on it—about the general corruption of life. And so it was understandable that they could breathe freely only once Irmimiás had gone, for he embodied not only the promise of a bright future, but also the fear of disaster: no wonder that it was only after he had gone that they dared truly believe that from now on "everything would be right as rain," and also only now that they could relax, let joy sweep over them, allaying their anxiety, and enjoy the sudden dizzying sense of liberation that could overcome even the usual "sense of apparently inevitable doom." Their boundless good cheer only increased when waving farewell to the landlord ('Serves you right, you old miser!"— shouted Kráner) who was leaning, exhausted, against the doorframe, his arms crossed, with rings under his eyes, watching the merry chattering band as they moved away, and capable—after having exhausted his self-consuming fury, long-simmering hatreds and the agony of his sheer helplessness—of nothing more than shouting after them: "Drop dead, you miserable, ungrateful bunch of bastards!" He had spent the night awake plotting ways—all ineffective, all flawed—of getting rid of Irimiás who had had the nerve to take over even his bed, so while he was debating with bloodshot eyes whether to stab him, strangle him, poison him, or simply chop him into pieces with his axe, "the hook-nosed swine" was happily snoring at the back of the store, not taking the least bit of notice. Talking had proved useless too, utterly useless, though he had done everything possible—in anger, in fury, in warning, or simply by pleading—to dissuade "these ignorant bumpkins" from this guaranteed disaster of a plan, a disaster that would destroy them all, but it was like talking to a brick wall ("Come to your senses, dammit! Can't you see he's leading you by the nose?!"), so there was nothing for it but to curse the whole world and admit the humiliating truth that he was ruined once and for all. For "what's the point of staying in business for just one drunken pig and one old tramp"—what could he do except to gather up his belongings and to do what everyone else was doing, to leave, to move back into his house in town, and hope to sell the bar, maybe even make some use of the spiders. "I could offer to sell them to someone for use in a scientific experiment; who knows, I might even get a bit of money for them," he pondered. "But that would be just a drop in the ocean ... The fact is I have no idea how to start over again from scratch," he sadly admitted. The intensity of his disappointment was only matched by the intensity of Mrs. Horgos's delight at his despair. Having surveyed "this whole idiotic ritual" with a sour expression, she had returned to the bar, to mock the landlord behind his counter. "You see. Just look at you! The horse has bolted, all right!" The landlord controlled himself but he'd happily have kicked her. "That's the way it goes," she went on. "Now up, now down. You'd better get used to it and accept it. See where all your bright ideas have got you? A lovely house in town, a car, your lady wife—but that's not enough for you. So now you can choke on it!" "Shut up with your cackling," the landlord growled back. "Go home and do your cackling there!" Mrs. Horgos downed her beer and lit a cigarette. "My husband was just like you, never satisfied. Nothing was ever good enough for him, not no how. By the time he realized his mistake it was too late. There was nothing left but to hang himself in the attic." "Why don't you just shut up!" the landlord snapped back. "Stop hassling me! Go home and look after your daughters before they run off too!" "Them?" Mrs. Horgos grinned. "Forget it. You think I'm simple or something? I've locked them up at home till this bunch on the estate are safely away. Why not? They'd leave me in my old age to look after myself. This way they can carry on looking after the farm—they've done enough whoring, after all. They might not like it, but they'll get used to it. It's only the kid, Sanyi. I'm cutting him loose. He can go where he likes. I can't see any use for him at home anyway. He eats like a pig. I can't support him. Let him go—wherever he wants. One less thing to worry about." "You and Kerekes can do what you like," growled the landlord. "But it's all over for me. That rat-faced bastard has ruined me for good." He knew that by evening, when he had finished packing—because until then nothing else could go in the van apart from the coffin, not next to it, not behind it, not on the seats, anywhere—once he had carefully locked all the doors and windows and was driving to town in his battered old Warszawa, cursing all the while, he wouldn't be looking back, wouldn't turn around once, but would vanish as fast as he could and try to wipe all trace of this miserable building from his memory, hoping it would sink from sight, and be entirely covered up, so that not even stray dogs would stop to piss on it; that he would vanish precisely the way the mob from estate had vanished, vanish without a last look at those moss-covered tiles, the crooked chimney, and the barred windows because, having turned the bend and passed beneath the old sign indicating the name of the estate, feeling elated by their "brilliant future prospects," they trusted the new would not only replace the old but utterly erase it. They had decided to meet by the old engine house in two hours at the latest, because they wanted to get to Almássy Manor while it was still light, and in any case that seemed ample enough time to pack their most important belongings, for what was the point of dragging stupid bits of bric-a-brac with you for ten or so miles, particularly when they knew they wouldn't lack for anything once they got there. Mrs. Halics had suggested they start straightaway, not bothering with anything, leaving it all behind to start in the spirit of Christian poverty, since "we are already blessed and well provided for with the Bible!" but the others—chiefly Halics—eventually convinced her that it was desirable to take at least a few basic personal necessities. They parted excitedly and feverishly set to packing, the three women going through their wardrobes first then emptying kitchens and pantries, while Schmidt, Kráner and Halics's first thoughts were for their tool cupboards, sorting out essentials, then checking everything else with eagle eyes in case the women in their carelessness had left "anything valuable behind." The two bachelors had the easiest job of it: all their possessions fit into two large suitcases: unlike the headmaster who packed fast but very selectively, constantly bearing in mind the idea of making "the best use of whatever the new place offers," Futaki quickly threw his belongings into the old suitcases left to him by his father and, quick as lightning, snapped the locks shut—it was like locking a genie back in its bottle—then put them in a pile and sat on them, lighting a cigarette with his trembling hand. Now that there was nothing left to remind him of his personal presence; now that, cleared of his clutter, the place that enclosed him was bare and cold; having packed, he felt he had left no sign that he had ever been part of this world, no shred of evidence that might have proved he once existed here. But however many days, weeks, months, perhaps years of hope lay before him—since he was quite sure his lot was finally cast for the better—squatting on his baggage now, in this drafty, foul-smelling place (of which he could no longer say, "I live here" though he was in no position to answer the question, "If not here, where?"), he found it ever harder to resist an increasingly suffocating sense of sadness. His bad leg was aching so he got off the suitcases and carefully lay down on his wire bed. For a few minutes he was overcome by sleep, then, having suddenly awoken with a fright, he clumsily tried to leap off the bed and his bad leg got caught in a gap between the wires so he almost fell flat on his face. He cursed and lay down again, putting his feet up on the bedstead, and examined the cracked ceiling for a while with a melancholy expression, before propping himself up on his elbows and making a survey of the bleak room. Doing so, he understood why he had, time and time again, put off the idea of making the decision to leave: he had rid himself of the one single security in his life and now he had nothing left; and, as before he hadn't had the guts to stay, so now he lacked the guts to leave, because having packed up for good, it was as if he had denied himself even greater possibilities, and had simply exchanged one trap for another. If, up until now, he had been a prisoner of the engine house and the estate, now he was subject to—in fact being exploited by—mere chance; and if he had until now dreaded the day when he wouldn't know how to open the door anymore and the window would allow no more light in, now he had sentenced himself to be the prisoner of some eternal momentum, a momentum he might equally well lose. "Another minute and I'll be on my way." He allowed himself some slight delay, and felt for the cigarette pack by the bed. He bitterly recalled the words spoken by Irimiás by the door of the bar ("From today, my friends, you are free!") because right now he was feeling anything but free and though time was pressing he was quite incapable of making up his mind to leave. He closed his eyes and tried to calm his "needless" worries by imagining his future life, but instead of being calmed he was seized by anxiety to such an extent that he had to mop drops of sweat from his brow. Because however he willed his imagination to move on, it was the same image that kept recurring time after time: he saw himself on the road in his ragged old coat and a torn carrier bag, trampling exhausted through the rain, then stopping and indecisively turning back home again. "Stop it!" he growled at himself in desperation. "Enough of this, Futaki!" He got up from bed, tucked his shirt back into his trousers, threw on his heavily worn overcoat and strapped the handles of his baggage together. He carried them outside under the eaves then—not seeing anyone else—set off to hurry the others. He was about to knock on the door of the Kráners, his nearest neighbors, when he heard a great clattering inside, as if several heavy objects had collapsed. He retreated a few steps because at first he thought there was a problem. But when he was about to try knocking again he could clearly hear Mrs. Kráner's gurgling laugh, then the sound, first of a plate, then of a mug being broken on stones. "What the hell are they up to?" He looked through the kitchen window, shading his eyes with his hand. He couldn't believe what he saw: Kráner, just raising a heavy-duty cauldron above his head, threw it with all his might against the door. In the meantime Mrs. Kráner was tearing the curtains from the back windows facing the yard before motioning the out-of-control Kráner to get out of the way and then dragging the empty sideboard away from the wall and effortfully pushing it over. The sideboard hit the stone flagging of the kitchen floor with a mighty crash. One side of it came away and Kráner kicked the rest to pieces. Then Mrs. Kráner climbed on top of the already broken pile in the center of the kitchen and, with one great yank, tore the tin light fixture from the ceiling, swung it above her head and Futaki had only just enough time to dive before it was flying toward him, crashing through the window, rolling a few yards and landing under a bush. "Hey! What are you doing?" Kráner shouted at him when he finally managed to inch the window open. "Good God!" screamed Mrs. Kráner behind him, watching pale-faced as Futaki cursed, got up, leaned on his stick and carefully shook the splinters of glass off his clothes. "You're not cut, are you?" "I came to get you," muttered Futaki, frowning, "but if I'd known this would be my reception I'd have stayed at home." Mrs. Kráner was dripping with sweat and however she tried she couldn't get rid of the look on her face, clearly intent on havoc. "Well, serves you right for peeping!" she retorted with a malicious grin. "Never mind. Come in, if you can, and we'll have a drink to make up!" Futaki nodded, beat the mud from his boots, and by the time he had succeeded in scrambling over parts of an enormous broken mirror, a dented oil stove and a shattered wardrobe in the hall, Mrs. Kráner had filled three glasses. "So what do you think?" Kráner asked with great satisfaction. "Nice work, eh?" "You should leave your things in one piece," Futaki replied, clinking glasses with Mrs. Kráner. "I'm not going to leave them for a bunch of gypsies to take away, am I? I'd sooner smash it all!" Kráner explained. "I see," Futaki cautiously answered, thanked them for the *pálinka*, and quickly left. He cut across the ridge dividing two rows of houses but took better care at the Schmidts' house, taking a sly look in at the kitchen window first. But there was nothing threatening here, only the wreckage, with Schmidt and his wife sitting exhausted on top of an overturned cupboard. "Has everyone lost their minds! What the hell has got into these people?" He tapped at the glass and gave the confused, round-eyed Mrs. Schmidt a wave to say they should hurry up because it was time to go; then started toward the gate but stopped after a few steps because he spotted the headmaster carefully creeping over the ridge, entering the Kráners' yard and peeping through their broken window, then—still thinking he wasn't seen by anyone (Futaki was hidden by the Schmidts' gate) he set off back to his own house, uncertainly at first, but then on his arrival, slamming the entrance door over and over again, ever more forcefully. "What's got into him? Have they all gone crazy?" Futaki wondered in astonishment, leaving the Schmidts's yard, walking slowly toward the headmaster's house. The headmaster was slamming his door ever more furiously, as if trying to work himself into a hysterical state, then, seeing he was having no success, lifted the door off its hinges, stepped back two paces then, using all his strength, smashed it against the wall. But this was still not enough to break the door so he jumped on it and kept kicking it until only a single plank of wood remained. If he hadn't happened to glance back and see the grimacing figure of Futaki he might have started smashing whatever furniture was still in one piece inside the house; but, having seen him, he was deeply embarrassed, straightened his heavy gray coat and gave Futaki an uncertain smile. "Ah, you see ..." But Futaki made absolutely no reply. "You know how it is. And besides ..." Futaki shrugged. "Obviously. All I want to know is when you will be ready. The others have finished packing." The headmaster cleared his throat. "Me? Well, I'm ready now. I just have to stack my baggage on the Kráners' cart." "Good. You can sort that out with them." "It's already settled. It cost me two bottles of *pálinka*. If things were different I'd make more fuss about it, but since we have, I suppose, a long journey before us ..." "Obviously. It's worth it," Futaki assured him then said goodbye and set off back to the engine house. The headmaster meanwhile—it was just as if he had been waiting for Futaki to turn his back—spat through the open doorway, picked up a brick and took aim at the kitchen window, and when Futaki, hearing the glass break, suddenly turned around, the headmaster dusted off his coat and, pretending not to have heard anything, tried to look as though he were busying himself with the broken bits of wood that lay about him. Half an hour later they were all at the engine house ready to go, and with the exception of Schmidt (he having drawn Futaki aside in attempt to explain whatever had happened, saying, "You know, friend, it would never have occurred to me to do that. It was just that a saucepan fell off the table and the rest just sort of followed.") it was only the flushed faces and the eyes sparkling with satisfaction that betrayed the fact that, for the others, "the leave-taking had gone pretty well." On top of the headmaster's two suitcases, most of the Halicses' possessions fitted easily on the Kráners' small two-wheeled handcart and the Schmidts had their own cart, so there was no need to worry that the journey would be slowed down by the weight of luggage. So there they were, all ready to go, and they would have started, had there been anyone to give the word. Everyone was waiting for someone else, so they just stood around in silence, staring at the estate in increasing confusion, because now, on the point of departure, they all felt some proper "words of farewell" to be appropriate, a matter in which they were most likely to trust Futaki but he, having witnessed all those incomprehensible acts of destruction, struggled for words, and by the time he found some that might do for an "in some way ceremonial" address, Halics had got fed up with waiting, grabbed the handles of the wheelbarrow, and grunted, "Right!" Kráner was in front pulling the cart behind him, leading the parade, Mrs. Kráner and Mrs. Halics supported the luggage on either side to prevent a suitcase or shopping bag being shaken off and close behind them followed Halics, pushing his wheelbarrow, the rear being brought up by the Schmidts. They passed through the old main gate of the estate and for a good while only the creaking of the wheelbarrow and cart's wheels could be heard, because, apart from Mrs. Kráner—who really couldn't hold her tongue for long and made frequent remarks about whatever happened to be the state of the luggage piled on their cart—not one of them was up to breaking the silence, if only because it was hard getting used to the peculiar blend of excitement, enthusiasm, and tension about their unknown future, a blend that only deepened the anxiety about their ability, after two long sleepless nights, to withstand the hardships of a long journey. But none of this lasted very long because they were all reassured by the fact that the rain had been light for hours and that they didn't expect the weather to take a turn for the worse, and because it became progressively more difficult not to give vent to their sense of relief and pride at their own heroic decision in words that anyone setting out on an adventure finds hard to contain. Kráner would happily have given a great whoop as soon as they hit the metaled road and set out in the direction away from town, leading to Almássy Manor, for the moment that the march got under way, the frustration of decades—only half an hour ago still oppressing him—utterly vanished and though the contemplative mood of his companions restrained him right until they reached the entrance to the Hochmeiss estate, his high spirits eventually got the better of him and he cried out in joy: "Damn those years of misery! We've done it! We've done it friends! My dear friends! We've finally done it!" He stopped his cart, turned around to face the others, and slapping his hand against his thigh, cried out again: "See here, friends! The misery is over! Can you believe it?! Do you get it, woman?!" He leapt over to Mrs. Kráner, picked her up as he would a child and spun her around as fast as he could, as long as he had the breath, then let her down, fell into her arms, and kept saying over and over: "I told you! I told you!" But by that time "the tide of feeling" had burst in the others too: Halics was first fluently cursing heaven and earth, before turning to face the estate to shake a threatening fist at it, then Futaki went up to the still grinning Schmidt and, in a voice trembling with emotion, simply said, "My dear friend ... !"; meanwhile the headmaster was enthusiastically explaining things to Mrs. Schmidt ("Didn't I tell you we should never give up hope! We have to believe, I say, believe unto death! Where would doubt have brought us? Tell me where?") while she, being just about capable of containing the tide of undiluted happiness welling up inside her but unwilling to draw attention to herself, forced an uncertain smile; and Mrs. Halics tipped her head back, cast her eyes up to heaven and, in a hoarse, tremulous voice, kept repeating "Blessed be Thy name" at least until the rain falling on her face prevented her, and in any case she'd noticed by then that she couldn't outshout this "godless crew." "Hey people!" Mrs. Kráner bellowed "let's drink to this!" and produced a bottle from one of her shopping bags. "God damn it! Well, you really have prepared for a new life!" Halics rejoiced and was quick to stand behind Kráner so that he might be first in line, but the bottle followed a completely arbitrary path from mouth to mouth and, before he realized it, there was just a mouthful left at the bottom. "Don't look so mournful, Lajos!" Mrs. Kráner whispered to him, even giving him a wink: "There'll be more, you'll see." After this there was no coping with Halics: it was as if he'd grown immeasurably lighter, and he started wildly dashing back and forth with his wheelbarrow, only calming down a little once he caught the eye of Mrs. Kráner a few yards away, and she gave him back a look as if to say, "Not yet ..." His great cheer naturally egged on the others and so, though they continually had to be adjusting now this bag, now that, piled on one or other of the carts, they made pretty good progress and soon they had left the little bridge over the old irrigation canal behind them and could see in the distance the great pylons carrying high-tension cables with the wires sagging and undulating between then. Futaki occasionally joined in the general chatter though it was he who found the march the most trying, since he had strapped his heavy suitcases—suitcases that, despite Kráner and Schmidt's best efforts, proved impossible to fit on any of the carts—to his shoulders which made it extra hard for him to keep up with the others, not to mention the trouble of his lame leg which cost him even more effort. "I wonder how they'll cope," he pondered. "Who?" Schmidt asked. "Well, Kerekes, for example." "Kerekes!" Kráner shouted as he turned back. "Don't go bothering your head on his account. Yesterday he went home, threw himself on his bed and, provided the bed hasn't collapsed under him, I don't suppose he'll wake up until tomorrow. He'll grunt and grumble at the bar for a while then he'll head off to Mrs. Horgos's for a good time. They're as like as two peas in a pod, those two." "No doubt of that!" Halics interrupted. "They'll get thoroughly smashed! You think they care about anything else? Mrs. Horgos had the mourning gear off the next day..." "I've just thought!" Mrs. Kráner butted in. "What happened to the great Kelemen? He vanished on the sly—I never saw him." "Kelemen? My bosom buddy?" Kráner grinned back. "He skipped yesterday, after lunch. He's had a bad time, he-he-he! I got the better of him first, then he took on Irimiás, the idiot. Well, he took on a bit too much there because Irimiás didn't stand for any of his nonsense, and told him to fuck off as soon as he started moaning on about this, that and the other, telling Irimiás what should be done, that the whole bunch of us should be in the clink, and that he himself deserved something a little better than the rest, that kind of stuff! Then he grabbed his things and fucked off without another word. What really finished him off, I think, was when he waved his volunteer police armband at Irimiás, and Irimiás told him to, pardon me, go wipe his ass with it." "I wouldn't say I missed the

bastard much," Schmidt noted. "But I could certainly do with his cart."
"I can well believe that. But how would we cope with him? That man
would pick a quarrel with a shark!" Mrs. Kráner made a sudden stop.
"Wait!" Kráner stopped the cart in fright. "Listen everyone! What are
we thinking of?!" "Go on, tell us," Kráner agitated: "What's the problem?" "The doctor." "What's with the doctor!?" They fell quiet. "Well,"
the woman began hesitantly, "well . . . I never said as much as a word to
him! Surely! . . ." "Come on, woman!" Kráner turned on her: "I thought
there was something really wrong? Why are you bothered about the
doctor?" "I'm sure he would have come. He'll starve to death by himself. I know him—how could I fail to know him after all these years? I
know he's just like a child—if I didn't put food in front of him, he'd
starve. Then there's the *pálinka*. And the cigarettes. The dirty clothes.
Give it a week or two and the rats will have eaten him." "Don't play the
Good Samaritan with us," Schmidt angrily retorted. "If you're so keen
on him, go back! I don't miss him! Not a bit! I think he'll be happy as
hell not to be seeing us . . ." Then Mrs. Halics joined in: "Quite right!
We should praise the Lord that that particular slave of Satan has not
come with us! He's definitely one of Satan's, I've known that a long
time!" Everyone having stopped, Futaki lit a cigarette, and offered
them around. "All the same, it's strange," he said, "didn't he notice anything?" Mrs. Schmidt, who hadn't said a word till then, now came up
and spoke. "That man is like a mole. No, worse than that! At least a
mole puts his head up above ground now and then. But it's like the
doctor wanted to be buried alive. It's weeks since I've seen him . . ." "For
heaven's sake!" Kráner exclaimed in delight. "He's perfectly all right!
Every day he gets nicely drunk and has a good snore because there's
nothing else for him to do. We needn't feel sorry for him! I wouldn't
mind having his maternal inheritance in my pocket right now! And in
any case, we've been standing round here long enough. Let's get going
or we'll never get there!" But Futaki was still not satisfied. "He sits the

whole day by the window. How couldn't he have noticed?" he thought
uneasily, and leaning on his stick, set off after Kráner. "He couldn't have
failed to hear that racket! And everyone milling around, all the carts,
all the shouting ... Well, I suppose it's possible he might have slept
through it all. It was Mrs. Kráner who spoke to him last, the day before
yesterday, and there was certainly no problem then. In any case, Kráner
is right, everyone should mind their own business. If he wants to meet
his maker there, that's fine by me. But I'll lay a bet on it: in a day or two,
when he hears what's happened, and thinks it over, he'll just pull himself together and follow the rest of us. He couldn't exist without us
there." After half a mile or so the rain started to come down more heavily and they went on their way grumbling as the bare acacias on either
side of the road thinned out: it was as if their life support was slowly
vanishing. Further on there were still fewer trees remaining on the rain-
sodden earth; then not a tree, not even a crow. The moon had risen in
the sky, its pale disc just about visible as it filtered through a solemn
mass of unmoving cloud. Another hour, they realized, and it would be
dusk, then night would suddenly fall. But they couldn't walk any faster,
and when exhaustion hit them, it hit them hard. Passing the storm-
ravaged tin figure of Christ at Csüd, Mrs. Halics suggested a brief rest
(as well as a quick Our Father ...) and they angrily rejected the
thought, convinced that, if they stopped now, they'd hardly have the
strength to start again. It was in vain for Kráner to try to cheer them up
with a few memorable incidents ("You remember when the landlord's
wife broke her wooden spoon on her husband's ass?" or "You remember how Petrina once salted that ginger cat's, begging your pardon,
asshole?"): rather than cheering up, they started cursing Kráner because he wouldn't stop talking. "Anyway!" Schmidt fumed, "who told
him he's in charge around here? What's he doing bossing me around?
I'll have a word with Irimiás and tell him to feed his balls to the sharks,
he's been so full of himself recently ..." And when Kráner wouldn't give
it up, and had another go at lightening their spirits ("Let's rest for a

minute and have a drink. Every drop is pure gold and we didn't get it from the landlord either!"), they grabbed at the bottle so impatiently it was as if Kráner had been trying to hide it from them. Futaki couldn't resist joining in. "You're full of cheer all right. I wonder if you'd be so damn cheerful if you were lame and had to drag these two suitcases around . . . ?" "You think this lousy cart is easy work?" Kráner threw back at him: "I've got no idea what to do when it falls to pieces on the damn road!" Insulted, he fell silent and from that time on spoke to no one but dragged the cart along, keeping his eyes on the road at his feet. Mrs. Halics was silently cursing Mrs. Kráner because she was as sure as could be that she wasn't doing anything useful on the other side of the cart; Halics cursed Kráner and Schmidt every time he thought of his aching hands because "Of course it's easy for them to be chatting away . . ." But it was Mrs. Schmidt who was the particular bugbear for everyone because now—if not before—it seemed obvious to them that she had been strangely silent ever since they set out, and what's more— "Hang on! when I think back," the same thought flashed through the minds of both Mrs. Kráner and Schmidt, "she has hardly said a word since Irimiás arrived . . ." and then, "There's something shady going on," thought Mrs. Kráner. "Is something bothering her? Is she ill? Surely not! Ah, no—she knows what she's doing. Irimiás must have said something to her when he called her into the storeroom last night . . . But what would he have wanted from her? After all, everyone knows what went on between them last time . . . But that was ages ago! How many years back?" "She thinks of nothing but Irimiás," Schmidt uneasily continued: "The look she gave me when Mrs. Halics brought the news! . . . Her look went straight through me! There can't have been a way . . . ah, no. She's not going to lose her head at this age. Yes, but . . . what if? She must know I'd wring her neck, just like that! No, she wouldn't do it. In any case, she can't possibly imagine that Irimiás fancies her now, her of all people! You've got to laugh. However much cologne she splashes on during the day she still smells like a pig. Oh yes, she's just Irimiás's type! He has more women than he can shake a stick at, each more gorgeous than the last, he's not going to be lusting after a country goose like her. Ah, no ... But then why are her eyes sparkling like that? Those two great cow's eyes of her? ... And how the hell does she have the gall to be making up to Irimiás, God blast her?! Well, of course, she makes up to anyone, it doesn't matter who, as long he's wearing trousers ... Well, I'll beat that out of her! If she didn't learn last time, I don't mind giving her another lesson. I'll make her come to her senses, don't you worry about that! May her tits dry up, the whore, and all the whores on this shithouse of a planet!" Futaki found the pace ever harder, the straps of his cases had rubbed his shoulders so raw they were bleeding. His bones seemed to be made of fire and when his bad leg got painful again he fell a long way behind the others though they didn't even notice until Schmidt turned round and shouted at him ("What's up with you? We're going slow enough as it is without you dragging us down") because Schmidt was growing increasingly furious with Kráner for "playing the big chief," and so he grunted at Mrs. Schmidt to keep up, while he himself began to scurry ahead on his tiny legs. He quickly caught up with Kráner's cart and stood at the head of the procession. "Go on then, rush ahead!" Kráner silently raged: "We'll soon see who can last!" "For heaven's sake, friends ...," Halics panted: "Don't be in such a hurry! These blasted boots are playing havoc with my heels, every step is agony!" "Don't go sniveling," Mrs. Halics hissed at him. "What's there to cry about? Why don't you show them what a real man you are, right here, instead of just in the bar!" Hearing this, Halics clenched his teeth, and tried to keep step with Kráner who was now in a private race with Schmidt, the two bitterly competing, first one then the other leading the procession. And so Futaki got ever more left behind and once the distance had increased to two hundred yards or so he simply stopped trying to keep up. He tried more and more ways of carrying the load of his ever-heavier cases, but however he adjusted the straps the pain wouldn't go away. So he decided not to torture himself any further and when he spotted an acacia with a broader trunk he turned off the road and, just as he was, baggage and all, he collapsed in the mud. He leaned against the trunk and spent the next few minutes painfully gasping for air before removing the straps and stretching his legs. He reached into his pocket for a light but suddenly sleep overcame him. He woke needing to piss, so he struggled to his feet, but his legs were numb and he immediately collapsed again, and was only successful on the second attempt of rising and staying on his feet. "What idiots we are ... ," he grumbled aloud, and having relieved himself, sat back down on one of the suitcases. "We should have listened to Irimiás. He told us to wait, and what did we do? We had to move right away! This very evening! Now here I am sitting in the mud, dog tired ... As if it made any difference whether we started today, tomorrow or in a week's time ... Irimiás might have got hold of a truck by then! But no, that's not what we do, oh no! Do it right now! ... Right away! ... It's chiefly Kráner's fault! ... But never mind ... it's too late to be sorry. We're not that far away now." He pulled out a cigarette and took a first deep lungful. He was already feeling better, though he was still a little dizzy and had a dull constant headache. He stretched his stiff limbs again, rubbed his numb legs, then started scratching the ground in front of him with his stick. It was growing toward dusk. The road was barely visible now but Futaki felt calm: you couldn't lose your way since the road went precisely as far as Almássy Manor and in any case over the years he had often made this journey because he had acted as a kind of funeral director for redundant machine parts, it being his task, among others, to remove ruined, no longer usable components and deposit them in the building that even then was in poor condition. "And when you think about it," he suddenly thought, "there is something else very strange about all this. I mean take this manor for a start. No doubt back in the count's time, it must have looked pretty good. But now? The last time I saw it the rooms were covered in weeds, the wind had blown the tiles off the tower, there wasn't a window or door intact, and even the floor was missing in places so you could see through to the cellar ... Best not to interfere, of course ... Irimiás is the boss, and he'll know why he picked the manor! Perhaps it's the very fact that it's so isolated that makes it the best place ... because, after all, there isn't even a farm nearby, nothing ... Who knows? It might be because of that." He didn't want to risk using a match since it would be hard to light in the damp weather so he lit the new cigarette using the still glowing end of the old one but he didn't throw the stub away yet, holding it between cramped fingers for a while because the slight warmth it gave out felt good. And then this whole thing ... that business yesterday ... "However I try, I still don't understand it ... Because he'd be confident that we knew him well enough. So why all the clowning? Talking like an evangelist preacher ... You could see he was suffering as much as we were ... I don't understand. He would have known what we wanted! And he'd have known the only reason we went along with all that nonsense about the idiot child was because we wanted him to say, 'OK, enough of all this! Here I am, boys and girls. What's all this moaning and groaning about? Let's pick ourselves up and do something clever for once. Any good ideas out there? ...' But no. It was all 'ladies and gentlemen' this and 'ladies and gentlemen' that, and you are all miserable sinners ... I mean, it's beyond belief! And who knows whether he's doing this in earnest or just messing around? There was no way of telling him to stop either ... And all that stuff about the retard ... So she ate a lot of rat poison, so what? It was probably the best thing for the sad creature, at least she's spared more suffering. But what's all that got to do with me!? There's her mother: it was her job to care for her! And then ... all that frantic searching through bog and brake, the whole day in awful weather, combing every inch of the place till we find the miserable little thing! ... It should have been that old witch, her mother, doing the searching. But that's how it is. Who can understand Irimiás? No one! It's just that ... he wouldn't have done this back then ... I mean I didn't know where to look, I was so surprised ... He has certainly changed a lot, that's for sure. Of course we don't know what he's been through in the last few years. But his hooknose, his checkered jacket, and his red tie—that's exactly the same! Everything's OK." He gave a relieved sigh, got up, picked up his bags, adjusted the straps on his shoulders then, leaning on his stick, set off down the road again. So that time might pass more quickly and to distract himself from the pain of the straps biting into his flesh, and lastly, because he was a little scared to be all alone here at the end of the world on a desolate road, he started singing, "How lovely thou art, our dear Hungary," but he had forgotten everything after the second line and so, because nothing else occurred to him, he sang the national anthem. But the singing only left him feeling more lonely so he quickly stopped and held his breath. He seemed to hear a noise to his right ... He began to walk more quickly, as far as that was possible given his bad leg. But then there was the sound of something cracking on the other side ... "What the hell is it ...?" He thought he'd better resume his singing after all. There wasn't such a long way to go. And it would fill the time ...

Bless the Magyar, Lord we pray,
Nor in bounty fail him
Shield him in the bloody fray
When his foes assail him ...

And now it was as if ... there was a shout or something ... Or not quite a shout ... no, it was someone crying. "No, it's some animal ...an animal whimpering. It must have broken its leg." But however he looked this way and that it was total darkness on either side of him now. It was impossible to see anything.

He whom ill luck long has cursed
This year grant him pleasure . . .

'We thought you'd changed your mind!" Kráner teased him once they spotted Futaki. "I recognized him by his walk," Mrs. Kráner added. "You can't mistake it. He hobbles along like a lame cat." Futaki put his suitcases down, slung off the straps and gave a sigh of relief. "You didn't hear anything on the way?" he asked. "No, what was there to hear?" Schmidt wondered. "Just a strange noise." Mrs. Halics sat down on a stone and rubbed her legs. "The only strange noise we heard was you coming up the road. We didn't know who it was." "Why, who would it be? Is there anyone else around here besides us? Thieves and robbers? . . . There's not a bird to be seen, let alone a man." The path they were standing on led to the main building and boxwood had been growing wild on either side for decades, surrounding the odd wide-trunked beech or fir, climbing above them with the same persistence as the wild ivy on the thick walls of the hall, so the whole "manor" (as they called it in these parts) had a silent, desperate feel to it, because though the higher reaches of the building were still uncovered, it was clear that within a few years it would surrender to the ruthless advance of the vegetation. The wide steps that led to the enormous doorway used to have two female nude statues, one on either side; statues that had made a deep impression on Futaki when he first saw them years ago, and his first impulse was to search for them nearby but in vain—it was as if the earth had swallowed them. The company trod the steps awkwardly, speechless and wide-eyed, because the silent hulk towering barely visibly in the darkness above them—despite the stucco having almost completely fallen away from the walls, and the old tower now so unstable it was clear it wouldn't withstand another major storm, not to mention the holes where the windows had been—still had a certain grandeur about it as well as an air of timeless vigilance, vigilance having been part of its original purpose. When they reached the top, Schmidt, without any hesitation, immediately stepped through the collapsed arch of the main door and reverentially, but without any fear, explored the house that rang with emptiness. His eyes quickly got used to the darkness and so, when he reached a small hall on the left-hand side, he could cleverly avoid the shattered ceramic tiles strewn on the floor as well as the rusty mechanisms and machine parts on the treacherously rotted floorboards and could stop in time before falling through the various gaps so clearly remembered by Futaki. The rest followed him some eight or nine steps behind and in this way they made a tour of the cold, deserted, and defunct "manor" with its chilly drafts, stopping occasionally at a window space to look down on the dangerously overgrown park, then, ignoring their tiredness, to stare at the still undamaged though rotting, fancifully carved windowframes and the oddly stiff plaster figures on the ceilings above them, surveying all this with the help of flickering matches; but the thing that made the deepest impression on them was a beaten copper stove that had toppled onto its side, on which the now highly animated Mrs. Halics counted precisely thirteen dragons' heads. But they were roused from their silent admiration by the harsh voice of Mrs. Kráner in the middle of the hall standing on her firmly planted powerful legs and raising her arms to cry out in sheer wonder: "How could anyone afford to heat all this?!" And because the question implied an answer they could only grunt to signify their own astonishment before returning to the entrance hall, where after some argument (Schmidt was particularly opposed to Kráner's suggestion, saying, "Right here? Here in this terrible draft? Yes, boss, brilliant idea, absolutely ...") they agreed with Kráner that "it would be best to camp here for the night. True, it's drafty like every other place here, but what happens if Irimiás arrives before first light? How the hell does he find us in this labyrinth?" They went out to their carts, in case the rain got really heavy during the night and the wind grew into a gale, to secure their luggage, and to take whatever they had brought with them—a sack, a blanket, an eiderdown—as a temporary bed. But once they settled down as best they could and their breathing had warmed them a little under their blankets they found they were too tired to sleep. "You know, I don't really understand Irimiás," sounded Kráner's voice in the darkness: "Can anyone explain it to me ... He used to be a simple man at heart, just like we are. He spoke like us too: it was just that his brain was sharper. And now? He's like a lord, like a real big shot!... Am I wrong?" There was a long silence before Schmidt added, "To be honest, it was rather odd. Why stir the shit like that? I could see he was very much after something but how could anyone know how it would turn out ...? If I'd known from the start what he wanted, I could have told him not to bother with all the heavy stuff..." The headmaster turned in his makeshift bed and stared uneasily into the darkness. "It really was a bit much, all that sinner stuff, I mean, and Esti this and Esti that! As if I had anything to do with that degenerate? I mean my blood boiled every time I heard her name. What's this about 'poor little Esti'? It's pure farce, I tell you. The girl had a proper name, Erzsi, but she was spoiled. Her father was far too soft with her and ruined her! But me? What was I supposed to do? After all, I did everything I could to help that girl stand on her own two feet!... I even told the old witch when she brought her home from special needs, that, as a matter of mutual business, I'd keep her in order if she sent her over to me every morning. But no, that wouldn't do. That well-off hag wouldn't spend a penny on the poor miserable thing! So I'm to blame! Pure farce, if you ask me!" "Pipe down a bit," Mrs. Halics hissed at them. "My husband's asleep. He's used to silence." Futaki ignored her. "What will be, will be. We'll find out what Irimiás meant soon enough. It will all be clear tomorrow. Or even before then. Can you imagine?" "I can," the headmaster answered. "Have you seen the outbuildings? There are at least five of them, I'm prepared to bet they'll be turned into workshops." "Workshops?" Kráner asked. "What kind of workshops?" "How should I know ... I suppose they're just workshops one way or another. What's all the fuss about?" Mrs. Halics raised her voice again. "Can't you all shut up? How's a person supposed to get any rest!" "Aw, shut up yourself!" snapped Schmidt. "What's wrong with people talking?" "No, I figure it'll be the other way around," Futaki continued: "Those workshops will become our houses and it's this place that will be turned into workshops." "You keep going on about workshops ...," Kráner objected. "What's the matter with all of you? Do you all want to be engineers? I understand about Futaki, but you? What will you do? Are you going to be the works manager?" "Enough chatter," the headmaster added coolly. "I don't think this is the best time for stupid jokes! In any case what gives you the right to go offending people! I ask you!" "Ah, for God's sake get some sleep!" Halics grunted. "I can't sleep with you all going on!" There was quiet for a few minutes but it didn't last because one of them accidentally let off a fart. "Who was that?" Kráner laughed and dug his neighbor Schmidt in the ribs. "Leave me alone," the other fumed as he turned over: "It wasn't me!" But Kráner wouldn't let it go. "Come on now, will no one own up to it!?" Halics was practically gasping with nerves, as he sat up. "Look, it was me," he pleaded: "I confess it all. Now will you please shut up ..." After this it finally did fall quiet and a few minutes later they were all fast asleep. Halics was being pursued by a hunchback with glass eyes and after a desperate chase he finally leapt into a river, but his position became even more hopeless because every time he came up for air the little hunchback hit him on the head with an enormously long stick, crying in a hoarse voice: "Now you'll pay!" Mrs. Kráner heard a noise outside but couldn't work out what it was. She slipped on her coat and started off in the direction of the engine room. She was almost at the metaled road when she suddenly had a really bad feeling. She turned around and saw the roof of their house licked by flames. "The kindling! I've left the kindling out! Merciful heavens!" she cried in terror. She rushed back because it was hopeless calling for help, everyone else seemed to have vanished into thin air, and dashed into the house to save what could be saved. Her first thought was the room and, quick as lightning, she grabbed the ready cash they kept hidden under the bed linen, then leapt over the flaming threshold into the kitchen where Kráner was sitting at the table calmly eating as if nothing had happened. "Jóska! Are you out of your mind? The house is on fire!" But Kráner never even flinched. Mrs. Kráner saw that the curtains were alight: "Escape, you fool! Can't you see the whole place is about to collapse?!" She rushed out of the house and sat outside, her fear and trembling suddenly gone, almost enjoying the sight of her possessions being reduced to ashes. She even pointed it out to Mrs. Halics who had appeared beside her. "Look, how lovely! I've never seen a more beautiful shade of red!" The earth was moving under Schmidt's feet. It was as if he were walking across a swamp. He reached a tree, climbed it, but felt it too was sinking ... He was lying on the bed and was trying to pull the nightshirt off his wife but she started screaming as he leapt after her and the nightshirt got torn. Mrs. Schmidt turned to face him, cackled, and the nipples on her enormous breasts bloomed like two wonderful roses. It was horribly hot inside, the sweat was dripping off them. He looked out the window: it was raining outside, Kráner was running home with a cardboard box in his hands but then the bottom of it flew open and the contents were strewn everywhere. Mrs. Kráner was shouting for him to hurry so he couldn't pick up the half of the stuff that had rolled away and he decided to come back for it the next day. Suddenly a dog darted at him and he cried out in fright kicking the creature in the face and it yelped once and collapsed, remaining there on the ground. He couldn't help himself: he kicked it again The dog's belly was soft The headmaster, deeply embarrassed, was trying with some difficulty to persuade a little man in a patched suit to accompany him to a little frequented place. The man seemed incapable of saying no and the headmaster could barely contain himself, and as soon as they reached the deserted park he even gave the man a push so that they might reach a stone bench that was densely overgrown with bushes where he laid the little man down and threw himself on him, kissing his neck, but at that moment some white-gowned doctors appeared on the path that was strewn with white gravel and he waved ashamedly to them to indicate that he too was just passing by though he went on to explain to the doctors that they really had nowhere else to go so really they should understand and that they should certainly take this into account and he began to abuse the embarrassed little man because by now he felt nothing but a deep disgust for him but whichever way he looked it made no difference the doctors stared at him with contempt then made a tired gesture as though there was nothing he could do about it Mrs. Halics was washing Mrs. Schmidt's back the rosary beads hung on the edge of the bath slid into the water a young scoundrel's face appeared glaring at the window Mrs. Schmidt said she'd had enough her skin was beginning to burn with all the scrubbing but Mrs. Halics pushed her back in the bath and carried on scrubbing because she was ever more fearful that Mrs. Schmidt was annoyed with her then she cried out angrily I hope the viper bites you and sat down at the edge of the bath and the young scoundrel was still glaring at the window Mrs. Schmidt was a bird happily flying through the milk of theclouds seeing someonedownthere wavingather soshedes cendeda littleland could hear Mrs.Schmidtbawling whyisntshecooking youscoundrelcomedownim mediatelybutshe flewoverher andshechir ruppedyou won'tdieof hun gerbeforetommorrow shefeltthe warmsunonher backsudden lySchmidtwas therebesideherStopit immediatelybutshe paid noattention anddescendedfurther shedhavelikedtocatchaninsect theywerebeatingFutakisback withanironrod Hecouldntmove hehadbeenboundwithropestoatree

tenselyshefelthow theropewasstraining alongopenwoundacrosshis-
back shelookedawayshecouldntbearit shewassittingonanexcavator
thatwasdigginganenormousditch amancameover andsaidhurry
becausesyourenotgetting anymorefuel howevermuchyoubegmeforit
shedugtheditcheverdeeper itkeptcollapsing she tri tr triedagain
butinvainandshecried asshewassittingattheengineroomwindow
andhadnoideawhatwashappening itwasdawnandgettinglighter oreve-
ningandgrowingdarker andshedidntwantitall evertocometoanend she-
justsatandhadnoideawhatwashappening nothingchangedoutside
itwasneithermorningnoreveningitjust carriedondawnortwilight-
whichever ...

IV

HEAVENLY VISION?

HALLUCINATION?

As soon as they rounded the bend and lost sight of the people waving and hanging around by the bar, his heavy-as-lead sense of exhaustion vanished and he no longer felt any of the agonizing sleepiness that had practically glued him to the chair by the oil stove, because ever since Irimiás had told him something he had never even dared to dream of ("All right, go and talk it over with your mother. You can come with me if you like ...") he couldn't bear to close his eyes, and spent the whole night turning over and over in his bed with his clothes on so as not to miss the arranged dawn meeting; and now, when, through mist and half-light, he saw the road ahead arrowing into infinity his strength was redoubled and at last he felt "the whole world opening up before him," and he knew that whatever happened he would stay the course. And however great the desire in him to give voice somehow to his enthusiasm he controlled it and unconsciously measured his steps in a more disciplined fashion, following his master even while burning with the fever of his election, since he knew he could only carry out the mission granted him if he responded not as a snotty-nosed kid but as a man—not to mention the fact that if he did speak without thinking the constantly irritable Petrina was bound to come out with some new mocking remark and he couldn't bear to be humiliated before Irimiás, not even once. It was perfectly clear to him that his own best option was faithfully to copy Irimiás in every small detail because this way he was sure not to get a nasty surprise; first he watched his characteristic movements, his long easy stride, his proud bearing and raised head, the now challenging, now threatening movements of his raised right forefinger the moment before he made a significant remark and, most difficult, the falling cadence of his voice and the heavy silence between the distinct elements of his speech, noting the control of his resonant proclamations, and trying to capture something of the undoubted confidence that so generously permitted Irimiás to articulate his thoughts with such precision. Not for a moment did his eyes leave his master's slightly stooped back and narrow-brimmed hat pulled firmly down so as to prevent the rain beating against his face; and seeing that his master paid no attention whatsoever to him because his mind was clearly intent on something else, he too walked on in silence with an earnestly wrinkled brow, because by concentrating his attention like this he liked to think that he was helping Irimiás's own thoughts reach their goal more quickly. Petrina scratched his ear in agony because, seeing the tense expression on his companion's face, he himself did not dare break the silence, so, however he tried to give the kid a look to indicate that he should keep mum ("Not a peep out of you! He's thinking!") he too felt constrained and was so desperate to ask questions he could only breathe with difficulty, making first whistling, then dry hoarse sounds as he did so, until eventually it became plain even to Irimiás that the heroic figure holding his tongue beside him was practically choking, so he made a face and took pity on him. "Go on, out with it! What do you want?" Petrina gave a great sigh, licked his cracked lips and started blinking rapidly. "Master! I am shitting myself here! How are we going to get out of this?!" "I must say I'd be pretty surprised if you weren't shitting yourself," Irimiás replied, annoyed. "Would you like some paper to wipe yourself with?"

Petrina shook his head. "It's no joke. I'd be lying if I told you my sides were splitting with laughter ..." "In that case shut your mouth." Irimiás gazed haughtily down the road fading in the distance up ahead. He stuck a cigarette in the corner of his mouth and lit it without breaking step. "If I were to tell you that this was precisely the opportunity we had been waiting for," he confidently declared, looking deep into Petrina's eyes, "would that reassure you?" His companion flinched a little under his gaze then bent his head, stopped and thought a little, and by the time he had caught up with Irimiás again he was so nervous he could hardly get the words out. "Wha ... wha ... what are you thinking?" Irimiás made no reply but continued gazing mysteriously down the road. Petrina was so tortured by anxieties that he tried to seek some explanation for the profoundly meaningful silence and so—despite knowing the effort to be vain—tried to delay the inevitable disaster. "Listen to me! I have stood by you all this time, through good times and bad times. I swear, if I do nothing else with my miserable life, that I will flatten anyone who dares to be disrespectful to you! But ... don't do anything crazy! Listen to me just this once! Listen to good old Petrina! Let's forget it, forget it now, immediately! Let's hop on the first train and get out! These people will lynch us the moment they discover the dirty trick we've pulled on them!" "No chance," Irimiás mocked him. "We are taking up the demanding, indeed hopeless, cause of human dignity ..." He raised his famous forefinger and warned Petrina, "Listen, jackass! This is our moment!" "God help us then," groaned Petrina, seeing his worst nightmares realized. "I've always known it! I trusted ... I believed ... I hoped ... and here we are! This is how it ends!" "You must be joking!" the "kid" behind them butted in: "Can't you take things seriously for once?" "Me?!" squealed Petrina, "me, I'm happy as a pig in shit, you can practically see me drooling ..." Grinding his teeth he looked up to the heavens and shook his head in despair. "Be honest with me! What have I done to deserve this? Have I ever hurt anyone? Have I spoken out of turn? I beg you boss, have some regard, if for nothing else, for these old bones! Take pity on these gray hairs!" But Irimiás was not to be swayed: his partner's words went in one ear and out the other. He just smiled mysteriously and said, "The network, jackass . . ." Hearing the word, Petrina immediately perked up. "Do you understand now?" They stopped and faced each other, Irimiás slightly leaning forward. "It's the network, that enormous spiderweb, as woven and patented by me, Irimiás . . . Am I getting this through your thick head? Has a light come on there? Anywhere?" Life began to seep back into Petrina, first as the faint shadow of a smile flickering across his face, then as a distinct sparkle in his beady eyes, his ears reddening with excitement until his whole being was visibly moved. "Somewhere . . . wait . . . Something rings a bell . . . I think I'm getting it now . . ." he whispered hoarsely. "It would be fantastic if . . . how shall I put it . . ." "You see," Irimiás gave a cool nod. "Think first, whine later." The "kid" was following at a respectful distance behind them but his keen ears helped him pick up their conversation: he hadn't missed a word and because he had not the slightest idea of what they were talking about he quickly repeated it all to himself so he wouldn't forget it. He pulled out a cigarette, lit it and, like Irimiás, slowly and deliberately pursed his lips and blew out the smoke in a faint straight line. He did not try to catch up but followed, as he had done, some eight or ten steps behind because he felt ever more hurt that his master had not chosen to "let him into the secret," though he should have known that he—unlike the constantly complaining Petrina—would have given his soul to be part of the plan: he had, after all, promised to be unconditionally faithful to the end. The tortures of jealousy seemed infinite, the bitterness in his soul growing ever more bitter since he was obliged to see that Irimiás thought him unworthy of a single remark, not one! His master ignored him altogether, as if "he simply wasn't there," as if the idea, "Sándor Horgos, who is not after all a nobody, has offered his services," meant absolutely nothing to him … He was so upset he accidentally scratched an ugly acne spot on his face and once they reached the fork at Póstelek he could bear it no longer but rushed to catch up with them, looked Irimiás in the eye, and trembling with fury, cried: "I'm not going on with you like this!" Irimiás regarded him with incomprehension. "What was that?" "If you have any problems with me tell me now, please! Tell me you don't trust me and I'll get lost right now!" "What's up with you?" Petrina snapped. "Nothing in the world's wrong with me! Just tell me whether you want me with you or no! You haven't said a single word to me ever since we set out, it was always just Petrina, Petrina, Petrina! If you're so fond of him, why invite me along?!" "Now hold on a second," Irimiás calmly stopped him. "I think I understand now. Listen hard to what I tell you because there won't be time for this later … I invited you because I need a capable young man like you. But only if you can do the following: One, you only speak when I address you. Two, if I entrust you with anything you'll do your best to get it done. Three, get used to the idea of not giving me lip. For the time being it is up to me to decide what I tell you and what I don't. Is that clear? …" The "kid" lowered his eyes in embarrassment. "Yes, I just …" "No 'I just.' Act like a man. In any case, I know what you're capable of, my boy, and I don't think you'll let me down … But enough now. Let's get going!" Petrina gave the "kid" a friendly slap on the back but then forgot to remove his hand and propelled him along. "See here, you little piece of shit, when I was your age, I didn't dare open my mouth when there were adults present! I fell silent, silent as the grave, if an adult was anywhere near! Because in those days there was no back talk. Not like today! What would you know about …" He suddenly stopped. "What was that?" "What was what?" "That … that noise …" "I don't hear anything," the "kid" said, puzzled. "What do you mean you don't hear anything! Not even now?" They listened, holding their breath: a few steps ahead of them Irimiás stood stock-still too, listening. They were still at the Póstelek fork, the rain gently pattering, not a soul to be seen anywhere, only a few crows circling in the distance. It seemed to Petrina that the noise was coming from somewhere above him, and he silently pointed to the sky but Irimiás shook his head. "From there, rather . . . ," he pointed toward the town. "A car? . . ." "Maybe," his master answered, clearly troubled. They did not move. The humming neither strengthened nor weakened. "Some kind of plane, perhaps . . . ," the "kid" tentatively suggested. "No, not likely . . . ," said Irimiás. "But in any case we'll take the shorter route. We'll go down the Póstelek road as far as Wenkheim Manor, then we'll take the older road. We may even gain four or five hours that way . . ." "Do you have any idea how muddy that road is?!" Petrina protested in fury. "I know. But I don't like this sound. It would be better for us to choose the other road. There we're sure not to meet anyone." "Meet who?" "What do I know? Let's get going." They left the metaled road, and set off toward Póstelek. Petrina was continually looking back over his shoulder, nervously scanning the landscape, but didn't see anything. By now he could have sworn that the noise was coming from somewhere above them. "But it's not a plane . . . It's more like a church organ . . . ah, that's crazy!" He stopped, went down on hands and knees and put an ear to the ground. "No. Definitely not. It's crazy!" The low hum continued, no nearer, no further away. However he searched his memory the humming wasn't like anything he had ever heard before. It wasn't the roar of a car or a plane or of distant thunder . . . He had a bad feeling about it. He swiveled his head left and right, sensing danger in every bush, in every scraggy tree, even in the narrow wayside ditch covered in frogspawn. The most terrifying thing was that he couldn't even decide whether the menace, whatever it was, was close at hand or at a distance. He turned a suspicious eye on the "kid." "Look here! Have you eaten today? It's not your stomach rumbling?" "Don't be an idiot, Petrina," Irimiás remarked over his shoulder. "And get a move on!" ... They were some quarter of a mile from the fork now, when they noticed something else besides the worryingly continuous humming. It was Petrina who first became aware of it: incapable even of saying a word, it was only through his eyes he could register the shock. His dull eyes started from their sockets, gazing at the sky, indicating the source. To the right of them above the marshy lifeless ground, a white transparent veil was billowing in a particularly dignified fashion. They hardly had the time to take it in before they were startled to see the veil vanish as soon as it touched the ground. "Pinch me!" groaned Petrina shaking his head in disbelief. The "kid" stood there open-mouthed with wonder, then, seeing that neither Irimiás nor Petrina was capable of speech, firmly remarked, "What's up? Never seen fog before?" "You call this fog?!" Petrina snapped nervously back. "Jackass! I swear it was a kind of ... a wedding veil ... Boss, I have a bad feeling about this ..." Irimiás was staring puzzled at the place the veil had disappeared. "It's a joke. Pull yourself together Petrina and say something sensible." "Over there!" cried the "kid." And not far from the last sighting of the veil, there was a new veil slowly drifting in the air. They stared mesmerized as it too touched down and then, as if it really were fog, disappeared ... "Let's get out of here, boss!" Petrina urged, his voice shaking. "The way I see it, it'll be raining frogs next ..." "I'm sure there's a rational explanation for this," Irimiás firmly declared. "I just wish I knew what the devil it was! ... We can't all three have gone mad at once!" "If only Mrs. Halics was here," remarked the "kid" grimacing. "She'd soon tell us!" Irimiás suddenly raised his head. "What's that?" Suddenly it was quiet. The "kid" closed his eyes in confusion. "I'm just saying ..." "Do you know something?!" Petrina demanded in fright. "Me?" grimaced the "kid." "Course I don't. I was just saying it as a joke ..." They walked on in silence and it occurred, not only to Petrina but to Irimiás too, that it might be wiser for them to turn back immediately, but neither of them was up to making the decision if only because they couldn't be sure that retracing their steps would be any less dangerous. They started to hurry and this time not even Petrina complained, quite the opposite in fact: if it was up to him they'd have broken into a run, and so, when they saw the ruins of Weinkheim ahead and Irimiás suggested a brief rest ("My legs have completely gone to sleep ... We'll build a fire, eat something, dry out, then go on ...") Petrina cried out in despair, "No, I couldn't bear it! You don't imagine I want to stay in this place a moment longer than I need to? After what's just happened?" "No need to panic," Irimiás reassured him. "We're exhausted. We have hardly slept in two days. We need a rest. We have a long way to go." "OK, but you go ahead!" Petrina demanded, and gathering up what courage he had left followed some ten paces behind the other two, his heart in his mouth, not even prepared to respond to the teasing of the "kid" who, seeing Irimiás calm, relaxed a little and aspired to be regarded as "one of the brave" ... Petrina waited till the first two turned down the path leading to the manor then, carefully, anxiously glancing left and right, scurried after them, but as he came face to face with the main entrance of the ruined building all his strength left him and—he saw in vain how Irimiás and the "kid" had quickly ducked behind a bush—he himself was incapable of moving. "I'm going to go mad. I can feel it." He was so frightened his brow was covered in sweat. "Hell and damnation! What have we got ourselves into?" He held his breath and, with muscles tense to the point of snapping, he finally succeeded in sidling—literally sideways—behind another bush. The sound of something like sniggering grew louder again: it was like a cheerful bunch of people making merry, it being perfectly natural for such a jolly crew to seek out this particular deserted spot and to spend their time carousing here in the wind, rain and cold ... And that sniggering—such a strange noise. Cold shivers ran down his back. He peeped out to the path, then, when he judged the moment to be opportune, set off like a lunatic and bolted over to Irimiás the way a soldier might leap, under enemy fire and at risk of his life, from trench to trench during battle. "Here pal . . . ," he whispered in a choking voice as he settled by the squatting figure of Irimiás. "What's going on here?" "I can't see anything at the moment," the other answered, his voice quiet and steady, in full control of himself, never taking his eyes off what used to be the manor gardens, "but I expect we'll find out soon." "No," grunted Petrina: "I don't want to find out!" "It's like they're having a proper party . . . ," said the "kid," excited, breathlessly impatient for his master to entrust him with something. "Here!" squealed Petrina: "In the rain? . . . In the middle of nowhere? . . . Boss, let's run now before it's too late!" "Shut your mouth, I can't hear anything!" "I can hear! I can hear! That's why I say we — " "Quiet!" Irimiás thundered at him. There was no sign of movement in the park where the oaks, the walnuts, the boxwood and flowerbeds were all densely overgrown with weeds, so Irimiás decided, since he could only see a small part of it, that they should carefully creep forward. He grabbed Petrina's wildly waving arm and dragging him behind him they slowly made their way to the main entrance, then tiptoed along the wall to the right, Irimiás at the head, but when he reached the corner of the building and warily looked toward the back of the park, he stopped dead in his tracks for a moment then quickly drew back his head. "What's there?!" Petrina whispered: "Shall we run?" "You see that little shack?" Irimiás asked, his voice tense. "We'll make for it. One by one. I go first, then you, Petrina, and you last, kid. Is that clear?" No sooner had he said it than he was off in the direction of the old summerhouse, running, keeping low. "I'm not going!" muttered Petrina, clearly confused: "That's at least twenty yards. We'll be shot full of holes by the time we reach it!" The "kid" pushed him roughly forward—"Get going!"—and Petrina, not expecting to be pushed, lost his balance after a few steps and lay sprawled in the mud. He immediately got up but then within a few yards threw himself face down again and only reached the summerhouse by crawling on his belly like a snake. He was so scared he didn't even dare to look up for a while, covering his eyes with his hands, lying perfectly still on the ground, then, once he had realized that "thanks to God's mercy" he was still alive, he plucked up his courage, sat up and peeked at the park through a gap. His already wrecked nerves were not up to the sight. "Down!" he screamed, and once again threw himself flat on the ground. "Don't scream, you idiot!" Irimiás snapped at him. "If I hear another peep out of you I'll wring your neck!" At the back of the park, in front of three enormous naked oaks, in a clearing, wrapped in a series of transparent veils, lay a small body. They might have been no more than thirty yards from it, so they could even make out the face, at least the part not covered by a veil; and if all three of them hadn't thought it impossible, or if they hadn't all helped place the body in the crude coffin Kráner had constructed, they could have sworn it was the kid's sister lying there, her face ashen white, her hair in blonde ringlets, in peaceful slumber. From time to time the wind lifted the ends of the veil, the rain quietly washing the corpse, and the three ancient oaks creaked and groaned as if about to fall ... But there was not a soul anywhere near the body, just that sweet, bell-like laughter everywhere, a kind of carefree, cheerful music. The "kid" stared at the clearing, mesmerized, not knowing what he should most fear, the sight of his sister, dripping, stiff, clad in white as pure as snow, or the thought of her suddenly getting up and walking toward him; his legs trembled, everything went dark, the trees, the manor, the park, the sky, leaving only her, glowing painfully bright, ever more distinct, in the middle of the clearing. And in that sudden silence, in the total lack of any sound, when even the raindrops broke silently as they fell, and they could well have thought they'd gone deaf, since they could feel the wind but couldn't hear it humming, and were impervious to the strange breeze lightly playing about them, he nevertheless thought he heard that continuous hum and tinkling laughter suddenly give way to frightening yelps and grunts, and as he looked up he saw them moving toward him. He covered his face with his arms and started sobbing. "You see that?" Irimiás whispered, frozen, squeezing Petrina's arm so hard his knuckles turned white. A wind had sprung up around the body and in complete silence the blindingly white corpse began uncertainly to rise ... then, having reached the top of the oaks, it suddenly rocked and, bobbling slightly, started its descent to the ground again, to the precise spot it had occupied before. At that moment the disembodied voices set to a fury of complaint like a dissatisfied chorus that has had to resign itself to failure once again. Petrina was gasping. "Can you believe that?" "I am trying to believe it," replied Irimiás, now deathly pale. "I wonder how long they have been trying? The child has been dead almost two days now. Petrina, perhaps for the first time in my life I am really frightened." "My friend ... can I ask you something?" "Go ahead." "What do you think ...?" "Think?" "Do you think ... um ... that Hell exists?" Irimiás gave a great gulp. "Who knows. It might." Suddenly all was quiet again. There was only the humming, a little louder perhaps. The corpse started to rise again, and some six feet above the clearing it trembled, then with incredible speed it rose and flew off, soon to be lost among the still, solemn clouds. Wind swept the park, the oaks shook as did the ruined old summerhouse, then the tinkling-chiming voices reached a triumphant crescendo above their heads before slowly fading away, leaving nothing behind except a few scraps of veil drifting down, the sound of rattling tiles on the fallen-in roof of the manor, and the frightening knockings of the broken tin gutters against the wall. For minutes on end they stood frozen staring at the clearing, then because nothing else happened they slowly came to their senses. "I think it's over," whispered Irimiás, then gave a deep hiccup. "I really hope so," whispered Petrina. "Let's rouse the kid." They took the still trembling child under the arms and helped stand him up. "Now come on, pull yourself together," Petrina encouraged him while just about managing to stand himself. "Leave me alone," the "kid" sobbed. "Let go of me! "It's all right. There's nothing to be scared of now!" "Leave me here! I'm not going anywhere!" "Of course you're coming! Enough of this pitiful crying! In any case there's nothing there anymore." The "kid" went over to the gap and looked over to the clearing. "Where ... where has it gone?" "It vanished like the fog," Petrina answered, hanging on to a projecting brick. "Like the ... fog?" "Like the fog." "Then I was right," the "kid" remarked uncertainly. "Absolutely," said Irimiás once he finally managed to stop his hiccupping. "I have to admit you were right." "But you ... what ... what did you see?" "Me? I only saw the fog," Petrina said, staring straight ahead and bitterly shaking his head. "Nothing but fog, fog all over the place." The "kid" gave Irimiás an uneasy glance. "But then ... what was it?" "A hallucination," Irimiás answered, his face chalk-white, his voice so faint that the "kid" instinctively leaned toward him. "We're exhausted. Chiefly you. And that's hardly surprising." "Not in the least," Petrina agreed. "People are likely to see all kinds of things in that condition. When I was serving at the front there'd be nights when a thousand witches would pursue me on broomsticks. Seriously." They walked the length of path, then for a long time down the road to Póstelek without speaking, avoiding the ankle-deep puddles, and the closer they approached the old road that led straight as a die to the southeastern corner of town, the more Petrina worried about Irimiás's condition. The master was all but snapping with tension, his knee buckling now and then, and often it seemed that one more step and he'd collapse. His face was pale, his features had dropped, his eyes were staring glassily at nothing in particular. Fortunately the "kid" spotted nothing of this partly because he had been calmed by the exchange between Irimiás and Petrina. ("Of course! What else could it be? A hallucination. I must pull myself together if I don't want them to laugh at me!..."), and partly because he was quite excited by the idea that Petrina had acknowledged his role in the discovery of the vision so he could now march along at the head of the procession. Suddenly Irimiás stopped. Petrina leapt to his side in terror, to help if he could. But Irimiás shoved his arm away, turned to him and bellowed, "You creep!!! Why don't you just fuck off?! I've had enough of you! Understand!!?" Petrina quickly lowered his eyes. Seeing that, Irimiás grabbed him by the collar, tried to lift him, and failing gave him a great push so Petrina lost his balance and, having scrambled a few steps, finished on his face in the mud. "My friend . . ." he pitifully pleaded, "Don't lose your—" "You're still talking back?!" Irimiás bawled at him, then sprang over, and with all his strength, punched him in the face. They stood facing each other, Petrina desolate and in despair, but suddenly sober again, utterly exhausted and quite empty, feeling only the mortal pressure of despair like a trapped animal that discovers there is no escape. "Master . . ." Petrina stuttered: "I . . . I am not angry . . ." Irimiás hung his head. "Don't be angry, you idiot . . ." They set off again, Petrina turning to the "kid" who seemed to have been turned to stone and waving him on as to say, "Come on, no problem, that's done with now," sighing from time to time and scratching his ear. "Listen, I'm an evangelist . . ." "Don't you mean an Evangelical?" Irimiás corrected him. "Yeah, yeah, that's right! That's what I meant to say . . ." Petrina quickly answered and gave a relieved sigh on seeing his partner was over the worst." "And you?" "Me? They never even christened me. I expect they knew it wouldn't change anything . . ." "Hush!" Petrina waved his arms in panic, pointing to the sky. "Not so loud!" "Come on, you big dope . . ." Irimiás growled. "What does it matter now . . ." "It may not matter to you, but it does to me! Whenever I think of that blazing comet thing I can hardly breathe!" "Don't think of it like that," Irimiás replied after a long silence. "It doesn't matter what we saw just now, it still means nothing. Heaven? Hell? The afterlife? All nonsense. Just a waste of time. The imagination never stops working but we're not one jot nearer the truth." Petrina finally relaxed. He knew now that "everything was all right" and also what he should say so his companion might be his old self again. "OK, just don't shout so loud!"

he whispered: "Don't we have enough troubles as it is?" "God is not made manifest in language, you dope. He's not manifest in anything. He doesn't exist." "Well, I believe in God!" Petrina cut in, outraged. "Have some consideration for me at least, you damn atheist!" "God was a mistake. I've long understood there is zero difference between me and a bug, or a bug and a river, or a river and a voice shouting above it. There's no sense or meaning in anything. It's nothing but a network of dependency under enormous fluctuating pressures. It's only our imaginations, not our senses, that continually confront us with failure and the false belief that we can raise ourselves by our own bootstraps from the miserable pulp of decay. There's no escaping that, stupid." "But how can you say this now, after what we've just seen?" Petrina protested. Irimiás made a wry face. "That's precisely why I say we are trapped forever. We're properly doomed. It's best not to try either, best not believe your eyes. It's a trap, Petrina. And we fall into it every time. We think we're breaking free but all we're doing is readjusting the locks. We're trapped, end of story." Petrina had worked his own way up to fury now. "I don't understand a word of that! Don't spout poetry at me, goddamnit! Speak plain!" "Let's hang ourselves, you fool," Irimiás sadly advised him: "At least it's over quicker. It's the same either way, whether we hang ourselves or not. So OK, let's not hang ourselves." "Look friend, I just can't understand you! Stop it now before I burst into tears . . ." They walked on quietly for a while, but Petrina couldn't let it rest. "You know what's the matter with you, boss? You haven't been christened." "That's as may be." They were on the old road by now, the "kid" eager for adventure scanning the terrain, but there were only the deep tracks left by cartwheels in the summer, nothing looked dangerous; overhead, an occasional flock of crows, then the rain coming down harder and the wind too seeming to pick up as they neared the town. "Well, and now?" asked Petrina. "What?" "What happens now?" "What do you mean what happens now?" Irimiás answered through gritted teeth. "From here on things get better. Till now other people have told you what to do, now you will tell them. It's exactly the same thing. Word for word." They lit cigarettes and gloomily blew out the smoke. It was getting dark by the time they reached the southeastern part of town, marching down deserted streets where lights burned in windows and people sat silently in front of steaming plates of food. "Here," Irimiás stopped when they reached The Scales. "We'll stop here for a while." They entered the smoky, airless bar that was already packed and, pushing their way past loudly guffawing or arguing groups of drivers, tax officials, workers and students, Irimiás made his way to the bar to join a long line. The barman, who recognized Irimiás as soon as he stepped through the door, skipped nimbly over to their end of the counter, remarking, "Well, well! Who do I see here! Greetings! Welcome, Lord of Misrule!" He leaned across the bar, extending his hand and quietly asked, "What can we do for you, gentlemen?" Irimiás ignored the proferred hand and answered coolly: "Two blended and a small spritzer." "Right away gentlemen," the barman answered, a little taken aback, yanking his hand back. "Two measures of blended and a small spritzer. Coming right up." He skipped back to his position at the center of the bar, poured the drinks and quickly served them. "You are my guests, gentlemen." "Thank you," replied Irimiás. "What's new, Weisz?" The barman wiped his sweaty brow with the sleeve of his shirt, glanced left and right and leant close to Irimiás. "The horses have escaped from the slaughterhouse . . ." he whispered excitedly. "Or so they say." "The horses?" "Yes, the horses—I just heard that they still haven't been able to catch them. A whole stable of horses, if you please, running amok in town, if you please. So they say." Irimiás nodded, then, raising the glasses above his head, cut his way back through the crowd and, with some difficulty, reached Petrina and the "kid" who had made a small place for themselves. "Spritzer for you, kid." "Thanks, I saw, he knows." "Not hard to guess. So. To our health." They threw back the

drink, Petrina offered cigarettes around, and they lit up. "Ah, the famous prankster! Good evening! Is it you? How the devil did you get
here! So pleased to see you!" A short, bald man with a beetroot-col-
ored face came up and extended his hand, friendly fashion. "Greetings!" he said and turned to Petrina. "So how are things, Tóth?" Petrina
asked. "Pretty well. OK as things go nowadays! And yourselves? Seriously, it must be at least two, no, three years since I last laid eyes on you.
Was it something big?" Petrina nodded. "Possibly." "Ah, that's different
…" the bald man acknowledged, embarrassed, and turned to Irimiás.
"Have you heard? Szabó is done for." "Uh uhm," grunted Irimiás and
threw back what remained in his glass. "What's new, Tóth?" The bald
man leaned closer. "I got an apartment." "You don't say? Congratulations. Anything else?" "Well, life goes on," Tóth answered dully. "We've
just had the local election. Any idea how many went to vote? Hm. You
can guess. I can count them all, from one to one. They're all here," he
said pointing to his own head. "Well that was big of you, Tóth," Irimiás
answered in a tired voice. "I see you don't waste your time." "Obvious
isn't it?" the bald man spread his hands. "There are things a man has to
do. Am I right?" Petrina leaned forward. "Indeed you are, now will you
join the line to bring us something?" The bald man was keen: "What
would you like, gentlemen? Be my guests." "Blended." "Coming up.
Back in a minute." He was at the bar in a matter of moments, waved the
barman over and was immediately back with a handful of glasses. "To
our meeting!" "Cheers," said Irimiás. "Till the cows come home,"
added Petrina. "So tell me what's new? What's new over there?" asked
Tóth, his eyes wide with anticipation. "Where?" Petrina wondered.
"Just, you know, 'there' … speaking generally." "Ah. We have just witnessed a resurrection." "The bald man flashed his yellow teeth. "You
haven't changed a bit, Petrina! Ha-ha-ha! We've just witnessed a resurrection! Very good! That's you, all right!" "You don't believe me?"
Petrina sourly remarked. "You'll see, you'll come to a bad end. Don't

wear anything too warm once you're at death's door. It's hot enough there, they say." Tóth was shaking with laughter. "Wonderful, gentlemen!" he panted. "I'll rejoin my associates. Will we meet again?" "That," said Petrina with a sad smile, "is unavoidable." They left The Scales and started down the poplar-lined avenue that led to the center of town. The wind blew in their faces, the rain drove into their eyes, and because they had warmed up inside they were hunched and shivering now. They met not a single soul until they got to the church square, Petrina even remarking on it: "What is this? A curfew?" "No, it's just autumn, the time of year," Irimiás noted sadly: "People sit by their stoves and don't get up till spring. They spend hours by the window until it grows dark. They eat, they drink, they cling to each other in bed under the eiderdown. There are moments when they feel everything is going wrong for them, so they give their kids a good beating or kick the cat, and in this way they get by a while longer. That's how it goes, you idiot." In the main square they were stopped by a crowd of people. "Have you seen anything?" asked a gangling man. "Nothing at all," answered Irimiás. "If you do, tell us immediately. We'll wait here for news. You'll find us here." "Fine. Ciao." A few yards on Petrina asked, "I might be an idiot, but so what if they're there? They were perfectly normal to look at. What were we supposed to have seen?" "Horses," Irimiás replied. "Horses? What horses?" "The ones that escaped from the slaughterhouse." They passed down the empty street and took a turn toward the old Romanian quarter, Nagyrománváros. At the crossing of Eminescu Street and The Avenue they spotted them. There they were in the middle of Eminescu Street, some eight or ten horses, grazing. Their backs reflected the faint streetlights and they carried on peacefully chomping the grass until they noticed the group staring at them, then suddenly, it seemed in unison, they raised their heads, one neighed, and within a minute they had disappeared down the far end of the street. "Who are you cheering for?" asked the "kid," grinning. "For myself," Petrina nervously replied. There was hardly anyone in Steigerwald's bar when they looked in and those who were there quickly left. Steigerwald himself was fiddling with the TV set in the corner. "Damn you, you useless bastard!" he cursed at the TV, not having noticed the newcomers. "Good evening," boomed Irimiás. Steigerwald quickly turned round. "Good Lord! It's you!" "No problem," Petrina reassured him. "No problem at all." "That's good. I thought . . ." the landlord muttered. "That rotten bastard there," he pointed to the television in fury: "I've been trying for an hour to get a picture out of it but it's gone and doesn't want to come back." "In that case, take a break. Get us two blended, and a spritzer for the young gentleman." They sat down at a table, unbuttoned their coats and lit more cigarettes. "Listen kid," said Irimiás. "Drink it up then go down to Páyer's. You know where he lives? Good. You tell him I'm waiting for him here." "OK," answered the "kid" and buttoned his coat again. He took the glass from the landlord's hand, threw back the contents, and was quickly out of the door. "Steigerwald," Irimiás stopped the landlord who, having put their glasses down in front of them, was on his way back to the bar. "Ah, so there is trouble after all," he groaned and planted his behemoth of a body on a chair beside them. "There's no trouble," Irimiás assured him. "We need a truck by tomorrow." "When will you bring it back?" "Tomorrow night. And we sleep here tonight." "All right," nodded the relieved Steigerwald then struggled to his feet. "When are you paying?" "Right now." "Pardon?" "You misheard," the master corrected him: "Tomorrow." The door opened and the "kid" rushed in. "He'll be right here," he announced and sat back in his chair. "Well done, sonny. Get yourself another spritzer. And tell the man to make us some bean soup." "With pork trotters," Petrina added with a grin. A few minutes later a heavily built, fat, gray-haired man entered, umbrella in hand. He must have been ready for bed because he hadn't even dressed properly but simply thrown a coat over his pajamas and put a pair of fake-fur slippers on his feet. "I hear you're back in town, squire," he said sleepily and gently let himself down into the chair next to Irimiás. "I wouldn't resist if you tried to shake my hand." Irimiás was gazing mournfully into space but at Páyer's words snapped to attention and gave a smile of satisfaction. "My deepest respects. I hope I have not awoken you from your slumbers." The smile did not wither on Irimiás's lips. He crossed his legs, leaned back and slowly blew out smoke. "Let's get down to business." "Don't go scaring me at the outset," the newcomer held up his hand, but he spoke with confidence. "Go on, ask me for something now that you've dragged me from my bed." "What will you have to drink?" "No, don't ask me what I want to drink. They don't have it here. I'll have a plum *pálinka*." He listened to Irimiás with his eyes closed as if asleep, and only raised his hand again to ask a question when the landlord arrived with the *pálinka* and he had thrown it all back at once. "Wait a minute! What's the hurry? I haven't been introduced to your esteemed colleagues . . ." Petrina leapt to his feet. "Petrina, at your command. I'm Petrina." The "kid" did not move. "Horgos." Páyer raised his lowered eyelids. "A well-mannered young man," he said and gave Irimiás a knowing look. "He has a bright future." "I'm pleased my assistants are slowly gaining your sympathy, Mister Bang-bang." Páyer raised his head as if by way of defense. "Spare me the nicknames. I'm not obsessed with guns as I believe you know. I just deal in guns. Let's stick with Páyer." "Fine," smiled Irimiás and stubbed out his cigarette under the table. "The situation is this. I would be most grateful for certain . . . raw materials. The more kinds the better." Páyer closed his eyes. "Is this a purely hypothetical inquiry or are you ready to back it up with a certain figure that might help me bear the indignity of simply being alive?" "Backed up, naturally." The guest nodded in acknowledgment. "I can only repeat that, as a business associate, you are a gentleman through and through. It's a pity that there are ever fewer well-mannered men of your profession to deal with." "Will you join us for supper?" Irimiás inquired with the same unwearying smile when Steigerwald appeared at the table with plates of bean soup. "What have you got to offer?" "Nothing," the landlord grunted. "Do you mean that whatever you bring us is inedible?" asked Páyer in a tired voice. "Right." "In that case I won't have anything." He got up, gave a slight bow and gave the "kid" a special nod. "Gentlemen, at your service. We'll deal with the details later if I understand you correctly." Irimiás too stood up and extended his hand. "Indeed. I'll look you up at the weekend. Sleep well." "Look, it is precisely twenty-six years since I last slept five and a half hours without waking: ever since then I've been tossing and turning, half asleep, half awake. But I thank you anyway." He bowed again, then with slow steps and a sleepy look he left the bar. Once supper was over, Steigerwald prepared beds for them in a corner, grumbling all the while, and gave the non-functioning TV set a frustrated nudge with his elbow as he was about to leave them to it. "You don't have a Bible by any chance?" Petrina called to him. Steigerwald slowed, stopped and turned round to face him. "A Bible? What do you need one of those for?" "I thought I'd read a little before I sleep. It always has a settling effect on me, you know." "How can you even say that without blushing!" muttered Irimiás: "You were a child the last time you read a book, and even then you just looked at the pictures..." "Don't listen to him!" Petrina protested, making an offended face: "He's just jealous, that's all." Steigerwald scratched his head. "All I've got here are some decent detective stories. Do you want me to bring you one?" "Heaven forbid!" cried Petrina. "That won't do at all!" Steigerwald looked sourly at him then vanished through a door to the yard. "That Steigerwald, what a miserable bastard...," Petrina mumbled. "I swear the starving bears I meet in my worst nightmares are friendlier than he is." Irimiás had lain down in the place prepared for him and covered himself with the blanket. "Maybe. But he'll survive us all." The "kid" turned off the light and they fell quiet. The only thing to be heard for a while was the sound of

Petrina mumbling as he tried to remember the words of a prayer he'd heard his grandmother say.

Our father ... um, our father
which art there, art, art in the sky, er,
in heaven, let us praise, er ... hallowed be
our lord Jesus Christ,
no ... let them praise ... no, let us praise
rather, let them praise Your name,
and give us this ... what I mean is,
let everything be according to, er,
whatever you want ... in earth as
it is on earth ... in heaven ...
or in hell, amen ...

III

THE PERSPECTIVE,

AS SEEN FROM THE BACK

Quietly, continually, the rain fell and the inconsolable wind that died then was forever resurrected ruffled the still surfaces of puddles so lightly it failed to disturb the delicate dead skin that had covered them during the night so that instead of recovering the previous day's tired glitter they increasingly and remorselessly absorbed the light that swam slowly out of the east. The trunks of the trees, the occasionally creaking branches, the sticky festering weeds, and even the "manor"—everything was sheathed in a refined but slimy gauze as though the elusive agents of darkness had marked them all out so that they might continue their work of corrosive, continual destruction the next night. When, far above the unbroken layers of cloud, the moon rolled unobserved down the western horizon and they peered blinking into the gaping hole that had once been the main entrance or through the high window cavities into the frozen light, they slowly understood that something had changed, that something was not quite where it had been before dawn, and having understood this, they quickly realized that the thing they had secretly most feared had actually happened: that the dreams that had driven them forward the previous day were over, and it was time for the bitter awakening ... Their first feelings of confusion gave way to a frightened acknowledgment of how stupid they had been to rush into "things"; their departure having been the result not of sober calculation but of an evil impulse, and that because they had, in effect, burnt their bridges, there was no chance now of taking the sensible course and returning home. It was dawn, the most miserable of hours: their stiff limbs were still sore and there they were, shivering in the cold, their lips almost blue, foul-smelling and hungry, struggling to their feet among the scraps of their possessions, forced to face the fact that the "manor" that only yesterday had seemed the fulfillment of their dreams, was today—in this pitiless light—simply a cold, relentless prison. Grumbling and ever more embittered, they roamed through the deserted halls of the moribund building, exploring in somber chaotic fashion the dismantled parts of rusted machinery and in the funereal silence the suspicion grew in them that they had been lured into a trap, that they were, all of them, naïve victims of a low plot to dump them there, homeless, deceived, robbed and humiliated. Mrs. Schmidt was the first that dawn to return to the miserable prospect of their makeshift beds; she sat down shivering on the crude bundles of their belongings and stared in disappointment at the light as it grew brighter. The eye make-up she had received from "him" as a present had smeared across her puffy face, her mouth was turned down in bitterness, her throat was dry, her stomach ached and she felt too weak even to attend to her tousled hair and crumpled clothes. Because it was all in vain: the memory of the few magical hours spent with "him" was not enough to allay her fear—especially now that it was plain that Irimiás had simply reneged on his promise—that all was lost now ... It wasn't easy, but what else could she do: she tried to resign herself to the fact that Irimiás ("... until this matter is finally closed ...") would not be taking her away, and that her dream of disentangling herself from Schmidt's "filthy paws" and taking her leave of this "stinking hole of a place" would have to be postponed for months, perhaps years ("Good heavens, years! More years!") but the terrible thought that even that might be a lie, that he was now over the fields and far away in search of new conquests, made her clench her fists. True, if she thought back to the other nights when she gave herself to Irimiás at the back of the storeroom, she had to admit that even now, at this most dreadful hour, it was no disappointment: those magnificent moments, those moments of extraordinary blissful satisfaction had to compensate for everything else; it was only the "betrayed love" and the crushing and besmirching of her "pure burning passion" that could never be forgiven! For after all, what could one expect when, despite the words whispered in secret at the moment of parting ("Before dawn, for certain!...") it finally became clear that everything was "a filthy lie"!... Without hope but still stubbornly longing, she gazed at the rain through the enormous gap where the main entrance had been, and her heart contracted, her entire body doubled up, and her tangled hair fell forward to cover her tortured face. But however she tried to concentrate on the thirst for revenge rather than on the agonizing sadness of resignation, it was the tender murmuring of Irimiás she kept hearing; it was his tall, broad, respect-demanding, solid body she kept seeing; the strong self-confident curve of his nose, the narrowing of his soft lips, the irresistible glow of his eyes, and time and again she felt his delicate fingers half-consciously playing with her hair, the warmth of his palms against her breasts and thighs, and every time she heard the slightest noise she imagined it might be him, so — when the others had returned and she saw the same bitter funereal expression on their faces as she felt on her own — the last weak barriers of her proud resistance were swept away by despair. "What will happen to me without him?!... For the love of God ... leave me if you must, but ... but not now! Not yet!... Not just at this time!... An hour more!... A minute!... What do I care what he does to them, but ... Me! Not to me!... If nothing else make him allow me to be his lover! His handmaid!... His servant! What do I care! Let him kick me, beat me like a dog, just ... this one time, let him come back just this one time!..." They sat by the wall, depressed, with humble packed meals in their laps, chewing away in the cold draft of ever-brighter dawn. Outside, the shaggy pile that had once formed the bell tower of the chapel to the right of the "manor"—that's when it still had a bell—gave a great creak and from within it came a suppressed rumbling sound, as if yet another floor had collapsed ... There was no doubt about it now, they had to admit it was pointless to hang around any longer since Irimiás had promised to come "before daylight" and dawn was practically over. But not one of them dared break the silence or pronounce the appropriately grave words "We've been completely screwed over" because it was extraordinarily difficult to regard "our savior Irimiás" as "a filthy liar" and "a low thief," not to mention the fact that what had happened was still something of a mystery ... What if something unexpected had delayed him?... Maybe he was late because of the bad roads, because of the rain, or because ... Kráner got up, went over to the gate, leaned against the damp wall, lit a cigarette and nervously scanned the path leading down from the metaled road, before furiously standing up and swiping at the air. He sat back in his place and spoke in an unexpectedly trembling voice. "Listen ... I have a feeling ... that ... we've been conned!..." Hearing this, even those who had been staring vacantly into space lowered their eyes. "I tell you, we've been conned!" Kráner repeated, raising his voice. Still nobody moved and his harsh words echoed menacingly in the frightened silence. "What's the matter with you, are you all deaf?" screamed Kráner, quite beside himself, and leapt to his feet. "Nothing to say? Not a word?!" "I told you," Schmidt cried out with a dark expression. "I told you right from the start!" His lips were trembling and he pointed an accusing finger at Futaki. "He promised," Kráner ranted on, "he promised to build a new Eden! There! Have a good look! There's our Eden! That's what we've come to, damn the miserable scoundrel! He enticed us here, here to this wasteland, while we . . . ! Fucking sheep! . . ." "While he," Schmidt picked up the thread, "gleefully scuttles off in the opposite direction! Who knows where he is now? We could be looking for him the rest of our lives! . . ." "And who knows in which bar he's gambling away our money?!" "A whole year's work!" Schmidt continued, his voice shaking. "A whole year of miserable scrimping and saving! I'm back where I was, without a penny again!" Kráner started stalking up and down like an animal in a cage, his fists clenched, giving more occasional swipes in the air. "But he'll regret it! He'll be damn sorry, the bastard! Kráner is not the sort of man to let such things go! I'll find him if I have to look in every nook and cranny! And I swear I'll strangle him with my bare hands. With these!" He held his hands up. Futaki raised a nervous hand. "Not so fast! Not so fast with that threat! What if he appears in a couple of minutes! Where's all this ranting going to get you then? Eh?!!" Schmidt sprang to his feet. "You dare to open your mouth?! You dare to say a word?! Where's that going to get us?! It's you I have to thank for being robbed! Who else but you?!" Kráner went up to Futaki and looked deep into his eyes. "Wait!" said Futaki and took a deep breath. "All right! We'll wait two minutes! Two entire minutes! And then we'll see . . . what will be will be!" Kráner pulled Schmidt along with him and they stood together at the threshold of the main entrance, Kráner spreading his feet and swaying back and forth. "Well! So now we're ready! And there he is, just coming," Schmidt mocked, turning to Futaki. "You hear?! Here comes your savior! You poor bastard!" "Shut up!" Kráner interrupted him and squeezed Schmidt's arm. "Let's wait the full two minutes! Then we'll see what he has to say, him and his big mouth!" Futaki rested his head on his knees. There was absolute silence. Mrs. Schmidt sat huddled in the corner, terrified. Halics gave a great gulp then, because he had some vague idea of what might happen, almost inaudibly said, "It's really awful . . . that even at a time . . . like this . . . I mean, each other . . . !" The headmaster rose. "Gentlemen," he addressed Kráner, trying to calm him: "What's all this?! This is no solution! Think it over and—" "Shut up, you ass!" Kráner hissed at him and seeing his threatening look the headmaster quickly sat down again. "So, friend?" Schmidt asked dully with his back to Futaki, gazing down the path. "Is the two minutes up yet?" Futaki raised his head and hugged his knees. "Tell me, what's the point of this performance. Do you really think I can do anything about it?" Schmidt grew beetroot red. "So who convinced me in the bar? Huh?" and he slowly moved toward Futaki: "Who kept telling me I should take it easy because this and that and the other will be all right, eh?" "Are you out of your mind, buddy?" Futaki replied raising his own voice, beginning to twitch nervously: "Have you gone mad?" But Schmidt was in front of him by then so he couldn't get up. "Give me my money back," Schmidt snarled, his eyes wide and bloodshot. "You heard what I said!? Give me back my money!" Futaki pressed his back against the wall. "There's no point in asking me for your money! Come to your senses!" Schmidt closed his eyes. "I'm asking you for the last time, give me my money!" "Listen everyone," Futaki cried. "Get him away from me, he's really gone—!" but he couldn't finish what he was saying because Schmidt, with all his strength, kicked him in the face. Futaki's head snapped back and for a second he sat absolutely still, the blood starting to gush from his nose, then slowly slipped to one side. By that time the women, Halics, and the headmaster had leapt over, twisted Schmidt's arm behind his back, and then with great difficulty, not without a violent struggle, dragged him away. Kráner grinned nervously in the entrance, his arms crossed, then started moving toward Schmidt. Mrs. Schmidt, Mrs. Kráner and Mrs. Halics were screaming and fussing in terror around the unconscious Futaki, until Mrs. Schmidt pulled herself together, took a rag, ran out to the terrace, dipped it in a puddle and ran back with it. She knelt down by Futaki and started wiping his face, then turned on the weeping Mrs. Halics, shouting, "Instead of blubbering you could do something useful like fetching another rag, a bigger one, to soak up the blood!" ... Futaki was slowly regaining consciousness and opened his eyes to stare blankly first at the sky, then at Mrs. Schmidt's anxious face as she leaned over him. Feeling a sharp pain, he tried to sit up. "For heaven's sake, don't do anything, just lie still!" Mrs. Kráner shouted at him. "You're still bleeding!" They laid him down again on the blanket and Mrs. Kráner tried to wash the blood off his clothes while Mrs. Halics knelt beside Futaki, quietly praying. "Get that witch away from me!" groaned Futaki. "I'm still alive ..." Schmidt was gasping for breath in another corner, clearly confused, pressing his fists into his groin as if that were the only way he could keep himself from moving. "Really!" the headmaster shook his head as he stood together with Halics with his back to Schmidt to block his way in case he tried to attack Futaki again. "Really, I can't believe what I'm seeing! You're a grown man! What are you thinking of? You just go and assault someone? You know what I call it? I call it bullying, that's what I call it!" "Leave me alone," Schmidt answered through gritted teeth. "That's right!" Kráner said, stepping closer: "This has nothing to do with you! Why are you so determined to poke your nose in everywhere? In any case the clown deserved it! ..." "You shut up, you lowlife!" the headmaster snapped back: "You ... you were the one who encouraged him to do it! You think I can't hear? You'd better keep quiet!" "What I suggest, pal ...," hissed Kráner with a dark look, seizing the headmaster, "What I suggest is that you get out of here while the going is good! ... I don't advise you to pick a quarrel with—" At that moment a resonant, severe, self-confident voice cut across them: "What's going on here?!" Everyone turned around to the threshold. Mrs. Halics gave a fearful cry, Schmidt leapt to his feet and Kráner took an involuntary step back. Irimiás stood there. His seal-gray raincoat was buttoned up to the chin, his hat drawn far down his brow. He stuck his hands deep into his pockets and surveyed the scene with piercing eyes. A cigarette dangled from his lips. There was stony silence. Even Futaki sat up, then tried to stand, swaying a little, but hid the rag behind his back, the blood still dribbling from his nose. Mrs. Halics crossed herself in astonishment then quickly lowered her hands because Halics was signaling to her to stop it immediately. "I asked what's going on?" Irimiás repeated threateningly. He spat out the cigarette and stuck a new one in the corner of his mouth. The estate stood before him, their heads hung low. "We thought you weren't coming..." Mrs. Kráner wavered and gave a forced smile. Irimiás looked at his watch and angrily tapped the glass. "It says six-forty-three. The watch is accurate." Barely audible Mrs. Kráner replied, "Yes, but ... but you said you'd come at night ..." Irimiás furrowed his brow. "What do you think I am, a taxi driver? I work my fingers to the bone for you, I don't sleep for three days, I walk for hours in the rain, I rush from one meeting to another to overcome various obstacles, while you ...?!" He took a step toward them, cast an eye at their makeshift beds then stopped in front of Futaki. "What happened to you?" Futaki hung his head in shame. "I got a nosebleed." "I can see that. But how?" Futaki made no answer. "See here ...," Irimiás gave a sigh, "this isn't what I expected of you, friends. From any of you!" he continued, turning to the others. "If this is how you start what do you think you are going to do next? Stabbing each other? Shut up ...," he waved away Kráner who wanted to say something, "I'm not interested in the details! I've seen quite enough. It's sad, I can tell you, pretty damn sad!" He walked up and down in front of them with a grave face then, when he had returned to his original spot at the entrance, he turned around to face them again. "Look, I have no idea what exactly happened here. Nor do I want to know because time is too precious to spend it dealing with such piddling matters. But I won't forget. Least of all you, Futaki, my friend, I'll not forget you. But I will overlook it this time, on one condition—that it never happens again! Is that clear?!" He waited a moment, ran his hand across his brow and with a careworn expression continued: "All right, let's get down to business!" He drew deeply on the tiny remnant of his cigarette then threw it down and stamped on it. "I have some important news." It was as if they were just now emerging from some evil spell. They were sober at a stroke but they simply couldn't understand what had happened to them in the last few hours: What demonic power had taken possession of them, stifling every sane and rational impulse? What was it that had driven them to lose their heads and attack each other "like filthy pigs when the swill is late"? What made it possible for people like them—people who had finally managed to emerge from years of apparently terminal hopelessness to breathe the dizzying air of freedom—to rush around in senseless despair, like prisoners in a cage so that even their vision had clouded over? What explanation could there be for them to "have eyes" only for the ruinous, stinking, desolate aspect of their future home, and completely lose track of the promise that "what had fallen would rise again"! It was like waking from a nightmare. They formed a humble circle around Irimiás, more ashamed than relieved, because, in their unforgivable impatience, they had all doubted the one man who could save them, a man who, even if he had been delayed a few brief hours, had after all kept his promise, and to whom they had every reason to be grateful; and the agonizing sense of shame was only increased by the knowledge that he had not the least idea how far they had doubted him and taken his name in vain, accusing him of all kinds of crimes, he who had "risked his life" for them and who now was standing among them as living proof of the falseness of their allegations. And so, with this extra load on their conscience, they listened to him with a greater and still more unshakable confidence, and were enthusiastically nodding even before they knew what he was talking about, especially Kráner and Schmidt who were particularly aware of the gravity of their sins, although the "changed, less favorable circumstances" Irimiás now referred to might well have soured their mood, since it turned out that "our plans for Almássy Manor have to be suspended for an indefinite period" because certain groups "wouldn't take" to a project with an "as yet unclear purpose" being established here, and had objected particularly, as they learned from Irimiás, to the considerable distance between the manor and the town that made getting to the "manor" all but impractical for them, which in turn reduced the prospect of regular inspections to less than the required bare minimum ... "Given this situation," Irimiás continued, sweating a little but still resonant, "the only possibility of bringing our plans to a successful conclusion, the only possible way forward, is for us to disperse into various parts of the country until these gentlemen entirely lose track of us, at which point we can return here and set about realizing our original objectives." ... They acknowledged their "particular importance in the scheme of things" with a growing sense of pride, especially prizing their privilege in being considered "the chosen few" while appreciating the recognition of their qualities of steadfastness, industry and increasing vigilance that were considered, apparently, quite indispensable. And if some aspects of the scheme lay beyond them (especially phrases like "our goal points to something beyond itself") it was immediately clear to them that their dispersal was just "a strategic ploy" and that even if they were to have no contact with each other for a while they would continue to be in lively, continual communication with Irimiás ... "Not that anyone should think," the master raised his voice, "that we can just sit and wait for things to improve by themselves during this time!" They registered, with an astonishment that quickly passed, that their task was to be the unceasing, vigilant observation of their immediate surroundings, meaning that they should rigorously note down all opinions, rumors and events which "from the perspective of our agreement might be of the utmost importance" and that they should all develop the indispensable skill of distinguishing between favorable and unfavorable signs, or, to put it in plain language, "knowing the good from the bad," because he—Irimiás—sincerely hoped that no one would seriously think it possible to take a single step forward down the path he had revealed to them in such painstaking detail without it . . . So when Schmidt asked "And what will we live on in the meanwhile?" and Irimiás assured them, "Relax, everyone, relax: it's all planned, all thought through, you will all have jobs, and to begin with you will be able to draw on basic survival funds out of mutual, accumulated funds," the last traces of their early morning panic vanished at a stroke and all that remained for them was to pack up their belongings and take them down to the end of the path where an idling truck was waiting for them on the metaled road . . . So they did pack up again in a feverish hurry and, after a little awkwardness, started chatting to each other as if nothing had happened, Halics setting the best example who, with a bag or suitcase in his hand, would follow now the bearlike Kráner, now the striding, manly figure of his wife, sneaking behind them like a monkey, imitating them, and who, once he had finished his own packing, carried the luggage of the uncertainly swaying Futaki over to the road, remarking only that "a friend in need is a friend indeed . . ." By the time they had succeeded in bringing everything down to the side of the road, the "kid" had managed to turn the truck around (Irimiás had, after long pleadings, relented and allowed him a go at the wheel), so there was nothing left after that than to take a brief silent look of farewell at the "manor" that was to be their future, and to take their places on the open truck. "So, my dear companions," Petrina stuck his head through the passenger's window. "Please arrange yourselves so that this dizzyingly fast miracle of transport might get us to our destination in at least two hours! Button your coats, on with your hoods and hats, hold on tight, and feel free to turn your back on the great hope of your future because if you don't you'll get the full force of this filthy rain in your faces . . ." The baggage took up a good half of the open truck so the only way they could all fit in was by huddling close to each other in two

239

rows, and it was no surprise that, when Irimiás revved the engine and the truck juddered and started back toward the town, they felt just the same enthusiasm for the warmth of "the unbreakable bond between them" as had sweetened their memorable journey the day before. Kráner and Schmidt were particularly loud in their determination never again to give vent to idiotic rages and to declare that, if there should be any future disagreement, they would be the first to put an immediate stop to it. Schmidt—who had tried in the midst of all this merry badinage to signal to Futaki to indicate that "he deeply regretted what he had done" (partly because he had somehow failed to "bump into him" along the path, but partly because he lacked the necessary courage)—had only now decided to offer him "at least a cigarette" but found himself jammed in between Halics and Mrs. Kráner, both of whom were immovable. "Never mind," he reassured himself, "I'll get around to it when we get off this damn wreck ... we can't part in anger like this!" Mrs. Schmidt's face was flushed, her eyes sparkling, as she watched the rapidly receding manor, that enormous building covered in weeds and rampant ivy, its four miserable towers extending at the corners, while the metaled road, billowing with ridges behind them, vanished into infinity, and her relief at the return of her "darling" so excited her that she didn't notice the wind and rain beating her face, though she had no protection against any of it however she pulled the hood over her head, because in the great confusing mêlée she found herself at the end of the rear row. There could be no doubt, nor did she feel any; nothing now could shake her faith in Irimiás. It was not like before because here, on the back of the speeding truck, she understood her future: that she would follow him like a strange dreamlike shadow, now as his lover, now as his maid, in absolute poverty if necessary, and in this way she would be reborn time after time; she would learn his every movement, the secret meaning of each distinct modulation of his voice, would interpret his dreams and should—God forbid!—any

harm befall him, hers would be the lap in which he would lay his head
... And she would learn to be patient and wait, to prepare herself for
any ordeal, and if fate decreed that Irimiás left her for good one day—
for what else could he do?—she would spend her remaining days quietly, knit her shroud and go to her grave with pride knowing that it had
once been given her to have "a great man, a real man" as her lover ...
Not were there any bounds to the good cheer of Halics, who was
squashed up beside her: not rain, not wind, not the bumpy ride, no
discomfort of any kind could deflate him: his corn-hardened feet were
flat and frozen in his boots, the water on top of the driver's cabin occasionally slopped down the back of his neck and powerful gusts of
wind from the side of the truck brought out tears, but he was cheered,
not only by the return of Irimiás, but by the sheer delight of traveling
for, as he had said often enough in the past, "he could never resist the
intoxicating pleasure of speed," and here was his big chance to enjoy it,
now, while Irimiás, ignoring all the dangerous potholes and ditches
along the road, had his foot on the gas right down to the floor, so whenever Halics was able to open his eyes, even if ever so slightly, he was
thrilled to see the landscape rushing by at dizzying speed, and he
quickly formed a plan, because it wasn't too late, in fact it was a very
good time, to make one of his long-cherished dreams come true, and
already he was seeking the right words to convince Irimiás to help him
realize it, when suddenly it occurred to him that the driver was obliged
to reject opportunities that he—alas!—"granted his old age" found
irresistible ... So he decided simply to enjoy the pleasures of the journey as far as he could so that later, over a friendly glass, he could conjure every detail to his prospective new friends, because simply imagining it as he had so far was "as nothing to the real experience ..." Mrs.
Halics was the only one who found nothing to enjoy in "this insane
rush" since, unlike her husband, she was firmly set against any kind of
new foolishness, and because she was pretty sure that if they carried on

this way they would all break their necks, and so she closed her hands, praying fearfully to the Good Lord to protect them all and not to desert them at this hour of danger, but however hard she tried to convince the others to do the same ("In the name of Our Savior, Jesus Christ please tell this lunatic to slow down just a little!") they didn't "give a hoot" either about the wild speed or her terrified mutterings, on the contrary, they "seemed to find pleasure in the danger!" The Kráners, and even the headmaster, were childishly exhilarated, proudly braced against the back of the truck squinting like lords at the barren landscape flying past them. It was exactly as they had imagined the journey, as fast as the wind, at mind-numbing speed, passing every obstacle—utterly invincible! They were proud to see the landscape vanish in a haze, proud that they could leave it behind, not like miserable beggars but—behold!—with heads held high, full of confidence, on a triumphant note ... Their only regret, as they rumbled past the old estate and reached the road-mender's house on the long bend, was that in their hurry they didn't get a glimpse of the Horgos family, or of blind Kerekes or of the landlord, his face purple with jealousy ... Futaki carefully tapped his swollen nose and considered himself lucky to have "got away" with nothing worse, not having dared to touch it at all until the sharp pain had completely gone, so he couldn't know whether it was broken or not. He was still not quite in control of his senses, and felt dizzy and faintly nauseous. His mind confused images of Schmidt's twisted scarlet face and Kráner behind him, ready to leap, with the stern gaze of Irimiás, a gaze that seemed to be burning him up. As the pain in his nose faded he slowly became aware of other injuries: he had lost part of an incisor, the skin on his lower lip was broken. He could hardly hear the consoling words of the headmaster crushed up next to him—"You shouldn't take it too much to heart. As you see, it has all turned out for the best ..."—because his ears were ringing and the pain made him turn his head this way and that, not knowing where to spit the salty blood still left in his mouth, and he only started feeling a little better when he caught a flash of the deserted mill and the sagging roof of Halics's house, but however he twisted and turned he still couldn't see the engine house because by the time he had got into position the truck was passing the bar. He cast a sly look at the squatting figure of Schmidt then confessed to himself that, however strange it sounded, he felt absolutely no anger toward him; he knew the man well and had always known how quick his temper was, and so—before any thought of revenge could occur to him—having wholeheartedly forgiven him, he decided to reassure him at the earliest opportunity because he could guess his state of mind. He watched the trees rushing past him on either side of the road with a certain sadness, feeling that whatever had happened in the "manor" simply had had to happen. The noise, the whistling wind and the rain that from time to time hit them from the side eventually drew his attention away from Schmidt and from Irimiás too for a while. With great difficulty he dragged out a cigarette and, by leaning forward and covering the match with his palm, eventually succeeded in lighting it. They had left the estate and bar a long way behind now and he judged that they could be only a few hundred yards from the electric generator, and therefore only about half an hour from town. He noted how proudly and enthusiastically the headmaster and Kráner, who was sitting immediately next to him, were turning their heads this way and that as if nothing had happened, as if all that had happened at the manor was hardly worth remembering and could rapidly be forgotten. He, on the other hand, was by no means sure that the arrival of Irimiás had solved all their problems. And while the sight of him standing in the doorway had changed everything for them while they were in despair, the whole mad scramble after it, and now this strange dash along a deserted highway, was not for Futaki any kind of proof that the rush was to some specific place; it seemed to him more like a kind of stampede, a "blind and uncertain rush into the unknown" that was somehow pointless: they had not the least idea what was waiting for them, that's if they ever stopped. There was something ominous about having no clue what Irimiás was planning: he could not guess why they were in such a panic to leave the manor. For a brief moment he recalled a terrifying image he hadn't been able to forget, not in all these years: once again he saw himself in his old tattered coat, leaning on his stick, hungry and infinitely disappointed, trudging down the metaled road, the estate fading into the dusk behind him, the horizon in front of him still far from clear ... And now, numbed by the rattling truck, his premonition seemed to be coming true: penniless, hungry, and broken in body, here he was, sitting in the back of a truck that had turned up out of the blue, on a road that led God knows where, heading into the unknown, and should they come to a fork in that road, he couldn't begin to decide which road to take because he was helpless, resigned to the fact that his fate was being decided elsewhere, by a noisy, rattling, ancient wreck of a truck over which he had absolutely no control. "It seems there's no escape," he reflected in apathy. "This way or that, I'm lost either way. Tomorrow I'll wake in an unfamiliar room where I won't know what's waiting for me, and it will be as if I had set out on my own ... I'll put my minimal possessions out on the table by the bed, if there is one, and there I am, staring out of the window at dusk watching the light fade all over again ..." It shocked him to realize that his faith in Irimiás had been shaken the moment he saw him at the "manor" entrance ... "Maybe, if he hadn't come back, there might still have been some hope ... But now?" Right back at the manor he had sensed the well-concealed disappointment behind the words, and saw, even as Irimiás was standing by the truck watching them loading up, how he was hanging his head, and that something was lost, lost forever! ... Now suddenly everything was clear. Irimiás lacked the strength and energy he once had; he had finally lost "his old fire"; he too was just filling in time, driven along by habit; and, realizing this,

Futaki now understood that the speech at the bar with its clumsy rhetorical tricks was simply a way of concealing from those who still believed in Irimiás the truth that he was as helpless as they were, that he no longer hoped to lend meaning to the power that was strangling him as much as it was them, that even he, Irimiás, could not free himself from it. His nose was pulsing with pain, his nausea refused to pass and even a cigarette did not help, so he threw it away without finishing it. They crossed the bridge over "the Stinker," a water stagnant with weeds and frogspawn, lying perfectly still, the roadside ever denser with acacia, and there were even one or two abandoned farm buildings in the distance, surrounded by trees. The rain had stopped but the wind was buffeting them ever more violently and they were worried in case baggage was blown off the top of the pile. For the time being there was neither sight nor sound of humanity and to their astonishment they met no one at all, not even when turning off at the Elek fork on the road leading into town. "What's with this place?" yelled Kráner. "They got rabies?" It reassured them to see two figures in raincoats swaying with their arms around each other by the entrance of The Scales, then they turned down the road leading to the main square, their eyes thirstily drinking in the low level houses, the drawn blinds, the fancy drains and the carved wooden entrances: it was like leaving prison. By now, of course, time was simply rushing by and before they could take it all in the truck braked right in the middle of the wide square in front of the station. "OK, folks!" Petrina stuck his head out of the cabin window and shouted. "End of the sightseeing tour!" "Wait!" Irimiás stopped them as they were preparing to get off, and left the driver's seat. "Just the Schmidts. Then the Kráners and the Halicses. Get your things together! You, Futaki, and you, Mr. Headmaster, wait here!" He led them with firm decisive steps, the herd after him struggling with their baggage. They entered the waiting room, piled the baggage in a corner and stood around Irimiás. "There's time enough to talk things over calmly. Are you very frozen?" "We'll be snoring to-night like nobody's business," sniggered Mrs. Kráner. "Is there a pub round here? I could do with a drink!" "Sure there is," Irimiás answered and looked at his watch. "Come with me." The waiting room was practically empty except for a railwayman leaning on a rickety counter. "Schmidt!" Irimiás spoke up once they'd downed a glass of *pálinka*. "You and your wife are going to Elek." He brought out his wallet and found a piece of paper that he pressed into Schmidt's hand. "It's all written down there, who you look for, what street, what number and so on. Tell them I sent you. Is that clear?" "It's clear," nodded Schmidt. "Tell them I'll be along in a few days to check up. In the meantime they are to give you work, food and rooms. Understand?" "I understand. But who is this person? What's the deal?" "The man's a butcher," said Irimiás, pointing to the paper. "There's plenty of work there. You, Mrs. Schmidt, you'll be on the counter, serving. And you, Schmidt, you're there to help generally. I trust you can manage this." "You bet your life we can," Schmidt enthused. "Fine. The train comes in at, let's see ..." and he looked at his watch again, "yes, in about twenty minutes." He turned to the Kráners. "You'll find work at Keresztúr. I haven't written it all down so make sure it's engraved on your memory. The man you want is called Kálmár, István Kálmár. I don't know the name of the street but go to the Catholic church—there's only one so you can't miss it—and to the right of the church there is a street ... are you remembering all this? You go down that street until you see a sign on your right saying Women's Tailoring. That's Kálmár's place. Tell them Dönci sent you, and make sure you remember that because they might not remember my usual name. Tell them you need work, accommodation and food. Immediately. There is a laundry room at the back where you are to sleep. Got that?" "Got it," clucked Mrs. Kráner brightly. "Church, road on right, look for sign. No problem." "I like that," smiled Irimiás and turned to the Halicses. "You two will get on the bus to

Póstelek: the stop is in front of the station in the square. Once in Póstelek you find the Evangelical rectory and look for Dean Gyivicsan. You won't forget?" "Gyivicsan," Mrs. Halics enthusiastically repeated. "Correct. You tell him I sent you. He's been after me for years to get him two people, and I can't think of anyone better than you. There's plenty of room there, you can take your pick, and there's consecrated wine as well, Halics. As for you, Mrs. Halics, you will clean the church, cook for three and look after the housekeeping." The Halicses were quite overcome with joy. "How can we possibly thank you?" Mrs. Halics declared, her eyes filling with tears. "You've done everything for us!" "Come, come," Irimiás waved her away. "There'll be time enough to be grateful. Now all of you, listen to me. To start with, before things settle down, you'll get a thousand forints each from the communal chest. Look after it well, don't waste it! Don't forget what it is that binds us! Never forget, not for one minute, what it is you're there to do. You must observe everything carefully in Elek, in Póstelek and in Keresztúr, because without that we won't get anywhere! In a few days I will visit all three places and look you up. Then we'll go into proper detail. Any questions?" Kráner cleared his throat: "I think we understand everything. But might I formally ... I mean ... in other words ... we'd like to thank you for ... everything you've done ... for us, since ..." Irimiás raised his hand. "No, friends. No gratitude. It's my duty. And now," he stood up, "it's time for us to part. I have a thousand things to do ... Important negotiations ..." Halics, deeply moved, leapt over and shook his hand. "Look after yourself," he muttered: "You know we care about you! We want you hale and hearty!" "Don't worry about me," smiled Irimiás, moving toward the exit: "You look after yourselves, and don't forget: constant vigilance!" He stepped through the station doors, went over to the truck and gestured to the headmaster, "Listen! We'll drop you at Streber Street. Go and sit in The Ipar and I'll come back for you in about an hour. We'll talk more then. Where's Futaki?" Here

I am," Futaki replied, stepping out from the other side of the vehicle. "You . . ." Futaki raised a hand. "Don't bother with me." Irimiás looked shocked. "What's wrong with you?" "With me? Nothing at all. But I know where to go. Someone is bound to offer me a job as a night watchman." Irimiás was irritated. "You're always so stubborn. There are better places for you, but fine, do what you want. Go to Nagyromán-város, the old Romanian quarter, and there next to The Golden Tri-angle—you know where that is?—there's a building. They're looking for a night watchman there—they'll give you a room too. Here is a thousand forints to be getting on with. Get yourself some dinner. I suggest the Steigerwald, it's within spitting distance. They have food there." "Thank you. You like the idea of spitting?" Irimiás made a face: "It's impossible to talk to you at the moment. Get your stuff. Be at the Steigerwald tonight. All right?" He extended his hand. Futaki accepted it uncertainly, gripped the money with his other hand, took his stick and set off toward Csokos Street, leaving Irimiás standing by the truck without a word. "Your baggage!" Petrina shouted after him from the driver's cab, then leapt out and helped Futaki get his luggage on his back. "Isn't that heavy?" the headmaster asked, feeling awkward, then quickly put out his hand. "Not too bad," Futaki quietly answered: "See you." He set off again with Irimiás, Petrina, the headmaster and the "kid" staring puzzled after him, but then they got back in the truck, the headmaster in the back and started back into the town center. Futaki was making halting progress, feeling close to collapse under the weight of his cases, and when he reached the first crossroad he dropped them, loosened the straps and, after a little thought, threw one of them into the ditch and went on with the other. He wandered aimlessly down street after street, from time to time putting his suitcase down so as to get his wind back, then off he went again with a bitter feeling . . . If he met anyone he would hang his head because he felt that if he looked into the stranger's eyes his own misfortune would seem even worse. He was after all a lost cause ... "And how stupid! How steadfast, how full of hope I was yesterday! And now look at me! Here I am stumbling down the street with a broken nose, cracked teeth, a cut on my lip, muddied and bloody as if this was the price I had to pay for my stupidity ... But then ... there's no justice in anything ... no justice ...," he kept repeating in a perpetual melancholy that remained with him that evening when he turned on the light in one of the sheds of the building next to The Golden Triangle, and noted his distorted image in the glass of a dirty window. He had a vacant look. "That Futaki is the biggest idiot I've ever met," Petrina noted as they drove up the street leading to the town center. "What's got into him? Did he think this was the Promised Land? What the devil does he think he's doing?! Did you see the face he made? With that swollen nose?!" "Shut up, Petrina," grumbled Irimiás. "You keep talking like that you'll get a swollen nose too." The "kid" behind them whooped with laughter, "What's up Petrina, has the cat got your tongue?" "Me?!" Petrina snarled back. "You think I'm scared of anyone?!" "Shut up, Petrina," Irimiás repeated in irritation: "Don't mumble at me. If you have anything to say spit it out." Petrina grinned and scratched his head. "Well boss, if you're asking ...," he started cautiously. "It's not that I have any doubts, believe me, but why do we need Páyer?" Irimiás bit his lip, slowed down, allowed an old woman to cross the road then stepped on the gas. "Stay out of grown-up business," he grunted. "I'd just like to know. Why do we need him? ..." Furious, Irimiás looked straight ahead. "We just do!" "I know boss, but guns and explosives ... really?!..." "We just do!" Irimiás shouted at him. "You really want to blow up the world and us with it ...?" Petrina spluttered with a terrified look: "You just want rid of things, don't you?" Irimiás didn't answer. He braked. They had stopped in Streber Street. The headmaster jumped off the back of the truck, waved goodbye to the driver's cab, then, with firm steps, crossed the road and opened the doors of The Ipar. "It's after eight-thirty. What will they say?" the "kid" wondered. Petrina waved him away. "The damn Captain can go to hell! What does it mean to be late? 'Late' means nothing to me! He should be pleased we are seeing him at all! It's an honour when Petrina comes to call! Understand, kid? Remember that because I won't say it again!" "Ha ha!" the "kid" mocked him and blew smoke in Petrina's face: "What a joke!" "Get it into your thick head that jokes are just like life," Petrina grandly declared: "Things that begin badly, end badly. Everything's fine in the middle, it's the end you need to worry about." Irimiás was looking up the road, not saying anything. He felt no pride now that it was all settled. His eyes stared dully ahead, his face was gray. He gripped the steering wheel tightly, a vein was pounding in his temple. He saw the neat houses on either side of the street. The gardens. The crooked gates. The chimneys belching smoke. He felt neither hatred nor disgust. His head was clear.

II

NOTHING BUT WORK
AND WORRIES

The document, having been corrected at eight-fifteen, was handed over to the clerks for the preparation of the draft a few minutes later, and the problem seemed all but insoluble. But they showed neither surprise nor anger, nor did they complain, not in the least: they simply looked at each other in silence as if to say—you see! the latest, undoubtedly convincing evidence of the tragically rapid general decline. It was enough to glance at the sloping lines and scratchy hand to see that the work before them was quite clearly an essay in the impossible because, once again, they had to bring some clarity, some fitting intelligible order to this "depressingly crude scrawl." The incomprehensibly short time at their disposal combined with the distant prospect of producing a usable document made them feel tense and yet urged them on to a heroic effort. Only "the experience and maturity of long years; the years of practice that demand respect" explained how they were able to detach themselves in a moment from the maddening racket of their colleagues dashing around and chattering—so that in a matter of moments they could focus their entire attention on the document. They soon got through the opening sentences where they only had to clear up a few common ambiguities, those clumsy attempts at subtlety that clearly betrayed a layman's touch, so the first part of the text might be said to have passed fairly smoothly into a "final draft." *Though only yesterday I stressed, several times, that I regard the writing down of such information as unfortunate, in order that he should see my willingness—and, naturally, as proof of my faultless devotion to the matter in hand—I am prepared to carry out his commission. In my report I take particular note of the fact that you have encouraged me to be strictly honest. At this point I should remark that there can be no doubt about the suitability of my workforce, and I hope to convince you of that tomorrow. I consider it important to repeat this only because it is possible for you to read the following improvised draft in ways other than intended. I particularly draw your attention to the condition that in order for my work to continue and to have a functioning basis it is vital that I alone should be in contact with my workforce, and that any other approach will lead to failure ... etc. etc. ...* But as soon as the clerks got to the part relating to Mrs. Schmidt, they immediately found themselves in the deepest difficulty, because they didn't know how to formulate such vulgar expressions as *stupid*, *big-mouth* and *cow*—how to retain the import of these crude concepts so that the document should be true to itself while at the same time retaining the language of their profession. After some discussion they settled on "intellectually weak female person primarily concerned with her sexuality" but they hardly had time to draw breath because next they came across the expression *cheap whore* in all its awful attendant crudity. For lack of precision they had to abandon the idea of "a female person of dubious reputation," of "a woman of the demimonde" and "a painted woman" and a mass of other euphemisms that seemed alluringly attractive at first glance; they drummed impatient fingers on the writing desk across which they faced each other, painfully avoiding each other's eyes, finally settling on the formula "a woman who offers her body freely," which was not perfect but would have to do. The first part of the next sentence was no easier but with a handy flash of insight they took the dreadfully colloquial *she hopped into bed with any Tom,*

Dick or Harry, and it was a matter of pure chance if she didn't and turned it into the relatively useful "she was the epitome of infidelity in marriage." To their genuine surprise they found three sentences one after the other that they could type up as the official version without any change, but after that they immediately hit another difficulty. However they racked their brains, however they lobbed potentially useful phrases back and forth, they couldn't find anything suitable for *the haunting compost smell that rose from her like a blend of cheap cologne and something rotting* and were on the point of giving up and passing the job back to the Captain on the excuse that there was something urgent waiting at the office when a shyly smiling old typist lady brought them cups of steaming black coffee and the pleasant scent calmed them a little. They started thinking again, considering new variants when— avoiding another stab of terror—they agreed not to torture themselves any longer but settle on "she tried unconventional means of covering up the unpleasant smell of her body." "It's dreadful the way time flies," said one to the other when they finally managed to finish the part referring to Mrs. Schmidt, the other man glancing with concern at his watch: too true, too true, there was only a little over an hour left before lunch. So they decided to try and deal with what remained at a slightly quicker pace, which in fact meant nothing more than that they tended to agree on less satisfactory solutions more readily than they had before, "though it's only fair to say that the results were at the same time, far from hopeless." They were delighted to observe that using this new method they got through the Mrs. Kráner parts much quicker. *That foul old bag of poisonous gossip* became the more reassuring "a transmitter of unreliable information" and the phrases *seriously, someone should think about sewing her lips together* and *fat slut* were solved without undue difficulty. It was a special joy to them that there were sentences they could simply lift and use in the official version and they started to breathe more easily when they reached the end of the text about Mrs.

Halics because the person here—charged with religious fanaticism
and certain peculiar traits—was characterized by certain old slang expressions that were child's play to translate. But on seeing the parts
relating to her husband, Halics, a passage full of horrifying obscenities,
they realized that the greatest difficulties still lay ahead, for whenever
they thought they could see through the dense texture of the witness
testimony they had to admit that, having finally reached the limits of
their combined talent for re-invention, they were utterly stumped once
again. Because while they could just about manage turning *wrinkled
drink-sodden dwarf* into the simple "elderly alcoholic of small stature"
they had—shame or no shame—no idea where to start with *stuttering
buffoon,* or *utterly leaden,* or indeed *blindly bumbling;* and so after long
agonized discussion they silently decided to leave the terms out, chiefly
because they suspected the Captain wouldn't have the patience to read
right through the whole document and that it would therefore find its
way—in a properly regular way—into the files anyway. They leaned
back in their chairs, exhausted, rubbing their eyes, annoyed to see their
colleagues chattering and preparing for lunch, making some minimal
order in their files, slipping into carefree conversation with each other,
carrying on, washing their hands and a few minutes later leaving in
twos and threes through the door leading into the entrance hall. They
gave a sad sigh and, admitting that lunch would be "something of a
luxury now," took out buttered rolls and dry cookies and started
munching them while getting on with the job. But as luck would have
it even this minimal pleasure was denied to them—the food lost its
flavor and chewing became a form of torture—because when they en-
countered the file on Schmidt it was clear they had arrived at a new
level of difficulty; the obscurity, incomprehensibility, and carelessness,
the conscious or unconscious attempt to blur everything they had to
sort out, amounted to what they agreed was "a slap in the face to their
professionalism, industry and struggle" ... Because what did it mean

to say that something represented *a cross between primitive insensitivity and chillingly inane emptiness in a bottomless pit of unbridled dark*?! What sort of crime against language was this foul nest of mixed metaphors?! Where was even the faintest trace of striving for intellectual clarity and precision so natural—allegedly!—to the human spirit?! To their greatest horror the whole passage about Schmidt consisted of sentences like this and, what was more, from now on the witness's handwriting, for some inexplicable reason, became simply illegible, as if the writer had grown progressively more drunk ... Again they were on the point of giving up and resigning because "it's really dreadful the way, day after day, people put such impossible stuff in front of us, and what thanks do we get?!" when—as once already that day, the delicious smell of coffee, delivered with a smile, persuaded them to reconsider. So they set about excising phrases such as *incurable stupidity, inarticulate complaint, irreconcilable anxiety petrified in the dense darkness of a reduced inconsolable existence*, and other such monstrosities, until, having reached the end of the character testimony but still wincing with pain, they discovered that all that remained untouched were a few conjunctions and two predicates. And because it was clearly hopeless trying to resolve the actual contents of what the witness had intended to say they took the cavalier course of reducing the whole febrile mishmash to a single, sane sentence: "His limited intellectual capacity and his tendency to cower before any display of strength makes him peculiarly suitable for the carrying out, at the highest level, of the act in question." The passage relating to the unnamed personage known simply as the headmaster was no clearer, in fact it seemed even more obscure, if that was possible: the confusion worse, the infuriating attempts at subtlety still more infuriating. "It seems," one of the clerks noted with a pale face, shaking his head and pointing to a dirty scrap of paper for the benefit of his tired colleague slumped behind the typewriter, "it looks as though the half-wit has completely gone off his head here. Listen to this!" And he read the first sentence. *Should anyone contemplating the advisability of leaping off a high bridge be in any doubt or prone to any hesitation, I advise him to consider the headmaster: once he has considered this ridiculous figure he will immediately know that there is simply no alternative but to jump!* Incredulous and exhausted, they stared at each other, their faces reflecting their utter exasperation. What is this! Do they want to ridicule us out of a job?! The clerk slumped at the typewriter gestured silently to his colleague as if to say, leave it, it's not worth it, there's nothing anyone can do, just carry on. *And as concerns his appearance he looks like a scrawny, dry cucumber left too long in the sun, his intellectual capacity below even that of Schmidt, which is truly saying something* ... "Let's write," the one by the typewriter suggested, "of worn appearance, lacking ability..." His colleague clicked his tongue, annoyed. "How do the two statements relate to each other?" "How should I know? What can I do about it?" the other snapped back. "It's what he wrote and we have to convey the content ..." "Oh, all right," his colleague replied. "I'll go on." ... *he deals with his cowardice through self-flattery, hollow pride, and enough stupidity to give you a heart attack. Like all self-respecting jerk-offs, he tends to sentimentality, and clumsy pathos, etc., etc.* Given all this it was plain that there was no point in seeking compromise, they had to make do with half-solutions, and, occasionally worse, with work unbefitting their calling, and so, after another long discussion they agreed on: "Cowardly. Of sensitive disposition. Sexually immature." Having dealt so brutally with the headmaster, they couldn't deny that their troubled consciences were slowly turning into fiery pits of guilt, so they approached the Kráner section with their hearts in their mouths, both of them growing ever more irritable as they saw how quickly the time was passing. One pointed furiously at his watch and indicated the rest of the office: the other just made a helpless gesture because he too had noticed the general sense of movement that suggested there were only a few minutes of official work time left. "Could it be possible?" he shook his head. "A man is just getting down to a job when the bell rings. I don't understand. The days fly by in a constant whirl..." And by the time they had converted the annoying phrase *a chump who puts one in mind of nothing so much as a slovenly ox* to "a powerfully built ex-blacksmith" and found an acceptable equivalent for *a dusky slob with an idiotic expression, a danger to the public,* all their colleagues had gone home and they had had to accept various mocking farewells, and signs of mock appreciation without a word because they knew that if they stopped working for just one moment they would be tempted to give vent to their anger and declare to hell with it!—with all the serious consequences that entailed. Around about half past five, as they painfully finished the final draft of the Kráner section, they allowed themselves a minute's cigarette break. They stretched their numbed limbs, grunting, they rubbed their sore shoulders and smoked the cigarettes through without a word, "All right, let's get on with it," said one. "Listen. I'll read." *The only one who presents any danger is Futaki,* the text began. *Nothing serious though. His tendency to rebel only means that he is all the more likely to shit himself eventually. He could add up to something but can't free himself of his stubbornly held beliefs. He amuses me and I'm sure we can count on him more than anyone ...* etc., etc. "OK, write this," the first clerk dictated. "He is dangerous but useful. More intelligent than the others. Disabled." "Is that it?" the other sighed. "Put his name down there. At the bottom. What does it say?... mmm, Irimiás." "What was that?" "I'll say it slowly: I-ri-mi-ás. Are you hard of hearing?" "Shall I write it just like tha—?" "Yes, like that! How else would you write it!" They put the file away in the folder, then slipped all the dossiers into the appropriate drawers, carefully locked them, then hung the keys on the board by the exit. They put their coats on without speaking and closed the door behind them. Downstairs by the gate, they shook hands. "How are you getting home?" By bus." "OK. See you," said the first clerk. "Pretty good day's work, eh?" the other remarked. "That? To hell with it." "If only once they'd notice how much work we put into it," the first grumbled. "But nothing." "Never a word of appreciation," the other shook his head. They shook hands again and parted and when they eventually got home both were asked the same thing on their arrival. "Did you have a good day at the office, darling?" To which they responded, tired—for what else could they have said, shivering in the warm room—"Nothing special. Just the usual, sweetheart ..."

I

THE CIRCLE CLOSES

The doctor put on his glasses and stubbed out the cigarette that had burned practically down to his nails on an arm of his armchair, then, checking that the estate was all right by looking through the gap between the curtains and the window frame ("Everything normal," he noted, meaning nothing had changed) he measured out his permitted quantity of *pálinka* and added some water to it. The question of the level, a question that needed to be resolved to maximum satisfaction, had required careful consideration ever since his arrival back home: the balance between water and *pálinka*, however tricky the problem, had to be referred to the advice of the hospital chief who, rather tiresomely, tended to repeat his clearly exaggerated warnings (as in, "If you don't stay away from alcohol and if you don't radically reduce the number of cigarettes you smoke you'd better prepare yourself right now for the worst and call a priest ...") so, after an agonizing internal struggle, he abandoned the "two-parts-liquor, one-part-water" formula and resigned himself to "one-part-liquor-to-three-parts-water." He drank slowly, drop by tiny drop and, now that he was over the undoubtedly agonizing "transitional readjustment period," he decided that he could get used to even this "infernal slop," and considering how he had spat the first taste of it straight out in disgust, he could swallow the stuff now without any major shock to the system and, he thought, might even master the art of distinguishing between the varieties of this "dishwater" that were beyond redemption and others that were tolerable. He put the glass back in its place, quickly adjusted the matchbox that had slipped off the cigarette pack, then ran his eye over the "battle order" of demijohns behind the armchair with a certain satisfaction and decided that he was now ready to face the approach of winter. That had not been "such a simple matter," of course, two days before when they released him from hospital at "his own risk" and the ambulance finally entered the gates of the estate, when his ever-keener anxiety had turned to what could simply be described as outright fear, because he was almost sure that he'd have to start everything afresh: that he'd find his room in a mess, his possessions all over the place, and, what was more, at that moment he did not think it impossible that the "thoroughly disreputable" Mrs. Kráner might have made use of his absence to go through the whole house in the name of cleaning "with her filthy brooms and stinking wet rags," thereby destroying everything that had taken long years of enormous care, not to mention exhausting work, to assemble. His fears proved groundless however: the room was exactly as he had left it three weeks earlier, his notebooks, pencil, glass, matches and cigarettes precisely where they had to be, and, better still, he was mightily relieved to note that when the ambulance drew up outside the house, there was not one inquisitive face at the neighbors' windows, nor did any of them disturb him when the ambulance crew—thinking to get a handsome tip—carried his bags full of food and the demijohns he had replenished at Mopsz, into the house. Nor indeed had anyone had the courage to disturb his peace after that. He couldn't console himself with the thought that anything of consequence had actually happened to "these moronic nincompoops" in his absence, of course, and indeed he was forced to admit that there had been some very minor improvement: the estate looked deserted, there was none of the usual ridiculous scurrying around, and the constant seasonal rain that had set in, as it unavoidably had to, seemed to have kept them huddled in their hovels, so it was no surprise that no one stuck their heads out of doors, except Kerekes, whom he had spotted from the ambulance window two days ago as the man ambled along the path from the Horgos residence toward the metaled road, but even that was only for a brief second because he quickly turned his head away. "I hope to see neither hide nor hair of them till spring," he noted in his journal then carefully raised his pencil so as not to rip the paper which—and this was something else he noted after his long absence— had grown so damp that it took only one clumsy movement for it to tear. There was no particular reason to be uneasy then, since "a higher power" had kept his observation post intact, and nothing could be done about dust or the damp for he knew that there was "no point in getting worked up" about the inevitable process of decay. He reassured himself of this because he had felt a certain shock on seeing everything in the place covered with a fine layer of weeks-old dust on his return, noticing how the delicate strands of the cobwebs that hung off the picture rails had more or less met in the middle of the ceiling, but he had quickly regained his composure, considering such things as unimportant trifles, and hastily dismissed the ambulance man who was waxing sentimental in expectation of an "honorarium" for which he was clearly preparing to thank him. Once the man had gone, he had taken a turn around the room, and though in a rather preoccupied state of mind, he started to note the "degree and nature of neglect." He immediately dismissed the thought of cleaning as "ridiculously excessive," then, moreover, as "pointless," since, it was perfectly clear, that would be to wreck the very thing that might lead him to more precise observation; so he simply wiped the table and what was on it, gave some of the blankets a shake, then set straight to work, observing the state of things as compared to weeks ago, examining each individual object—the bare bulb in the ceiling lamp, the light switch, the floor, the walls, the collapsing wardrobe, the pile of trash by the door—and, as far as possible, tried to give an exact account of the changes. He spent the whole of that night and most of the next day hard at work and, apart from a few brief moments of snoozing, allowed himself no more than seven hours of sleep and that only once he thought he'd done an accurate job of stock-taking. When he finished he was delighted to observe that, considering his enforced break, his strength and stamina seemed not only undiminished but even a little increased; though, at the same time, it was no doubt true that his capacity to resist the effects of "anything out of the usual" had noticeably weakened, so while the blanket that kept slipping off his shoulder as it always did and the glasses that kept sliding down his nose did not in the least disturb him, the tiniest variance in his actual surroundings now demanded all his attention, and he could only recover his train of thought once he had dealt with various "annoying trifles" and restored "the original conditions." It was this neglect that made him, after two days' struggle, get rid of the alarm clock he had bought, albeit only after a thorough examination and a lot of bargaining, at the "secondhand" store in the hospital, with a view to strictly regulating the order in which he took his prescribed pills. He was simply unable to get used to its earsplitting ticktock, chiefly because his hands and feet naturally adapted to the clock's infernal rhythm, so that one day, when the contraption had delivered its terrifying alarm call precisely on time, and he found his head nodding along to the satanic thing, he took it and, trembling with fury, cast it into the yard. His calm was immediately restored and, having enjoyed a few hours of his all-but-lost silence, he couldn't understand why he hadn't decided on the deed earlier—yesterday or the day before. He lit a cigarette, blew out a long line of smoke, adjusted the blanket slipping off his shoulders, then leaned over his journal again and wrote, "Thank God, it's raining without interruption. It's the perfect defense. I feel tolerably well though still a little dull after all that sleep. No movement anywhere. The headmaster's door and window are broken: I can't begin to guess why, what has happened and why he doesn't repair them." He jerked his head up and listened intently to the silence, then the matchbox caught his attention because, just for a moment, he had a decided feeling that it was about to slip off the cigarette pack. He watched it and held his breath. But nothing happened. He mixed another drink, pressed the cork back into the demijohn, and topped up his glass from the jug of water on the table—he had bought the jug at Mopsz for thirty forints. Having done so, he pushed the jug into place and threw back the *pálinka*. It made him feel pleasantly woozy: his corpulent body relaxed under the blanket, his head tipped to one side, and his eyes slowly began to close, but his doze did not last long because he couldn't bear for longer than a minute the awful dream he immediately entered: a horse with bulging eyes was rushing at him and he was clutching a steel rod with which, terrified, he hit the horse's head with all his power, but having done so, however hard he tried he couldn't stop hitting it until he glimpsed within the cracked skull the slopping mass of the brain ... He woke up and took, from the orderly column next to the table, a notebook headed FUTAKI, and continued his observations there, noting, "He's too scared to come out of the engine house. Probably collapsed on his bed, snoring, or staring at the ceiling. Or tapping the bedstead with his crooked stick like a woodpecker, looking for deathwatch beetles. He has no idea that his actions will produce precisely what he most fears. See you at your funeral, you halfwit." He mixed another drink, threw it dourly back, then took his morning medicine with a gulp of water. In the remaining part of the day he twice—at noon and at dusk—took note of the "light conditions" outside, and made various sketches of the continually changing flow of the field's drainage, then, when he had just finished—having done the Schmidts and the Halicses—a description of the likely state of the Kráners' kitchen ("stuffy"), he suddenly heard a distant bell. He was sure he remembered, just before he went to hospital, in fact the day before he was taken in, hearing similar sounds, and was as sure now as he had been then that his sharp ears were not deceiving him. By the time he had leafed through to the diary notes he had made that day (though he found nothing there referring to it, so it must have slipped his mind or he didn't think it particularly important) it had all stopped ... This time he immediately recorded the extraordinary incident and carefully considered the various possible explanations for it: there was no church nearby, that much was certain, unless one regarded the long disused, ruined chapel on the Hochmeiss estate as a church, but the distance meant he had to exclude the possibility that the wind might have carried the sound. For a moment it occurred to him that Futaki, or maybe Halics or Kráner, might be playing some kind of joke but he rejected the idea because he couldn't imagine any of them being able to imitate the sound of a church bell ... But surely his educated ears couldn't be wrong! Or could they?... Was it possible that his highly developed faculties had become so sensitive that he really could hear a distant, slightly muffled ringing behind certain other faint but close sounds?... He sat puzzled in the silence, lit another cigarette and, nothing having happened in a long time, decided to forget the matter for now until some new sign appeared to point him to the right solution. He opened a can of baked beans, spooned out half of it, then pushed it away because his stomach was incapable of taking more than a few mouthfuls. He decided that he must stay awake because he couldn't know when the "bells" would start ringing again, and if they were audible for as brief a time as they'd just been, it would be enough to fall asleep for a few moments and he'd miss them ... He made another drink, took his evening medicine, then pushed the suitcase from under the table with his feet and took a long time picking a magazine from among the rest. He filled the time till dawn by leafing through and reading a little here and there but it was a pointless vigil, a hollow triumph over the desire to sleep, because the "bells" refused to ring again. He rose from the armchair and relaxed his stiff limbs by walking around a bit, then sat back again, and by the time the blue light of dawn surged through the window he had fallen fast asleep. He woke at noon, drenched in sweat and angry, as he always after a long sleep, cursing, turning his head this way and that, furious at the wasted time. He quickly put on his glasses, reread the last sentence in his journal then leaned back in the chair and looked through the chink in the curtain at the fields beyond. There was only a faint drip of rain but the sky was the usual dark gray as it glowered over the estate, the bare acacia in front of the Schmidts' place obediently bending before the strong wind. "They're dead, all of them," the doctor wrote. "Or they're sitting at the kitchen table leaning on their elbows. Not even a broken door and window can rouse the headmaster. Come winter he'll freeze his ass off." Suddenly he sat up straight in his chair as a new thought dawned on him. He raised his head and stared at the ceiling, gasping for breath, then gripped his pencil ... "Now he is standing up," he wrote in a deepening reverie, pressing the pencil lightly in case he tore the paper. "He scratches his groin and stretches. He walks around the room and sits down again. He goes out for a piss and returns. Sits down. Stands up." He scribbled feverishly and was practically seeing everything that was happening over there, and he *knew*, was deadly certain, that from then on this was how it would be. He realized that all those years of arduous, painstaking work had finally borne fruit: he had finally become the master of a singular art that enabled him not only to describe a world whose eternal unremitting progress in one direction required such mastery but also—to a certain extent—he could *even intervene* in the mechanism behind an apparently chaotic swirl of events! ... He rose from his observation post and, eyes burning, started to walk up and down from one corner of the narrow room to the other. He tried to keep control of himself but without success: the realization had come so unexpectedly, he was so unprepared for it, so much so that in those first few moments he even wondered if he had lost his mind . . . "Could it be? Am I going mad?" It took him a long time to calm down: his throat was dry, his heart was beating wildly and he was pouring with sweat. There was a moment he thought he'd simply burst, that he couldn't bear the weight of this responsibility; his enormous, obese body seemed to be running away with him. Out of breath, panting hard, he slumped back in his chair. There was so much to consider *all at once* all he could do was sit in the cold sharp light, his brain positively hurting with the confusion inside him . . . He carefully grasped the pencil, pulled out the SCHMIDT file from among the rest, opened it on the appropriate page, and uncertainly, like a man with good reason to fear *the serious consequences of his actions,* wrote the following sentence: "He is sitting with his back to the window, his body casting a pale shadow on the floor." He gave a great gulp, put down the pencil and, with trembling hands, mixed himself another *pálinka,* spilled half of it and downed the rest. "He has a red saucepan in his lap, containing spuds in paprika. He isn't eating. He isn't hungry. He needs a piss so he stands up, skirts the kitchen table, goes out to the yard and through the back door. He comes back. Sits down. Mrs. Schmidt asks him something? He doesn't answer. Using his feet, he pushes away the saucepan he had put down on the floor. He's not hungry." The doctor's hands were still trembling as he lit a cigarette. He wiped his perspiring brow then made airplane motions with his arms to let his armpits breathe. He adjusted the blanket across his shoulders and leaned over the journal again. "Either I've gone mad or, by God's mercy, this morning I have discovered that I am the wielder of mesmerizing power. I find I can control the flow of events around me using nothing more than words. Not that I have the least idea yet what to do. Or I have gone mad . . ." He lost confidence at this point. "It's all in my imagination," he grumbled to himself, then tried another experiment. He pulled out the notebook headed KRÁNER. He found the last entry and feverishly began to write again. "He is lying on his bed, fully clothed. His boots hang off the end of the bed because he doesn't want to muddy the bedding. It's stifling hot in the room. Out in the kitchen Mrs. Kráner is clattering dishes. Kráner calls her through the open door. Mrs. Kráner says something. Kráner angrily turns his back to the door and buries his head in the pillow. He is trying to sleep and closes his eyes. He is asleep." The doctor gave a nervous sigh, mixed another drink, and anxiously looked around the room. Scared, touched by an occasional doubt, he once again resolved: "There can be no doubt about the fact that by focused conceptualizing I can, to some degree, decide what should happen on the estate. Because only that which has been conceptualized can happen. It's just that, at this stage, of course, it is an utter mystery to me what I should make happen, because ..." At that moment the "bells" began to ring again. He only had time enough to decide he had not misheard last evening, he really did hear "sounds," but he had no opportunity to consider where the clanging noises were coming from because no sooner had they reached him than they were were absorbed in the permanent hum of silence and once the last bell died away he felt such emptiness in his soul he was sure he had lost something of deep value. What he thought he heard in these curious distant sounds was "the lost melody of hope," a kind of objectless encouragement, the perfectly incomprehensible words of a vital message, of which the only part he understood was that "it means something good, and offers some direction to my, as yet unresolved, power." ... He put an end to his feverish jottings, quickly put his coat on and stuffed cigarettes and matches into his pocket because he now felt it more important than ever to seek out, or at least try to seek out, the source of that distant ringing. The fresh air dizzied him at first: he rubbed his burning eyes, then—so as not to rouse the least attention of the neighbors at their windows—left by the gate leading to the back garden and, as far as possible, tried to hurry. Reaching the mill, he stopped dead for a moment because he had no idea whether he was heading in the right direction. He stepped through the enormous gates of the mill and heard yelping sounds from one of the upper stories. "The Horgos girls." He turned and left. He looked around not knowing where to go or what to do. Should he skirt the estate and set out toward the Szikes? ... Or should he go by the metaled road that led to the bar? Or maybe it was worth trying the road to Almássy Manor? Maybe he should just stay here in front of the mill in case "the bells" started again He lit a cigarette, cleared his throat, and because he really couldn't make up his mind one way or the other he nervously stamped his feet. He looked at the enormous acacias that surrounded the mill, shivered in the sharp wind, and wondered if it wasn't a stupid idea going out just like that, on the spur of the moment, whether he hadn't acted too precipitously, since, after all, a whole night had separated the two peals of bells. So why should he expect another so soon ... He was about to turn around and go home where there were warm blankets waiting for him until the next time, when, just at that moment, "the bells" started ringing again. He hurried over to the open space in front of the mill and by doing so managed to solve one mystery: "the bell sounds" seemed to be coming from the other side of the metaled road ("It could be the Hochmeiss estate!...") and it wasn't simply that he could now work out the direction but that he was now convinced the bells represented a call to action, or at least an encouragement, a promise; that they were not merely the products of a sick imagination, or a delusion produced by a sudden rush of emotion ... Enthusiastically, he set out for the metaled road, crossed it and, taking no notice of mud or puddles, made his way toward the Hochmeiss estate, his heart "buzzing with hope, expectation and confidence ..." He felt "the bells" were compensation for the miseries of his entire life, for all fate had inflicted on him, that they were a fitting reward for stubborn survival ... Once he succeeded in fully understanding the bells, everything would go well: with this power in his hands he would be able to lend a new, as yet unknown momentum "to human affairs." And so he felt an almost childish joy when, at the far end of the Hochmeiss estate, he glimpsed the little ruined chapel, and while he didn't know whether the chapel—it had been destroyed in the last war and had never shown the least sign of life since then—contained a "bell," or indeed anything else, he didn't think it beyond imagination that it might ... After all no one had been down this way for years, except perhaps some simpleminded tramp needing shelter for the night ... He stopped by the main door of the chapel and tried to open it but however he wrenched and struggled, using his whole body weight, it wouldn't budge, so he skirted the building, found a small rotted side door in the crumbling wall, gave it a little push and it creaked open. He ducked and stepped in: cobwebs, dust, dirt, stench and darkness. There wasn't much left of the pews, only a few broken pieces, which was more than could be said of the altar which lay shattered everywhere. Weeds were growing over the gaps in the brickwork. Thinking he heard a hoarse gasping from the corner by the front door, he twisted around, moved closer and found himself confronting a huddled figure, an infinitely aged, tiny, wrinkled creature lying on the ground, his knees to his chin, shaking with fear. Even in the dark he could see the light of his terrified eyes. Once the creature saw he'd been discovered he moaned in despair and scrambled over to the far corner to escape. "Who are you?" the doctor asked in a firm voice, having overcome his momentary fright. The shrunken figure didn't answer, but drew further back into his corner, ready to spring. "Do you understand what I'm asking?!" the doctor demanded, a little louder. "Who the hell are you?!" The creature muttered something incomprehensible, raised his hands in front of him by way of defense, then burst into tears. The doctor grew angry. "What are you doing here? Are you a tramp?" When the homunculus failed to answer and just continued whimpering, the doctor lost his temper. "Is there a bell here?" he shouted. The tiny old man leapt to his feet in fright, instantly stopped crying, and waved his arms about. "El!... el!" he piped and waved to the doctor to follow him. He opened a tiny door in a niche beside the main portal and pointed upward. "El!... el!" "Good God," muttered the doctor. "A lunatic! Where have you escaped from, you half-wit!" The creature went on up the stairs leaving the doctor a few steps further back, trying to climb up by the wall in case the rotted, dangerously creaking stairs collapsed beneath him. When they reached the small bell tower of which only one brick wall remained, the rest having been brought down ages ago either by the wind or a bomb, the doctor immediately woke as if from "hours of a sickly, nonsensical trance." A quite small bell was hanging in the middle of the exposed, improvised structure, suspended from a beam, one end of which was propped on top of the brick wall, the other on top of the newel post. "How did you manage to raise the beam?" the doctor asked. The old man stared hard at him a moment than stepped over to the bell. "Uh— ur—ah—co-i! Uh—ur—ah—co-i!" he screeched, grabbed an iron bar and started ringing the bell in terror. The doctor had gone pale and was leaning against the wall of the stairs for support. He shouted at the man who was still feverishly striking the bells "Stop it! Stop it at once!" But this only made things worse. "Uh—urk—ah—co-i! Uh—urk— ah—co-i! Uh—urk—ah—co-i!" he kept screaming, hitting the bell ever harder. "The Turks are coming?! Coming up your mother's ass, you fool!" the doctor yelled back, then gathering up his strength climbed down the tower, hurried from the chapel, and tried to put as much distance between himself and the madman—anything not to hear the terrifying screech that seemed to follow him like a cracked trumpet all the way back to the metaled road. It was growing toward dusk by the time he got home and he assumed his position by the window again. It took some time, several minutes in fact, to regain his composure, for his hands to stop trembling enough for him to be able to lift the demijohn, mix himself a drink and light a cigarette. He downed the *pálinka* then picked up his journal and tried to capture in words all he had just suffered. He stared at the paper then wrote: "An unforgivable error. I took a common bell for the Great Bells of Heaven. A filthy tramp! A madman on the run from the asylum. I'm an idiot!" He covered himself with his blankets, leaned back in the chair, and looked out over the field. The rain was quietly pattering. His composure was back now. He went over the events of the early afternoon, over his "moment of enlightenment," then pulled out the notebook headed MRS. HALICS. He opened it on the page where the notes ended and started writing. "She is sitting in the kitchen. The Bible is in front of her and she is quietly muttering some text. She looks up. She is hungry. She goes to the pantry and returns with bacon, sausage and bread. She starts to chomp her way through the meat and takes a bite of the bread. Occasionally she turns the pages of the Bible." Writing this down had a calming effect, but, when he leafed back to what he had written earlier about SCHMIDT, KRÁNER and MRS. HALICS, he was disappointed to note that it was all wrong. He stood up and started walking about his room, stopping now and then to think, then moving again. He looked around the narrow limits of his home and his attention was caught by the door. "Damn it!" he groaned. He took a box of nails from under the wardrobe and, with a few nails in one hand and the hammer in the other, went over to the door and started beating in the nails with increasing fury. Having finished, he calmly returned to his chair, covered his back with the blankets, and mixed another drink, this time, after some consideration, in half-half proportion. He gazed and thought, then suddenly his eyes brightened and he took out a new notebook. "It was raining when ...," he wrote, then shook his head and crossed it out. "It was raining when Futaki awoke, and ...," he tried again, but decided this too was "poor stuff." He rubbed the bridge of his nose, adjusted his glasses then propped his elbows on the table and put his head in his hands. He saw before him, as clear as if by magic, the path prepared for him, the way the fog swam up from either side of it and, in the middle of the narrow path, the luminous face of his future, its lineaments bearing the infernal marks of drowning. He reached for the pencil again and felt he was back on track now: there were enough notebooks, enough *pálinka*, his medication would last till spring at least and, unless the nails rotted in the door, no one would disturb him. Careful not to damage the paper, he started writing. "One morning near the end of October not long before the first drops of the mercilessly long autumn rains began to fall on the cracked and saline soil on the western side of the estate (later the stinking yellow sea of mud would render footpaths impassable and put the town too beyond reach) Futaki woke to hear bells. The closest possible source was a lonely chapel about four kilometers southwest on the old Hochmeiss estate but not only did that have no bell but the tower had collapsed during the war and at that distance it was too far to hear anything. And in any case they did not sound distant to him, these ringing-booming bells; their triumphal clangor was swept along by the wind and seemed to come from somewhere close by ('It's as if they were coming from the mill ...'). He propped himself on his elbows on the pillow so as to look out of the mousehole-sized kitchen window that was partly misted up, and directed his gaze to the faint blue dawn sky but the field was still and silent, bathed only in the now ever fainter bell sound, and the only light to be seen was the one glimmering in the doctor's window whose house was set well apart from the others on the far side, and that was only because its occupant had for years been unable to sleep in the dark. Futaki held his breath because he wanted to know where the noise came from: he couldn't afford to lose a single stray note of the rapidly fading clangor, however remote ('You must be asleep, Futaki . . .'). Despite his lameness he was well known for his light tread and he hobbled across the ice-cold stone floor of the kitchen soundless as a cat, opened the windows and leaned out ('Is no one awake? Can't people hear it? Is there nobody else around?'). A sharp damp gust hit him straight in the face so he had to close his eyes for a moment and, apart from the cockcrow, a distant bark, and the fierce howling of the wind that had sprung up just a few minutes earlier, there was nothing to hear however hard he listened but the dull beating of his own heart, as if the whole thing had been merely a kind of game or ghostly half-dream ('. . . It's as if somebody out there wants to scare me'). He gazed sadly at the threatening sky, at the burned-out remnants of a locust-plagued summer, and suddenly saw on the twig of an acacia, as in a vision, the progress of spring, summer, fall and winter, as if the whole of time were a frivolous interlude in the much greater spaces of eternity, a brilliant conjuring trick to produce something apparently orderly out of chaos, to establish a vantage point from which chance might begin to look like necessity . . . and he saw himself nailed to the cross of his own cradle and coffin, painfully trying to tear his body away, only, eventually, to deliver himself—utterly naked, without identifying mark, stripped down to essentials—into the care of the people whose duty it was to wash the corpses, people obeying an order snapped out in the dry air against a background loud with torturers and flayers of skin, where he was obliged to regard the human condition without a trace of pity, without a single possibility of any way back to life, because by then he would know for certain that all his life he had been playing with cheaters who had marked the cards and who would, in the end, strip him even of his last means of defense, of that hope of someday finding his way back home. He turned his head toward the east, once the home of a thriving industry, now nothing but a set of dilapidated and deserted buildings, watching while the first rays of a swollen red sun broke through the topmost beams of a derelict farmhouse from which the roof tiles had been stripped. 'I really should come to a decision. I can't stay here any longer.' He snuck back under the warm duvet again and rested his head on his arm, but could not close his eyes; at first it had been the ghostly bells that had frightened him but now it was the threatening silence that followed: anything might happen now, he felt. But he did not move a muscle, not until the objects around him, that had so far been merely listening, started up a nervous conversation (the sideboard gave a creak, a saucepan rattled, a china plate slid back into the rack) at which point ..."

"'Reality examined to the point of madness.' What would this look like in contemporary writing? It might look like the fiction of László Krasznahorkai, the difficult, peculiar, obsessive, visionary Hungarian author.... Very long, breathing, unstopped sentences, at once literary and vocal, have been almost inseparable from the progress of experimental fiction since the nineteen-fifties. Claude Simon, Thomas Bernhard, José Saramago, W. G. Sebald, Roberto Bolaño, David Foster Wallace, James Kelman, and László Krasznahorkai have used the long sentence to do many different things but all of them have been at odds with a merely grammatical realism, whereby the real is made to fall into approved units and packages. In fact these writers could be called realists, of a kind. But the reality that many of them are interested in is 'reality examined to the point of madness.' The phrase is László Krasznahorkai's, and, of all these novelists, Krasznahorkai is perhaps the strangest.... His work tends to get passed around like rare currency.... One of the most profoundly unsettling experiences I have had as a reader."
—James Wood, *The New Yorker*